STORM SONG

RICH BULLOCK

Rich WORDS
PRESS

DEDICATION

For all artists who tell stories through song.
Artists create the music that inspires us. I always listen to music while writing,
but with Storm Song, the music became the story I had to tell. Without music,
the world would be a dull place indeed.

STORM SONG

CHAPTER ONE

"Ten minutes, Miss Van Onweer," the stage manager's voice sounded outside the dressing room door.

"Thank you." Regen tilted a bottled water to her lips, but pulled it away without drinking. She'd be running to the bathroom between every song.

The woman staring back in the mirror *looked* composed, confident. "Pretense, that's what counts," Aunt Ruth had always told her. But that was years ago in Nebraska before Regen van Onweer existed, not here in Rotterdam.

Her cell phone vibrated an excited dance on the dressing table. Unknown Caller ID. Only a few people had her new number. Her hand trembled as she pushed the answer button.

"Hello?"

A voice whispered, "Did you get my *gift*?"

Regen's eyes cut to the trash bin and the hideous flower as she jabbed the disconnect button. How had he gotten this number?

The door clicked, opened inward, and Regen shot to her feet, sending the cell phone to the hard tile floor where it split into its component pieces. They spun to a stop at the feet of the woman in the doorway—Lorna Nairne, her costume and hair expert. Lorna's smile faded at

Regen's shuddering breath. Bending down, Lorna scooped up the battery, cover, and phone, while Regen worked air into frozen lungs.

"You okay, Ree girl? You look a little spooked." Lorna's accent rolled off her tongue like the Jamaican native she was, though Regen had heard her speak flawless King's English when it benefited her. Lorna deposited the electronic parts into Regen's cupped hands.

Regen nodded her response. She swiveled toward the dressing table, fingers trembling as she inserted the battery and snapped on its cover. "I'm just nervous, you know." Her voice sounded as phony as a B-movie actress. Pretense wasn't up to par. With battery in place, the phone buzzed happily, rebooting and searching for the cellular network, readying itself for the next call. She held her breath until the display went dark.

Lorna laughed in lilting tones, moved behind Regen, and watched in the mirror as she tugged her black wig right and left until satisfied. She gave Regen a calculated once-over in the glass, then nodded.

"Yes, dis is a big night, Regen, but you are ready." She massaged Regen's shoulders. "You may not think it too much right now, but you are."

Regen closed her eyes under Lorna's kneading fingers. The Dutch police still had no leads on the caller, but security at the Ahoy Rotterdam had been beefed up for tonight's concert. There was even an Interpol inspector onsite. He'd checked in with her earlier.

Lorna had Regen stand and pirouette. The wide, multilayered Victorian skirt dusted the floor on the sides and back, but had a front cutaway to show off black leather knee boots that each sported a dozen silver buckles.

The cell phone buzzed and Regen's eyes jerked toward the lighted display. A text message from Unknown Sender:

Save your last breath for me.

When the display blinked out, she powered off the device and dropped it into her purse stowed under the counter. She'd have to change the number—again.

A rap rattled the door, and Regen jumped. "Two minutes!"

Lorna shot her a look.

Regen ignored the obvious concern. "Time to go."

She led the way out of the suddenly claustrophobic room, every cell in her body yearning for the open stage. The stage manager, a petite man with a bad comb-over and thin mustache, danced in front of them, first forward, then backward, punctuating his rapid mix of French and Dutch with his cluttered clipboard. Regen paid little attention and outpaced him with her long strides as she wove between props, costume racks, ropes, and towering draperies. Stagehands parted like the main curtain when they recognized her.

Tonight was the culmination of months of hard work, not to mention a boatload of money. Casting off the doubts, she began layering herself with the persona of Regen van Onweer, queen of Europe's symphonic metal bands. Her chin came up, her shoulders squared. She marched forward, authority ringing with each strike of her four-inch heels. She stretched her arms wide visualizing music flowing from her core, down her arms, and exiting her splayed fingers—lightning bolts seeking each member of the audience. Feeling better already, she winked at Lorna over the head of the little man clucking like a frantic fowl.

"Over here, Miss Van Onweer," a stage tech beckoned and checked his watch. He took her gloved hand and helped her onto a four-foot square of stage floor. A small railing of black pipe at the back edge of the platform provided the only handhold, and she steadied herself while Lorna tucked the voluminous skirts of ruffled red taffeta between Regen's legs.

"Now you hold these with your knees so your dress won't snag when you pass through the main level." Lorna gave Regen a wide grin. "Wouldn't want the queen to arrive onstage skirtless now would we?"

Regen concentrated on the muted roar of the audience. The warm-up group had exited the stage and the fans were impatient for the main act. Elusive Hope. Their band. *Her* band. She strained for breath against the stiff black leather corset, wishing it a little looser. Above, a bass drum began a slow, steady kick, quickly echoed by at least seven thousand pairs of stomping feet. After a few measures, the string ensemble played a long, extended note, slowly building intensity.

The tech handed Regen the in-ear monitors, which she deftly inserted. The custom-made IEMs were hideously expensive—a treat after last year's tour—but they muted the band enough to protect her hearing while providing a clear monitor mix. The tech inspected her cheek microphone and hooked everything up, then stuffed the transmitter/receiver pack down the back of her corset, cinching the garment tighter still.

Regen closed her eyes, visualizing the stage above. A single blue spot would illuminate drummer Danny Haynes, with soft amber bathing the string players. More spots as Hans Vicker's fuzzy lead guitar and Eva Wolf's bass joined Danny. Then everything went silent, and Regen counted the beats: *two, three, four*...Pieter Rademaker's electronic keyboard filled the hall with the glorious sound of a Baroque pipe organ. The plywood beneath her boots vibrated as huge subwoofers reproduced the organ's heart-stopping bass, and she couldn't help grinning at Lorna. Ever since they'd all attended an organ festival at Basilica St. James in Prague, Pieter had tried to mimic the magnificent three hundred year-old instrument, but he'd never before had use of the fantastic sound system here at the Ahoy. As the organ backed off to a more moderate volume, Regen pictured, as much as heard, the woodwinds, chimes, and the other more subtle instruments of the twenty-five-piece orchestra unite from stage left.

Lorna leaned close. "Do good, baby girl." With Regen's ear monitors in place, Lorna sounded as if she spoke through a pillow. Four ornate gold rings adorned her hand as she teased one wayward curl away from Regen's face.

She caught a whiff of spices and grinned at Lorna. "Are we having cinnamon rolls after the show?" The Jamaican's baking talents kept all the band members on her good side. "Be a nice reward—Thomas said we sold 7,500 tickets."

Lorna stepped away from the platform and shouted over the music. "I heard him say close to nine thousand a bit ago. You brought 'em out of the woodwork, girl."

Regen relaxed a little. Maybe the money wouldn't be a problem after all.

Each thump of Danny's bass drum vibrated the railing beneath her hand, and Hans let loose on a long guitar solo intro for their first song.

"Five seconds," the tech barked, reading a cue sheet. Regen didn't need one—she'd written the production outline herself. He moved to a control box. "Up you go." He pushed a green button, and the platform started upward.

At twelve feet, she rose through the main stage, and the sound increased dramatically. She continued upwards beneath the massive staircase that sloped toward the front of the stage. Her very bones hummed in response to the music, and her breathing increased as she continued rising. Music swelled in her IEMs as the sound tech brought them up to the predetermined volume, and her heart beat faster in response to the familiar strains.

Through the cracks in the scaffolding, bright light flashed as the first of the pyrotechnics exploded on each side of the platform, eliciting cheers in the auditorium. The orchestra and band picked up the tempo, and she threw her head back and shook her curls, grinning in spite of lingering nerves. This was so cool!

She stared at the underside of the forty-foot wide staircase. Red-illuminated fog erupted from twin volcanoes and poured down through the opening above like molten lava.

Raoul Kloepper faded into the folds of a curtain as Regen van Onweer's assistant hurried by on her way to the stage-right observation area where a small group of production people consulted clipboards, spoke into radios, and sent stagehands scurrying on the endless errands necessary to pull off the concert production. He chuckled to himself. They had no idea how big tonight would be. It was time to move.

His black clothes and knitted cap matched the other workers, and several nodded to him as he made his way through the backstage maze of props, smoke machines, curtains, and miles of electrical cords. It always amazed him how accepting people were if he looked and acted like he belonged. And he *did* belong in this world—at least enough to know his way around. Theater and concert venue jobs in Germany, Belgium, and the Netherlands had prepared him. It had taken months of diligent training, but now he was part of their world, *her* world.

He stepped into a hallway that led to the empty upper dressing rooms used by larger productions. Illuminated by a single fixture at the far end, the worn, gray tile reflected minimal light.

The red fire hose cabinet sat recessed into the white wall, probably unopened since its last inspection. Well, that's what everyone assumed, if they thought about it at all. He freed the latch and swung the door open. Tucked under the hose reel lay a long black leather pouch, right where he'd hidden it four days ago.

The choir, orchestra, and band swelled, measure by measure, and the audience exploded to new heights of applause as Regen's head emerged from the billowing crimson cloud. The platform jolted to a stop, and she stepped cautiously forward, blinded by over two hundred white and colored lights. Odors of sulfur, make-up, plywood and sweat tickled her nostrils. As her eyes adjusted, she made out the steps sloping down to stage level, lit on each side by flickering electric torches. Deep purple and magenta gauze draped the set creating a rich, Gothic aura.

Regen spread her arms high, raised her face to the lights, and sang the opening song, "Red Rain," as lava-like smoke cascaded down the stairway and spread among her bandmates.

Her clear soprano sounded strong, even in the tiny ear monitors, and her voice lifted as she crafted the story of a young girl, Marielle—her happy life interrupted. While the music's base was the heavy metal rock of her band, the story and entire performance were pure opera, including costumes, dramatic staging, and heart-rending emotion. Regen's vocals tied it all together.

The audience quieted as, in the third verse, misery and pain rained down, transforming Marielle's idyllic childhood into despair and darkness. Regen offered only a glimpse of hope woven subtly in these first lyrics. Those who followed the band relived the girl's pain, but waited for the finale.

The microphone pack dug into Regen's back with each breath, and soon sweat trickled down her neck from under the thick wig, but she ignored the discomfort and descended the stairs. She stopped three-quarters of the way down, where the steps divided around Danny's huge drum kit. Polished brass and chrome glittered like jewels, and Danny's shaved head sparkled with sweat as his colorfully tattooed arms marked a commanding rhythm for the rest to follow. A two-story shimmering curtain of tinsel danced in the air, simulating rain, and lightning flashed, spilling a million reflections off the metal as massive subwoofers thundered. The audience cheered, obviously not minding the dark message—they knew Marielle's journey had only begun.

Raoul noted the small plaque beside the door—*E31*—and today was the thirty-first of the month.

"Yes, it's meant to be," he proclaimed to the empty passageway.

The small room contained an electrical sub panel and was perched one floor up from the main control room at the back of the theater. His hand shook as he twisted the unlocked knob and opened the door. Music blared through a one-foot square opening in the far wall. Abandoned bolt holes in the floor indicated this had once housed projection equipment.

He crossed to the opening and dropped to his knees. He could have set up back stage, but it had been far too crowded with stagehands and theater people. Sharing Marielle wasn't part of his plan. This room was perfect.

The aperture gave a limited view of the balcony, mezzanine, and main floor of the auditorium. Those weren't important to him. Only the view of the stage mattered—a clear shot, so to speak.

Sixty meters away, Regen van Onweer stood center stage, one arm raised as she sang. Several songs into the concert now, she had changed into a beautiful, formfitting, black leather dress and wine-colored boots with black laces. The skirt had slits up each side, held together by ten short, red belts and buckles—he'd counted them in her dressing room. A jeweled collar sparkled around her throat, sending shafts of red and amber over the seats, and the curls of her burgundy wig brushed her shoulders as she raised her eyes, staring straight at him. A sigh escaped his lips.

Marielle. So beautiful.

With clumsy fingers, he pulled a wrinkled sheet of paper from his pocket and carefully smoothed it on the window ledge, the original of the copy he'd slipped into the pocket of the very dress Regen van Onweer wore now. Had she found his note? Had she brushed her fingers along the paper as the words teased her ruby lips?

Music burst from the stage as Elusive Hope transitioned into a new song, and he whispered Marielle's poem for no one except himself and Marielle as he watched Regen van Onweer.

"Save your last breath for me, my lovely white dove,
    Don't sing too loud or long.
    Yellow fades and black overwhelms, like cold fog.
    I will release air from your lungs,
    Embrace my gift of freedom."

CHAPTER TWO

"Green Wind" brought soft lights, billowing gauze, and a sweet choral overlay as gentle as a spring meadow to the edginess of the band. Pieter's keyboard accompaniment and the strains of the orchestra strings floated through Regen's ear pieces as she sang of new birth, a turning of luck, joy. Spring held promise of good things to come and an end to pain and darkness. Dancers in diaphanous gowns slowly twirled through pools of light around Regen as she sang of hope and love.

But then the music turned chaotic, heavy, true hard rock. The light darkened. The choir sang counterpoint to Regen's mournful soprano. Marielle's love had fled as fast as it had come, leaving her devastated. Regen fought for control as her own emotions surged. She reminded herself this was Marielle's story, not her own. Even so, salty tears ran into her mouth as the last quiet notes faded away on a wisp of the harp's note, as piercing as a twisting knife. Quiet shrouded the auditorium except for hushed breathing and several muffled sobs. In the dark, Regen wiped her eyes and took a cleansing breath, glad to be through the toughest number. She knew from past concerts there would be tears on the faces of young girls, and of some males, too.

Raoul pressed his temples and wiped his wet cheeks, then sat back on the dusty floor, rocking in sorrow.

Marielle. My beautiful Marielle.

He'd been lost, a captive of Marielle's song. Panic brought him to his knees. But how long? Was his opportunity past?

Music swelled as the next number began, and he glanced through the window. Dancers in blue gowns, spun in time to the beat. The stage was lit in undulating deep blue, and computer controlled lights transformed the stairs into a waterfall flowing around Regen van Onweer and Danny Haynes, two performers marooned on an island in the middle of a raging river. The choir joined their voices with the orchestra.

Raoul let out a breath and relaxed. These dancers performed two songs before the final number. The finale, a masterpiece of emotional impact, would milk every last tear from the audience. Plenty of time, but he couldn't let himself be carried away like that again. He pulled a pill bottle from his pocket and shook out a red capsule, then added a second, swallowing them without water. Ian had said never to take more than one at a time and he'd already had one while back stage, but he needed them now, to concentrate, focus. His fingers shook a little more as he struggled to replace the protective cap.

He removed the black leather pouch from where he'd strapped it on the inside of his right leg under his baggy cargo pants. The package had been short enough to allow a normal gait as he traversed the theater halls, carrying a bulging clipboard and non-working radio. His friends, Ian, Beth, and Jorge, were on the floor of the auditorium beside his empty seat, thinking him in the toilet due to bad Indian cuisine. He'd joined them once, then excused himself again with apologies and donned his stage uniform and identification. He would meet them afterward for beers where they would commiserate that he had missed the most shocking event of the decade—all because of an irritable bowel.

He unzipped the pouch and removed the stock of the Armalite AR-7, .22 caliber rifle. He twisted off the butt pad, pulled out the barrel, main action and magazine, then deftly snapped and screwed the parts together. When finished, he pulled his cell phone from his belt and programmed a delayed update message to his blog.

Save your last breath for me, my lovely white dove,
  Don't sing too loud or long.
  Yellow fades and black overwhelms, like cold fog.
  I will release air from your lungs,
  Embrace my gift of freedom.
  Dark rain will fall from your eyes,
  From your body, like notes spilling from a score.
  I drink its life; you sustain me.
  Give me what you promised.
  Save me,
  And I will remain with you always.

Then he added,

Tonight the present is transformed into history, all by my hand, the same hand that delivers the tulip rose.

Most people—including his moronic friends—didn't understand how a moment in time could gain historic significance, if only someone knew how to freeze it. Lee Harvey Oswald had done it. So had John Wilkes Booth.

He lovingly stroked the weapon's barrel. He had that power. And with it, he'd take away Marielle's pain and make her his—forever.

The leather pouch gave up two more items: a noise suppressor and a clear plastic tube containing a final tulip rose, a twin of the one delivered to Van Onweer's dressing room. Two lovely flowers, their black and red petals meticulously woven together, made into a thing of beautiful horror. Fitting for Regen van Onweer. He placed the flower on the floor beneath the small window and then slipped the noise suppressor onto the gun barrel.

After sixteen songs and five major costume changes, Regen was both exhausted and energized. Danny said performances were like winning a marathon—elation balanced by physical depletion. Some nights after a large-venue concert, while the other band members wanted to go out and party, it was all she could do to bathe and crawl into bed.

Tonight she'd traced Marielle's story through sorrow, self-reliance, strength, and finally a new, tentative vulnerability in "Lemon Snow." The teeming crowd had demanded more from Regen than ever, and she was glad she'd invited Dolina Macgowan, an up and coming Goth band singer from Edinburgh, to join in on five of the songs. Their voices blended well, Regen's soprano and Dolina's raspy alto producing a combined power Regen couldn't achieve alone. Dolina's only fault was she tended to sing too loudly on quiet passages, and Regen had cautioned her about that during rehearsal.

The band began the last song, "Indigo Sun." It was nearly eight minutes long, but the first two minutes were instruments and choir, so Regen sipped some water behind the stairs to soothe her vocal cords while Lorna replaced Regen's wig with one containing blue extensions. The programmed lighting would turn it a luxurious indigo.

The players increased the tempo, and the orchestra's timpani bolstered Danny's kick drum, shaking the foundation of the auditorium. She took a breath. *Here we go.*

Regen strode onto the stage, the white Victorian skirt swirling around her boots. She sang the opening verse at the footlights only inches from the mosh pit fans. This was the finale and everyone was on their feet. Spotlights raked the audience, and her lingering doubts about whether they could pull off such a huge concert left her as she saw how many sang along.

Hundreds of hands strained for her as she moved cross stage, and she brushed them with her right hand. At the end of the stage she turned and ascended the staircase. She paused midway for the second verse, concentrating on breath control as she strained for the higher notes. Several feet below, Danny poured passion into the music, his arms whipping faster and faster across the drums and brass. Sweat drops flew from his skin, falling stars caught momentarily in the bright lights. His enthusiasm flowed into her, washing away the weariness of only moments before.

When Regen reached the top platform, Dolina emerged from billowing purple fog, and they came together at the center, singing of

Marielle's battle with her lifelong nemesis. It was the moment of climax for the story. Marielle and her reunited true love faced ultimate vindication or utter defeat. Everything rested on this pivotal confrontation.

Nine thousand voices joined with them for the emotional verses, overshadowing the choir, the orchestra, even the band. Dolina's eyes widened, mirroring Regen's own feeling of awe as goose bumps prickled her neck and arms. Neither had been part of something so moving, something that so deeply impacted thousands of people.

Regen grinned at Dolina, then hooked arms with her as they walked to the edge of the platform. Every inch of Regen's skin tingled with Marielle's triumph.

When Hans's guitar solo led them into the final verse, Regen stretched her arms wide and slowly raised them to the heavens. She belted her signature smooth, piercing high note, joined a third below by Dolina. A little too loud again, and Regen compensated.

Gas jets flashed from each side of the stage and across the top of the staircase, perfectly timed with Danny's pounding beat. Shimmering curtains undulated yellow and indigo, and warm spotlights scribed a circle where she and Dolina stood, bringing the power of hope through brilliant color. The audience raised their arms with Regen, anticipating Marielle's imminent victory.

More fireworks exploded, and something slammed into Regen's left thigh. Her breath left her, and she crumbled sideways in a mass of white satin at Dolina's feet. Regen's IEMs rang with music from all other sources, but her own voice had stopped.

Bewildered, she struggled to her knees. Her left leg began burning like a white-hot blade had sliced through the muscle. Had she been hit by some kind of shrapnel from one of the flash pots? She set her teeth and grabbed Dolina's extended hand.

Dolina opened her mouth, then jerked and toppled onto Regen, slamming her head hard against the platform. The weight slid away. Regen got to her hands and knees and stared in Dolina's direction, but she couldn't see anything beyond the spotlights and dazzling reflection off her white gown.

Where had Dolina gone?

The choir chanted victory and triumph. Hans Vicker's guitar riffs pierced the air, building, building. Regen knew that none of the other performers on the main stage could see her at the top of the stairs, but the crowd could, and a murmur washed across the stage above the pounding music.

As she rose to a kneeling position, two gouges appeared by magic in the black wooden platform inches in front of her, carved by an invisible claw that raked the surface. Buttery plywood splinters sprayed into the air, oversized dust motes twirling in the bright light.

Another punch in her arm coincided with the snap of bone so sharp it vibrated her torso like one of Danny's kick drums. Regen stared at the blooming red above her left elbow. This time the pain was immediate, scalding elbow to shoulder, then up her neck until her scalp burned in agony and turned her vision crimson.

The music continued, but the lyrics fled from Regen. She lifted her hand as if she could grip the swirling words, force them back into her mouth so she could finish Marielle's story, but they vanished into the flowing indigo mist that surrounded her.

Against her will, Regen's body hunched forward, seeking an instinctive fetal position to guard against further agony. She extended her right hand to catch herself as she fell, but in the blinding spotlights and fog, Regen misjudged how close the edge of the platform lay.

Her hand plunged into empty space.

CHAPTER THREE

The bicycle's tires crunched as Raoul turned off the paved road and coasted down the gravel driveway along the side of the house in Boskoop, South Holland. A decrepit Peugeot hunched at the far end, listing to one side in the tire ruts. He stashed the bike behind leafy shrubbery that enclosed a garden no larger than the automobile and turned to the cottage. Although he'd watched this house from a distance, he'd never been inside.

The doddering couple next door had thwarted his plans for two days, gardening in their yard and painting lawn furniture, but they'd finally left in their own ugly little car. They were fortunate. He wasn't waiting another day.

Now no one would interrupt him.

The house's bright red side door had glass in the top half and a single lock. He debated breaking the glass and reaching through, but instead retrieved a pry bar from his backpack and wedged the end between the door and frame. One push on the bar and the door popped silently open. He stepped into a cozy, serviceable kitchen, and turned slowly in the still air, breathing in.

Regen van Onweer's home.

Traditional black and white tiles covered the floor of the galley-style kitchen, dividing sink and cabinets on one side from the stove and refrigerator on the other. He ran his fingers over the cup and plate in the wooden dish rack, then opened a cupboard where her tea and coffee were stored. Her favorite varieties, chosen by her hands at the market. He pocketed several packages of tea before moving on. The small refrigerator contained an assortment of milk, chocolate custard, cheese, and vegetables. He closed the door.

A pair of Delft canisters sat on an open shelf near the stove, their trademark blue and white out of place, he thought, against the room's yellow walls. He picked up the larger of the two and held it to the light streaming in the diamond-paned window above the sink. The lid had a few small chips, but the piece was well made. Old. Perhaps valuable. He opened his hands and watched the container tumble to the tile floor. The ceramic shattered, sending jagged chunks every direction. A mushroom cloud of flour spread under the stove and open sink space. White powder covered his shoes.

"Not valuable anymore." He retrieved a glass from the cupboard, filled it with water at the sink, then swallowed two more of the red pills from his pocket. He'd have to get more from Ian.

Beyond the broken pottery and through the doorway lay the living room. Bile rose in his throat as he observed the shoddy furnishings there. Marielle deserved better. A small sofa had patterned fabric so thin he could see the underlying foam in places, and the table before it had nicks along the edges. A television with a missing knob perched on a wooden crate partially draped with a panel of blue cloth. The lamps and single dining chair were clearly second-hand. Cut flowers—fresh a few days ago—drooped in a blue vase. This was no way for her to live.

The rest of the décor held little interest—except for the painting opposite the sofa. He moved closer. Vermeer's *Girl With a Pearl Earring*. The oil was a copy, of course, but a very good one. The frame was of exceptional quality, and its carved surface shone with years of polish.

"Another favorite." Removing it carefully from the wall hanger, he lifted it high, then brought it down hard on the television. Wood splintered and the canvas tore as he struck it again and again, until only a scrap of the girl's blue scarf shone from the pile on the floor. He sifted through the mess until he found the piece with the earring. This he ripped free and slipped the remnant into his pocket.

Next he moved on to the bedroom. White eyelet curtains framed tall windows that overlooked the garden. Outside, a window box exploded with yellow and purple flowers. He pulled the blind down to hide the distraction. This room was where Regen van Onweer lived, where Marielle undressed. After running a soapy sponge over her limbs in the hallway bath, she slipped between soft sheets on the bed he was destined to share.

Her fragrance permeated the duvet, the throw rugs, and the containers lining the top of the painted chest of drawers. His eye began twitching—a sign he'd taken too many pills, Ian had said—but he squeezed the lid closed as he stretched his trembling hands to a tiny amber bottle and unscrewed its gold cap. Unconstrained, the bouquet slithered into his nostrils and into his lungs.

So strong!

Marielle's essence tore through his body, into his brain where electrical charges crackled across the nerve synapses, bathing him in pleasure. He tilted his head back as love welled inside. She was here in this very room, wanting him.

But his satisfaction transformed, became a grasping fist shoving inside his gut, rending upward, separating muscle from bone, determined to rip his heart from his chest. Too strong. *Too strong!*

With a roar he hurled the vial against the hanging mirror, splintering his reflection into kaleidoscope shards of light and dark. The liquid dripped down the patterned wall like golden blood, and its fragrance filled the room, driving him mad with desire.

"Marielle!" His eyelids twitched erratically, and he yanked his hair with both hands trying to create more space in his skull for his sizzling brain. He spun, first right, then left in her bedroom. Marielle was his. They were meant to be.

Faster and faster the objects in the room flowed around him. Mirror, dresser, window, bed. Mirror, dresser, window, bed. Destroying Regen van Onweer would free Marielle, allow her to come to him willingly. *Faster.* Mirror, dresser, window, bed.

Miniature periwinkle flowers on the wallpaper blurred in looping blue arcs, curving up and down, up and down, like a carnival ride. *Faster. Faster.* Her fragrance—Marielle's essence—filled him with longing and fury. Regen van Onweer held the young girl hostage. He had to release Marielle.

CHAPTER FOUR

"Rayne? Are you with us again?"

Regen cracked her eyes open, squinting against harsh light glaring from every corner of the white ceiling. Even stage spotlights weren't this intense.

She needed a hot washcloth to dissolve the glue of her fused eyelids. How long had she been asleep? Her mouth tasted like she'd eaten a cardboard sandwich stuffed with sawdust.

"Rayne?"

She couldn't see the woman, but the voice was familiar. She attempted a question, but managed only a croak. The owner of the voice moved into view. Blonde, dressed in a camel cashmere sweater and crisply ironed beige slacks. The haircut followed the jaw line, tips sharp enough to injure the unwary.

Mother.

Regen's head rapidly cleared. She should have known. No one else called her Rayne. Not anymore.

Her mother moved closer and Regen turned her head, but the slight movement increased the deep throbbing that threatened to push her eyeballs right out of their sockets. She closed the lids to hold them in place. What was her mother doing here? And where was *here*?

A straw touched her lips and Regen opened to allow it in. Though tepid, the water tasted heavenly as it dribbled down her throat. Bracelets jangled on her mother's arm as she set the water back on the stand.

While Regen let the water revitalize her mouth, she dared open her eyes again to take in the surroundings. "Here" was a medical facility of some sort, complete with chrome side rails on the bed. An intravenous line snaked from a hanging sack filled with clear liquid to the back of her right hand where it was secured with strips of thin white tape. The walls were painted lettuce-green, and a small television perched on a shelf, with cords stretching to outlets somewhere below. Colored pictures moved silently on the screen, but Regen didn't have the energy to decipher them.

Food smells and voices floated from the hall. German? No, Dutch. She was still somewhere in the Netherlands.

"Rayne?" The voice brought Regen's attention back to her mother. Worry lines creased the carefully applied makeup.

Rayne. Her old name. Who she used to be. The memories slid sideways, and Regen couldn't seem to hold them in place.

"I'm going to get the doctor." Her mother pivoted and clicked out of the room. High heels. Cordelia Evans always wore high heels.

Regen lifted her head and spikes of pain—oddly both severe and distant—shot up her scalp. She fell back with a groan. A doctor was definitely in order. What had happened?

Her left thigh felt like one of the over-ripe watermelons her uncle used to grow on his farm near Omaha. The touch of a knife tip was all that was needed to split the melon wide open. She wiggled her toes and saw the sheet moving at the end of the bed. Still attached. Good.

A cast covered her left arm from armpit to wrist, but her fingers responded to commands, albeit weakly. She didn't hurt as long as she didn't move her head, but she felt a little out of body, like Julia Roberts in *Flatliners*. Or was it Kiefer Sutherland or Billy Baldwin? One of them died, or all of them did, she couldn't remember. She'd have to rent the DVD again. Maybe that's what was on the TV. She stared at the screen's changing images but couldn't make them hold still long enough to recognize more than colored shapes. She let her eyelids descend and block the confusion.

Thoughts swirled like colored fog, indistinct but oddly familiar, and she had no idea how much time had passed when a knock roused her. A tall man with close-cropped hair stepped into the room, followed by her mother. The ends of a stethoscope stuck out of the left pocket of the man's white lab coat. She forced herself to concentrate.

"Hello, Miss Van Onweer. Good to see you with us again." He spoke in English, but with the almost musical cadence of the Dutch. A broad smile emphasized deep creases at the corner of each eye, reminding her of the actor Max von Sydow. She hoped he wasn't playing a villain like he so often did. "I'm Doctor Ostrander, head of the trauma center here."

She focused on him again and licked her lips. "Where's 'here'?"

"Oh, sorry." His accent made the 'o' into a long vowel, and this simple difference was a comfort. "This is the Erasmus University Medical Center, Rotterdam. You're familiar with us perhaps?" His eyebrows rose.

She nodded and immediately regretted the movement. Had someone beaten her with a baseball bat? The doctor withdrew a small flashlight from his pocket and passed it back and forth in front of her eyes. Seemingly satisfied with blinding her, he replaced it in his coat.

"You don't remember my other visits?" The doctor pressed his index finger vertically to his lips as if contemplating her answer before she gave it.

"We've talked before?" Regen watched him nod, and noted her mother's worried expression where she stood behind the doctor. Regen touched her forehead and encountered a thick bandage wrapping her head. "I'm a little fuzzy." More than a little.

"Well...not unexpected," the doctor said. "You've had quite an injury, Miss Van Onweer." He reached out to adjust the drip on the hanging bag. "A two-weeks coma is very serious, you know. And we're giving you something for the pain."

Two weeks. Regen struggled to remember what had happened. A concert—she'd been singing. A big stage. Other than that, the image of what it looked like and how it sounded wouldn't form, no matter how much she strained.

Her eyelids grew heavy with the effort, and she let her right hand thump to the sheet like a hunk of driftwood from Katwijk aan Zee. She wanted answers, needed them. But they wouldn't happen now. The people in the room no longer seemed important as sleep pulled her down. One last question came from her mother.

"Doctor? Will she ever remember?"

A knock sounded on the hospital door, and Regen turned. Danny Haynes, with his shaved head and a small bat tattooed on the side of his neck, stood in the doorway.

"Danny." She reached toward him with her good hand.

"Well, it's not Kojak, babe." He stepped into the room, grinning tentatively at the shared joke.

Regen's lips were like cracked paint on an old building, and she gestured toward the water bottle. "Could you...?" Danny caught her intent and held it for her while she sipped. At least her brain was working today now that they'd decreased the pain killers.

"God, Regen. You scared us to death."

Now that he was closer, she noticed dark stitches in a cut above his right eyebrow. And when he turned to replace the water bottle, she saw an orange and purple bruise on the back of his head. She reached toward his face.

"You're hurt."

"This?" He touched the wound above his eye. "Nah, it's nothing." He cleared his throat. "Not compared to you, anyway." He looked down as if unable to face the reality of how she looked. "I just found out you woke up. I came by and ran into your mom in the waiting room."

She grimaced. "Sorry about that. I should have warned you about her."

Danny had the grace to laugh. "Oh, it wasn't so bad." He grinned again, the old Danny back. He admired his colorful arms. "Actually, she's kind of taken with my tattoos. I think I talked her into getting a butterfly on her shoulder, or maybe an ankle chain."

Regen didn't give him the satisfaction of reacting until she saw his lips twitch and the corners of his mouth turn up. Danny could never hold a straight line for long. But she finally did laugh, imagining her society mother with a tattoo of any kind. Regen wondered if her mother had noticed the inked blue-green waves on the inside of Regen's right wrist. If so, had she suspected their meaning?

Danny took her hand, carefully avoiding the IV line, and she relaxed at the touch of those familiar, calloused fingers. She sank into the bed, feeling better than she had since first waking—well, the first time she could remember. Maybe it was euphoria from the pain medication working its magic, but it was so good to have someone she could talk to, a friend who knew her life here in Holland.

But now an awkward silence fell between them. They couldn't simply talk about what friends were doing, or the weather, or music—at least not without getting the important thing out first. Regen took a breath, fighting the lassitude that threatened to drag her into yet another nap.

"I… Danny, I can't remember what happened. And my mother won't tell me a thing." She had to stop and catch her breath. Could two weeks in a coma do that? Or maybe it had more to do with the answer he'd give her.

Surprise had widened his eyes. "You don't know?"

"The doctor says my brain's a little shook up. I can't recall some things." Most things. It had improved a little each of the last two days, so that gave her hope. She had remembered the nurse's name from yesterday. But the accident that had put her in the hospital was still a blank. Her mother flatly refused to talk about it and unplugged the television soon after Regen woke from the coma. But Danny would tell her.

Evidently it was Danny's turn for dry lips as he licked them repeatedly. He blew out a deep breath. Stalling.

"I remember singing…somewhere," she prompted, even as her eyes grew heavy. She mentally shook herself, the way she did to keep from falling asleep when driving. "I raised my arms and…that's all."

Danny nodded, licked again. "Okay."

Snatches of memory flashed as he told the story, familiar scenes as if from an often-watched old movie, disconnected from her present reality. But some things were new, like how the shooter had hidden at the back of the theater, and how Dolina had been shot, then fell off the back of the platform.

"She didn't…she's not…" Regen's throat clenched shut.

"No, no. She's alive." Danny wiped his eyes and took a breath. "She was shot in the shoulder, but it missed the bones. And her leg's broken. But she's recovering well."

"You've been to see her?"

Danny nodded. "Couple of times. She asks about you."

Regen imagined the young girl's fear—the pain of a bullet wound, then plummeting off that high platform. Perhaps having a fuzzy memory was a blessing. She prayed Dolina didn't remember, either.

Danny mumbled something, too quiet for Regen to make out. "What?"

"Lorna. She's injured, too."

Danny's voice was quiet, and Regen gripped his hand tighter. "Tell me."

"Lorna was walking behind the platform carrying some of your costumes." He paused for a breath. "When Dolina fell, she landed on Lorna."

"Danny?" Regen prompted when he didn't continue right away.

"Lorna has a broken neck."

After a few minutes of Danny's reassurances that the doctors were optimistic about Lorna's recovery, Regen closed her eyes. Even then, the tears still leaked out, hot streams down to her ears and neck before finally soaking into the stiff pillowcase.

Dolina and Lorna so badly injured, and all because some psycho shooter had targeted Regen. She thought again of the threatening texts and calls, the weird flower. This was far worse than she'd imagined. With luck she'd forget it all again by tomorrow, or lapse into another blessed coma.

CHAPTER FIVE

Using her right hand and foot, Regen rolled the wheelchair through her mother's living room, past new glass and metal tables and thin-cushioned, angular divans with tubular chrome legs. Sunlight streamed hot and bright through the full-height windows that overlooked Atlanta's commercial and residential rooftops.

"Where the lesser people live and work," her mother said when Regen first arrived in Georgia's capital a week ago.

The view was far prettier at night when the city's lights came on and darkness obscured the maze of satellite dishes, air conditioners, and electrical conduits. This morning's searing sun revealed every grisly flaw, like daylight on the Las Vegas Strip.

A sigh escaped her lips as she carefully jockeyed around yet another glass end table holding a glass vase filled with glass flowers arranged in clear glass marbles. Way too much glass.

She missed her comfy house in Boskoop where she could go outside without using an elevator and plant living flowers in real dirt. Wonderful neighborhood flowers surrounded her little home there, with colors so bright on a sunny day they hurt your eyes. One of the frequently used canals meandered along just across the narrow road out front. Sometimes at night when quiet settled over the land, she could hear the tiny slap of water against the steep banks. The only thing she could hear at night in her mother's loft was the rumbling air conditioning unit, car horns, and sirens.

Regen's idea of home was where smells triggered good memories, where the house muttered dependable nightly groans as it cooled, and where the weather always arrived from the expected direction. None of those happened in this house, at least not for Regen.

Cordelia Evans had moved five times in the fifteen years Regen had lived in Europe, hopscotching across Indiana and Kentucky before landing here in Georgia. This current home of six months was a loft conversion in Midtown, far from the original Nebraska house little Rayne Evans had grown up in. Even that old house with its peeling paint would be preferable to this angular world her mother had chosen. Last night she showed Regen a brochure from a new condo complex on a beach near Jacksonville, Florida. A man her mother knew had invited her to the Sunshine State, and Regen could tell another move was imminent.

She hoped the Florida condo would be an improvement on this kitchen that lay before her. A doctor could operate in this room. No homey memories would ever spark from this expanse of granite and stainless steel. Looking out of place, a brightly colored package of cupcakes lay on the counter, as close to fresh baking as her mother got. Daddy had been the baker in the family.

A calendar in a shiny frame mocked her from its place beside the phone. One week. She shook her head. It seemed like she'd been here a month—at least.

Even while growing up, she'd never understood her mother. Daddy had worked hard as a grocery deliveryman for a regional chain, regularly putting in overtime hours. But even as a child, Regen noticed how her mother's subtle but constant hints about how they could "better" their status wore on him. Then one day shortly before Regen's high school graduation, Daddy hadn't come home after work. A coworker had found him curled over on the seat of his old pickup, cold hand twisted in his shirtfront.

"Oh, man." Regen swiped her eyes. Recalling her dad's heart attack hadn't made her cry in years. Maybe this kitchen *did* stir up memories. Bad ones.

With her left thigh bandaged and bent only slightly at the knee, turning the wheelchair around in the narrow space between the island and stove left her forehead damp with sweat. While each day brought slight improvement, her progress was agonizingly slow. Bullet wounds on TV were nothing like the real thing. Heroes got up and chased the bad guy minutes after being shot. Regen could barely make tea.

After turning on the burner under the kettle, she pulled the basket where her mother kept the tea into her lap. Empty.

"Correction. I *can't* make tea." She flung the empty container onto the counter and turned off the stove. She hated being helpless, but even more, detested being depressed about it. However, with her left arm cast from shoulder to wrist, there was no way to lift herself out of the chair to reach the upper cabinet where her mother kept the full stock of tea and coffee. Regen's bruised spine twisted in rebellion each time she did too much. And the physical therapist wouldn't be here for another hour.

Regen stuffed one of the cupcakes into her mouth and wheeled back to the refrigerator where she pulled out a can of Diet Coke—more appropriate in Atlanta than tea anyway.

"Did I tell you I'm only three blocks from Pemberton Place?" her mother had reminded Regen at least three times. This to-die-for location was named after the inventor of Coca-Cola, and housed the World of Coca-Cola exhibit. Evidently living in the shadow of the great man lent prestige and upped property values.

Regen finished the cupcake, popped the can's top, and raised it toward the window in a toast. "Here's to you, Mr. P." She took a long swig. Her mother would chastise her that nine-thirty was too early for sodas, but so what? She wasn't guzzling a Heineken or Grolsch. Plus, it was six hours later in Holland—well into the afternoon. She tilted the can again.

As she rotated the wheelchair toward the living room, Regen whacked her left leg on the kitchen island. Dagger-like pricks shot up her leg and into her lower back, and she swore. Perspiration beaded her brow. The urge to jump up and sprint out of the building nearly overwhelmed her. She wanted *out* of here. It wasn't home.

But then her home wasn't what it used to be either.

Tears stung at the thought of her cottage. Smashed furniture, glassware, and dishes had greeted Danny when he went to retrieve some clothes for Regen while she recovered in the hospital. Except for a few T-shirts, her everyday clothes and performance costumes had been slashed to rags. Police suspected a meat cleaver or hatchet had been used to chop her boots and shoes. Light fixtures were torn from ceilings, mirrors smashed, bedding shredded, sinks cracked, doors ripped from their hinges. The intruder had emptied every liquid in the house onto the floors, ruining the carpets.

She couldn't imagine the scene and sure didn't want to see it. Even the walls had deep slashes, like claw marks made by some rabid animal. Three parallel lines, exactly like her dressing room at the Ahoy. A shiver walked up her spine on cat's feet, and she shifted back to the tall windows to watch heat shimmers rising from rooftops.

Authorities had found one of the strange flowers on the windowsill above her kitchen sink, and another at the Ahoy Rotterdam in a room at the back of the theater where the shooter had hidden. It took one of their experts only a few minutes to determine the flower was rose and tulip petals, crudely hot-glued together on a stem. The black tulip petals appeared to have been frozen, preserved from spring for use later. It wasn't that the flowers were so creepy that weirded her out; it was his ability to gain access to her world. Her home would never feel the same again no matter how hard she worked at it.

Danny had arranged for basic cleanup and new locks, but those bills nearly drained her bank account, leaving her with little more euros than for her airfare to the United States. Plus, she still owed performance pay to Danny—she'd managed to pay everyone else. He'd waved off her attempt and had told her to pay him later. She bit her lip. That could be awhile.

Many of her loyal fans, initially both horrified and ecstatic to witness her being shot live onstage at the big finale, had been quick to accept a full ticket refund and free admission to another concert as a blatant bribe to keep any from suing the concert organizers and the auditorium. This decimated the income from ticket sales. In Nebraska-speak, she'd bet the farm...and lost—thanks to whoever wanted her dead. Almost thirty-six years old, no money, and living with her mother. Not the success she'd dreamed about.

The doorbell jangled, and she checked the mirrored wall clock. The physical therapist was early. Time for cruel and unusual punishment.

Halfway to the door, the coke in Regen's lap tipped, spilling cold liquid between her legs and puddling in the seat under her. She snatched the can and set in on an end table as she passed. Great. Now she'd have to do her exercises while soaked. This day just kept getting better.

The cheery doorbell tones filled the entryway again as her chair bumped against the door. The peephole was too high for her to reach. Regen unlocked the deadbolt and kicked back so she could pull the door inward. It wasn't the easiest maneuver, and it took a minute before she got the door open wide.

A slender, gold box with matching ribbon and bow sat outside the doorsill, but there was no one there. Regen scanned the hallway. It was twenty feet to the corner that led to the elevator and stairs. Whoever delivered the box must have left right after the last push of the doorbell.

A white card imprinted with colorful balloons lay next to the box: Greater Atlanta Delivery Service. Something for her mother. Maybe from her "man friend" in Florida. Regen smiled. In spite of their differences, she really did wish her mother happiness. Maybe this next move would be good for her.

Regen bent and strained, barely hooking her thumb and index finger under the ribbon and lifted the box to her lap. Another card was tucked under the ribbon, and she flicked it open. Blank.

"Well, that's helpful." Regen slipped the ribbon aside and lifted the end of the box.

No! Panic snatched away her breath.

She hurled the container to the floor, and the single black and red flower tumbled into the hall. She kicked at the box, the doorway, anything she could reach to get away from the thing. The wheelchair spun around, sending the door all the way open against its stop and leaving Regen completely exposed. She twisted, ignoring the pain in her leg, and managed to snag the doorknob. With a heave, she slammed the door and twisted the deadbolt, only slightly relieved by its resounding *thunk.*

Sweat ran down her neck, and her right hand slipped on the chair wheel as she pushed for the phone. One week. One stinkin' week. Who was this guy and why was he tormenting her?

She dialed 1-1-2 twice before remembering the States used 9-1-1 for emergencies. The operator took her information and promised a patrol officer would be there soon. He wanted to remain on the line, but Regen disconnected after she convinced him she was safe behind a locked door. She felt anything but safe. She couldn't stay in Atlanta and couldn't go home until this nut was behind bars. She had to get out of Georgia without being followed, and then stay out of sight where no one would think to look.

There was only one person she could call—the last person she wanted to talk to.

———

Raoul Kleopper crouched in his rental car a block from the complex where Regen van Onweer stayed and lifted his binoculars as a vehicle emerged from the underground garage. The lights by the exit revealed a lone male in the driver's seat. The car headed the opposite direction, and Raoul lowered the glasses and rubbed his eyes. The pills didn't work as well anymore, but he consumed two more, forcing them down with warm water from a plastic bottle.

It had been eleven hours since the police car arrived with flashing lights and sirens blaring. Two more followed minutes later, one blocking the exit from the underground garage. It had all been very exciting, but now the other cars had departed, leaving only a single patrol car parked in front of the high rise's main entrance. The bored-looking officer inside filled out paper work, rarely looking up.

Evanescence sang on the car's radio, and he turned up the volume. Although no Regen van Onweer, Amy Lee was a passable soprano, and My Immortal was one of her best songs. Resting his head against the reclined seat, he wished he'd brought an Elusive Hope CD.

It would have been so easy to take Regen van Onweer earlier at the condo, but the address hadn't matched the date or any other numbers meaningful to him. As much as it frustrated him, the timing wasn't right.

Plus, it was satisfying to imagine Van Onweer cowering in fear. She'd emerge soon enough, if only to check in with her local doctor.

Besides, Marielle couldn't be in a wheelchair, unable to dress for him. He needed her healed, whole. Yes, he must wait even longer, until she was finally ready for him.

Save your last breath.

Regrettably, he no longer had access to her like he did in his roles as part of the stage crews. How many times had he walked behind, breathing her fragrance? Or brushed her arm as he passed on some important errand? He needed a new plan to connect with her. He didn't know if she had a new cell phone yet. But it didn't matter. Soon.

Dark rain will fall from your eyes
    From your body, like notes spilling from a score.
    I drink its life; you sustain me.
    Give me what you promised.
    Save me
    And I will remain with you always.

At one o'clock in the morning, he drove to his hotel to sleep, but he was back in his car by 5:00 am. When he pulled into his covert parking place, he immediately noticed that the police car was missing from the front of the condo unit. A smile tugged the corners of his mouth. Had she run? It might take him hours to confirm, yet he suspected so. Like prey scurrying in vain to escape the jaws of Raoul, the hungry wolf. His smile grew wider.

"You can't keep Marielle from me, Regen van Onweer. I will find you, and your last breath will be mine."

CHAPTER SIX

The train trip up the California coast lasted a lot longer than Regen imagined. She'd grown used to distances in Europe, where one could drive across two countries in a day. California was huge, and it didn't help that she was sleep-deprived from flying out of Atlanta at three in the morning.

As she turned to watch the view from the window, the muscles in her back spasmed again, sending shooting pains down her left hip and thigh. With a groan, she used her good arm to lift herself from the wheel chair, taking the weight off her butt for a minute. She longed for a bed or sofa —even the ground would do. Anything to get prone.

After landing in Los Angeles, she'd opted for the train up the coast, thinking a spacious coach car would be easier than squeezing onto one of the tiny commuter planes that offered the only air service to Mission Peak, the closest town to her destination. Plus, the train was a lot cheaper. But she hadn't counted on the delay while busing to Union Station, then having the train stop at practically every crossroads with a population greater than twelve. Most stops, no one got on or off, but still the train waited, maybe in hope someone would screech into the parking lot at the last second.

The boy across from her—about fifteen and wearing a white T-shirt

under a black leather jacket studded with enough metal to fill a shoebox
—stared openly, as he'd been doing for two hours or more. With the
tattoo on his neck, he looked like a junior Hell's Angel and had *surly*
down pat. Quarter-inch plugs pierced each earlobe, their hollow black
coordinating with the jacket. His endless scrutiny was starting to
seriously annoy her, but she didn't want to draw any more attention to
herself. The ear buds from his music player buzzed tinny notes.

To him, she must look like a car crash victim with her left arm in a
cast, the wheelchair, stiff left leg, and fading bruises across her face. The
straw hat and sunglasses her mother had thrust upon her looked out of
place inside the train, but without them she'd frighten small children and
parents alike.

At least when she'd flown from Rotterdam to Atlanta, her mother
had been with her to help—the most motherly thing she'd done in…
well, ever. Plus, she'd been on serious painkillers and didn't remember
much about the trip. Regen had woken the next morning in the guest
room at her mother's loft. Oh, for one of those little pills right now, but
they were buried in her bag.

She lifted her sunglasses and checked her watch: about thirty minutes
to go. The rails had curved away from the ocean, guiding the train and
passengers past farmland with arrow-straight rows of crops sighting the
looming foothills.

Fighting the cramp in her hip, Regen wished she'd given in to Ben's
insistence he pick her up at LAX and drive her to the house on Storm
Lake. But that would have meant him driving five hours each way. She'd
refused to tell him the flight information until he'd given in. Stubborn
man.

Regen bit her lip. It had been so long. Shouldn't the guilt be gone? Yet
unlike yogurt or milk, remorse never seemed to expire.

She grunted and jerked as another spasm hit, aware she'd be lying
down by now if she'd taken the commuter flight. Talk about stubborn.
She glanced at her watch again and found only two minutes had passed.
"Please make it go faster," she muttered to no one. Biker boy lifted a
brow, but didn't move, other than to bob his head in time to the buzzing
earphones. He continued to stare.

Ben Conner checked his watch for the tenth time in as many minutes as he paced to the southernmost end of the Mission Peak Amtrak platform. The schedule board optimistically showed the train "On Time," but evidently that didn't mean as much as it had forty years ago when his grandfather had been an engineer with the Southern Pacific. Ben stared down the empty tracks, willing the train to materialize.

"They just radioed," a voice called from his left. Ben turned to the platform conductor wheeling a large aluminum baggage cart toward the edge of the platform. "Four minutes out."

"Oh. Thanks."

"Looked like you needed to know." The man tipped his hat to Ben and gave a knowing smile.

Ben frowned at the steel ribbons. He just wanted to get this over.

Three and a half minutes later, he spotted the train's headlamp coming around the shallow uphill curve, followed seconds later by the thrum of the diesel. The engine's tone changed as it slowed and glided past the station, bringing the passenger cars in alignment with the raised platform. The cars braked to a smooth stop without so much as a squeal.

A light breeze blew diesel fumes back along the platform in a pungent cloud—a powerful reminder of Ben's childhood. The oily fuel had been his dad's weed killer of choice for years along their gravel driveway, long before anyone knew the environmental dangers of such action. Sure had killed the weeds, though.

As passengers began debarking, Ben stepped forward, rubbing his damp hands on his pants. He looked down at the faded denim. A frayed hole was beginning on the right pocket where he kept his keys. Maybe he should have dressed up a little. He grimaced, feeling like a character in an old west movie. If he'd had a hat, he'd be doffing it and slicking down his hair, waiting for the little lady. He exhaled and shook out his hands.

Only this was no little lady. Never had been. Not unless you described little ladies as heavy metal rockers with a will of steel. No, *demure* didn't describe Rayne Evans, especially not her stage presence of Regen van Onweer.

Sweat trickled down Regen's back and soaked into her blouse where she leaned against the seat. This was by far the dumbest thing she'd ever done, and she wasn't thinking about the train ride. Before the coach had stopped, everyone around jumped to their feet, gathering backpacks, duffle bags, water bottles, and children. She couldn't seem to move.

Maybe she should have accepted Danny's offer to stay at his house in Amsterdam. But no, that had seemed way too close to whoever was trying to kill her. Or she could have… But that was the rub, wasn't it? There was nowhere else to go. She'd tried her mother's, but had been found in short order. It wasn't that hard to figure out her mother's name and address using the Internet, not with the Dutch newspapers running non-stop stories about the shooting and Regen's hospital stay. Paparazzi and legitimate press had photographed and interviewed everyone working at or visiting the hospital. Even though her mother hadn't spoken with the press, Regen's picture had appeared in several articles.

Regen massaged her forehead. Maybe she should just stay on the train and keep going to San Francisco or Seattle. But what then? She didn't know a soul in those cities. She hadn't been on the West Coast in fifteen years, not since…

Regen scattered the thoughts with a shake of her head. She couldn't go there right now. That was the past. She looked out the window at the golden rolling hills, so familiar—a sight she had never planned to see again.

A hand touched her shoulder, and she looked up with a start. Biker Boy stood next to her, buzzing earphones draped over his shoulders.

"Do you need help with your bag?" He gripped his own badly worn backpack by its top handle. Did he have the barest smile? He seemed sincere as he gestured toward her carry-on wedged under the seat.

Now she felt bad for not trying to talk to him during their journey from Los Angeles. She'd become distrustful of people. And, truth be told, he looked like the majority of her fans in Europe. His neck tattoo—a red and black Celtic cross with a green snake coiled at the base—was pretty mild compared to what she often saw. Even on her band. She smiled at him.

"What's your name?"

"Oh, it's Josh. Joshua." He accepted her extended hand using a firm grip. Most teenagers wimped out when shaking hands. Her father had always said you could tell a lot by a handshake. "What's yours?"

"I'm Re... uh, Rayne."

"Like a rain storm?" Josh asked, raising one brow. Her smile slipped, but she covered it with a cough.

"Not exactly. I spell it R-a-y-n-e." Josh had no idea he'd hit exactly on the meaning of her assumed Dutch stage name. Regen van Onweer: rain of the storm.

"Cool. What happened to you? Car accident?" he asked bluntly. He'd certainly had plenty of time to catalogue her injuries during the trip. And now that he'd started talking, he didn't seem inclined to stop.

Regen turned away slightly. "Something like that." Except for the bullets. From the corner of her eye, she saw him give a shrug, then bend and pull her bag from under the seat. Without another word, he turned and headed for the exit, her bag slung over his shoulder. She had no choice but to follow.

So much for staying on the train and running away. Like last time.

The stream of riders exiting the train slowed to a trickle, but Ben saw no sign of Rayne. There were five doors with conductors manning each opening. He stood in the middle of the platform, turning each way to cover them all.

At five foot eleven inches, she always stood out in a crowd. Her height had surprised him when they first met. He'd never dated anyone as close to his own six one. With heels, which she rarely wore, they were eye-to-eye.

Ben's teeth ground together. That had been a long time ago. So much had changed since then. Still, when she'd called last night totally out of the blue, he hadn't turned her down.

He walked to the northernmost door, but as he arrived, the conductor signaled waiting passengers to begin boarding. Obviously everyone was off this end of the train. Ben spun around and headed the other way, passing a conductor helping off-load a wheelchair-bound old lady in a straw hat. He got a dozen feet past them.

"Ben."

The single, half-whispered name stopped him dead. He turned, expecting to find her striding toward him—or rather using crutches since she said she'd been attacked and injured. But there was no one except the old lady and a punker teenager. Maybe she'd called from the station building?

Then the woman in the wheel chair removed her sunglasses and tilted her head up. The kid set a bag beside the chair and walked away.

"Hello, Ben."

Even from this distance, Ben recognized the vibrant green eyes of Rayne Evans.

His ex-wife.

CHAPTER SEVEN

The look in Ben's eyes at the station had swept her back through a decade and a half, brushing away Regen van Onweer in one stroke and replacing her with Rayne Evans. Now, riding in the truck to Ben's house, she marveled how it had happened.

She had lived as Regen for over twelve years, ever since she assumed the stage name as her own. Regen was stronger, more assured than Rayne had ever been, perfect for commanding the stage, negotiating with concert promoters, and handling cantankerous band members. Becoming Regen had set her career on a new path, and doors opened for the Dutch singer that had been closed to any American. She'd never lied to anyone about her nationality, but her fluent Dutch fooled most people, and she simply didn't correct their assumption.

She thought of herself as Regen, bought clothes as her, performed as her. It was only in the quietest hours of the long nights that she occasionally dreamed as Rayne. Even in Atlanta with her mother calling her Rayne, her brain automatically translated it to Regen. Especially in her mother's home, she'd needed Regen's strength.

But Regen had never driven on these familiar California roads that wound through golden hills dotted with hunter green oaks draped with Spanish moss. This was where Rayne had lived, and it would be better to think of herself that way once again while here. She leaned against the headrest, wondering how she could make such a transition without losing too much of herself.

Of course Ben knew her stage name. But it would be far safer if no one else did. She *had* to let Regen go—at least temporarily—and she found that frightening.

The forty-minute drive from Mission Peak to Perilous Cove, then up and over the hills to Storm Lake and Ben's house, set a new level of discomfort. Not from physical pain like on the train—she had popped two pain pills before they left the station, even though the bottle called for one. The effective chemicals were pleasantly coursing through her veins. No, the strain in the truck was purely emotional.

She glanced at Ben, his strong jaw set, eyes straight ahead. When they had been married and he'd gotten angry, he always clammed up. And he hadn't said ten words to her since he finally recognized her in the wheel chair. Nope. Just helped her into the truck and driven off.

But it wasn't too surprising. Ben Conner didn't owe her any more than that. Not even that much, really, after what she'd done to him. Still, it would have been nice to be welcomed back. *"How are you doing, Rayne? Good to see you. And why didn't you tell me about all the bullet holes?"*

A giggle escaped her lips. Ben's eyes cut to her, anger replaced by confusion...and something else. But the winding road and pain meds had her head spinning, and it was too much work to think. All she wanted was for everything to stop moving so she could rest.

Ben's attention returned to the road, but she noted the anger was gone. She relaxed at the sunlight flickering through the trees and warming her face.

Fifteen minutes later, they slowed and turned down a sloped driveway. The blacktop curved through majestic oak trees for a hundred yards before opening into a compound-like, paved yard in front of a four-car garage. Ben always liked his projects, both cars and woodcrafting. It appeared he had plenty of room.

But her relief was short-lived when she realized Ben would have to lift her again, this time to help her down from his crew-cab pickup. He unloaded her wheelchair from the bed, but then, to her dismay, carried it up the three stairs and through the front door into the house. He then returned and opened her door.

"What are you doing? I need—"

"It's easier this way."

'This way' turned out to be slipping his arms under her and lifting her from the truck. She automatically hooked her right arm around his neck, regretting both the intimacy it implied and the stretched muscles of her back. A groan slipped between her lips.

"Sorry," Ben said. "Are you okay?"

Rayne nodded. "Just go easy."

By the time Ben edged sideways through the front door, she was panting against the pain, and sweat beaded her forehead and lip.

Gently, Ben lowered her into a cushy leather recliner and, for a moment, time slowed. Bent at the waist, his arms were still under her as she settled into the chair, his face only inches from hers. So close. Her breath caught, but not before drawing in his familiar aftershave. What brand was it? She'd bought it for him that one Christmas together, but couldn't remember. No matter what the name, the fragrance surfaced unbidden memories of beach sand and crashing surf, suntan lotion, of splashing cold lake water on days with sky so blue it looked like cutout craft paper pasted overhead. Ben's eyes dropped to her mouth. Involuntarily, she wet her lips. What was he…?

But as she wondered, he slid his arms from beneath her and straightened. An unreadable expression crossed his face, then he turned and walked down a hallway to what Rayne presumed was the bedroom area. Her breath came in stuttered gulps. Whoa. What *was* that?

Her head fell back into the soft headrest, but her betraying heart kept up a staccato beat. She glanced down at her sticky shirt, expecting to see movement from the traitorous organ in her chest. When they'd been together, she'd rarely known what Ben was thinking. And the man was as irritating as ever, always doing the opposite of what she… Wanted?

No.

With a decisive mental sweep, she cleared the incident, if that's what it was, from her mind. And, since he seemed to be taking his sweet time doing whatever down the hall, she surveyed what she could see of the house.

This was obviously the great room. Its vaulted ceiling of whitewashed knotty pine reflected light from windows set high in the peak, bathing the walls with a late afternoon pale gold. Furnishings were sparse, but shouted craftsmanship. The glass-topped coffee and end tables were hand-hewn from four-inch-round logs with a burnished satin finish that appeared to be hand-rubbed.

The family room opened to a spacious kitchen, complete with whitewashed pine cabinets, beautiful green-veined granite countertops, and stainless steel appliances. The same materials that seemed so cold at her mother's looked warm and inviting here. Everything appeared new, yet not ostentatious. Having been out of the country so long, Rayne didn't know much about current American kitchens, but she liked this one.

Through triple French doors she saw a flagstone patio with a low fire pit to one side. Beyond the patio, the yard sloped away to an unobstructed, jaw-dropping view of Storm Lake. This was nothing like the tiny log cabin they'd lived in so long ago. Aspens flanked by majestic pines filtered the sun, dappling the patio and yard with ever-shifting patterns. Two comfy looking chaises were perfectly positioned for lounging away an afternoon with a good book and cup of cocoa or glass of wine, depending on the season. She imagined sitting in one with her notebook, working on song ideas while the sun played on the water.

"What do you think?" Startled, she found Ben standing nearby, a damp washcloth in one hand.

"It's magnificent." Her voice came out a whisper, sounding way too... Something. She cleared her throat and pushed as upright as she could get in the impossibly comfortable chair. "I mean it's very nice. You must have looked a long time to find such a nice place." Nice. Sheesh. She sounded like an idiot. Sweat broke out on her skin again.

Ben handed her the washcloth, and she placed it against her forehead. For a moment, she closed her eyes at its cool comfort, then she slid it down her face and made a couple of quick passes around her sticky neck. After a whole day of travel, she needed a bath, but it felt so good to sit in something besides the wheelchair, that she didn't want to move.

"I didn't find it."

For a moment, as she held the damp washcloth against her skin, she couldn't remember the question she'd asked. It must have showed in her expression.

"The house. I built it." Ben slipped onto the arm of the sofa. "Well, rebuilt it, really. A *lot* of remodeling," he said, a smile caressing his rugged features.

She looked around with new awareness. Everything looked new, like he'd moved in only a few days ago. But it was all so comfortable, too, like a home well lived in. A family's home. Had he built this for someone? A special someone? She sought out framed photos in the bookcase, on the hand-carved fireplace mantle, but they were all too small to make out. Was Ben married? She'd been so panicked when she'd called yesterday, she never thought to ask, but now...

A door slammed somewhere beyond the kitchen and her heart jumped. His wife?

"Hi, Quin," Ben called, even though no one had come into the room. "Come in here. I want you to meet someone."

A slender, brown-haired boy of twelve or thirteen came in from the kitchen, a backpack slung over one shoulder. He let it slide to the floor and came to stand beside where Ben sat. Ben reached out and squeezed his shoulder.

"Quin, I'd like you to meet Rayne Evans. She's the woman I told you about."

The boy mumbled "Hi," all-the-while taking in her bandaged leg and arm cast, the red scars on her face.

"Rayne, I'd like you to meet Quin Walker. My son."

As Quin stepped forward to greet her, Rayne couldn't help staring beyond him, wondering if his mother would arrive next.

Later, in her bedroom, Rayne stared out the tall window. Four pine trees towered over the north end of the property, filtering the view of the sparkling, blue water as a light breeze ruffled their boughs. The tranquil setting did little to calm her churning emotions.

Ben had a son. She shook her head. Hadn't seen that one coming.

Even as she'd fled to her room—with Ben's help, of course, since she couldn't move without her wheelchair and, thereby, making the whole fleeing thing kind of moot—his explanation that he was adopting Quin hadn't answered nearly all her questions. Same old Ben, he didn't seem inclined to expound. And really it wasn't any of her business anyway, so she couldn't very well demand the full story.

But that didn't stop the questions.

Who was Quin's mom? Had Ben married her? What kind of situation had Rayne inserted herself into?

With a sigh, she turned her chair and rolled past the four-poster bed and into the spacious attached bathroom. Travertine floor tiles stretched right into a walk-in shower with no door or curtain. The same green-hued granite as in the kitchen made up the long countertop that included dual sinks. An arrangement of candles and a basket brimming with bath beads, shampoos, and other small bottles were the only items on the smooth stone. A woman *had* to live here.

A large soaking tub occupied one corner, flanked by forest-view windows with sage sheers and matching tiebacks. The tub was partially recessed into the floor, providing low access. Her leg wound was sufficiently healed, so the only thing she had to worry about was her arm cast. Rolling over to the tub, she eyed the edge, its depth, and a stainless grab bar. She could get in. The question was, could she get out? Well, as Aunt Ruth used to say, what's life without a challenge?

Ninety minutes later, she'd successfully bathed, gathered up the wet towels she'd spread on the floor to roll out onto after her bath, and dressed. It had left her panting, but clean and feeling like a new woman —or at least as new as she could feel in her battered body.

Now, dressed in thin cotton sweat pants and a black Elusive Hope T-shirt, she rolled into the kitchen area. Ben was at the counter, chopping carrots and dropping them into a large, steaming pot on the six-burner stove. Aromas of onions and browned meat filled the air, flooding her with childhood memories of visiting her grandmother on her father's side.

"Is that stew?"

Ben finished the last carrot with a chop, chop, chop, then turned toward her. "Are you hoping for a yes?"

Irish stew had become an instant favorite dinner during that visit to her grandmother, and she'd begged her mother to fix it when she got home. Her mother said any kind of stew, especially Irish stew, was a poor person's meal. They'd had veal instead and never spoke of stew again. One time when her mother was away on a trip, her dad had fixed it using her grandmother's recipe. It had been their secret.

"Sorry," Ben said. She looked up to find his lips drawn in a tight line. "I can make something else if you like."

"Oh, no." Rayne realized the memory of her mother had pulled her mouth into a frown. "I'm sorry—bad memory." She corrected it with her widest smile. "Stew is my favorite meal—especially with crusty French bread." She nodded toward the long loaf on the counter.

His expression softened. "Thought I had that right, unless your tastes changed with all the high living in Europe."

Yeah, right. A rueful smile curled her lips. Two-day-old bread and simple meals had been her standard fare up until two years ago when things started to turn for the group. For ten years she'd supplemented her income by waiting tables at various restaurants in and around Boskoop. Neither the pay nor the tips were great, but at least she got the occasional meal included with her work. And often she'd take home some leftovers set aside by the cooks she made a point of befriending. Many times she'd lug her keyboard to work and play during breaks between waiting tables. That always increased the evening's tips.

But even with the band's recent success, she'd continued to live a frugal lifestyle. Having seen so many other bands rise to the top and disappear overnight, she never held anything too tight.

"Ben, could you help me tie my hair back?" Rayne held up a scrunchie, one of the few things recovered undamaged from her house. Ben gave her a considered look, then moved behind the chair and ran his fingers along her scalp as he combed the long curling strands back. It felt so good, that he'd done it several times before she remembered to hand him the scrunchie. He doubled it around her thick mane, let it fall against the back of her chair, and then stepped where she could see him.

"Your hair didn't used to be black." He regarded her with hooded eyes. It was such an obvious statement of fact, she almost laughed. Then she remembered this was Ben. Lucky he even noticed the different hairstyle. Sometimes he'd been so caring; then, other times, he hadn't paid any attention to her at all. At least that's the way she remembered it. Had he changed?

"It's been a bunch of colors. Part of the profession," she said, trying to keep things light. "Symphonic metal queen, you know?"

He nodded and his eyes cut to the delicate sea-green waves tattooed on the inside of her right wrist. She pulled her arm into her lap. She'd never been self-conscious about her tattoo before, but then again, the inked design had no special meaning to most of her friends. But as Danny said, every tattoo was significant to the person wearing it for life.

Rayne kept her eyes down as she addressed him. "I know I've asked a lot of you, Ben, calling out of the blue and asking if I could stay here. And I should have told you the extent of my injuries." She fiddled with the edge of her T-shirt. She'd been thinking only of herself when she'd telephoned him. He could have been in the middle of a divorce, moving, dying of some disease; none of these had occurred to her. "I didn't even ask about... I mean—"

"Rayne. It's okay."

He was letting her off the hook, and she snagged the overture like a rope from the lifeguard he'd once been.

"I'm still sorry." Rayne wished she'd stayed on the train bound for San Francisco. And now for the next hard thing. "I'm going to need some help. I should be doing physical therapy, but the truth is, I can't afford it. When I was at my mother's, she paid for someone to come in and work with me, but—"

"Rayne." Ben gave her an exasperated look. "Why didn't you say you needed money? I can—"

"No!" It came out stronger than she intended, and her upraised palm surprised her. So did the hurt that flashed across Ben's face. But she didn't want his money. Asking for a place to stay, him feeding her was bad enough. She dropped her hand and continued more softly. "No. I can pay a little, but not for a professional. Do you know anyone, a girl or woman, who could work with me for a few weeks? Ideally, she could help me wash my hair, as well as work through some of the physical therapy exercises.

"Also, I've got to find a doctor out here. My doctor in Rotterdam said this cast could come off in five to six weeks, and next week is week five. If it had been just a clean break, I'd use one of your saws and hack the thing off myself. But with the bullet wound, I have to make sure everything is healing as it should."

Ben rubbed his chin. Despair weighed on her shoulders. She might have to advertise in the newspaper or something.

"There's a good doctor up in Deer Cove, so that's no problem." Then Ben's eyes crinkled, and the corners of his mouth turned up. "And I think I know just the person for your other needs. Although you might get more than you bargained for."

Rayne glanced at the clock and wondered if it was too late in the day to catch a northbound train.

CHAPTER EIGHT

Rayne sat on one of the kitchen chairs, enjoying a cup of coffee. Only one day and she'd already fallen in love with Ben's view. This afternoon, the water sparkled like a million diamonds in the breeze that pebbled the lake's surface. Small boats carved furrows through the liquid blue, the purr of their outboard motors growing distant and then fading completely.

Ducks landed and took off regularly, the lake their migration refueling station, while squirrels darted across the grassy bank looking for any food they could stockpile for the coming winter.

She hadn't been mature enough to appreciate the beauty when she'd lived here. The lake had become a place of confinement, keeping her from music and performance. But now... She longed to be a simple passenger in one of the boats skimming across the glimmer. The air might be cool enough to wear a warm jacket, but it would buffet her cheeks to a healthy pink and fill her lungs with clean, pure nature.

Rayne breathed deep. Even inside the house the air smelled fresh. She'd just determined to climb back into her wheelchair and maneuver onto the patio when the deep gong of the doorbell sounded.

From upstairs Quin yelled, "I got it!" He flew down the stairs, skidding to a stop at the front door and leaving the oval throw rug in a mound. He pulled the door open.

"Mandy!"

"Hey, boat boy, how's it going?" The girl, evidently named Mandy, ruffled Quin's hair as she stepped inside. He ducked out of her grasp and grabbed his coat off the hook by the door.

"I've gotta give Mrs. Hamilton a ride to the doctor," Quin told Mandy. He swung around and pointed to Rayne. "That's her over there." With that glowing introduction, Quin darted out the door, letting it slam behind him.

"Well," Mandy said, arms akimbo as she leaned close to the door. "Good to see you, too, Quin." She pivoted, focused on Rayne, and headed her way, a big, lopsided smile lighting her face.

She was tall—perhaps taller than Rayne's own 5'11"—and she had short, but spiky black hair which added to her height. Rayne checked the girl's feet. No added height from the flat boat shoes that matched her snug red T-shirt. Denim Capri pants with four-inch cuffs revealed deeply tanned, muscled calves. Red and blue striped hoop earrings coordinated with a small handbag.

The simple stroll across the great room qualified her for the finals of any modeling contest, but it wasn't pretentious. Rayne didn't think the girl even knew she was doing it. She had the natural grace of a dancer or athlete. Given the girl's broad shoulders, Rayne was betting on sports of some kind.

Mandy extended her hand. "Hi. I'm Mandy," she said in a sexy alto.

Rayne accepted the girl's handshake. "Good to meet you, Mandy. I'm Rayne…uh…Evans."

Mandy tilted her head to one side, eyes narrowing as she continued to grip Rayne's hand. "Have we met before?"

"I'm sure we haven't." Rayne retrieved her hand. "I've been out of the country for many years." Closer now, the girl looked younger than Rayne first thought. Probably seventeen or eighteen, though something in her dark eyes spoke of wisdom and experience that couldn't be counted in years.

"No accent," the girl observed. "You must have been born in the

U.S." She tapped one unpolished fingernail on her lips, forehead slightly furrowed. "Kansas?"

"Nebraska," Rayne laughed. "So, should we—"

Mandy stopped her with an outstretched palm. "Coffee first." She skirted the breakfast bar and headed into the kitchen. "Ben's not here, is he?" she cast over her shoulder as she reached for a mug.

"Uh, no. He's in Mission Peak on a job today." He'd left before eight this morning, reminding her through her bedroom door that someone—evidently Mandy—was coming by today. "Why?"

Mandy waived a hand as she poured with the other. "Oh, he never lets me drink coffee. Says it'll stunt my growth." She added a heaping teaspoon of sugar from the bowl, then a splash of milk from the refrigerator. "As if," she muttered to herself, but loud enough Rayne heard.

"You're certainly old enough to drink coffee," Rayne said, nodding as Mandy lifted the carafe in her direction.

"Yep, that's what Sam says, too. But the guys never listen," Mandy said as she topped off Rayne's cup.

Now Rayne was completely confused. Who were 'the guys,' and why wasn't Sam one of them? "Sam. Is he a friend?"

"Oh," Mandy said, retaking her seat at the table. "No. Sam's a girl. Woman. She's my..." The girl's voice grew quiet, and suddenly she looked younger. For a minute Rayne wondered if she would answer, but then she perked back up as if a switch had been thrown. "She's my mom. Well, not yet, but soon," Mandy said, and sipped her coffee, as if that explained it all.

Good thing Rayne wasn't prone to headaches. Although many of her fans in Europe were this girl's age, Rayne didn't hang out with teens or young twenties on a regular basis. They switched conversational directions faster than she remembered from her growing up years. Maybe it was all the texting and social media posts.

"So, Mandy, you deduced me as an American. Let me see how *my* powers of deduction are. Sam's your soon-to-be mom. You're probably an athlete. I'm stretching, but perhaps you do some modeling? Maybe in college—nineteen?"

Mandy choked on her drink. "Nineteen? You think I'm nine-*teen*?"

Rayne realized her mistake immediately. It was never a good thing to under-guess a young person's age. They all wanted to be older. To have someone think you younger was a disaster of global proportions.

"I'm sorry, Mandy. I've never been good at guessing ages. You're older? What, twenty-two?" She hoped that was high enough. With skin so perfect, Mandy couldn't be much more than that. A wide grin spread across the girl's face before she reined it back into a serious expression.

"Twenty-two, huh?" Mandy leaned back in her chair and chewed on the words for a minute, face masked in total seriousness. Then she leaned forward, grabbed Rayne's right hand, and said conspiratorially, "We're going to get along great. You know why?"

Rayne shook her head. Better to stay quiet at this point.

***

Ben pulled into the driveway at 6:15, turned off the engine, and stretched his neck, wincing at the kinks. He'd spent half the afternoon in an eighteen-inch-high crawlspace above a commercial building in Mission Peak, installing surveillance camera wiring. Whoever had dropped the ceiling on the late 1800s structure hadn't figured on a man his size squeezing between cripple walls and cross-bracing to get to the various locations. To make it worse, the space had been partially stuffed with fiberglass insulation. A hot shower couldn't come soon enough.

He snatched up the two extra-large pizzas and a large salad from Wave Pizza in Perilous Cove and climbed out of the truck. The only pizza place here at the lake was at Deer Cove, and he hadn't had the energy to drive up there and back around the lake. Plus, The Wave, as locals referred to it, was around the corner from the Last Drop, so he'd grabbed a large coffee and traded stories with the coffee shop owner, Conrad Langworth, while waiting for the pizza.

Juggling the food while reaching for the doorknob, Ben heard the telltale sound of an outboard motor. He walked to the end of the porch where he could see the lake. An aluminum fourteen footer arrowed toward the dock, its perfect V wake glinting in the waning sunlight. He recognized Quin's reversed Dodgers baseball cap and black windbreaker. Ben set the salad on the porch rail and waved, but

Quin was concentrating on slowing and maneuvering to the tie-up at their dock and didn't see him. Ben went inside and headed for the kitchen.

He spotted Mandy's purse on the breakfast table at the same time he heard laughter from the hallway leading to the guest suite—Rayne's room. In spite of his fatigue, he grinned, wishing he'd been a fly on the wall when Rayne met Mandy. His brother's daughter made quite the first impression. Whip-smart, tall, and gorgeous, Mandy had moxie to spare—a gift from her Italian mother.

Mandy had other talents, too, including her dead aim with a handgun—she'd acquired that skill from her dad. And good thing. Not too many months ago, she'd taken a bullet in the shoulder and, in turn, later shot the would-be governor of Missouri, saving Samantha Riley's life and maybe her dad's life as well. Mandy might be a teenager, but she'd been forced to grow up fast, acquiring a maturity beyond her years.

In the kitchen Ben battled between eating or heading upstairs for a shower. He hadn't decided one way or the other when the laughter grew louder. Rayne hobbled around the corner into the great room, Mandy lending a supporting hand under her shoulder. Pain creased Rayne's brow with every step, but she wasn't letting on to Mandy. With a sigh and rapid breathing, Rayne sank into a kitchen chair, taking the weight off her healing leg.

Ben relaxed and let out his own breath. "Well, looks like you two met." They hadn't seen him as he leaned against the far counter, and both turned in surprise.

"Ben!" Mandy danced toward him, but he warded her off with outstretched palms and explained about his insulation-covered clothes.

"It's *Uncle* Ben to you, young lady. And have you been drinking coffee?" He nodded toward the two mugs on the table. "Again?"

"Rayne thinks I'm old enough to drink coffee," Mandy said, ignoring Ben's uncle status and turning a smug expression to Rayne. "Don't you?"

Rayne's jaw dropped open. "Well, I...I mean, well you are quite...did you say *uncle*"?

Mandy spun to Ben, smugness replaced by sophistication. "Rayne thinks I'm *twenty-two!*" she nearly squealed, and Ben turned to Rayne, who had gone contrite. He raised his brow.

Color flooded up Rayne's neck. She raised her good shoulder in a shrug, then used a napkin to dab her forehead. "I was trying to guess her age. I had no idea she was your... Well, I may have guessed a smidge high," she finished in a weak voice, barely meeting his eyes.

Mandy squealed again just as Quin—holding his ears—came through the garage door and into the kitchen.

"Sounds like a girl party in here." No one said anything for a second, leaving him time to sniff loudly. "Hey, pizza!" He looked around and spotted the flat boxes behind Ben. He had a lid up and was reaching for a slice before Ben stopped him.

"Hold it, sport. Let's wash up and sit down at the table with Rayne." He pointed Quin toward the sink. "Mandy, can you set the table?"

"Sure can, *Uncle* Ben," she purred in her sweetest I-want-something alto, but she didn't elaborate.

Whatever her scheme, he was too tired to get into it right now. As he passed Rayne on the way to wash up himself, she touched his hand.

"She's Addison and Elizabeth's daughter?" Rayne whispered under Mandy and Quin's banter.

He gave a single nod, realizing she'd left before Elizabeth had given birth to Mandy. He'd written to Rayne once, informing her of Elizabeth's death. He couldn't remember if he'd mentioned their daughter's name.

They devoured three-quarters of the pizza in short order, along with all the salad. Quin told them about his trip across the lake to take Olivia Hamilton to and from her doctor appointment in Deer Cove.

While Quin talked, Ben found himself watching Rayne as she, in turn, watched his niece and Quin. Occasionally, a flash of sorrow shadowed Rayne's countenance, especially when she glanced his way. Most people wouldn't have noticed it, but he knew what to look for. Sadness for life missed?

Well, she'd chosen her path. No matter how successful, or how much power or fame one gained, nothing replaced family in his mind. It was the reason he'd stayed in Storm Lake so long ago, the reason for adopting Quin now. The boy needed a father. No one should go through life without close family. Maybe Rayne was finally learning that lesson.

These kids had been through so much: Mandy had lost her mother, Elizabeth, to cancer a few years ago, and Quin's father had died in a car accident a little over two years ago. Now Mandy had Samantha Riley in her life, and Quin had Ben. Things had a way of working out. He hoped Rayne's presence wouldn't throw a wrench in the works.

Ben stood, gathered the boxes, and headed for the kitchen. He kept his back to the group while he wrapped up the remaining pizza, then ducked into the half-bath to blow his nose. When he emerged, Mandy, who'd struck a pose at the counter, caught his eye.

"So, *Uncle* Ben." The purring had returned and Ben braced himself. "Now that I'm going on twenty-*two*, how about taking me driving in your truck?" The girl had the nerve to bat her eyes at him.

Well there were two ways to play this game. He gave her his biggest smile and cleared his throat.

"Oh, okay. Sounds like a good idea, young lady, now that you have your learner's permit—" he made sure he had Rayne's eye "—and you're almost *sixteen*." Rayne looked properly chagrined. He let Mandy's surprised expression turn into a full-blown grin before he dropped the punch line. "I assume by *truck*, you mean the Bronco. Good idea, since that's what your dad and I drove when we were young."

Mandy crossed her arms. "You expect me to drive that rattletrap piece of junk? No way."

"You need some experience in a classic vehicle. I think a '66 is just the thing."

"It hasn't even got a decent radio," Mandy pouted. "It's barely got a floor."

"Ben, don't tell me you still have that decrepit Ford?" Rayne asked.

Mandy's pout turned into a surprised frown, and her gaze ping-ponged between Rayne and Ben before stopping on Rayne. Mandy's eyes narrowed. "Wait. How'd you know about the Bronco?"

Ben shot Rayne a look. She had guilt written all over her face, but it was too late to take back her words. While Mandy turned her focus on Ben, Rayne mouthed, "*Sorry.*" Mandy's brows were higher than he'd ever seen them, which was pretty high for this passionate teen.

Oh, man.

CHAPTER NINE

"I can't believe you and Uncle Ben were *married*," Mandy gushed for at least the fifth time as she washed Rayne's hair the next day.

On the flip side, Rayne couldn't believe this was Addison's daughter. She had grown from baby to a young woman while Rayne had been gone. It didn't seem possible, but Rayne had missed this girl's entire lifetime so far. That felt incredibly wrong.

The more Mandy talked about Rayne and Ben's past marriage, the more enthusiastically she scrubbed. Rayne's scalp was beginning to hurt, but it felt heavenly to get her hair completely clean. Her mother hadn't wanted to wash it—she'd just had a manicure—so Rayne had done the best she could in Atlanta using one hand and the bathroom sink.

"I mean, I *wondered* why you were here, but I thought it had something to do with his security and protection business. But *married*. Wow!" Mandy shook her head. "I never saw that one coming."

Rayne hadn't seen it coming either. She'd been young and dumb. *Really* dumb. Oh, she'd thought herself so sophisticated. She'd spent a year with her aunt and uncle in Amsterdam on a study abroad program, going to school and playing music in clubs every chance she got. The rock music scene had been booming, and she'd loved every minute of it. Coming home to Milhone, Nebraska, had been a huge letdown after the glitz and glamour of the cultural capital of the Netherlands. She'd made —and left behind—her best friends across the pond.

"You have to tell me everything," Mandy said, pushing suds through Rayne's long curls. She was propped on a stool, head back in the bathroom's oversized sink and a towel under her neck while Mandy squeezed and agitated her hair.

So Rayne told her story. How she'd always loved music, gone to the Netherlands, and returned to Nebraska to graduate high school. She'd planned to go back, but her aunt and uncle retired and left Amsterdam for Alabama.

"Then the high school and junior college in Milhone did a joint, West Coast choir tour in the fall. They needed a keyboard player, and I'd never been to Disneyland…"

"Major perk," Mandy nodded.

"Absolutely. After the Magic Kingdom, we headed up the coast, stopping in Mission Peak to sing at a street fair." It had been a disastrous performance, the worst of the tour. The makeshift risers collapsed, tumbling the singers to the sidewalk. And the shuffling crowds kicked out the power cords for the amps, lights, and her keyboard four times.

To make matters worse, twenty-nine-year-old Ben Conner had taken a chair in the front row, all surfer-dude-blond-in-need-of-a-trim cute. During the performance, his blue eyes never left her, and she fat-fingered too many notes to count that night as her eyes continually strayed to the T-shirt drawn tight across his defined chest and flat abs.

When the production mercifully ended, the director gave everyone two hours to enjoy the street fair. Rayne fled to the bus to pack her keyboard in the luggage bin, wanting nothing more than to crawl in after it and pull down the hatch. After performing semi-professionally in Europe—she got paid a little for the club gigs, and even performed at a couple of weddings—tonight was totally embarrassing. She rose, put her hands in the small of her back and stretched cramped muscles. When she turned, surfer boy stood right behind her, holding out his hand.

"Hi. I'm Ben Conner." The corners of his eyes crinkled when he smiled.

She shook his damp hand. Was this great-looking guy nervous? "Rayne Evans." He cleared his throat a couple of times and for a moment seemed at a loss for words. She lowered her head. "Look, I'm sorry about that disaster performance."

"You're sure tall, for a girl," he blurted.

Her head snapped up, and she burst out laughing, tension sliding from her like water from a swimmer's body. When she regained control, she leaned one hip against the bus and regarded him more seriously.

"That's an unusual pickup line. Does it usually work for you?"

He rubbed his chin, considering her question for moment. Then he shook his head. "Not on short girls."

She laughed again. "What about tall girls?" she asked, raising a brow. This time, he didn't hesitate.

"Never talked to one as tall as you. You'll have to let me know." The twinkle in his baby blues won her over. If there was one thing she'd learned in Europe, it was how to be aggressive when appropriate. She stepped forward and laced her arm through his.

"I *will* let you know." She smiled and pulled him toward the noisy crowd a block away from the parked bus. "Come on, Ben Conner. You're buying me a Coke."

Mandy wrapped a towel around Rayne's hair and squeezed out the water. "That's such a great story." She snapped on the blow dryer, shouting above its whine. "I hope I can meet a guy just like that someday."

"You will, Mandy. Don't be impatient. Wait for the right one." In the mirror, Rayne could see Mandy considering the admonition before responding.

"I guess your meeting Ben didn't have a storybook ending."

"Not exactly." Rayne liked Mandy's straightforward manner, but this one hurt. Or maybe it was the truth that caused the painful memories. After several minutes, Mandy turned off the hair dryer.

"Will you tell me how you got married and…what happened?"

Rayne stared at Mandy's reflection. Although she didn't look it, she was such a young girl. Fifteen, going on…well, twenty-two thanks to Rayne's mile-off guess. But Rayne had been eighteen when she and Ben met, and only nineteen when they married. Four years older than this girl. Life happened so fast, and young people were always in a hurry to move it along. Looking back, Rayne had been no exception.

She'd fallen in love fast, married fast, and fled—fast. Hurrying produced nothing but big mistakes...and heartbreak. The last fifteen years had been good, steady years, building a respected career, even if she'd missed seeing Ben's niece grow into this beautiful young lady.

But there was only so much time in life, and a person couldn't do everything they wanted. Besides, she had a lot of good music years ahead of her when she returned to Holland.

Ben entered the house from the garage and set the grocery sacks on the kitchen counter. Usually he worked later, especially if Quin had delivery jobs to do on the lake, but today he felt drawn home early. He didn't want to admit it, but the house seemed different with Rayne here. It was more than that, though. Quin lived here full-time now, too, and the house felt...full, like he'd always intended it to be when he'd worked all those months hauling concrete, drywall, wood, and tile.

He checked the wall clock; Mandy should be here today. A stack of bills waited for him in the office, but he heard voices coming from the hall, so he headed that direction. He'd nearly reached the guest room doorway when the hair dryer came on. The women's voices grew louder.

"I hope I can meet a guy like that someday."

"You will, Mandy. Don't be impatient. Wait for the right one."

"I guess your meeting Ben didn't have a storybook ending."

Ben's smile faded at Mandy's statement, then left his face completely at Rayne's answer.

"Not exactly."

Ben turned away and strode back through the kitchen and into the garage, looking for something to do. After a minute, he opened the far garage bay door and lifted the hood of the old Bronco. The dirty engine compartment stared back.

Familiar smells of oil, gas, and grease flowed over him like a salve. In minutes, he had the distributor cap and spark plug wires spread across the workbench. One by one, he removed the cracked wires and replaced them with new ones, cutting each to length. Next he pulled, cleaned, and replaced the spark plugs.

Years ago when his dad was alive, the two of them had pulled out the tired six-cylinder engine and replaced it with this 289 V8 out of a wrecked Mustang. A string of other modifications followed, including a lift kit to raise the body, rebuilt suspension, reupholstered seats, and new wiring. Still, there was always something that needed fixing.

He snapped the distributor cap back on, connected the new wires, and turned to get his timing light when he noticed Mandy leaning against the frame of the open bay door, watching him with a pensive expression. He grabbed the timing gun and snapped the leads onto the battery and number one spark plug. Out of the corner of his eye, he saw Mandy move to the driver's side of the Ford and, without a word, climb into the cab. The old springs of the truck creaked under her weight.

Ben straightened, holding the timing light wires away from the engine fan. "Do you remember how to start her up?"

Mandy leaned out of the window. "Pull out the choke, turn the key, pump the gas three or four times. When it starts, push the choke in slowly as the engine warms up." She raised a brow for confirmation of the process.

Ben gave her a thumbs up and Mandy turned the key. The starter ground and growled, then the engine coughed and backfired mightily, scattering a group of crows from the driveway.

"Hold it a minute," Ben called to her. He loosened the distributor and retarded the timing a little. "Okay, try it again."

This time the engine started on the second revolution. Mandy gave it some gas, keeping the idle up while the engine warmed. The crows deemed it best to stay away as the yard filled with a cloud of white exhaust.

Soon the motor ran smoothly, and his niece hopped out of the cab and came to the front. "Can you show me how to do it?" she asked, indicating the timing gun he held.

Ben demonstrated where to point the light while keeping the wires clear of the radiator fan, then handed her the instrument. She deftly shined the strobing light on the spinning crankshaft pulley, and Ben showed her how to rotate the distributor until the chalk mark lined up properly with the metal indicator, then he tightened the hold-down bolt. She handed him the light and reached into the cab to turn off the engine.

He supposed it appropriate that mechanics referred to timing lights as timing guns, due to their similar shape. Mandy seemed comfortable with anything with a trigger. And he had no doubt she could do this on her own next time. That was one of the things he liked most about her—she never forgot a lesson. Just like Quin.

Ben was no slouch in the quick-learning department, either. He hadn't forgotten what Rayne taught him fifteen years ago: never hang on too tight or risk too much—at least not with her.

He tossed the wrenches in the cabinet and shut the drawer a little too hard. Mandy shot him a questioning look, but he ignored her and concentrated on lowering and latching the hood.

"Got your license with you, young lady?" Mandy looked wistfully toward his much newer F-150. Ben shook his head and pointed to the Bronco. She sighed dramatically, then brightened and sprinted into the house.

Rayne pulled the old fleece jacket of Ben's tighter against the afternoon breeze as she sat on the porch, watching Mandy struggle to back the Bronco out of the garage. Rayne remembered well the confusing column shifter, touchy clutch, and the lack of power steering on the old beast.

Mandy revved the engine too high and released the clutch too fast. The rear tires chirped and the engine stalled. The girl let out a grrrr, then restarted the motor. After a couple more tries, she had the vehicle in the middle of the yard, pointing up the driveway. Ben sat patiently in the passenger seat, quietly giving hints. Mandy lurched the truck forward, stopped, and backed up, then went forward again, more smoothly each time. Then she drove in a tight circle around the small courtyard.

Ben had shown Rayne the same patience as she'd driven the stick shift for the first time, spinning the tires in the gravel yard of their rustic, rented cabin. Now, with a toot of the horn, Mandy and Ben headed up the driveway. The engine roared briefly as they reached the lake perimeter road, then slowly faded away, leaving Rayne with the so familiar pungent exhaust, and a lot of memories.

Those first few months of marriage had been so full of energy, of life.

Everything was new, exciting, and she'd loved him so. They were young, but they were two joined together, taking on the world. They swam in the lake, fished, went to the beach at Perilous Cove, and ate canned beans and hot dogs over an open fire in their backyard while watching shooting stars in the night sky.

Then... Well, nothing went right after—

"Hi."

Rayne jerked in the chair. Quin stood in the open doorway, sucking a Big Stick, his lips ruby red.

He held up the frozen treat. "Want one? Ben bought two boxes yesterday."

The weather had turned this afternoon, and the nip on the wind let her know Halloween wasn't too far off. Still... She eyed the Popsicle as Quin rotated it on his tongue.

"He said they're your favorite."

Her breath caught. "Ben said that?" He remembered. She shook her head. Best to leave that thought alone. In a few weeks at most, she'd return to Holland, to her home, her friends, her music. By then, the authorities would surely have caught whoever shot her and Dolina, and hurt Lorna. Rayne still hadn't heard from her friend.

As mystical as Storm Lake had been once, perhaps still was, this wasn't the real world—not for her, anyway, and certainly not for Regen van Onweer.

"Was he wrong?" Quin asked, still eyeing her as he licked the sides of the multicolored ice. He was asking about food, but his question addressed the bigger one—the future. This might be the life for Ben. In fact, it was perfect for Ben, Quin, Mandy, and her family. But *Regen* didn't belong here.

Rayne shook her head. "No, Quin, Ben wasn't wrong." She smiled, though it felt short of genuine. She'd been the one in the wrong, both back then and again now for coming here. Problem was, she had nowhere else to go. "I'd love one. But first, how about helping me into the house. Then I want to hire you for an errand."

CHAPTER TEN

"Hi, Mandy," Rayne called from the kitchen as she heard the front door open. In the week Mandy had been helping her walk a little and do painful extension exercises, Rayne's leg had improved rapidly. The thing holding her back now was the cast on her left arm. Running from shoulder to palm, the plaster hampered every task and she was dying to be rid of the thing.

"What's up for today, Rayne?" the girl asked, dropping her sling-bag backpack on the bar. She had hitched a ride with her friend, Tori, who lived in Perilous Cove, was eighteen, and worked four afternoons a week at the small store here in Shelter Cove. It worked out perfectly for Mandy to hitch a ride with the girl as far as Ben's house.

Rayne had yet to meet the mysterious, soon-to-be-Mandy's-mom Sam Riley, and she hadn't seen Ben's brother, Addison, who was Sam's fiancé and a very in-demand security expert. Mandy also talked about her soon-to-be little sister, Star who, like Quin, wasn't related to any of them. If one more person popped up, Rayne would need an org chart to figure out Ben's family.

"How would you like some driving experience this afternoon?" Rayne asked.

Mandy's eyes lit up, then she frowned. "I can only drive with an adult who is licensed."

Rayne waved her wallet. "I keep my Nebraska license current. Plus, I have an international diver's license. I'd think those would satisfy the requirements, don't you?" The Dutch police had found her purse intact under the smashed dressing room vanity. They said she was lucky.

"All we have is the Bronco, and it sucks gas like a black hole," Mandy complained, then brightened. "Where do you want to go?"

"Doc Arnold's in Deer Cove. I called him earlier. I'd have Quin take me, but there's no way I can climb in and out of his boat with this cast, and Doc's office is closed by the time Ben gets home. They have a cancellation this afternoon and can fit me in." She studied the teen. It was near impossible to think of her as only fifteen, and she didn't want to ask too much of her. "Are you comfortable driving that far?"

Mandy's mouth curled into her trademark lopsided grin. "Absolutely."

Mandy drove cautiously, slowing at each curve and whenever another vehicle approached, but she handled the old truck well, even mastering the column shifter. Due to numerous washouts years earlier, the road no longer circled the north end of the lake where steep canyons channeled a dozen small streams to the main body. Instead, they had to drive south and around the bottom of the lake before heading up the west side to Deer Cove.

Rayne suspected Mandy was competent at anything she pursued. Last time together, the girl had come with a library book on physical therapy, its pages marked with numerous Post-it Flags. She had Rayne working up a sweat in no time and was talking a possible career in PT.

Twenty minutes later, they were cruising through Deer Cove. The small village looked much the same as she remembered. Some of the business names had changed, but the buildings hadn't. The flower shop, ice cream store, post office, gift stores, and deli reminded her of the Boskoop neighborhood where her cottage was. On a back street, Mandy parked the Bronco in front of the doctor's office, a western façade complete with wood plank porch and authentic hitching posts. Rayne smiled as she exited the Bronco. It probably hadn't been too many years since horses spent an hour or two tied to these well-worn rails.

Inside, Rayne waited only a few minutes before the receptionist helped her down the hall to an exam room. Following a small knock on the door, a man entered and introduced himself as Doc Arnold. Rayne appreciated his cheerful attitude. He complimented the Dutch doctors on how they had left an opening in the cast for cleaning and dressing the bullet wound and pinning incision.

In short order, he x-rayed her arm and compared the new films with those digitally transmitted from Rayne's doctor at the hospital in Rotterdam. While everything looked good, he wanted her to keep the cast on for another week, but when she begged and promised she'd be really, really good, he cut it off and fitted her with a padded blue sling.

Her skin looked like overcooked whitefish layered with cottage cheese. And even though the doctor had wiped it down, the unwashed arm smelled like an old, wet tennis shoe. She begged a handful of alcohol wipes from the receptionist, but couldn't wait to get home and give it a good bathing.

Proud of getting her way, Rayne hobbled through the empty waiting room and outside into the gloom of early evening where Mandy leaned on the hitching rail and chatted with two boys who looked old enough to be in college—or graduated. Better if she broke this up before Ben found out.

"Time to go," Rayne said. She opened the passenger side of the truck and climbed in.

The two boys gaped when Mandy swung into the driver's seat of the elevated vehicle.

"This is yours?" one of them asked, new admiration in his eyes. His friend ran his palm along the oxidized front fender as if it were a concourse restoration. Rayne couldn't tell if they were more impressed with the ancient four-wheeler or the knockout behind its steering wheel.

Mandy threw them a grin as she started the engine and deftly backed out of the parking space. Before pulling out on the road, she revved the engine and called out the window in her sultry alto, "Bye, boys," and then accelerated down the road, smoothly hitting every shift and grinning ear to ear. Rayne scrunched down and peeked in the right side rearview mirror. The two young men were standing in the middle of the parking lot, mouths open.

"They never stood a chance," she said to Mandy.

"I know," Mandy said, still grinning, and winked at her. "Kind of sad, huh?"

A few minutes later, Mandy steered the bucking Bronco, much like its namesake, to a pullout on the perimeter road and rolled to a stop as the engine died.

"Rats! I can't believe this." The headlights shone gamely in the gathering dark. The motor cranked but wouldn't restart.

Rayne looked around. "Is there a flashlight?" Aided by the inadequate dome light, Mandy rummaged around under the seat and came up with a battered ribbed tube, more brass than chrome. Rayne held out her hand, and Mandy gave her the ancient flashlight. The RAY•O•VAC Sportsman was the one her dad had given her before he died. It was the only thing of his she had when she came to Storm Lake, and she had presented it to Ben one morning after they'd broken down in the Bronco and had to walk two miles home. Rayne slid the switch. Miraculously, the thing still worked.

"Thanks, Dad," she whispered.

"What?" Mandy asked, halfway out her open door.

"Nothing." Rayne climbed down. "Let's take a look under the hood."

"Do you know anything about cars?" Mandy asked as she worked the latch and lifted the hood. Rayne put the rod into place to hold it open.

"Only this one." She played the light around the engine compartment, tugging on wires until one came loose in her hand. "Ah, ha!"

"What is it?"

"The coil wire," she said, pushing the end of the pencil-sized wire securely back into the coil socket. "That should do it. Give it a try." Mandy climbed in and turned the key. The Bronco roared to life.

"I'm impressed," Mandy said as she jumped out and helped Rayne close the hood.

Full dark had fallen by the time they turned down the driveway. The headlight beams swept across a stern-faced Ben standing on the porch. Tori was next to him, her car parked beside the stairs, obviously done with work and wanting to head home.

Without a second glance at him, Mandy triggered the garage door opener and proceeded into the bay.

"I hope Ben won't be mad at us for being out after dark with you driving," Rayne said as she gathered her purse and opened the door. Mandy only smiled in the dim light of the dome.

They climbed out, and Mandy helped her across the yard toward the house. Just when Rayne thought Ben was going to say something, Mandy stopped and, being careful of the sling, enveloped Rayne in a long hug.

"Thank you for a wonderful afternoon," she said, loud enough for Ben to hear. "I had the best time."

"Uh. Okay?" Rayne said, surprised by the girl's affection, and conscious of the two observers coming down the steps. Ben's stern countenance had been replaced by one of surprise mixed with confusion. Then she got it: anyone who made Mandy happy, made Ben happy. The girl was *good*.

"Hey, Tori," Mandy said, pulling away and heading to the girl's car. "Sorry we're late getting back. Ready to go?" She turned to her uncle. "Uncle Ben, Rayne's kind of tired. She could use your help getting up the stairs." Then Mandy slipped into the passenger seat of the small sedan. "Bye, Rayne."

Rayne waved as Tori started the engine and backed up. When Ben came near, Rayne put her arm around his waist and eased the weight off her aching left leg. "Help me get inside? I'm beat." He slid his arm around her. It felt as natural as all time, and at the same time, totally foreign. Together, they climbed the porch steps.

At a toot of the horn, they turned to see Mandy leaning across the front seat of the car. Through Tori's open window she said, "Have a good evening, you two," and waved as they drove off.

Ben only grunted.

Inside, he settled Rayne in the leather sofa in front of the fire, then lifted her right hand up to the flickering light. Black smudges covered her fingers and palm.

"Minor car repair," she said, meeting his level gaze, aware of the heat of his hand, her delicate fingers captured by his callused ones. They'd been apart for nearly fifteen years. How could his touch feel so natural, even comfortable? She'd held hands with other men over the intervening years, of course. Even Danny Haynes held her hand once in a while when they were walking or sitting in a theater, but this was different. Something she didn't want—or couldn't have. She tugged her hand free. "You left the coil wire loose. Like last time."

Of course 'last time' had been long ago indeed. And now, even within the radiating warmth of the orange flame, her hand felt empty and cold.

CHAPTER ELEVEN

"Have a good evening, you two."

Yeah, right. Thanks, Mandy.

Ben banged around the kitchen making more noise than necessary before finding the pot he wanted. Chicken broth, canned tomatoes, carrots, celery, and onion went in, followed by cut up chicken he'd sautéed this morning before heading to work. He opened the spice cupboard and pulled out a half-dozen bottles, adding shakes, pinches, and sprinkles to the steaming pot.

"You never told me how you learned to cook," Rayne said as she slipped onto a barstool. Ben took time out to pour her some coffee, then continued rummaging through the spices. He'd never been one to follow recipes except for baking—couldn't fudge on that.

"I never told you about Gramma C?"

Rayne shook her head.

"Grandma Conner—my dad's grandmother, known as Gramma C to everyone around the lake. She opened a small eatery in Deer Cove when she first moved here in the early 1900s. Dad took me there when I was really young."

He remembered visiting the rustic shed built of grayed barn wood siding, its rough, planked porch and roof supported by irregular peeler logs worn smooth by the passage of thousands of hands, young and old. The corrugated tin roof had large rusted splotches, and Ben had asked his father if the place was going to fall down. His dad laughed and said, "Probably not today," as he led Ben by the hand into the dark, warm, and oh-so-fragrant interior.

"Gramma C was about eighty years old then. And while the building wasn't much, its appearance didn't keep the hungry away." Ben sprinkled in spices, then continued his story.

"Her cooking drew full-on crowds coming during the summer months when families camped, fished, and boated all around the lake, then kept a steady stream of locals off-season. Each summer, Gramma C's family erected a tent awning on one side of the building, dragged some old picnic tables from around back, and strung a long strand of dim, bare bulbs from the large oak to the porch."

Ben fitted a lid on the soup pot, and then leaned against the counter with his own coffee.

"Every Friday night, neighbors showed up with blankets and lawn chairs, ate fried chicken or Gramma C's famous ribs or venison, and listened to locals play guitars, banjos, or whatever they had." He grinned at her. "I remember being particularly fond of kazoos."

"Ah, a man of sophisticated musical tastes." Rayne returned his grin.

"Once in a while a talented singer performed a few songs. But I think my favorite time was early fall. The evenings got cold, and Gramps would stoke up an open campfire in the front yard. My friends and I would spread blankets and lie like the spokes of a wheel around the fire. Our hair nearly caught fire while we flicked bits of bark and twigs into the flames. We made up points for accuracy, distance, or the biggest spark."

"So your great-grandmother taught you to cook?" Rayne asked, shifting on the stool.

Ben detected pinching weariness around her eyes, so he helped her back to the couch in the great room and sat on the other end facing her.

"Gramma C never owned a cookbook. She kept two battered shoe boxes full of notes scratched on bits of paper bags, torn-out pages from magazines and newspapers, and letter paper from her mother, sent from back East. Some of those still smelled like perfume."

Ben remembered sitting at a scarred work table in the old kitchen, sorting the contents for her, straightening bent edges and smoothing creases. There was no filing system—she knew the recipes by shape and paper type, and could find one in a few seconds whenever she chose to look. He was too young to know it back then, but his dad told him years later that Gramma C cooked by feel, adding ingredients 'because they go together' and leaving out things that 'don't belong.'

"I must have inherited at least her cooking method if not her actual skill. It works for me, and I haven't killed off anyone yet."

In the kitchen, the pot lid began rattling, indicating the stew had started to boil. He got up to check it, added more garlic, and turned the burner down to simmer. In the pantry, he found a box of corn bread, but the soup needed to cook a bit before he started the bread.

He glanced in at Rayne and saw her eyes were closed, head resting against the soft leather. Completely relaxed, she looked so young, innocent, and he found his mind wandering to what-ifs. Dangerous territory. Instead of traveling that unproductive road, he quietly left the kitchen through the door to the garage, then went out the back door to the yard.

Crickets, their nightly chorus slowed by the cool air, joined the slap of wavelets on the rocky shore. Ben zipped his fleece vest and stuffed his hands into his jeans as he followed the well-worn path down the slope toward the lake. The chill filled his lungs with sage, oak, and the scent of fresh water that always reminded him of trout fishing, swimming off Breaker's Point as a kid, and drinking from the clear spring that fed the lake near the tiny town of Gift—where he and Rayne lived when they were married.

To the west, lights from a few homes to the south of Deer Cove rippled in the restless water. Many were second homes, occupied by part-timers or rented by vacationers during the busy summer months. But now that school had begun, cabins and houses sat empty, boarded up until spring or merely locked until the next convenient weekend when they'd come alive with laughter, food, and families.

To his right, needles of the four pines shushed in the barest breeze. Tonight's calm masked dangerous potential. Fall and winter storms originating in the Pacific Northwest could sweep over the coastal hills and down the lake canyon, churning the surface into violent upheaval in only a few minutes, sinking boats, and battering docks with floating logs and debris.

He well remembered as a boy sitting beside his grandmother as Nellie Farnsworth recounted the story of men lost in her family during the great storm of 1908. He'd been wide-eyed as Nellie told how her grandfather and two of his brothers had been out fishing in one of the thirteen boats lost that day. The bodies of her grandfather and one brother were found with two others on Graveyard Beach the next morning, while the body of the other brother was discovered floating in thick reeds at the south shore by Flume. Locals had called it Storm Lake ever since.

Despite its clouded history, people loved this lake, Ben included. He'd grown up here, traveled away, and then returned, never finding anywhere else quite like it. When he and Rayne first moved here, he'd thought…

Well, that was the past now. He'd seen the international calling card Quin had purchased for her on one of his errands. And he'd heard her talking with members of her band, discussing song ideas and next year's tour dates. She'd be gone soon, just like before.

Ben scuffed the shore rocks with his boot until the dim light spilling from the kitchen glinted off the one he wanted. With a sideways whip of his arm, he sent the flat stone skipping toward Deer Cove and the yellow lights. He counted six skips before it shattered the faint illumination and sank to the bottom.

The lonely screech of a night hawk winging somewhere overhead drew Ben's attention back toward the house. Warm light showed from the bare kitchen windows. From this angle, he couldn't see into the living room, but flickering firelight danced on the ceiling. He loved the way the beams caught the light, painting their shadows in long lines. Above the kitchen, Quin's room was also lit. He was probably doing homework, struggling with Miss Eaton's latest evil math assignment.

The pretty blonde teacher had been the willing focus of many matchmaking attempts by Ben's friends. He couldn't count the times some well-meaning woman asked, "Who are you building that gorgeous house for, Ben Conner?" The asker always had a twinkle in her eye, like she possessed insider information requiring immediate action so he wouldn't miss the investment.

But Ben never had an intelligent answer, not for the well-wishing meddler, or for his own heart. No one had seemed the right fit. Maybe he was as risk-averse in relationships as his broker said he was financially. He'd dated, but never more than a few times with any one woman. Then last summer, Quin had come into his life and everything changed, giving him purpose and a reason to be a better man as he took on the role of *dad*. Not that he could ever replace Quin's true father. But he would do his best, even if it turned out to be only the two of them.

Ben hiked up the path and reentered the house, assailed by delicious smells that set his mouth watering. He stirred the soup, turned the oven on bake, and peeked into the living room to see if Rayne wanted another cup of coffee. Quin sat on the left end of the couch, sock-covered feet stretched toward the crackling fireplace, reading a book.

Ben opened his mouth, but Quin placed a finger on his lips and pointed to Rayne. She lay on her side, head propped on the armrest, long lashes closed in sleep. The blanket rose and fell slightly with each soft breath. Strands of hair had escaped her hair band, casting thin shadows across her skin with every flicker from the fireplace. She looked so young. Vulnerable. Beautiful.

Their little cabin here at the lake had been too small for a proper sofa, but they'd found a used loveseat at a garage sale, and she had jumped up and down in excitement. He would have taken an extra job if he had to so they could buy it. Fortunately, the old man selling it met their meager offer and they'd hauled it home. Ben always kidded her he had to sit on the floor because she so often stretched out for naps, curling her legs underneath, exactly as she had now. When he bought this couch, he made sure to get one big enough for... He stopped the memories, rubbing his face.

Ben slid his eyes back to Quin who'd evidently been staring at him, asking silent questions to which Ben had no answers. Quin glanced at Rayne, then back to Ben, and a smile tugged at the corners of his mouth before he shifted on the soft leather and returned to his book.

Two souls, content before a warm fire. Why did Ben feel only dread of what was to come?

CHAPTER TWELVE

For three days, Raoul had slipped into a fog of anger after losing Regen van Onweer in Atlanta. She hadn't outsmarted him. No. It had to have been her mother's plan to spirit her daughter away in the middle of the night. Van Onweer could be anywhere in the world now.

Finally, it came to him how he could locate her. He'd returned to Holland, spending more of his dwindling savings on the plane ticket, and set his plan in motion.

It had only taken Raoul a few days to ferret out the weak link in Doctor Ostrander's Rotterdam staff. Femke Verhoeven left work at precisely 4:50 each afternoon. Raoul had strategically positioned himself on a bench and said hello the first two days as she exited the doctor's office building. On the third day, she stopped to admire the fuzzy little dog he'd stolen from a yard across town.

"Oh, she's such a cutie," Femke gushed, scratching the dog's chin. "What's her name?"

Whether Coco was the correct name for the mutt or not, he neither knew nor cared, but that's the one he gave. He'd learned long ago that most women couldn't resist a cute little dog. Femke rewarded him with a shy smile.

That the woman wasn't his type at all, in the end probably saved her life. Dishwater blonde hair parted in the middle—its only redemption being the scarf disguising most of it—hung limp as a mop to shoulders too rounded for a woman in her early thirties. She wasn't completely ugly—well, except for the shoes that protruded from beneath her plain dress—but she wouldn't win any contests, either.

He pasted a smile in place, chatting with the woman as he fabricated a history of traveling the world for several years before recently moving from Germany and not having friends yet.

"I found a little shop that has the best koffee and hapjes. Just there." Femke's eyes followed his finger as he pointed across the green parkway at an establishment with several tables on the sidewalk. "Perhaps you'd join us, Coco and me, for a snack and be my first friend?"

Femke hesitated, her openness drawing in on itself like a flower closing against the cold night. For a minute, Raoul thought he'd pushed too far.

The dog squirmed in his arms. He withheld a grimace as the dog's pink tongue darted out and licked the woman's acne-marked skin. Femke laughed.

Clearly the dog lacked good taste, but he'd reward the animal with a treat tonight for such perfect timing.

The next day, Raoul surprised Femke with flowers at the doctor's office where the rest of the workers oohed and aahed over them. By the end of the week, he'd taken her to dinner, found out she was responsible for opening the office each morning, and moved her to tears with the heart-wrenching white lie that little Coco had been run over and killed by an unsympathetic Citroën driver. Femke had proved very consoling that night. After she fell asleep, he'd stolen her office keys and had them duplicated before "finding" them the next day in a flowerbed near her house where, he convinced her, she must have accidentally dropped them.

On Sunday night, Raoul let himself into the doctor's office with his shiny brass key.

"Now, Regen van Onweer," he asked the thousands of records on the racks stretched before him, "where are you?" Femke had shown pride as she emphasized the importance of a proper filing system, describing the system used in the office.

In less than ten minutes, he found Regen van Onweer's records. The final notation indicated they had been faxed to a Dr. Arnold, Deer Cove, California, USA.

"Ah, there you are." Raoul's hand trembled as he placed the sheet on the copier. He popped two of the red pills into his mouth and gulped them down.

After returning all of Regen van Onweer's papers to their proper place on the shelves, he scattered random folders in the wire trash bins and set them on fire. By the time emergency vehicles began arriving, he was a block away, walking the very-much-alive little Coco, just another Nederlander with a touch of insomnia circling around to watch the firemen at work.

He hadn't had to torch the office—he'd been careful to wipe down anything he touched. And he'd left Regen van Onweer's records intact. But if she heard about the break-in and fire, she would wonder. Fear would eat away her sanctuary.

"Yes, Regen van Onweer. I've found you." A smile touched his lips as he turned and headed away from the smoldering building. "I'm coming, Marielle." *Save your last breath for me.*

He dropped Coco off on her street before sunrise and watched the dog scoot up the path to her house. Then he went home to pack.

CHAPTER THIRTEEN

Two days after getting the cast off, Rayne had Mandy drive her back to
Deer Cove. Her left arm felt like a cooked strand of angel hair pasta. She
couldn't even lift it to shoulder height, let alone wrestle the manual
steering and column shift of the old truck. It would probably be two or
three weeks before she could drive, and by that time Rayne would be
back in Boskoop, putting her life back together.

Meanwhile, Mandy had a mission to get Rayne's arm up to at least
under-cooked pasta status by the end of the week, and Rayne continued
wearing the sling like a good patient.

But today's visit to Deer Cove had nothing to do with her arm. They
drove through the small town until the buildings grew sparse. At the
northern edge, situated at the front of a field still used for crops, stood a
majestic western barn with a tall center section, high hayloft door
complete with rope and pulley, and two lower-roofed side wings. The
words Bibs' Beauty Barn stood out in faded white against the weathered
vertical planks. The yard approaching the structure was paved, and lined
with a dozen flower planters made from wine barrels cut in half. They
overflowed with nasturtiums, marigolds, impatiens, and other varieties
of flowers Rayne couldn't name. Aspens rimmed the edges of the neat

parking area, their round leaves shimmying in the afternoon breeze, as if impatient for the first cold snap.

The story, as Rayne remembered it, was that Bibs's husband named her business as a joke by painting it on their old barn after his wife hosted a beauty party for some of her friends. She fooled him by turning it into a thriving business for at least the last forty years. The husband was gone, but Bibs' Beauty Barn lived on.

Mandy edged the Bronco into an available spot between an aging Pontiac and a Honda Civic parked half onto the line. Rayne held her breath, but the girl made it look easy. Rayne slid to the ground, wincing as she put weight on her left leg. Mandy had been working her hard, and her range of movement had improved greatly, but that didn't keep it from hurting.

"I've driven by this place," Mandy said, "but never stopped. Looks like it's seen better days."

Two siding boards were loose at the corner and dangled in the breeze. Directly in front of the wide door, a willowy mannequin posed in high heels, perfect makeup, a styled purple wig, and a sequined evening gown. One finger pointed at all comers, and a sign strung around her neck warned, "Don't get me started."

"Wouldn't think of it," Mandy muttered, as they sidestepped the lady and entered the barn. The fragrance of flowers outside gave way to acetone, hair spray, and other potent chemicals. Six stations lined the area, and several shampoo sinks were fastened to a half-wall that divided the cavernous space. Even the whine of hair dryers dissipated in the lofty rafters.

"How do they heat this place in the winter?" Mandy whispered in Rayne's ear as they approached the main desk. In spite of the chill in the air outside, the room felt comfortable.

"Good afternoon," a gravelly voice called, and they turned to a woman sitting—ensconced like a queen on her throne would be a better description—in a worn blue velour recliner straight out of someone's living room. The chair, resting on a foot-high platform, looked completely out of place in the rustic barn, but gave the woman a clear view of all the goings-on in the room.

Rayne recognized Bibs immediately. No taller than five two, the woman was nearly as wide, overflowing the arms of the lounger as she pushed the reclining lever forward and surged to her feet on stubby legs. Thinning, fiery red hair still hadn't turned white—or wasn't allowed to. Bibs had seemed old to Rayne fifteen years ago; how old she actually was, no one knew, and Bibs wasn't saying. Rayne smiled as the woman took her place behind the glass display counter.

"Hi. I hope you can help me." Rayne explained what she wanted while Mandy went to check out hair gels displayed on a shelf under the front window. Bibs squinted at Rayne and cocked her head, then came around the counter and lifted her hair, separating the curls and studying her roots.

"Could take awhile." Bibs gave a decisive nod, then turned to Mandy, eyeing her spiked, black hair. "You ready for a change, too?" she asked, moving closer.

Mandy retreated a step, palms out. "Nope. I'm just fine, thank you." Mandy cut a glance at Rayne.

Bibs pursed her lips as if considering an argument about whether Mandy's locks were fine or not, but reconsidered, probably thinking the job on Rayne would be challenge enough. "Then you'd better find something to do, young lady," she said, and linked her arm through Rayne's. "Change like this takes time."

"I'm going to die soon." They all turned to the petite woman sitting in a rocking chair a few feet away. She had a cloud of gray around her head, and her skin had that puffy white softness all grandmothers should have—at least grandmothers of a certain age. Knitting needles clicked furiously in the woman's hands, and Rayne swore she could perceive the garment lengthening as a huge ball of yarn rotated in a knitting bowl beside the rocker.

"Oh hush up, Irene," Bibs chided. "You're not going to die."

"Am so." Irene never missed a loop.

Bibs rolled her eyes at the other woman's comment. "Sisters," she said, as if that explained it all. Then she leaned closer and stage-whispered to Rayne, "Always thinks she's going to kick the bucket. Been saying that for twenty years now and she's still healthier than me." Bibs tapped one polished fingernail against her temple as if that explained it all.

"I'll just wait out in the car," Mandy said, wide-eyed and backpedaling out of the room.

With Bibs waddling and Rayne limping, they looked like two fugitives from a three-legged race as they made their way to the one stylist without a customer. Bibs introduced the woman as Linda, and Rayne was somewhat relieved to see she had normal-looking brown hair in an attractive cut.

Two and a half hours later, Rayne stopped at the front counter to pay, and Bibs levered out of her chair. The old woman cocked her head as she approached, assessing Linda's work. Then her eyes caught Rayne's.

Bibs gave a decisive nod. "Rayne Conner. Ben's wife. Thought it was you when you come in, but wasn't sure with all that black hair. 'Course you're older." She winked at Rayne. "Me too."

Rayne Conner. No one had called her that for a long time, not since she'd gone back to Europe. She opened her mouth to correct Bibs when another woman approached from Rayne's right. She turned to find an old woman standing five feet away, peering at her with rheumy eyes more angry than curious. Her wet hair hung limp in gray strands, soaking the salon smock and dripping on the polished concrete floor.

The woman glared at Rayne, then turned on Bibs. "Rayne Conner you say?" She whirled back to Rayne, advancing cautiously closer. "Well, that explains it." Rayne hugged her sling close to her body.

"Nellie Farnsworth, what are you blathering about now?" Bibs asked, obviously used to the woman's peculiar manner. "Explains what?"

Surprise widened Nellie's eyes. "Why the signs, of course. The signs," she said to Bibs, as if it were obvious.

Rayne edged back, until her legs bumped the counter, stopping further retreat. Nellie Farnsworth was definitely a strange bird, and Rayne wished she could head for the door, but she hadn't paid yet.

Bibs, intrigued or irritated, Rayne couldn't say, rapped her fingernails on the glass counter to get Nellie's attention. "Would you just speak English, woman? What are you talking about?"

"The crows. Thirteen crows flew over my house this morning, and I knew bad times was comin'. Broke a mirror, too, my favorite hand mirror my mother left me."

"The crows broke your mirror?" Bibs asked.

Nellie lowered her gaze to the floor, as if looking for answers, shaking her head slowly, side to side. "Not the crows. Me," she answered, more to herself than Bibs. Then, abruptly, she fired a dark look at Rayne. "You're the cause. You brought the trouble, she said, loud enough that others in the salon turned."

"Trouble?" Rayne asked. "I haven't done anything."

Nellie pointed a crooked finger at Rayne, and for a second reminded her of the mannequin out front. *Don't get me started*. Well, someone had obviously gotten Nellie Farnsworth started, and Rayne didn't like it one bit. She'd dealt with rude audiences in clubs, stood up to conniving pub owners who tried to cheat her out of a night's wages, and even learned to tolerate her own mother—well, at least to a point. But this woman...

Before Rayne could garner a reply to Nellie's accusation, Bibs moved spry as a cat around the counter and stopped directly in front of Nellie. She grabbed the woman's raised finger and pushed it down.

"Now you listen to me, Nellie Farnsworth. You leave Rayne alone. She's obviously had a bad time recently, and she doesn't need any of your superstitions to make her life harder. You mind your own business, you hear?"

Every dryer had gone silent in the old barn, all conversation ceased. Everyone stared, first at Nellie, then at Rayne. Suddenly, numerous whispers sprang up as older women shared comments, pointed and nodded. Everyone on the lake would now know about the return of Ben Conner's long-lost wife, the one who ran away fifteen years ago and left him worse off than a grieving widower. Rayne felt a headache coming on, and she couldn't blame it on the toxic chemicals.

Nellie suddenly sagged and, if Bibs hadn't caught her, Rayne thought the old woman might have toppled to the hard floor. Nellie looked around, bewildered, and glanced at Rayne without any recognition at all. After several seconds, her eyes focused on Bibs, questioning. Bibs took the woman's arm and turned her toward the main work area.

"Nellie, let me take you back to your chair, and Faye will finish up your cut." Nellie stumbled a bit as she let Bibs lead her away, as if her feet weren't fully in agreement. "And how about we add a few highlights to brighten your beautiful hair? No extra charge being it's so close to your birthday, you know."

"But... but my birthday isn't until February," Nellie protested in a voice lacking all the conviction of only a moment ago.

"Well, that's close enough, dear." Bibs patted the old woman's hand as she settled her in Faye's waiting chair. "Won't it be good to see another birthday? We have to take all we can get, don't we?"

A few minutes later, Rayne stepped outside on shaky legs. Rays from the disappearing buttery orb in the sky penetrated her skin and brought warming relief, as if she'd emerged from one of the ice caves she'd visited with Danny on their tour in Norway.

Mandy, reading in the Bronco, glanced up, down, then abruptly jerked up straight. Behind the windshield, her mouth opened in a silent "Wow." Rayne opened the passenger door.

"You look *amazing!*" Mandy turned sideways as Rayne used the pull strap to hoist herself in.

"Thanks. It was time for a change."

"Change?" Mandy waved her hands in the air. "A change is two inches off the length and a bangs trim. Holy cow, Rayne. Ben's gonna *die* when he sees you." Mandy continued to stare, and Rayne felt heat rising on her neck.

Ben? Rayne hadn't done this for Ben. She'd done it for herself. She'd changed her hair a dozen times in the past fifteen years, and never for Ben. He wasn't in the picture.

"Man, oh man," Mandy continued. "You know...I've got some eyeliner with copper accents that would—"

"Can we just go? I'm kind of tired." She didn't want to hear about what Ben would think or why he would even care. Mandy gave her a 'whatever' shrug and started the truck. She backed out of the lot and accelerated down Lake Road.

Rayne had nothing to feel bad about. In all these years, she'd done fine on her own and, evidently, so had Ben. They'd never been right for each other—a bad match as her mother had put it. It was simply a hormonal attraction that brought them together in the first place.

Her world had been music and performance, crafting works that inspired the soul. She loved to challenge and change people's outlook on life through her work, encouraging them to treat others better, to *be* better.

Ben's life had a more elemental base: the lake and land, creating in wood, family. He'd always been close to his family; it was one of the things that had drawn her to him. Except for her dad, her own family never had that closeness, that love for each other that defended and protected against all comers. Dad had been the glue that held Rayne and her mother together. Without him, they simply fell apart.

Of *course* she'd thought her marriage to Ben could work. But they'd been so different. She wanted to travel to Europe and work in music. Maybe only for a few years, but wouldn't it be fun to travel, see new places? Her dream was to form her own band and perform on big stages. Ben didn't want her to go, wanted her to stay with him at Storm Lake. He had a good job, and in a couple of years, they could build a place of their own, somewhere they could raise a family.

Discussions turned into frequent arguments. She was being childish, selfish; he was a stubborn man with no sense of adventure. With Ben a firstborn and she an only child, they'd battled like two alpha dogs for leadership of the pack, neither willing to roll over in submission.

So stupid. And a classic case of differing expectations never discussed before tying the knot.

And then Ben's mom, Erlene, got sick. At only fifty-two years old and excited about having two new daughters-in-law—and with Addison's wife, Elizabeth, expecting her first grandchild—Erlene had everything to live for. But the cancer struck hard and proved relentless. The doctors designed aggressive treatments, toxic concoctions of drugs and radiation that resulted in crisis after crisis of drug reactions, high fevers, infections, and emergency room visits. Addison and Elizabeth were living in Missouri then and could only come home occasionally, so the burden of support for the Conners fell on Ben.

It was the worst possible timing—for Rayne, at least. She'd already planned to leave. Just for a few months to get back to the music scene where she could create and perform. Then maybe she could return and figure out how to be content in the small community after seeing the world's bigger stage. To Rayne, it felt like Erlene Conner became part of the conspiracy to trap Rayne at the lake. She knew at the time that was absurd, but it still felt that way. The Conners needed Ben more than ever, and Rayne felt like an outsider, someone who siphoned Ben's time from his parents.

It was a telephone call one morning when Ben was at work that set things in motion. Danny Haynes, who'd been on that one junior college choir tour with Rayne, was leaving for the Netherlands to start a band, and he needed a keyboard player. Would she be interested?

A week later, after one particularly horrible argument with Ben, Rayne packed her bags, caught a train from Mission Peak, and left Storm Lake—and Ben Conner—behind.

Rayne stared at the road winding before her. Too bad she hadn't left the guilt behind, too. Or maybe she had, and now she'd returned to reclaim it.

The road grew darker, and the Bronco's headlights seemed to brighten as Mandy drove the winding road toward Ben's home, but Rayne barely noticed. She stole glimpses in the right-side mirror until the light failed. For almost as long as she'd been singing in Europe, her hair had been dyed black. It was her trademark, born out of her earlier years in Goth bands. A couple of times she'd cut it short and even changed the color several times, but wigs kept her signature look alive during her concerts. Even her silver, dark blue, and red wigs used in concerts matched the long, wavy style. And for the last two years, she'd let her hair grow long again and kept it black.

The woman in the Bronco's mirror seemed a stranger, or at most a distant memory. In all the times she'd changed her hair, she hadn't gone back to this style and color: exactly as she'd had it when she and Ben met and married. Rayne fingered the jaw-line cut of rich auburn, straightened and free of curl—a softer version of her mother's. Had she picked this because of Ben? With her useless left arm, short hair was far more practical; she should have cut it weeks ago.

Mandy said something, dragging her from her thoughts.

"Sorry. Daydreaming," Rayne admitted. "What did you say?"

"I said you're awfully quiet." In the twilight, Mandy's eyes twinkled in amusement. "Wondering what Ben's reaction will be?"

Suddenly afraid of what she'd started, she wished she could have Mandy turn around and race back to the Beauty Barn for a redo. She glanced in the dark side mirror again, remembering Mandy's statement from earlier.

Ben's gonna die *when he sees you.*

"Do you really think she'll like them, Ben?" Quin scooped the last of the Rice Krispies treats onto a platter of layered wax paper. Ben had read off the ingredients, but Quin had mixed everything and done the cooking.

Quin's dad hadn't had time to show him how to cook, so Ben tried to teach the boy something every week. This month was desserts. Next month, vegetables. Quin wasn't looking forward to those lessons.

"Absolutely she'll like them." Ben patted Quin's shoulder. Physical touch was still awkward for both of them, but he was working on it. It must be different when you raised a child from a baby. He'd never know that experience, but he was glad, *very* glad, for Quin. In every way, Ben wanted the boy to be his son, and ws fortunate Mrs. H had introduced him to Quin months ago.

"How did you know she likes the cocoa ones best?"

Ben opened his mouth but didn't answer right away. Ben had asked Mandy not to tell Quin that he and Rayne were once married. The roar of the Bronco coming down the driveway saved him—this time. The noise of the garage door going up rumbled through the wall.

Quin's eyes lit up. "They're here!"

Ben handed him platter. "Let's move these to the coffee table so she'll see them when she sits down by the fire."

Quin carried it to the living room, while Ben rubbed his palms on his jeans. Why was he nervous? It was Quin, not he, who'd wanted to do something special for Rayne.

Ben had to keep a distance with Rayne, while not creating one between Quin and himself. Rayne would be leaving again in a few weeks or a month. She'd been talking with a couple of her band members, as well as a woman named Lorna who had evidently been injured in the attack, but was recovering. Ben tried to stay out of those conversations. Much as he hoped differently, they only confirmed she'd be leaving. Still...

The kitchen door opened, and Mandy came in from the garage. She closed the door behind her.

"Where's Rayne?" Quin asked, sliding back into the kitchen on his socks.

"You'll see," Mandy answered melodically, not quite succeeding in keeping a huge grin from spreading across her whole face. "She's coming in the front door," she said, and ushered them into the great room right when the front door swung open, and Rayne stepped in.

Mandy bounced up and down, clapping her hands. "I give you the all new, improved Rayne Evans!"

Ben didn't know what to say. Did he laugh at her great joke? Was a compliment appropriate? His jaw clenched.

"Well, what do you think?" Mandy squealed, grabbing Ben's hands and dancing him toward Rayne. "Doesn't she look absolutely *amazing*?" Mandy pulled him to a stop a yard from Rayne.

Rayne met his gaze for a moment, then, when he didn't react, looked away.

"Well, *say* something," Mandy implored, her grin faltering at his expression.

What words could describe seeing his wife again as she'd been years ago?

Rayne watched Ben turn without a word and head upstairs. Pain clawed her insides, far worse than the bullet that had ripped her flesh. This had been such a bad idea. Why did she do it? Stupid, stupid.

She heard Mandy say something to Quin, and then Quin, too, ran past and pounded up the stairs. A moment later came the sound of his bedroom door slamming.

Tears blurred the flames of the fire as she sank into the soft leather and stared at the fireplace, seeing only the disappointment on Ben's face —and Quin's. That puzzled her. She could understand Ben's reaction, though she'd hoped for a different one. But why had Quin been upset? Was it seeing Ben's response and recognizing things were wrong in the adult world? She didn't know a lot about kids, but knew they picked up on more than adults gave them credit for.

A car horn tooted outside and, with obvious mixed emotion, Mandy gathered her backpack, then knelt and placed a hand on Rayne's knee.

"I'm sorry, Rayne. I have no idea what happened, and I feel so bad for leaving right now, but I promised Sam and Star I'd be home early to help with stuff for their wedding." She squeezed Rayne's knee. "Are you going to be all right?"

Rayne muttered assurances and promised to explain later. It wasn't the girl's fault. Rayne wasn't sure *fault* was the correct word for describing what just happened, but the weight of guilt pressed her down into the sofa as if someone had loaded her arms with firewood. If anyone was to blame, she was.

The door clicked softly behind Mandy, and Rayne heard the car drive off seconds later. Needing something to do, Rayne shook off the burden and leaned forward to stand. It was then she noticed the platter of cocoa Rice Krispies treats on the coffee table. A small, tented card stood on one side, her name printed neatly on the front. Rayne freed its edges from the sticky squares and opened the card.

Dear Rayne,

I made these for you. Well, Ben helped a little. Hope you like them. Ben said they are your favorite—besides the popsicles.

Your friend, Quin.

She swiped at new tears, touched by Quin's thoughtfulness—and Ben's memory. He seemed to remember so much about her, them, their life together, as short as it was. Did she remember as much about him?

More than she'd been willing to admit until she stepped—or was carried—into this house. She remembered the way he looked her in the eyes the second before kissing her. The way his hands felt on her back. His aftershave lotion in the morning before leaving for work. And the way the water sluiced off his body when he emerged from the lake.

Rayne closed her eyes, pushing away what she no longer had. Eventually she'd have to deal with Ben, but first, she wanted to know what she'd done to hurt Quin. He'd gone to a lot of trouble to fix these treats for her, then he'd bolted. Somehow, she didn't think it was because of Ben.

Rayne picked up one of the gooey squares and inhaled deeply. Chocolate, sugar, and marshmallows: what could be better? She didn't feel like eating a thing, but her stomach betrayed her attempt to remain in guilt. The first bite burst with sweet flavor and crunch, exactly as she remembered from her grandmother's house—and from Ben. He'd made them for her at least once a month while they were married, even that last month. The chewy goodness reminded her of all they'd been, all they'd intended to be.

Rayne got a saucer from the kitchen and transferred four squares from the platter, then started up the stairs. With each step, pain shot up her left leg, and the muscles threatened cramps. It was probably good exercise, but how would she get down without help?

Three rest stops later, she reached her goal and rested a moment against the railing, panting. She hadn't been on the second floor yet, but she knew by Quin's description his room was the last door on the left. When she reached it, she knocked softly. A muffled "Come in" followed, and she opened the door.

Quin sat at his desk in front of the large dormer window that overlooked the lake. Ben said the boy would sit for hours at night, using his binoculars to scan every visible part of the shore and water. He loved Storm Lake. That had been the reason Ben initiated the adoption process so quickly, so Quin wouldn't have to leave when his much older sister and her family moved away.

"Thank you for the Rice Krispies treats, Quin," Rayne said, walking around the end of the bed with its ducks and waterfowl bedspread. Crossed fishing rods hung above the headboard, and at least a dozen boat models covered a dresser and the nightstand. "I tried one. They're the best I've ever had."

Quin didn't turn, so Rayne sat on the far side of the bed, closest to his desk.

"I didn't know if you'd had any, so I brought some to share. Want one?" Rayne offered the dish. Quin turned in his chair and reached for a square. His eyes were red, cheeks smeared, but he didn't seem angry. More sad, as if he'd lost something of great importance.

He tended to be quiet and rather reserved, choosing to remain in the background of most conversations. The exception, according to Ben, was out on the lake in his boat. Then Quin came alive and would talk enthusiastically about all things boating related.

She and Quin were alike in this way. As much as fans assumed otherwise, Rayne was an introvert, seeking quiet, not parties, after concerts and tours. True, she absolutely loved stage performance, but that's what it was: a performance. And that was different from interacting with people. The guys in the band, including Lorna and Dolina, loved to go out clubbing after rehearsals or gigs. Rayne gained strength from solitude—hence her little house by the canal in Boskoop overlooking her neighbors' tulips.

So she waited, munching on another gooey treat. "We're thoroughly ruining our appetites for dinner, you know?" she confessed. "But this is the best dessert I've had for a long time."

Quin relaxed in his chair, and Rayne could see the desktop. He'd been drawing on a large pad, a colored pencil sketch of a shoreline with tall reeds, a boat dock, and brightly colored mallard ducks bobbing in the shallows. Up the slope she recognized this house, complete with patio occupied with a man, a boy, and a woman. The faces weren't defined, but she recognized Ben's stance and Quin's shock of brown hair. The woman had nothing to distinguish her, as if that part of the family hadn't solidified. Obviously the boy had dreams. Didn't they all?

"Quin, you're a very good artist. Are you taking lessons?"

He nodded, reaching for treat number two. "Mrs. H teaches me some things after I finish my jobs. She says I have natural talent."

Rayne smiled at his objective proclamation. He wasn't bragging, just stating the facts as given by Olivia Hamilton. Cautiously, Rayne stood and guided her index finger above the family. "I think I recognize Ben and you, but who is this?" She wasn't sure she wanted to know, but couldn't not ask.

For what seemed like several minutes, Quin didn't respond, chewing methodically while staring at the drawing. Then he wiped his fingers on some tissues and went to the closet. He knelt in the open doorway and pulled out shoes, a soccer ball, a fishing tackle box, and finally a small, scarred cardboard box. He brought it back to the bed and sat down beside her, the box on his lap.

Then he opened the flaps, which were floppy to the point of nearly breaking off. Inside were papers, a couple of paperback books, a wallet, and a man's reading glasses and wristwatch. Quin moved the contents around before finding a yellowed envelope. A single color photograph slid into his cupped palm, where he cradled it a moment, not touching the surface, before presenting it to Rayne.

"These are my parents."

Lying in her palm, the picture of a man and woman held weight far exceeding the paper itself. She instantly recognized the man—maybe late twenties—as an older version of Quin. Same eyes and unruly brown hair. The man gazed at the young woman at his side, but she had turned as the photo was taken and stared into the distance, as if looking ahead—or away. The style of her hair stopped Rayne's breath. The woman's hair was styled in an asymmetrical cut, sweeping right to left across her forehead. Cut short in the back, the sides matched the slope of the jaw line.

No wonder Quin fled the room when Rayne came in the front door. While she and the woman in the photo had different facial features, Rayne's new hairstyle was an exact match to his mother's.

CHAPTER FOURTEEN

Ben punched the power button on the remote, and his bedroom TV went dark. For an hour he'd been staring at ESPN with the sound muted. Now he couldn't even remember what sport had been on. Though he'd heard Rayne and Quin talking earlier, everything was quiet across the hall, and the only noise came from the gears grinding inside his skull. He'd come to the place where he wanted answers.

Why had Rayne done it? Had she no idea the effect her presence had on him? Long ago he'd given up hope they'd ever be together again. Yet old hope evidently took a long time to die—maybe an eternity. His brother told him to never give up, that Rayne would come to her senses one day. Addison hadn't counted on the strength of Rayne's independent streak.

"Admit it, Conner. She wouldn't be here now if she had anywhere else to go."

He tossed the remote onto the nightstand and went into the bathroom where he splashed cold water on his face. What had he gotten himself into when she'd called and asked to come? He hadn't even taken ten seconds to think about it, just responded immediately, as if no time had passed between them.

Water dripped from his chin as he stared in the mirror at a face too old to do such a dumb thing. Yet what *else* could he do? Someone had tried to kill her—nearly succeeded—and had then tracked her to her mother's house in Atlanta. Should he have suggested a hotel room in some distant city? Maybe. It wasn't too late. He'd even pay the bill.

But even as he thought it, he knew he couldn't send her away. After she healed, when she left as she planned, how much would it hurt? That was easy: it would hurt incrementally more for every single day she remained here. Each hour brought the old feelings closer to the surface. And as much as he denied it, he still cared.

Before Addison and Elizabeth had gotten married, Ben asked him how he knew he loved her. Addison laughed, then said, "When I realized I care more about her happiness and safety than I do about my own."

Maybe it was as simple as that. Or maybe it was that whenever Ben touched Rayne, it felt so perfect he never wanted to let go. Once, as the minister said, they had become one. How do you tear something like that apart and not be left with two jagged halves? When she left in a few weeks, it would be like ripping open a partially healed wound.

Disgusted with himself, he dried his face with the hand towel and left the room. He'd skipped dinner and hadn't fixed anything for Quin, either. The boy's room was dark, so Ben headed downstairs; he didn't like Quin having to fend for himself for food. As he rounded the corner of the kitchen, he spotted a fire out on the patio. The sliding glass door stood open a few inches, and through it he heard the crackling flames rising from the stacked-stone pit. The dancing light bathed the flagstone and planters in a warm glow. Rich pine smoke seeped into the house.

Quin sat next to Rayne on the two-seat glider, which moved gently back and forth. They had blankets bundled up to their armpits and were eating sandwiches, a half-gone platter of Rice Krispies treats resting on the side table.

Ben stepped into the dimly lit kitchen and stood still, taking in the scene on the other side of the glass. Quin faced away from the house, only the right side of his face visible in the firelight, while Rayne faced the house. Ben could tell that the boy was talking a streak, gesturing with his free hand and sometimes waving the half-eaten sandwich with the other. The kitchen counter was strewn with open jars of peanut butter and Concord Grape jelly, a loaf of bread, two smeared knives, wadded napkins, and a half-spilled bag of potato chips.

Laughter drew his attention back outside where he saw Rayne's new short hair shaking as she responded to something Quin said. Her face was three-quarters lit by the fire, and it was covered by a beautiful smile as she concentrated bright eyes on the boy, sometimes leaning closer, then back. Other than Mandy and Olivia Hamilton, this was about the most he'd seen Quin talk to anyone in the months he'd known the boy.

God? Why did you bring her back into my life?

Ben tossed two slices of bread on a plate and spread peanut butter and jelly on them. He'd lifted it to his mouth when he noticed Rayne's gaze pinning him over Quin's shoulder. Quin noticed where she was looking and turned toward Ben as Rayne raised one brow in question— or was it invitation? Quin motioned for Ben to come join them.

Although reluctant to intrude on their shared moment, Ben carried his sandwich outside and pulled a chair next to Quin.

"I see you two found some dinner."

"Yep," Quin said. "We weren't real hungry after the Rice Krispies treats, but Rayne said we should have something with protein. Peanut butter has protein in it. Did you know that?"

Ben said, "Yes," around a gooey bite of his sandwich. Quin went on to explain about all the food groups they were learning in school. Evidently food was one of the more interesting topics in the class where the teacher solicited samples of dishes from parents to share with the students. Ben wondered which parent would draw vegetable day and hoped it wasn't him. He stank at vegetables.

"Sounds like you spend most of your time eating," Ben said, as Quin enthused about the chocolate cupcakes they'd had. Over the boy's shoulder, Rayne hid a grin behind her hand as she caught Ben's eye.

Suddenly, Quin jumped up, sending the glider swinging. "I've got to finish my homework," he said, handing Ben his blanket. "Here, you take my seat by Rayne. It's closer to the fire, and you can reach the dessert."

Quin stood with the blanket extended, so Ben had no choice but accept it and shift to the glider as the boy waited. Only after Ben settled into the glider did Quin head into the house. A minute later, his bedroom light came on, and Ben imagined him at his desk in front of the window. Talk about an easy kid. Ben never had to remind him about homework.

"You're doing so well with him," Rayne said, her voice soft in the fragrant night air.

Ben turned to her. The glider had seemed bigger when occupied by Rayne and the boy. But now, as he and Rayne sat facing each other, it seemed tiny, yet oddly not uncomfortable.

"I can't take the credit," he said. "His dad did an excellent job. Too bad he's not here to see it."

Rayne shifted, flexing her left leg a few times. "He told me the story of his parents, how his mom left when he was only a baby, how close he was to his dad, and how he learned of his dad's accident." She grew silent for a few minutes before continuing. "That must have been so terrible for him."

Ben's throat tightened as he remembered how tough it had been when his own father died three years ago. He managed only a croaked agreement. At forty-three, losing his dad was really hard. What was it like at not quite thirteen? Ben vowed again to give Quin a rock-solid home the boy could always depend on.

A gust of lake-scented air rushed up the slope, sending leaves scurrying and fanning the fire. A column of sparks rose several feet above the pit, and Ben traced their path until they winked out, as if the black sky morphed them into the twinkling stars that filled the heavens.

The heat of the fire warmed his skin, driving the cold fall air back a few feet, but he felt Rayne shiver as another gust came.

"Do you want to go in?" he asked, relieved when she shook her head. By mutual agreement, or perhaps distant memory of nights by an open fire together, Ben spread his blanket behind them and drew it tight, their hands touching where they grasped the ends together. He leaned his head on the back of the seat and sent the glider in motion with one foot as he stared above, the stars scratching white arcs with each swing. Heat from Rayne's body melted the last vestiges of his earlier anger, dissolving the protective barriers he'd erected years ago. It was dangerous, yet he felt compelled to accept this moment, as if no other course was an option.

The old wood glider creaked beneath them, as if unused to this much weight but willing to give it a try. Maybe that's what Ben needed to do too.

"I like your hair," he said to the sky.

She was quiet for nearly a minute, and then her voice brushed a bare whisper against the night sounds. "I'm sorry."

They were silent for a long time, the glider joining nature's night song. Just when he thought she wouldn't say more, she turned her face toward his. In the flickering light, they were inches apart, yet continents separated them.

"I don't know what I was thinking, Ben."

He had no idea whether she was speaking of her haircut or issues of far greater consequence. Their lives had been propelled by internal drives and external forces since they first met at that street fair in Mission Peak. Like every couple, he supposed. He'd loved her but had felt compelled to stay and help his family when his mother got sick. Those were tough years, but he was glad he'd stayed and helped his father. And if he'd gone, he would have missed the last years with his mom.

Rayne had been—was still—driven by her career and the compulsion to create and tell stories in music. He understood she couldn't *not* do it, anymore than John Steinbeck could not tell a story, or George Lucas could not make movies. Rayne's art was who she was, not work she did.

He watched the flicker of light reflecting in her Celtic green eyes until her lashes dropped, and she drifted into sleep, lulled by the glider's back-and-forth path. He tucked her closer against his side and watched the fire until only warm coals remained, while reliving every moment of their brief courtship and marriage. He wished he knew what the next weeks would bring, but he remembered something his grandmother told him when he was a boy: *"Ben Conner, if it's meant to be, then it's meant to be. Sometimes that's all the answer we get."* She died less than two weeks later.

When the wind off the lake overpowered the last embers, Ben gathered Rayne into his arms, blankets and all, and carried her into the house. She stirred briefly in protest, still more than half asleep, but he shushed her and carried her relaxed, warm body down the hall to her bedroom. There he removed her shoes and the patio blankets and tucked her into bed, clothes and all.

CHAPTER FIFTEEN

"Hi, Danny. It's good to talk to you."

Ben watched Rayne carry the portable phone to the great room and ease into the recliner. Since Quin had purchased the phone card for her, she'd called most of her band mates. Danny had evidently been a little difficult to track down—until this morning. Ben glanced at the clock, doing mental calculations. It should be about six or seven o'clock in the evening, depending on what country Danny was in.

"Yeah, thanks. I'm doing okay; healing up, you know. I got the cast off. There's a girl here who's helping me with physical therapy."

Rayne laughed at something Danny said, and Ben tried to tune out her conversation while he packed a picnic lunch. He didn't want to think about her life in Europe, the life to which she'd return in the too-near future.

He spread out the sandwich fixings. Quin liked American Cheese with mayonnaise only. Ben fixed his own with a spicy brown mustard but couldn't get the boy to try it. Well, Ben hadn't liked a lot of foods as a boy, either. Some things came with time and growing older. Maybe all of life was like that.

He and Quin were taking the boat around Breakers Point and up toward Gift to see if they could trick some of the bass onto the grill for tonight's dinner. The fish were wily this year, skittish even, hiding in the shore reeds and ignoring fishermen by the hundreds. Of course, this meant bigger fish below and more determined men in boats above.

The water would be crowded with out-of-towners sporting the best gear money could buy, and locals trying secret bait recipes handed down for generations. Quin's wasn't a fancy bass boat with swivel seats and trolling motor, but it didn't make any difference to the two of them—they weren't high-end fishermen. Just being out on the lake on a sunny Saturday with a cooler stocked with food and drinks fulfilled their idea of a great day. A fish or two would be icing.

"No, I hadn't heard that," Rayne laughed, clearly enjoying the conversation. She asked Danny if he'd heard from Lorna. Then, "Interpol? Okay, let me write that down." She made some notes on her legal pad, then steered the conversation to music.

Ben headed out to the garage and set his small toolbox by the back door. On the way home, he wanted to cross over to Olivia Hamilton's house south of Deer Cove and repair her screen door. He smiled, remembering how he'd first met Quin at her house. The boy had been trying to fix the railing around her dock, but the boards were rotted beyond use. Ben had shown up, suggested he bring some new materials the next day and they could work on the railing together.

That was the beginning, and it had been a pretty quiet one at that, both of them working in comfortable silence except for an occasional "pass the hammer." He'd let Quin try all the jobs that day, measuring, sawing, and nailing, even though Ben on his own could have finished the repairs in half the time. He never suspected Quin would be living here only a few months later, and that Ben's attorney would be drawing up adoption papers. Life was weird and so darned fast.

Ben brought an ice chest in from the garage and set it on the counter. He dropped half a dozen sweet pickles into a baggie, then pulled out potato chips and added them to the food pile. Two nectarines and some cookies completed the feast. In the other room, Rayne sounded like she was wrapping up her conversation.

"I know. Soon, I hope." She paused, waiting for Danny. Then, "It *does* make a difference, Danny." Ben listened closer as he detected strain in her voice. She shifted from casual to professional.

"I don't mind doing special songs with Dolina, but I don't want her a regular part of the band." Another pause. "No. Yes, of course she's got a good voice and stage presence, but—"

While Danny talked, Ben packed the cooler with the food, ice packs, and sodas, feeling only slightly guilty at being quiet about it so he could hear.

"Danny." Rayne's voice cut with sharp-edged frustration. "No. Listen to me. I'm not saying she's a bad singer. She's great. It's just, well…it's like she tries to one-up me. You don't see it because you're playing and concentrating on the band."

Ben stepped forward so he could see into the great room. Rayne's head was bowed and she rubbed her forehead in tiny circles. Suddenly she sat straight up.

"You *what*? At Dark Chocolate?" Rayne's breathing sped up as she struggled to her feet with her weak arm and began pacing in front of the cold fireplace. "Did you do a few songs, or what…?" Pause "Two *nights*?" She stopped the pacing and sagged against the wall as Danny talked.

Finally she'd had enough.

"No, Danny, I won't allow it." Pause. "No, not with my band." Pause. "Yes, *my* band. I'm the one who fronts the money. I take the risks. You're not pushing me aside just because I'm in Cal… In America. I'll be back soon, two or three weeks at most."

Icy fingers tightened around Ben's heart at the words, and he snapped the cooler lid closed. He'd been stupid to let his guard down around her when down deep he'd known this would happen.

"I don't care about the investigation," Rayne said. "The Dutch police haven't found anything in the last couple of weeks. Maybe this guy is long gone." She started pacing again while Danny spoke. "Danny. Danny, stop. I'm not going to let some whacko derail my whole career. I can hire a body guard or something." Pause. "Yes, I'll call the inspector." A longer pause, and Rayne visibly relaxed. "Do you really think so?"

Ben moved back a little as Rayne turned his direction and stared out across the patio at the crystal blue lake. He didn't think the view even registered to her.

"All right. I've got to go; the phone card's telling me I have less than a minute left. I'll get another one and we can discuss this more in a couple of days." Pause. "Okay. Send me an email about it and I can— Ughhhh!"

Rayne punched the phone's end call button and, for a moment, Ben thought she might hurl it into the fireplace. he retreated into the kitchen as Rayne limped past the bar and replaced the handset in its base station.

"Guess you heard that," she said, and slumped onto one of the wrought iron stools.

"Parts," Ben admitted. He got a glass down, filled it with lemonade, and set it before her.

Rayne took a long drink. "Thanks." She was silent for a couple of minutes while he put the lunch fixings back into the refrigerator. He studied her profile as she sat with her head propped in her right hand, left idly tracing the moisture on the sweating glass.

"What about the people the police questioned?"

"Last they told me, they had interviewed all the backstage crew— except one they haven't tracked down yet. No one seems to know his name."

"But no arrests."

She shook her head. "You heard. I'm supposed to call an inspector with Interpol. Maybe he'll know more."

"Rayne, I know it's not my business…"

She cut her eyes at him, narrowed in warning. Finally she sighed and said, "No, go ahead."

"Well, it sounded like they did something—the band, I mean—that you didn't like." Ben poured lemonade for himself as he waited to see if she would answer. Since she'd arrived, they hadn't really talked about her music, the band, touring—her whole life overseas. He knew so little about that part of her, other than the shooting and how she'd lost most of her money on that last concert. Fifteen years of her life, a mystery to him. These past weeks, they'd started over like that long interlude hadn't happened, picking up from when she'd left Storm Lake, and ignoring the gap. Now, this conversation injected that distant life right into his world. He didn't like it, but there was no going back. And it was past time.

"You're right," she said. "The band played two nights at a club in Amsterdam."

"Dark Chocolate?"

She raised a brow. "It's a hot spot—does an incredible business, both locals and internationals. Bands stand in line to get in there. Great exposure." She took another sip of lemonade. "Somehow Danny wrangled an invite. No doubt me getting shot helped. They brought in Dolina Macgowan to sing. Guess she recovered from her injuries faster than I have." Rayne turned to Ben, green eyes flashing. "*My* songs, Ben. I wrote them—most of them, anyway. They didn't even have the courtesy to call me."

"I thought they couldn't call you, that you didn't give anyone the number here or even want them to know you are in California."

"Well, email then," Rayne said, swatting away the detail that she'd been hiding out since leaving her mother's in Atlanta. "Danny could have sent an email and told me about it. Instead, they just went ahead and did it."

Ben topped-off her glass and dumped some dry roasted peanuts into a bowl. He felt like a bartender listening to a patron's sad story as Rayne tossed a handful of nuts into her mouth and chomped hard.

"Guess that's why I could never reach Danny until today. He had the nerve to tell me they got a standing ovation." Another nut succumbed to mad-female-diva chewing. "I need a favor. Can you pick up another international phone card for me today while you and Quin are out? I've got to stay on this. Plus, Danny said there's an Interpol inspector who's trying to reach me. I need to call him and find out if he knows anything."

Sure. He'd help her rebuild her life overseas. No problem making it easy for her to walk away from Quin, a boy who deserved better than to have people drop out of his world, either by death or by choice. Why not help her go back to the life she loved while leaving behind the people who loved her?

Sure, he could do that. Ben lifted the cooler, glad at a chance to escape the kitchen before he said something he'd later regret.

He exited the garage from the rear door and headed down the path to the lake where Quin, clearly excited about a day fishing, readied the boat and equipment. At the dock, Ben set the ice chest down and turned back to the house. Its tall, peaked windows reflected the flawless blue sky. Nearby a meadowlark ran through its repertoire, and a squirrel chittered at them from high in one of the pines. All was right with the world this sunny Saturday. Why did he feel as if a nasty storm loomed just beyond the horizon?

Rayne watched from the kitchen window as Ben and Quin loaded the boat, then Ben held one of the tie lines as Quin fiddled with the motor. She saw Ben's hand reach for his cell phone, hold it to his ear. A frown followed. He retied the rope to the dock and walked a little ways away on the planks, shaking his head. Finally, Ben checked his watch, nodded and put away the phone. Quin's shoulder's slumped as Ben knelt and talked to him.

Rayne felt bad for the boy. Even though he was out on the lake two or three days a week on errands for people, he'd been so looking forward to fishing with Ben. But something had obviously come up that interrupted their plans.

Ben's small security systems company did installations throughout the county. He said he had a couple of good people working for him who could handle anything, but that evidently wasn't true in this case. A few minutes later, he came into the kitchen from the garage, running his hand through his hair.

"Something at work?" she asked.

"Yeah. Kurt's installing a new system at a bank this afternoon and some of the system parts are missing. I swear they were all there last week, but I know I have what he needs at the warehouse."

"Can't he go get them?" Rayne asked, but Ben shook his head.

"Not enough time. He's way down in South County. The bank's closed this afternoon specifically for this install, and the security guard can only stay until five o'clock. It's today or we'll have to wait over a month for the next opportunity. Kurt has to keep working while I pick up what he needs and get it to him."

Ben grabbed his keys. A minute later, Rayne heard his truck rumble up the driveway. She turned to the lake view and spied Quin trudging up the path with the small cooler, each step slower than the previous.

Rayne hated to see the boy's disappointment. He obviously cherished his time with Ben far more than just fishing. Rayne flexed her newly freed left hand. Her whole arm was still weak, but stronger than yesterday. At least she could move.

With instant decision, she slid open the kitchen window. "Hey Quin. I've got an idea."

Ten minutes later they were motoring full-throttle across the water, the bow slapping through light chop and sending spray over them.

"Hey, easy there, hotrod," Rayne called to Quin who, grinning wide, had one hand on the outboard tiller while his other held fast to the aluminum seat. His comfort with the craft showed with everything he did, from tying knots, to stowing gear, to how he balanced when moving around the boat. She had complete confidence in him.

Getting into the boat had been a bit of a challenge. Quin had supported her with surprising strength as she carefully descended the path from the house to the dock. Her left leg still spasmed when she least expected it, especially going downhill. The path had been difficult, but they'd made it. Then came the boat. Quin showed her how to sit on the edge of the dock and slide into the boat. It worked like a charm, even with her sling. She wasn't sure how easy getting back out might be, but she didn't worry about that now as they sped across the water.

The air held all the promise of fall: a bite that cut through Ben's light coat she'd borrowed, and the scent of wood smoke rising lazily from cabin chimneys they passed along the shore. Some homes had small gardens, filled mostly with moldy leaves and vines this late in the year, and dotted with bright orange pumpkins primping for their glory holiday of Halloween, only a week away.

Quin slowed and gave her a narrated tour as they passed the tiny huddle of cabins called Gift, retelling the story of how the first area settlers discovered a gushing spring, bubbling up the purest water any had tasted in years. It could be they were simply thirsty after a long day in the saddle coming over the mountains from the parched inland valley, but before they reached the lake, they'd stumbled on a rocky wall with water erupting from its base. According to legend one of the men said,

"This sweet spring is a gift from God, like Moses received in the Old Testament," and they'd named it Gift right on the spot and set up camp.

Rayne's chest felt heavy with each word he spoke. Ben had told her the same story, *exactly* the same, word for word, when he'd first brought her to Gift fifteen years ago. He'd learned it from his father. Obviously, now Ben had taught it to Quin. Ben was passing on his history to his son.

Father to son, father to son,
Stories of our histories passed down,
Anchoring us to the past
As we reach for the future.

Ideas flew in her mind, and Rayne breathed a sigh of relief when she found a small notebook and pencil in the pocket of Ben's coat. Quickly she wrote the words she knew would soon be lyrics. Rayne filled page after page with ideas for the theme of verbal family histories. There were other stories here at Storm Lake. Like Bibs' family who went back at least a couple generations, and there were the men who'd died in the storm of 1908. Nellie Farnsworth's family had lost someone; she'd have to research that, although she wasn't sure including anything about Nellie would be wise after the scene at the Beauty Barn.

As she took in the beauty around her, music began playing in her head. She envisioned oboes, strings—lots of strings—French horns, and Danny's massive drums, all set up on the flat area behind Bibs' Beauty Barn. Rayne remembered a sloping hill along one edge. With a little work, it could be a great amphitheater.

Melodies flowed to her. Music had to be tuned to nature, made to lift the stories, and take them soaring against the night air. Cricket and night songbirds, owls, coyotes and hawks, the wind whispering through the pine trees planted by Olivia Hamilton's husband, John, in his effort to replenish what early settlers and loggers had decimated. Rayne's vocal cords nearly vibrated with desire to lift the unwritten songs.

She looked around as they motored past granite cliffs north of Gift, embedded mica sparkling in the sun. Birds whirled and darted to and from nests high in the protective crevices, and Rayne flipped to a new page. Animals would play a big part in telling the story of Storm Lake and families.

Her burst of creativity began to play out, like adrenaline seeping from an athlete after a contest. Or, she realized, how her own body came down after the high of a concert. When the final notes had been played and the last word sung, when the applause died away, and she retreated to her car or a dressing room if the club had one, her body cooled from the heat of performance. It wasn't loss, but rather accomplishment; a job well done, complete, like a craftsman finishing a piece of fine furniture, or an artist brushing the last stroke of her signature on a masterpiece.

"Rayne?" Quin's voice registered dimly. She blinked, willing herself back to the present. Sounds rushed in: the purr of the motor, the slap of waves against the creaking aluminum bottom. She turned to the boy steering the craft. He'd been talking to her.

"What did you say, Quin?"

"You're crying."

Wetness had materialized on her cheeks as if by magic, and grew cold in the breeze. Rayne wiped her face dry with her hand, sniffing. "Sorry about that."

Quin eyed her, but his expression showed concern, not scorn.

Rayne indicated everything around them with a lifted hand. "It's just so beautiful out here." She sniffed again and wiped her nose on the sleeve of Ben's coat. She'd have to wash it when they got home.

Quin silently observed her, their surroundings. Then he nodded and smiled. He understood, Rayne realized. That's why he used every excuse to come out on the lake. Though his mom had abandoned him, his dad died, and his sister moved, Quin had forged a place for himself in this valley and, like generations before when settlers first discovered the area by horseback, the lake had become his. He belonged here.

Just like Ben.

New tears threatened, and Rayne turned back toward the bow so Quin wouldn't see. Yes, Ben belonged here. He needed this community of nature and people. This was his family—some related, some not. He'd been unable to pull up those historical stakes when she had. She understood that now, whereas back then she'd wondered why he hadn't joined in her adventure, or at least come after her to carry her home.

But where *was* home? Not where she'd grown up in Nebraska—not after her dad died. Certainly not with her mother in Atlanta. Holland felt good to her, and she had loved her little house. Now it felt violated, destroyed, as if the big bad wolf had blown her house down and she had no place to live. Was home the little cabin they'd first shared right here in Gift?

Wind stirred something in her lap, and she looked down at the little notebook's flapping pages. She'd filled the last page and covered the cardboard backing as well. Ideas for stories in song, stories of home, family, traditions, love, and future.

Rayne closed the notebook, stilling the pages. Her own life felt like a page torn out and cast on the winds or water, with no anchor to hold her in one spot. Was that what she wanted? An anchor? Did an anchor tie you down like a prisoner, or did it free you to grow deep? She tucked papers and stubby pencil securely in the coat's inner pocket.

Quin slowed the motor to an idle and maneuvered the craft to "the perfect spot," evidenced by the presence of at least a dozen other boats within casting distance. Some of the boaters waved, and a couple called Quin by name. All seemed to look at Rayne with scrutiny, but probably it was the sling she wore on the outside of the jacket.

Quin cut the motor and, except for water slapping the boat bottom, the lake reverted to silence. With quiet expertise, as if the fish below had listening devices to detect the enemy above, he showed Rayne how to rig the pole and ready a cast. She didn't have a fishing license, so she couldn't have a pole of her own or reel in any fish if they got lucky, but Quin let her cast the line.

"Wow, you're pretty good at casting, for a girl," he said, as he watched her drop the bait right where he'd pointed. "One-handed, too."

She grinned at him as she awkwardly cradled the pole and rotated the crank a half turn to lock the reel. Then she handed the rod to him.

Propping an extra life vest against the side, she lay back and let the fall sun bathe her skin. She didn't tell Quin, but Ben had taught her to fish right here, and many nights they counted on that meat as their main course. Money had been scarce, but they hadn't starved. Funny, she'd worked hard all her life, and she still didn't have any money. At least Ben had done well for himself.

There was no money in CD sales these days with the production costs and the industry changing. Their recording company said her music didn't suit itself well to digital downloads, and maybe if she wrote more popular songs, ones that would catch airtime on radio stations, she could make more that way. Otherwise, it was the big concert tours that brought in the best money. Of course, you had to spend money to make money, and she'd certainly done the spending part.

Suddenly the boat rocked.

"Rayne!" Quin called, and pointed to where the tip of the fishing pole dipped into the water.

CHAPTER SIXTEEN

Ben shut off the truck engine and climbed out onto the driveway in the dark, stretching his back to one side, then the other. Since it had taken longer than he'd planned to gather up all the spare parts needed, he'd stayed to help Kurt finish the installation. Too much of that time he'd been at the top of a ladder, his torso twisted into tight crawl spaces in the bank's attic, pulling wires to cameras and sensors. At six one, he was too big for that, but Kurt outweighed him by a good sixty pounds, so Ben had drawn the short straw.

After locking the truck, Ben mounted the porch. Quin was still small; maybe Ben should hire him to help on these difficult jobs. That brought a smile as he pictured prying Quin away from the lake and his boat. What he couldn't picture lay immediately in front of him as he walked through the great room to the kitchen.

"Stop it, Quin!" Rayne laughed. "The flour is supposed to go on the fish, not on me."

Quin cackled like only a middle school boy can do as he flicked a tiny cloud of flour dust toward a spatula-brandishing Rayne. Her nose and cheeks were covered with white smears.

"Back off, you cur, or I shall slice you open like that cold-blooded vertebrate." She raised her chin and swished the air with the spatula/rapier, which caused Quin to dance away and laugh harder still. She looked like Catherine Zeta Jones when she accosted Antonio Banderas in the horse stable in *The Mask of Zorro*. Only better.

Strands of hair had escaped from her short ponytail and framed rosy cheeks. That's what got him. Rayne was truly happy right this minute. In the warm kitchen lighting, she glowed in a way he hadn't seen since he'd carried her across the threshold of their rented cabin in Gift and dumped her on the squeaky, open-spring bed. Their bed. They used to laugh out loud at how much noise it made every time they...

Ben cleared his throat, and they both turned as one.

"Oops," Rayne said.

"Uh, oh," Quin said.

Ben strode closer. Flour and breadcrumbs covered the granite counter and sprinkled the floor. A cast iron skillet radiated heat on the stove, oil beginning to smoke.

"Did I hear you mention trout?" Ben asked. Rayne moved aside. Behind her lay two good-sized fish, cleaned and coated in the thick breading. His stomach rumbled, and he remembered he'd missed lunch.

"We were waiting for you before we put them in the pan. Potatoes are baking in the oven."

"There's two more in the fridge." Quin pointed.

Rayne lifted a brow. "Hungry?"

"Starved. Better get the other two fish ready. Since you caught and are cooking, I'll..." He frowned, surveying the messy kitchen before finishing, "...clean up." He turned toward the stairs, but not before he saw Quin give Rayne a dusty high five and hear them whisper in unison, "Yes!"

Rayne cupped her chin in her hand as Quin recounted their day, describing in detail how the other fishermen in boats had stared open-mouthed as he pulled in one fish after another while their own lines lay limp in the waters around Bass Point.

"You should have been there!" Quin innocently told Ben. The boy didn't notice the guilt lines around Ben's mouth, and Ben did a good job encouraging Quin and making him promise to teach Ben his fishing secrets.

It was late when they finished dinner. While Ben cleaned the kitchen, Quin laid a fire for Rayne in the indoor fireplace. With expert hand, he stacked paper, kindling, and finally the larger pieces. In less than two minutes the flames surged a foot above the wood as edges of the logs grew cherry. Quin, punchy after the long day, sat swaying on the edge of the sofa before she urged him to shower and go to bed.

With a weary sigh of her own, she sank deeper into the soft leather and stretched her legs out toward the crackling flames. During dinner, a gust had blown open the patio doors, swirling a frigid mini-tornado around the table until Ben got them closed again. She still hadn't warmed up all the way. She could have sworn the doors had been locked when she and Quin left in the boat, but maybe Ben had them open earlier in the day.

She thought again about the letter that arrived in today's mail, and whether she should show it to Ben. The Dutch police had informed her there'd been an arson fire in her doctor's office in Holland. Many records had been destroyed, but the staff had found hers in its normal place. They didn't think it had anything to do with her case, but they wanted to let her know about it. Maybe that's what the Interpol inspector wanted to tell her about. In Ben's busyness with the install today, he had forgotten to pick up a new calling card for her, but promised to do it tomorrow.

Soon he joined her, carrying two steaming mugs of hot chocolate made with milk, not water, and blanketed in colored miniature marshmallows, exactly like she liked it. The letter could wait.

Rayne studied his profile over the rim as she sipped the scalding liquid. This man knew her so well. He paid attention to details, remembered what she said, what she liked and didn't like. It only took one time with Ben—the next time he had it down, remembering for fifteen years.

It wasn't only with her; she saw how he related to Quin, too. He knew when Quin needed a firm command or a joke, some space or a warm hand on the boy's shoulder. Ben was a rare breed: an encourager, someone who preferred helping others be successful and achieving their dreams. Why hadn't it worked with her? She shifted her thoughts away from the troubling past.

"Sorry about the cooking mess. We got a bit carried away. Thanks for cleaning up."

"It was worth it." At first, she thought he was talking about the tasty fried fish, which she had to admit turned out superbly, but then he said, "I haven't seen Quin laugh that hard. Ever."

She opened her mouth to say thanks, but the intensity of his gaze pinned her.

"You're really good with him, Rayne. For eleven years he's wondered what it would be like to have a mother." Ben said no more, only watched her over his own mug as her throat constricted to the size of a squished straw.

She looked away, to the room, the fire, anywhere except his blue eyes. She was no one's mother. Couldn't be. She—rather Regen van Onweer— was the reigning queen of metal music in Europe. It was like a destiny, demanding fulfillment. Sort of like the Queen in England. No one just gives that up, leaves it behind. She couldn't. Not after all the years of hard work. No, it wasn't possible.

Yet, for the first time, a shred of doubt niggled at a corner of her being. Once, when she'd been eight or nine and challenged by her piano instructor to play a difficult piece in a recital, she'd whined and cried to her Aunt Ruth, saying it was too difficult. Her aunt had agreed it was a little beyond Rayne's ability. But when she had Rayne's attention, she said, "You know who you *are*, Rayne, but who are you willing to *become*?" She'd practiced for hours and hours for two weeks and aced the recital.

Rayne could keep touring and singing for years, but no one stayed at the top for long. Audience's tastes changed, and others, like Dolina Macgowan, would rise up to eclipse Regen van Onweer. If she wasn't careful, she'd end up on some oldies tour in Branson, Missouri, doing duets with videos of Kenny Rogers. A shiver rippled her shoulders. Ben noticed and added another log to the already hot fire.

Who are you willing to become?

But didn't she have at least a few more good years? Time to make a significant mark? There *was* work to be done, a legacy to build. She needed, *wanted*, to go back and pick up her work with Elusive Hope. But that didn't mean she couldn't spend a few more weeks here with Ben and Quin. She would do everything possible to help build their two-person family in the time remaining. And while here, she could work on new music, something to cement that local family legacy.

Staring into the flames, Rayne said. "I wish I had our old piano. Or at least something to use for practice as my arm gets stronger." Ben had discovered the instrument in a genuine western saloon east of Paso Robles. The leaking building had been closed for years, but someone had wisely thrown a tarp over the piano. He'd bought it for her as a wedding gift and had a friend help move it into their cabin. The spinet, small as it was, dominated their living area, but she'd loved it the first time she ran her fingers over its age-cracked finish. She polished it daily, rubbing a bit of gleam into the cracked brown varnish. Using one of his small wrenches, she'd tuned the strings herself and then played for hours. He probably sold it after she'd left. No reason to keep something that would remind him of their failed marriage.

Ben rose and held a hand out. Hesitating a moment, she took it and let him lead her down the hall on the other side of the great room to an area of the house she hadn't explored. Ben showed her a tiny office where he paid bills but otherwise rarely used. Past it was a TV room, and then, at the end of the hallway, was a closed door.

She supposed it to be another bedroom. Ben pushed open the door, stepped aside, and let her enter first. It contained a floor lamp and no other furniture—except for a spinet piano with matching bench. He leaned against the door as she limped to the instrument and ran her hands across the perfect mahogany surface. A very thin film of dust covered it, but not more than a day or two. Someone dusted it regularly. Ben?

It was the same brand and model as the one they'd had, but this one was perfect, every surface smooth and richly grained, protected with a glossy deep finish. The manufacturer decal shone rich gold against the dark surface.

"Ben, it's beautiful." She looked back at him. "May I?" He nodded, so she slid onto the bench and folded back the hinged key covers. The white keys gleamed bright and even in color, and the black ones looked like poured lacquer. Rayne slipped her arm out of the sling, positioned her hands, and began to play the last song she'd never finished, "Indigo Sun." This unplugged version sounded completely different without the choir, orchestra, and band, but it was Marielle's triumph, and the power emerged.

The empty room had a lot to do with it. Hardwood floors and beamed ceiling reflected and magnified the perfectly tuned strings until the very air vibrated with music like a fine concert hall. She played slowly, her weak left hand struggling to keep up and depress the keys with just the right touch. After one verse and the chorus, she let her hands drop to her lap, letting the last notes linger on the air for several seconds before releasing the sustain pedal. Sweat beaded on her lip from the strain of holding her left arm in place. Grateful for the sling, she slipped her quivering appendage into its resting place.

She closed the key cover, and it was then she noticed the keyhole for the lock. Unlike the rest of the quality restoration, the brass surround hadn't been fully refurbished. Although polished, its rim evidenced the dents and wear of time. She bent forward in the dim light to get a closer look. The brass reflected her dress, but when she shifted slightly to the side she could make out two words engraved on the oval: *Rayne Conner.*

Startled, she sat straight, looked at the small circle with the keyhole, then at Ben. A smile tugged the corners of his mouth before he turned and walked down the hall, leaving Rayne alone with the piano. *Her* old piano.

She stared at the empty doorway, wondering if Ben had done the work himself. And why had he kept the engraved keyhole cover? She couldn't picture Ben sitting around, pining after his lost love. Clearly he'd gotten on with his life, building this home, his business, and taking in Quin. Had he fostered hope she'd return one day, that the love they'd once shared would bloom again? Rayne swiveled on the hard wood and leaned her back against the piano and listened as the fire crackled in the distant great room.

But she *had* returned, hadn't she? When the world became dangerous, she sought out the one place—the one man—she knew would give her sanctuary. The thing that scared her most was, what Ben Conner wanted in return.

CHAPTER SEVENTEEN

Monday changed everything for Rayne. First, Bibs called her at Ben's and asked her to play for the Harvest Festival she hosted on Halloween each year behind the Beauty Barn. Evidently Rayne wasn't the first to notice the natural amphitheater. Bibs had a rancher delivering bales of hay, and musicians from all around the area, everything from mariachi bands to high school kids lip-syncing, would be there from three o'clock on. Bibs's granddaughter had games planned for the kids. An old-fashioned fall party with lots of food and fun. Rayne tried to say *no*, but Bibs was insistent, so they settled on two songs, all she thought her arm could handle.

Then, when Mandy showed up and heard about Rayne's planned performance, the girl designed an aggressive physical therapy schedule to get her arm in shape. Besides range of motion exercises, Mandy thought of filling the bathtub in Rayne's suite to the brim, then having her kneel and swish her left arm back and forth through the water while gripping a hand towel for extra drag. The resistance taxed every muscle in her fingers, arm, shoulder, and back. Who knew such a simple exercise could have her sweating in two minutes?

By day three, Mandy added a tennis ball for Rayne to squeeze while doing the water therapy. After the tub torture, Mandy tossed a dry tennis ball to Rayne, forcing her to both catch and throw with her left hand. Between Mandy's grueling routine and Rayne's practice on the piano, she felt much stronger by the evening of the festival.

Ben had finally brought home a new international calling card, and she'd left a message on Inspector Wolfe's voicemail this morning, telling him she couldn't be reached directly and that she'd call back. There was nothing more she could do on that front.

"Come on. It's time to go," Quin called, tromping blindly down the stairs while pulling a sweatshirt over his head. Rayne watched in horror from the great room, expecting him to tumble to the bottom. Hands tangled in the sleeves, he yanked the garment's neck past his eyes and jumped the last three steps, landing at her feet with a mighty thud. When he saw her expression and hand over her mouth, he grinned. "What?" he said, all innocence.

"What indeed, you maniac." Rayne laughed and finger-combed his tousled hair. That only caused his grin to expand. Scoundrel. Ben came in from the garage as she adjusted Quin's twisted sweatshirt. He watched her with the strangest expression, a combination of hopefulness and something else. Rayne stepped away from Quin and reached for her own coat, a plum-colored ski jacket borrowed from Mandy.

She couldn't encourage Ben, let him think there was a chance she'd stay. That wasn't going to happen. Using his laptop, she'd been in touch by email with all her band members: Pieter, Hans, Eva, and Danny. She frowned as they climbed into Ben's truck, thinking of Pieter's and Eva's messages. They'd been playing with other bands, catching gigs where they could, including with Dolina. Hans had guitar studio work lined up for several weeks on a major album project for a band from Germany. If she didn't get back soon, everyone would scatter, and she'd have to recruit anew—never a fun task.

Or Dolina Macgowan would take Rayne's place. She had to admit, the girl could sing, easily able to front a rock band. Not everyone could do that. Oh, many could perform well in a studio with a sound tech mixing down the instruments and boosting the vocals, but performing live with drums pounding, guitar and bass amps blasting...that took a strong singer whose vocals could stand on top with clarity; no easy task.

Rayne had that ability. So did Dolina. And she had a commanding stage presence, too.

"Something wrong?" Ben asked as they drove around the lake perimeter. Quin sat between them, and he looked up at her.

She gave what she hoped was a small smile. "Just thinking about music, I guess. Sorry."

"You looked mad," Quin said, clearly too observant for his own good.

"Did I? I'm sorry." She took his hand and squeezed with her newly-strong left hand. "I'm fine."

Her apology might have reassured Quin, but Ben wasn't buying it. She turned away from his gaze and watched the lake peek through the trees and rocks as they drove.

Cars filled the Bibs' Beauty Barn lot, and a pear-shaped Batman with a forty-six-inch waist was directing vehicles down a dirt path that led to the back field. Another Batman, this one skinny, motioned them into a line of cars waiting to park side by side. As soon as they exited the Ford, the air filled with music from loudspeakers and delicious smells of Santa Maria-style barbecue, distinctive even at a distance for its rich spices and oak wood coals. Kids surrounded a cotton candy machine, and Quin sprinted ahead to get in line.

"Guess he'll be spoiling his dinner first thing," Ben said, but a smile eased his features. "He deserves all the fun a boy can have."

"He's the least spoiled boy I know."

"Do you know many young boys in Holland?"

Rayne turned, startled by Ben's mild confrontation. He never asked about her life at home in the Netherlands. In fact, he avoided the subject, as if ignoring it might make it go away. But it wouldn't.

"Of course. My friends have kids. I see them when we have get-togethers." Okay, only Murita had kids, and they were ages two and four, and only the four-year-old was a boy, but he qualified as a young boy, didn't he? Time to change the subject. She pointed toward the back of the Beauty Barn.

"Look. Bibs has a drink stand set up. How about getting me a diet soda, no ice?"

"Don't you want something to eat, too?" He indicated the rapidly growing line by the barbecue pit. "We should get in line soon."

Rayne shook her head. "I'm too nervous to eat before I play. Maybe after." Her stomach felt like a tangle of irate squirrels fighting over the last acorn of the season. "But I'll hold a place for you," she said, limping toward the food queue. She wasn't scheduled to sing for an hour, and the closer she got, the better the meat smelled. At least thirty huge tri-tips sizzled over one end of the monster grill, which had a big wheel at one end for raising and lowering the grate. Chicken halves roasted over the center section, and a dozen loaves of French bread toasted on the far end. Two men in chef's hats used long tongs to prod and turn the items. One had a black apron with lime-green lettering that read, *Ghouls make the best goulash.*

Strands of colored lights and hay bales ringed the area beyond the cooking. Rayne spotted the low stage erected on one side. Black and orange crepe paper wrapped the corner posts and crisscrossed the top. More colored lights outlined the latticework canopy, casting a soft glow on drums, guitars, and microphones that stood ready alongside what looked to be a decent-quality keyboard. Her fingers tingled, anticipating the touch of the keys.

She'd always struggled with nerves, but there was comfort in most concerts where the vast majority of the audience were strangers. But here, while it was true she didn't know a *lot* of people, it felt like performing for family and friends. Everyone would watch in curiosity, to catch a glimpse of the woman who'd run out on Ben Conner. She wiped her hands on her slacks, glad for the moisture absorbing cotton.

Dusk fell while Ben ate, and Rayne nibbled some of his garlic French bread and sipped at her soda. The hay bale where they sat gave off a sweet fragrance in the cool night air that swept away civilization and returned her to a simpler time when communities gathered and entertained each other. A bluegrass band played several songs, followed by a high school group and a cowboy poet who had them all laughing at his unusual rhymes. People milled around, about half in costumes or simple masks. Two bales down, the front and back halves of a cow sat eating heaping plates of barbecue beef in flagrant insensibility to their animal costume.

Ben's brother, Addison, arrived with Mandy, his fiancé Samantha Riley—Mandy's soon-to-be mom—and Star Trafford, a redheaded spitfire who was Sam's adopted daughter. Mandy gave Rayne an enthusiastic hug and introduced her to Sam and Star. With cute professionalism, Mandy inquired about Rayne's arm. Rayne assured the budding therapist the arm was doing fine. In the seconds before they ran off, Rayne noticed the way Star mirrored the older girl, and not for the first time Rayne wished for a sister of her own.

She shook hands with Sam and dutifully admired the sparkling engagement ring, uncomfortably conscious of her own bare left hand.

"Good to see you again, Rayne," Addison said and gave her a stiff hug. He was as handsome as she remembered, maybe more so with the character lines around his eyes. It might have been her imagination, but his gaze seemed a warning not to cause his brother further hurt. Paranoid or not, she filed the unspoken message.

After eating, Sam and Addison left to help with the kids' games, which included tossing various items at targets and maneuvering through a huge maze constructed of duct-taped refrigerator boxes. Ben left to find Quin—they hadn't seen him in an hour, but most of the bigger kids had headed toward a large bonfire thirty yards away in an open area. Adults were supervising and handing out materials for s'mores.

While Ben was gone, a group began playing oldies, everything from Sinatra to the Beach Boys, and many couples took to the plank dance floor, some dancing at tempo, while others swayed slowly. What she noticed, though, was not the dancing, but the history that pervaded this place and these lives. Unknown to Rayne until they arrived, Bibs had begun the festival twelve years ago, quickly establishing a lake tradition. Usually the weather cooperated, though one year they had to move everything into the barn, squeezing in between the open back area and the beauty shop in the front.

Rayne watched an elderly couple take the floor. They danced slowly, oblivious to those stepping and twirling around, staring into each other's eyes. At the end of the song, the man dipped the woman who was tuned to his every lead. As she rose, he gave her a kiss and the woman lifted one leg at the knee, like in a scene from a movie. Hand in hand they strolled from the circle.

Suddenly, Rayne's view was blocked by a white wall, and she looked up to find the Lone Ranger directly in front of her, complete with white cowboy hat, matching pistols, and a black mask across his eyes. He tipped his hat and bowed at the waist.

"Eve'nin, little lady," he drawled and extended a hand. "Can I have the pleasure of this dance?" The band began playing Simon & Garfunkel's Bridge Over Troubled Waters. A girl of about eighteen sang in a clear soprano. Rayne didn't want to disappoint the man in white, but she had enough trouble walking.

"Oh, I'm afraid not," she said as kindly as possible. "I'm healing from a leg injury and wouldn't be much good out there. But thank you for asking."

"I completely understand." He indicated Ben's vacant spot. "May I sit down?"

"Oh, of course," she said, scooting to the right edge of the bale to make room.

His eyes roved the dancers and spectators. "Beautiful evening, isn't it?"

They chitchatted about the festival. Rayne learned he had a cabin nearby, but didn't get a chance to stay in it often since he traveled a lot. She was looking for Ben when the man pulled a notebook out of a pocket.

"I wonder if I could get your autograph. I'm a fan."

Rayne froze at the words. Had he recognized her from a concert or a CD cover? He hardly seemed the type to follow symphonic metal groups thousands of miles away, but then there were a few older fans in every audience.

Her voice quavered as she answered. "How...how do you know me?" After that horrible flower showed up at her mother's place in Atlanta, she'd done everything possible to keep her location secret. No one, not even Danny, knew where she was, other than somewhere in the United States.

People around the lake knew her as Ben Conner's runaway bride, the former Rayne Evans, who'd lived here for less than a year a long time ago. She'd never mentioned her life in Europe or Regen van Onweer. They couldn't know.

"I mean a *future* fan, I'm sure," he responded quickly, but Rayne got the feeling he was covering. He pointed back toward the barn. "Bibs mentioned you were going to sing tonight and said you play beautifully."

At Bibs's name, Rayne relaxed a little. He knew Bibs. The woman had been so excited to have Rayne sing, she'd probably told everyone who stopped for two seconds.

He held out the paper and a pen hopefully. "Maybe you'll be famous someday, and I'll have an original autograph."

Rayne tried to keep her hands from shaking as she took the pen and notebook. There was something...his voice? She glanced at him one more time before concentrating on the paper. She signed her first name, Rayne, then she hesitated, unsure of what she should use as a last name. Conner? Evans? Van Onweer? It was getting tough to keep her aliases straight. All her autographs in Europe had been Regen van Onweer. It felt very strange to sign an autograph as Rayne Evans, but that's what she settled on.

"Interesting tattoo you have there," Lone Ranger said, pointing at Rayne's wrist. "Does it symbolize anything?"

Rayne handed back the pen and notebook, and rubbed the ink as if she could trace the sea-green lines. How could she explain to a stranger that she'd been feeling down after a tough month shortly after she'd moved to the Netherlands? That Danny had picked her up for a Sunday afternoon picnic and, after two bottles of wine in the warm sun, they'd ended up in his favorite tattoo parlor in Amsterdam. He'd gotten another adornment to his spreading collection, while Rayne, head still spinning from the alcohol, opted for the simple wave lines that reminded her of the Pacific Ocean, Storm Lake...and Ben Conner.

A hand touched her shoulder, and she jumped. Bibs stood behind her, nodding toward the stage.

"You're on, hon."

CHAPTER EIGHTEEN

Ben and Quin walked up to the entertainment area as Rayne stiffly mounted the single step onto the stage. A guy in a Lone Ranger costume occupied the hay bale where they'd been earlier, so Ben and Quin remained at the edge of the ring. As Rayne adjusted the height of the stool and the position of the mic, Ben noticed people converging on the stage. They streamed from the bonfire, the drink area, and the dark reaches of the field. And, while they came to see and hear Rayne, they couldn't seem to resist frequently glancing Ben's way. Interest in him ceased as soon as Rayne played the first note.

She'd chosen "Indigo Sun," the same song she'd first played on her piano—their piano. The words recounted the story of a girl, a woman, named Marielle, who at first had a charmed life. But tragedy followed, then betrayal by those she loved. Marielle proved to be a fighter, never giving in to the forces that conspired against her, turning defeat into victory.

Ben shook himself out of trance-like wonder. Rayne's voice filled the festival area, then rose into the black night, enveloping the area in a protective blanket and transforming the merely adequate amp and speakers into a world-class sound system. No one around the square stirred: not a glass moved to lips, no fork of barbecue finished its path to waiting mouth, no one spoke. Even the kids stilled on parents' laps; crying babies quieted instantly. Ben noted many partly opened mouths as Rayne sang of beauty in the midst of pain, solace from simple things, and strength from faith.

When the last triumphant note echoed away to be replaced by crickets, no one moved, including Rayne who sat in her own world, staring across the stage, but not seeing anything here in this earthly place. Tears streamed down her cheeks, and Ben felt corresponding wetness on his own cheeks. Finally, after what seemed like thirty seconds, Ben heard quiet clapping and looked down to see Quin lead everyone in respectful applause. It grew and grew. People paused to wipe their eyes, then rejoined the tumult with renewed vigor.

Rayne bowed her head, dabbing with a tissue, but never acknowledged the noisy acclaim. Finally, she again lifted her hands to the keys. That simple movement instantly shushed the onlookers. She played a few chords, but then turned to the audience. Ben followed her eyes to the bale where they'd sat earlier. The Lone Ranger was gone and four pre-teen girls squished onto the hay. Rayne searched the ring until she spotted Ben and Quin. She smiled radiantly.

"How many fathers and sons do we have here tonight?" She continued to play as cheers went up, men and boys waving all around. Beside him, Quin let out a whoop and waved wildly at Rayne. She grinned back and Ben waved, too, proud to at last be a father. It was something he never thought would happen. And it didn't come about the way he'd imagined. But gazing down at the enthusiastic brown-haired boy next to him, he had no doubt things had worked out okay.

As the noise subsided, Rayne said, "Well this is a special song, written for fathers and sons everywhere, but *especially* those right here at Storm Lake."

The melody was simple, joyful.

Father to son, father to son,
   Stories of our histories passed down,
   Anchoring us to the past so dear
   As we reach for the future so clear.

She sang of fathers teaching boys to fish, how to tie knots and knot a tie, how to treat a girl. Dads told stories of their own childhoods: where they played, who taught them the rules to the games, songs they sang around campfires in Gift, Flume, and Deer Cove. Fathers recounted how their ancestors discovered Storm Lake either long ago or more recently, and the tales they heard of those first settlers.

People laughed at times, nodded, and held each other as Rayne sang on, telling how fathers left a legacy *in* their children, not *for* them, building the next generation on the strength of the previous.

At one point, Quin leaned into Ben's side, and he slipped his arm around the boy's shoulder. Quin grinned up at him and Ben had to look away, blinking hard.

Rayne had everyone sing along at the final chorus:

Father to son, father to son,
   Stories of our histories passed down,
   Anchoring us to the past so dear
   As we reach for the future so clear.

When she ended with a flourish, mad applause broke out, joined by cheers and whistles as adults once again reached for Kleenex and smiled at each other and their children with renewed love.

By the time they'd said goodbye to everyone and climbed into Ben's truck, a northern front had blown through the pass and over the upper lake, fanning the water into small whitecaps and dropping the temperature fifteen degrees in as many minutes.

Rayne's breath clouded the frigid cab, as she willed warmth to flow from the heater vents. As it always happened after a performance, adrenaline drained from her body like water out of a bathtub, leaving her depleted and cold. Tonight's chilly weather made it worse.

The heater finally kicked in, and Ben kept it at full blast, obviously noticing her shaking shoulders. Quin talked excitedly about the games, s'mores, barbecue, and the bonfire. He sorted through his candy stash showing off his best pieces, and told Rayne over and over how 'awesome' she'd been on stage, and how Mandy had flirted with college boys at the fire. Ben's eyebrows lifted at that one, but Rayne only smiled. Mandy had more smarts than any girl she'd ever known. The boys had better watch out.

When they entered the house, they realized they'd left the kitchen window open while they were gone, and cold wind swirled through the rooms. Ben closed it and turned up the thermostat, then went to check the other windows. Rayne kept her jacket zipped while putting on water for something hot.

"Ben! Where do you keep the hot chocolate?" She was rummaging through the walk-in pantry when Ben stepped in behind her and reached over her shoulder. Even through her jacket, she felt his warmth, and her body leaned into his heat.

"Looking for this?" His breath brushed her neck as he lifted a can of powdered chocolate before her eyes.

She turned, but he hadn't stepped back. The tiny room seemed smaller than ever. What was she looking for? Oh, yes. He held the can, but she wondered what *he* was asking about. His eyes dropped to her mouth and her breath caught. Again. Why did it keep doing that every time he looked at her mouth?

"Yes," she whispered. "That sounds good." She had no idea what she meant. Maybe he didn't either, but it didn't seem to matter. Ben closed the gap between them, hovering briefly, as if waiting for her. Then he lowered his mouth and kissed her.

She leaned into his gentle touch, relishing his warm lips tasting of barbecue with a hint of cotton candy. His weight shifted, pressing against her, heating her body head to toe. Her right hand was curling into his surfer hair when Quin popped his head in the doorway.

"Wow!"

Rayne jumped away from Ben, banging her head on a shelf hard enough to rattle cans. Ben dropped the chocolate container. The plastic seal flew off and brown powder rained on their shoes.

Quin stood there grinning ear to ear. "Are we having hot chocolate?"

Ben murmured something, picked up the container, and brushed past Quin who still filled half the doorway.

Rayne's neck was on fire, and a hot drink was the last thing she needed. One minute she'd been freezing, now sweat broke out all over. Before Quin backed up and let her exit the claustrophobic space, he gave her an exaggerated wink. She stripped off the jacket and hurled it toward one of the bar stools. The boy had been hanging out with soon-to-be-cousin Mandy way too much.

To Rayne's relief, Ben had disappeared upstairs, and Quin fixed his own hot chocolate since Rayne no longer cared for any. She muttered goodnight, ignoring his continuous grin, and stumbled straight through her dark bedroom to the shower. Leaving her clothes in a heap, she eased under the spray, letting the water soak her hair and run down her back. She'd washed her hair this morning but felt the need to do it again.

What had she been thinking, letting Ben kiss her like that? At *all*. She pressed her forehead against the cold tile under the shower head. Idiot. This was all such a bad idea. She should have stayed on that train to Portland or wherever it went. Alaska would be perfect. From there she could hop a fishing boat to Russia, hide out in a gulag somewhere.

"Ughh!"

She scrubbed her hair even though it didn't need it, shaved her legs though they weren't hairy, and finally climbed out of the shower seconds before she used up every drop of hot water in the house. At least her body temperature had stabilized—as long as she didn't think about the kiss. She leaned back into the shower to wring the excess water out of her hair, then twisted a towel around her head and used another to dry her body.

After blow-drying her hair, Rayne walked into the bedroom. She started to fall back on the bed when she noticed something centered on the white bedspread, barely visible in the dim light. She reached out and touched the object, stroking its silky texture. A single red rose petal.

CHAPTER NINETEEN

"What do you mean you're leaving?" Mandy demanded across the granite breakfast bar Monday afternoon.

Rayne inwardly cringed at the stricken expression on the girl's face. But the sooner Rayne left, the quicker things would get back to normal for everyone.

"But Dad and Sam's wedding is less than three weeks away. You said you'd be there."

Addison and Sam were getting married the Sunday before Thanksgiving at the Perilous Cove Community Church, a white New England style chapel on the hill overlooking the Pacific Ocean. The same place Rayne and Ben had gotten married. Only a week ago, Rayne planned to attend the service, then head back to the Netherlands as soon as Thanksgiving travel calmed down. She hadn't anticipated what sparked between Ben and her. The rose petal he'd left on her bed had been the deciding factor. If she stayed any longer...

"Earth to Rayne." Mandy was waving a hand in front of her face. "Major discussion here. Focus."

"What?" It came out sharper than she intended. "Sorry, Mandy. I'm a little uptight."

"Understatement," Mandy mumbled, and headed for the coffee pot. "What's happened, Rayne? Why do you suddenly have to leave?"

Let's see, Quin wanted—no needed—a mother and had his sights set on Rayne; Mandy hoped Ben and Rayne would reunite, or *ig*-nite, which they nearly had last night; Danny announced that Elusive Hope—*Rayne's* band—was performing next weekend in Amsterdam with Dolina Macgowan singing the lead; and last but certainly not least, Ben was… was…

"Something's come up—business stuff…personal—and I need to get back." It sounded lame, and Mandy's eyes narrowed. Rayne hated to disappoint Mandy by leaving early. As it was, she still hadn't found a flight she could afford. Just yesterday she'd gotten the bill for Doc Arnold, chewing yet another hole in her ragged resources. One possible flight had her connecting through three US cities, then London to Frankfurt and back to Amsterdam. The thought alone of that convoluted route exhausted her, and she never understood why the farther she flew, the cheaper the fare. The flight wasn't until Saturday, too late to overtake the concert plans, but at least she'd be in the country shortly afterward and be able to regain control. This was her career, her future. She wanted it.

She let out a sigh. But it was a stupid plan. Even that serpentine flight wasn't cheap enough. She'd arrive flat broke. No money to pay the back rent on her house or to fix the slashed tires on her Peugeot. She still hadn't paid Danny what she owed him. And then there was the cost of an alarm system to provide a modicum of security for her home.

She walked to the kitchen sink and watched the rain dimpling the window. Its gentle patter belied a frosty core. Only the cold air spilling across the stone countertop hinted at the outside temperature. The headache she'd had off and on all day returned with a vengeance, and she pinched the bridge of her nose. It didn't do any good, but at least it shifted the pain from one place to another, kind of like life.

As a seventeen-year-old, Rayne had relished the year abroad study in the Netherlands. She'd eagerly traded the loneliness of her dysfunctional family in Nebraska for being a stranger in a country where she didn't speak the language or understand social customs. But she'd learned fast by immersing herself in the deep end of the pool. While school friends and shopkeepers all wanted to practice their English on Rayne, she resolved to speak only Dutch. Her biggest mistake had been to come back to the states at the end of her school term.

No, that wasn't true. Her *biggest* mistake had been to go on that junior college choir tour that put a California beach kid named Ben Conner in the front row of their sloppy performance in Mission Peak. Maybe going out with him had been the biggest mistake—or marrying him. Definitely the marriage. She shook her head. What was she thinking, getting married at nineteen? Someone should have arrested her.

"Rayne? I can see the wheels spinning. Are you listening to me at *all*?"

Rayne turned back to the girl, who'd obviously been speaking for some time. "Sorry. What did you say?"

"I said, someone shot you—twice. Is it safe for you to go back? Did they catch the guy?"

"I think they're close." She hoped that was true. Regardless, she had to take her life back. The time for hiding was over.

She walked back to the breakfast bar, trying to concentrate on Holland, Elusive Hope, the next tour. But her mind meandered back to that warm evening at the street fair in Mission Peak. Though it had been fall and the cornstalk-decorated fair booths sported pumpkins and gourds by the thousands, a mild Santa Ana wind had come from the desert and pushed the typical coastal cool air far out to sea, providing a gorgeous evening of enticing foods. Stars sparkled overhead when they made their way from the downtown lights and crowds to the quiet, dark, mission gardens where Ben had kissed her under a spreading oak.

Yeah, it sounded like a romance novel, but that's how she remembered it. Did Ben have the same memories of that evening?

"I *so* totally give up," Mandy said, drawing Rayne's attention as the young woman threw up her hands. "You know, you artists are really weird. You tell me you're leaving, and now you're smiling. What's *that* about?"

"Oh, nothing. Just thinking about...a music tour." Rayne brushed some imaginary crumbs into a napkin, but she caught Mandy's hangdog expression—tinged with a hefty dose of anger.

The girl heaved a sigh. "When are you leaving?"

Why did her stomach twist in knots at the prospect of telling Quin? And Ben. "I haven't decided. Soon, maybe." She stalled at Mandy's confused expression. With another sigh, she explained. "The truth is, Mandy, I'm broke. Oh, not completely, but flights to Holland aren't cheap right now."

"Holland? Ben said you came here from Atlanta." Mandy's expression ran from mad to confused to hurt as the realization took hold that Rayne had lied to her—or at least withheld the whole truth about who she was.

For a brief second, Rayne considered telling Mandy the whole story. Surely she'd heard the news, even here in California where hardly anyone knew of Elusive Hope. But she didn't want to put Mandy in the position of keeping a secret, or dealing with things that would push the young woman further away from innocence.

"I...lost most of my money on a business deal, an investment gone wrong." It was the truth—mostly. "I have to get back to the Netherlands and see if I can recoup my money."

It was plain by the set of her jaw that Mandy didn't believe the fabrication.

"This is sounding more and more like a movie," Mandy said, then held up her hands when Rayne opened her mouth. "Since your mind is obviously lost in your plans or whatever"—Mandy waved her hands above her head, indicating clouds—"we might as well work on your body."

Rayne nodded. "Good idea. I've got to get my leg in shape."

"Yeah, so you can outrun the bad guys." She shook her head. "Grab your jacket. We're going for a walk."

Rayne glanced outside. "Are you kidding?" Water now sluiced down the windows in a waterfall. The weatherman had predicted three to four inches of rain, and it looked like the main storm was upon them. "It's wet and freezing out there," she said, feeling the need to state the obvious in case the girl had been lost in daydreams of her own.

Mandy slid her arms into a warm fleece and layered it with a poncho from the closet. She snatched another one of the hooded plastic garments and tossed it to Rayne. "Come on. It's just water. Where's that North Sea spirit? Don't you Nederlanders stick your fingers in the dikes when it rains?"

"They have maintenance crews for that now."

Mandy rolled her eyes. "Whatever. Besides, I've got an idea for how you can earn some bucks, but I'll only tell you outside." She headed for the door.

Raoul Kloepper couldn't believe his good luck as he caught a flash of movement in the rearview mirror. He'd been huddled in his Volkswagen wedged between two trees on the road above the house, waiting for something to happen. But all that had materialized so far was rain. Besides the drips hitting the steel dome above his head, a tear-shaped droplet originated on the upper left corner of the windshield, vibrated briefly, and fell with a splat onto his black jeans.

He'd picked up the 1975 Super Beetle in Los Angeles from a private party ad; however, there was no longer anything super about the car. The heater only worked in warm weather, the motor ran on three rather than four cylinders most of the time, the upholstery lay beneath layers of scratchy Navajo blankets, and the dash had a jagged cavity where the radio should be. But it did have one redeeming quality: the dark gray primer body had as much rust as paint, giving it natural camouflage.

Crouching low in his seat, Raoul watched through the left side mirror as two women trudged up the long driveway from the Conner house, heading to the main road behind him. Dressed in dark pants and tan rain parkas, hoods pulled tight around their faces, they were indistinguishable from one another. Except that one had a noticeable limp.

"Ah," he whispered, his breath fogging the cold glass. "Hello, Regen van Onweer. Nice to see you again."

When they were gone from sight, he slipped from the car, retrieved his heavy backpack from the passenger seat, and pushed the door closed with his hip. His coat was nowhere near heavy enough for the late afternoon. The weather had turned on a dime. If his car had a radio... Well, at least the jacket was semi-waterproof.

He lost his footing twice on dead leaves and mud, sliding down the steep hill to the side of the garage. Once there, he made his way around to the lakeside entry door. It was locked, but he retrieved the key from under a loose rock by the path, pocketed it, and slipped inside. The interior of the three-car garage was marginally warmer, though a cloud of vapor appeared with each breath.

He hadn't been able to see much of the interior of the house from outside since most of the uncovered windows faced the lake, and there were no hiding places on that side of the property. He'd first had to break in a few days ago when no one was home—a simple feat for a man with his skills—and physically survey the floor plan. Regen van Onweer's room was on the first floor, logical with her injuries. The break-in also gave him time to drill holes and push in miniature cameras. The camera wires weren't long enough to attach to the main control box—that was his task today.

Quietly, he grabbed the suspended rope for the crawl space stairs and pulled them down from their nested frame in the garage ceiling. He appreciated the architect's thoughtful design for the house. The stairs not only gave access to the storage space under the steep pitched roof of the garage, but also led to crawl spaces for some of the main floor rooms as well as the upstairs attic through a steel fire door. Originally intended for access to the pipes and electrical conduits that disappeared into the darkness, the space was perfect for his uses.

He pulled up the stairs after himself, then strapped on knee pads and an L.E.D. headlight from his pack. Sliding on his elbows and knees, he inched his way down the two-foot wide by three-foot high channel above the downstairs hallway until he reached her bedroom. The wires from his previous camera installs lay curled where he'd shoved them. At the first one, he tilted the headlamp downward to light his hands as he spliced the short leads to the long spool he carried. He did the same for the hall camera. He wished he could have installed one in the bathroom, but there hadn't been a good hiding place in the brightly lit room. Any camera in the ceiling or corners would be noticed.

He wired the two cameras in the great room, one pointing toward the front door, the other toward the kitchen, then two more in the garage to cover the interior and the view outside toward the driveway. Next, he connected the wires to the main control box—one of his own specialized design—then used a standard co-ax cable to link it to the main cable TV splitter for the house. Lastly, he attached the battery backup to keep the signal flowing in case of a power outage.

Raoul was halfway down the lowered stairs when headlights flashed across the garage door windows and one of the garage doors began to open. He scrambled up again, then yanked the stairs up to their closed position, but not before headlights swept them momentarily. He lay on his back, still as possible, breathing through his mouth while the vehicle, probably Conner's big truck from the sound of it, pulled into the garage. Without a sound, he extracted his street-purchased .38 revolver from the backpack and rested it on his chest.

As soon as the garage door finished rising, Ben let off the brake and wheeled the Ford into its space. A flash of white from the left side of the garage caught his eye, but just as he looked closer the windshield wiper swiped across the glass, smearing and streaking. When the blade retreated, all he saw in the garage was dark cabinetry. He set the parking brake and climbed out. Water dripped from the cold steel of the truck, puddling on the concrete. He listened for a moment. Other than the ticking of the cooling engine and the drip of rain off the house, all was quiet.

He grabbed a folder and shut the truck door, started for the house, then stopped when he noticed scuffs of mud and a few wet leaves near the door leading to the outside. The trail led partway across the garage before fading out. Quin wasn't home—he'd gone straight from school to a friend's house to study and have dinner. Why would Rayne use this door, especially on a cold, wet day? Ben twisted the doorknob. It wasn't locked, but that wasn't too unusual; they locked the front door of the house and the patio slider at nights and when they were both away, but this back exit often got left open. He pushed the door ajar and looked out. A stiff wind carried moist air and raindrops inside. Wet leaves and mud covered the outside doormat, as if someone had wiped their muddy shoes on it.

Ben closed the door and flipped on the interior light switch. Four long fluorescent fixtures hummed to life and bathed his workspace in blue white light. He did a quick check of his tools, opening cupboards and drawers, but nothing seemed to be missing. With a sigh, he turned off the lights, locked the door, and pushed the button for the rollup door and waited while it rumbled closed.

There had been a few break-ins over the years, but generally it was the more isolated homes, and especially those occupied only part-time. He'd have to talk to Quin about locking this door, though. The lake was changing. He might even install some of his own security products, as much as he hated to concede the loss of a time when people trusted each other and left buildings and vehicles unlocked. His business was successful because people demanded security systems, and he was good at installing them. But personally he disliked the idea of living in paranoia.

The warmth of the kitchen seeped into his clothes, gradually chasing away the cold as he poured a cup of coffee. Rayne must have made it recently since it wasn't bitter. He searched the ground floor and called her name, but received no answer. Mandy's backpack sat on a barstool, and the Bronco had been in its place on the far side of the garage. Dark clouds swirled over an angry surface, and fat drops smacked the glass in intermittent fusillades. Surely they hadn't gone for a walk.

He had the fire roaring when he heard footsteps on the front porch. The door opened and in poured a wave of laughter and wet plastic. Even with the rain gear, the two women were soaked. They supported each other as they removed their shoes, socks, ponchos, and jackets. Water dripped from limp hair, and Rayne squealed when Mandy shook her head like a dog after a swim in the lake.

"Ooh, a fire!" Mandy said, then added, "Hi, Ben," as she ran on squeaking feet and plopped down in front of the fireplace.

"That's Uncle Ben to you, young lady," he corrected. Rayne followed more slowly, wincing with each limping step. He slid a footstool forward and helped down her onto it.

"Thanks," she smiled up at him, sighing as she settled into the soft leather. She stretched her bare feet toward the fire and rubbed her hands in the radiating heat. "Feels good."

"It should," he said. "What were you thinking, going out in this storm?"

"Umm, that would be your niece's idea of physical therapy. Builds character."

"Yup," Mandy said, scooting nearer the fire. "Character. And wet underwear." They broke out laughing again.

Ben shook his head, but got towels from the hall linen closet and handed one to each woman. Mandy's hair, being much shorter, dried almost immediately with vigorous rubbing, while Rayne's new cut hung somewhat shapeless without benefit of a styling brush and blow dryer. He sank to a cushion at her side, leaning back on his arms as she toweled her neck and behind each ear.

Rayne's skin had always been velvet soft, like a perfect rose petal. He'd touched her so many times. The first weeks of their marriage, he'd been fascinated at the simplest, private things: how she leaned toward the mirror when removing and applying makeup; the way her rear end wiggled when she brushed her teeth; how she sat in the middle of their bed with one knee tucked to her chest while painting her toenails, humming tunes and making music notes on her ever-present composition book until she would catch him staring and grin, "What?" He felt his own mouth curve into a smile at the memory of her impish love of life.

In some ways, she hadn't changed much. He'd seen the young woman she'd been when she talked with Quin, giving her full attention like he was the only one in the whole world. Every day the boy opened himself more to Rayne. And, while Mandy could befriend nearly anyone, the two women had a depth of communication lost to him—perhaps to *every* male. They'd be working in the kitchen, and then some kind of telepathy caused them to glance at each other. A raised brow, the slightest nod, a smile—then they'd go back to their work without a word. But Ben had the feeling whole conversations had taken place, and too often he figured he was the topic.

Although still too thin, in his opinion, Rayne had put on a little weight since coming here. Quin's Rice Krispies bars had helped. Carrying her into the house that first day had been far too easy for her five-eleven height. Band life was tough. Playing clubs and touring probably didn't promote regular eating. In the flickering light, her high cheekbones were a little less pronounced, and her lips... Those full lips had been his downfall that night in Mission Peak, and he hadn't let her go without tasting them.

He was staring at Rayne's mouth when Mandy, sitting on Rayne's other side, gained his attention and offered him a smile. Before he could look away in embarrassment at being caught, sadness filled her eyes, and she turned to the fire, as if looking for answers in the flickering tongues.

He frowned. The girl had been blatantly pushing him toward Rayne these last few weeks. If Mandy had her way, she'd lock them in the house and make them work out their future. So why was she now not pressing her advantage?

Lights and the toot of a horn announced Tori's arrival, and Mandy grabbed her stuff and worked on her shoes sans wet socks. Before leaving, she stood solemnly in front of Rayne, looking her straight in the eye. Then she knelt and pulled her into a tight embrace. Mandy faced away from Ben, but he heard her whispering something, causing Rayne to squeeze her eyes shut as she returned the hug. Mandy disengaged and left without a backward glance or word, unique for his niece.

Ben started to ask Rayne about it, but she avoided his eyes, slid off the ottoman, and curled up on her "good" side on the mound of cushions, feet toward Ben. He reached out and squeezed her cold ankle.

"Are you hungry? Would you like some soup?"

She shook her head, eyes closed, lashes wet. Ben rose, grabbed a throw blanket off the sofa and covered her. She mumbled thanks as he added two logs to the fire.

Ben retreated to the kitchen. Something had changed between Rayne and Mandy today. Whatever good times the two had walking in the freezing rain had come to a crashing halt once they returned to the house. He could understand Rayne's exhaustion after a tough hike, but Mandy had enough energy for three people. Normally. But then, when had anything about this situation been normal?

Cold fingers of air slid across the stone countertop and slipped into his gut. He'd thought things were changing. Rayne's connection with Quin, her performance at the fair, the kiss in the pantry. But it wasn't just the kiss—it was that she'd pressed close, like it was what *she* wanted, too. He'd let hope gain a foothold, and there was nothing worse than dashed hopes and dreams.

He won her once, then let her go. At the time, he'd had to choose between his rebellious wife and his dying mother, then his grieving father. As the years passed, it had been easy to doubt the love they'd once shared. Now it had sparked again. But this time she'd never promised anything other than to leave again. And he couldn't follow— not with Quin as a new responsibility. Like a fool, he'd let her inside both his home and his heart. When she left, she would tear a large hole in both.

CHAPTER TWENTY

Something woke Rayne. Was it a bump against the side of the house? She lay still, barely breathing, straining. But no more sound came. She shifted onto her side, beat the pillow with her fist, and forced her eyes closed. Probably an animal. They'd seen wild turkeys crossing the yard in the past weeks. They made a mess of flowerbeds, uprooting flowers and small shrubs in their never-ending hunt for bugs. Rayne had also spotted five deer two days ago. Quin tried to convince her bears roamed the night, but she wasn't buying that story due to his half-hidden grin.

A smile curved her lips as she turned to the window; no light filtered through the shades. She worked her sore leg, stretching across the comfy bed. Mandy's forced march in the rain last night had nearly done her in, but it felt better now after a few hours of rest. She rubbed her eyes, sat up, and stretched her arms above her head. She'd slept too long by the fire last night, and she was paying for it. Might as well do something productive.

Guided only by the nightlight in the bathroom, she dressed in sweats and thick socks, brushed her teeth, and ran a comb through her hair. Her leg ached with her weight on it; she'd have to do more stretches later—if she could get down to the floor. Considering it hadn't been long ago she'd been in a wheelchair, she was pleased with her progress.

Pausing in the great room to pick up her music notation pad, she glanced at the black rectangles overlooking the lake. A couple of lights glistened on the distant shore, indicating she wasn't the only one up this early. She crossed into the hallway on the other side of the room, stopping at a closet to retrieve a thick towel, then stepped into the room with the piano. She closed the door and sealed its bottom with the rolled towel.

Cold from the piano bench made her glad she'd picked sweats. The automatic thermostat wouldn't kick on the house heat for another hour or two, and she didn't want to alert Ben she was awake by manually overriding it. Before folding back the keyboard cover, Rayne stroked the glossy finish. Its incredible depth shone like a fine mirror. She still couldn't believe he'd restored it himself, but Ben was a true craftsman as well as a jack-of-all-trades. There wasn't much of anything he hadn't tried—from building this home to rebuilding cars. But bringing back an old piano with peeling veneer and worn out mechanics? He was nothing short of amazing.

He'd probably even designed this room for music. The wood floor and vaulted ceiling augmented the quietest note, while the floor-to-ceiling windows suffused the room with wonderful light. The man was a wonder. And he hadn't even admitted to restoring the instrument. Quin had revealed that bit of information while they sat by the fire one night, proud of his soon-to-be dad's abilities.

The music room faithfully echoed Rayne's sigh as she pondered once again the coming changes in these crazy Conner families. Everyone was or had a *soon-to-be* of some sort: sisters, cousins, husbands, wives, sons, daughters, moms, dads. What did *she* have? In a few weeks she'd be back to her old life in the Netherlands, void of any *soon-to-be*'s. The thought chilled her more than the room, and she shrugged her shoulders in an attempt to dislodge the empty feeling. Once she got home, she'd be fine. She had friends. She had her band. Life would be good again.

She spread out the pages of lyrics, scored melody lines, and written themes she'd been fiddling with the last two days. Keeping her left foot firmly on the soft pedal to minimize the volume, Rayne played the verse of the most complete work. The song, when polished, would introduce the story of Storm Lake: its geological history, its animals—even pesky wild turkeys—the beauty of the seasons, and the people who made it home in both the past and present. Her father-and-son legacy song would be a repeated reprise, weaving itself through the opera.

Ideas burst in her mind like bubbles rising to the water's surface, so many that she broke her pencil several times while writing as quickly as possible. She re-sharpened it in Ben's office, then brought a fistful of fresh pencils back with her.

She blocked the songs across multiple pages, sketching squares with working titles and themes, then went back and filled in detail and drew relationship lines between songs. Ten works took shape, each telling a particular aspect of the story. Melodies flowed as quickly as the topics, and she played and notated line after line, using her color concept for songs like she'd done for Marielle's story, but changing it to fit the colors and seasons of the lake: blues for water and sky, green for trees and grass, red and orange for fall, and white and gray for winter.

A soft click was all the warning she had that she was no longer alone. The bath towel shushed across the hardwood as the door swung open, and Rayne spun on the bench to face the intruder.

Ben swayed sleepily in the doorway on bare feet, dressed in low-hung pajama bottoms and a threadbare U2 T-shirt he'd had when they were married. He blinked in the bright overhead light and brushed his hand over blond hair that looked like someone had taken an eggbeater to it. Soft whiskers blunted the sharp lines of his jaw. Rayne's breath skipped as she remembered the mild rashes those whiskers had once caused on the mornings they lingered in bed. Her fingers strayed to her neck before she could stop them, and his eyes tracked their movement before settling on her lips.

"What are you doing up so early?" His hoarse voice broke her spell, and she blinked back to the present. Her eyes cut to the windows where light peeked around the edges of the plantation shutters, the previous evening's storm obviously past. How long had she been working? That was Ben's next question, so she answered them both.

"Working and don't know." Ben had always been an early riser. This was the first time she'd beaten him up since she'd come.

"Coffee," he mumbled, and headed for the kitchen, leaving the door ajar.

Rayne turned back to the piano. At least forty pages of music covered its top, the music rack, and spilled onto the floor in a semi-circle around the bench. She carefully stretched her arms overhead until her shoulder blades popped, rotated her neck, and exhaled a deep breath as she brought her hands back to her lap. It felt good to get back to her "normal" routine of work, which was really no routine at all, just complete flexibility.

It was the way she'd always been, which was one reason college had been tough—scheduled classes got in her way. Some nights at home in Boskoop she'd power through till dawn in wave after wave of inspiration before dropping in exhaustion on her still-made bed and sleeping past noon. Other nights, like this one, she'd wake after a couple of hours, mind flying with ideas that required capture before they evaporated like mist in morning light.

A frown touched her mouth. That had been one of the problems living with Ben in the tiny cabin. His work schedule demanded he be up early most days, while she craved the freedom to work whenever inspiration struck. They'd never been able to resolve the issue, and it led to increasing fights.

Ben had obviously remedied that by putting this music room at the end of the house, far away from the bedrooms. Their long-ago conflict seemed petty now, diminished by time and, she hoped, maturity. Not that any of this mattered.

As she gathered the sheets and put them in order, she wished she had more than a few days to work on the music. Her gut told her this could be good, great even. Already, she had visions of the premier behind Bibs' Beauty Barn, a ring of colored spots bathing the stage in the mood of each song. The music called for a robust string section, heavy on cellos— kind of like Copland's Rodeo, but less of "Hoe-Down," and before American TV commercials ruined it forever with "Beef, it's what's for dinner."

Rayne liked using orchestra strings to carry the highs, using only a little brass, mostly French horns and trombones. She wasn't sure how a bona fide conductor would describe it, but she felt lower range instruments moved people at a deeper level, evoking emotion from their hearts and souls rather than blasting at ears and heads. In her mind, Yo-

Yo Ma and his cello trounced any violin soloist she'd ever heard, at least in evocative music.

She had yet to hit on a main character for the story, like Marielle in her last concert, but she was leaning toward something completely different...and challenging.

With a sigh, she slipped all the pages into her notebook. This work was American West, through and through, not suitable at all for the European rock scene. Her fans, no matter how loyal, would never accept it. Danny and the band would hate it. She should probably put it aside and work on next year's program so she'd have something to present when she arrived home.

Speaking of going home, she needed to tell Ben her plan to leave. He'd be mad, that was a given. She could handle mad. It was hurt that had her stomach in a knot. A noise drew her attention to the doorway. Ben stood there still looking all just-out-of-bed sexy, sipping a cup of coffee and holding one out to her. Rayne covered a sigh as she rose to accept the steaming mug. Maybe now wasn't the best time to bring up leaving.

It was nearly nine in the morning before Raoul made his escape from the attic. The boy had gone to school, and Conner, after taking his own sweet time, finally left in his truck. The pipes hissed as Regen van Onweer turned on the shower or bathtub. Inching along quietly, he made his way to the garage stairs, pushed them down, and climbed down on legs stiff from nonuse. He quickly folded the stairs up into the ceiling, then slipped out the garage door.

His first act was to hobble to the nearest tree and relieve himself, sending a steaming stream into the wet pine needles and leaves. Releasing a deep sigh, he hoped he hadn't permanently damaged his bladder by holding it so long.

When finished, he zipped his fly, only then surveying his surroundings in the tree-filtered light of morning. The sun, traveling below the mountain peaks this time of year, had reached the house in the previous thirty minutes or so, warming the frigid attic a little, but he felt the lingering chill right to his German bones, and stamped his feet to get the blood flowing.

Raoul found his decrepit Beetle where he left it and unlocked the door. Why he bothered securing it, he didn't know; surely no one would steal the thing. Fortunately, he hesitated before stepping in. Black water stood three inches deep in the driver footwell. Using a fast food cup from the debris in the back seat, he bailed out as much water as he could, then climbed in. Too late he realized the seat was soaked as well, and icy water saturated his pants down to the backs of his knees. He banged his head on the steering wheel a few times and swore. He didn't deserve this.

Well, nothing to do about it now. He needed to get back to his cabin and clean up. Fiberglass from the attic insulation had worked its way into every crevice of his skin and itched mercilessly. He turned the key. The starter growled, turning the engine with agonizing slowness.

"C'mon you piece of..." The engine wheezed, stuttered, then chugged weakly when he feathered the gas. He had to let it warm up for several minutes so it would have any power at all before turning around and heading south around the lake.

Going north and around the top of the lake would have been much shorter, but a few hundred yards past Deer Cove the pavement ended at a sign that read, End County Maintained Road. The proprietor at the bait shop told him the road had once been in good shape all the way around the north end, but mudslides several years ago had damaged so much of the roadway that the county determined it wasn't cost effective to keep it up.

Raoul's cabin was on the last relatively good section of road out of Deer Cove that led to North Beach. Beyond that the road rapidly deteriorated, cut through in several places by runoff from ravines. That section was a favorite for four-wheel drive enthusiasts.

At the rental, he parked the VW under the large oak in the yard and cranked down the windows so it could air out. Then he headed inside. Nothing fancy, it suited his purposes. The doors had adequate locks and, most importantly, the owner had installed cable TV.

Raoul retrieved an aluminum case from the closet. Nestled inside was a receiver box, the other half of the transmitter at Conner's house. He connected the receiver between the incoming television cable and the cabin's twenty-seven inch TV. He powered up the TV and tuned it to channel 3.

"Just like watching HBO." He chuckled as the screen filled with a picture of Conner's garage. Raoul's transmitter and receiver worked over the regular cable lines, using a different frequency so as not to disturb the normal broadcast television channels—at least that was the theory. Different cable providers used different frequencies, so there was always a chance his signals could screw something up. But so far, so good. Using a selector knob on his receiver, he switched from camera to camera.

"Now…what are you up to, Regen van Onweer?"

CHAPTER TWENTY-ONE

Rayne dried her hair, still shocked at how little time it took with her shorter cut, then dressed in jeans and a white T-shirt with Bibs' Beauty Barn tastefully embroidered above the left breast. Under the lettering, a flame-red lipstick imprint set at an angle added a splash of color. The shirt was a gift from Bibs in appreciation—her words—for all the business Rayne brought her after the festival concert. Rayne knew that wasn't true. Bibs was just being nice. Truth was, Rayne liked the old woman, regardless of her rough exterior, and Bibs had invited her for lunch today at 12:30 sharp. She still had a little time yet.

Ben was busy at a new job site, and Quin was doing boating errands after school, so Rayne was on her own all day.

After applying makeup from her limited supply, Rayne snagged a huge beach towel from the closet, walked through the great room, and stepped through the patio doors. A couple of puffy clouds still floated above the lake, but the storm had passed, leaving the air washed and diamond clear. She inhaled deeply, head slightly back, reaching her arms as high as she could, palms flat against the cerulean canopy. Her left arm wouldn't extend fully and she didn't push it, letting the easy stretch relax the damaged tissue. Earthy air filled every cavity in her lungs, and she held the position a moment before exhaling as her arms lowered to her sides. She repeated the movement four times.

Lorna was prone to trying any number of health kicks. If it wasn't a cutting-edge diet, it was a new exercise and, like any good fanatic, she insisted all her friends join her in the promised benefits, however transitory. One of her more useful health flavors of the month was yoga. Rayne wasn't into the mystical aspects of the exercise, but she liked the quieting of mind, concentration, and the stretches required by many of the positions. It always left her physically whipped and mentally charged, perfect for tackling songwriting. Lorna gave it up after four months—a near longevity record in her case—but Rayne had continued at home with a couple of yoga DVDs.

She spread the towel on the damp patio stone and sat with her legs out straight in front, then bent forward to touch her toes. Pain in her left leg and arm warned her to back off for a breather, then she pressed forward again, curling her back. Each repetition brought her closer to those elusive toes. The sound of water lapping at the shore swept up the bank, and her soul floated in nature, discomfort forgotten. High overhead, above the leaves rustling in the gentle breeze, a red-tailed hawk screeched, and even the distant roar of an outboard motor added to the unified ambience of this place.

Rayne wondered, not for the first time, if God lived in this beautiful corner of the world. She had visited several stunning locations in Europe and the Mediterranean while touring with Elusive Hope. Of all the places, lakes were her favorite: Lake Lucerne in Switzerland, Lake Como in northern Italy, and the spectacular Lake Bled in Slovenia with its medieval castle on the north shore. More than oceans, lakes, with their clear waters, rippled surfaces, and reflected light, inexplicably called her to stay, settle down, take root.

Storm Lake was no different. Was it because she and Ben lived here in their first little place? Did beginning a marriage in such a magical setting spoil a person for all other locations? Rayne lay back on the towel, feeling the solid, cold stone and letting it seep into her burning thigh. She longed to be anchored, set in the soil. Her fear back then had been getting stuck, like an old rowboat rotting away in the clinging mud. Fear propelled her to leave home, to keep moving. But now she was beginning to realize the benefits—no, the power—of settling. Not settling for *less*, but settling *down* and drawing on the strength of her surroundings, both nature and people.

Perhaps this was what moved her about her new music: the legacy of the land, how it cared for and challenged its people, on the one hand providing food and clothing, but on the other, causing hardship and toil. And the legacy passed down in families likewise proved both challenging and comforting. Certainly Rayne's relationship with her mother was more challenge than comfort. Oh, her mother loved her; Rayne didn't doubt that. But theirs had been an uneasy connection, not like the Conner family. She wondered if she would ever experience that again.

A cloud in brilliant white relief floated across the blue canvas, and Rayne followed its reshaping as it slid between treetops and finally disappeared. If God did create the world, he'd done a remarkable job. Who could dream up something as simple as a cloud, but with ever-changing design as it lived and traveled?

Something nudged her right tennis shoe. Rayne lifted her head slightly, and a chipmunk scampered off the patio and bounded onto one of the log planters that ringed the area. The animal's tail twitched as it glared at her. How dare she invade its private living space.

"Hey, little guy. Looking for a treat?" Its tail twitched, but the chipmunk kept quiet. She sat up and squinted through the kitchen window at the clock. It was almost noon. She'd been out here over an hour, when she only intended a few minutes. And right when she needed a little extra time, too.

She locked the doors, tossed the towel over the barstools so it could dry, and got her jacket and wallet. In the garage, she snatched the Bronco keys from the peg by the door, the metal fob icy against her skin. The garage hadn't warmed in the low sun, but when she opened the rollup door, warmer air washed in from the yard. Using her right hand, she grabbed the pull-strap above the Bronco's driver door and hoisted herself into the high cab.

"Come on, baby." Rayne pulled out the choke, cranked the engine until it started, then feathered the choke knob back in as the motor smoothed out. It was amazing how some things were locked in her memory. She'd never planned to return to the lake, to Ben, or drive this vehicle again, but here she was, doing all the old actions as if it were yesterday. Fumes filled the garage, so she closed the driver door and placed her left foot on the clutch pedal. Today was another step in her recovery—literally, she hoped.

An automatic transmission wouldn't have been a problem, but using a clutch would be difficult with her weakened left leg. And she'd have to be careful with her left arm. Doc Arnold better not catch her driving this thing or he'd put her back in a cast and throw away his plaster saw.

"Here goes."

She depressed the clutch and shifted into reverse, wincing only a little as muscles protested. Letting the clutch out evenly proved more difficult, but she managed to get the truck out of the garage without stalling it. Soon she was up the driveway and turning onto the perimeter road toward Deer Cove. Since her right foot worked fine, she gunned the V8, enjoying the connection between the sole of her shoe and the mechanical beast as it throbbed beneath her. Riding with someone else wasn't at all the same, nor was driving her diminutive Peugeot back in Boskoop.

At some point, Ben had replaced the hand crank windows with power ones. He said he was always improving the old truck. Mandy might want a new floor, but Rayne appreciated the ease of pushing a button to lower the passenger window. The swirling air caused goose flesh on her arms, so she boosted the heater to max and lowered the driver window an inch as well, grinning as cold air smelling of wet earth and clean pine mixed with blasting hot. Often, she and Ben had driven this same road, windows down and heater on, Rayne snuggled under his right arm as he steered with his left.

Nighttime rides had been her favorite, their future together clear only thirty or forty yards ahead, yet that was enough. Sometimes they'd drive down to Perilous Cove and turn toward the beach north of the point. Wrapped in a scratchy wool blanket, they'd sit on the sand as close to the waves as they could get and eat crackers and cheese or popcorn, sharing a Pepsi while watching for shooting stars over the constant, turbulent sea. Whoever saw a shooting star first got to tickle the other person. Ben always had the fastest eyes … and hands. He never discovered she'd let him win most of the times.

"Simple times, simple things," she whispered, and made a mental note to write that down. A song hid in those words, waiting for someone to coax it out. Life had been simple then, but not empty or boring. It was only when Ben had to work long hours that the emptiness began.

Rayne turned into the lot in front of the barn and switched off the engine. She laid her forehead on the steering wheel. If only she'd known then what she knew now, been wiser. She could have done so much more to strengthen their marriage. It wouldn't have been that hard to plan more picnics, outings with friends and Ben's family—especially when his mom got sick. Instead, Rayne had looked for a way out, like with her own family when she'd gone to Holland the first time.

She'd escaped her family, Ben's family, then the tiny family of her and Ben. With painful understanding, she realized none of them had been the ones to leave; each time it had been her decision, her choice. Now she planned to do it again, only this time the family had expanded to Quin, Mandy and her family, and new friends like Bibs.

She looked up to see the old woman waving from the barn door, motioning Rayne to join her inside. With a sigh, Rayne opened the truck door and eased to the asphalt. Maybe being broke was a blessing in disguise. If so, it was a very good disguise indeed. At least she couldn't take off just yet—the little matter of her minuscule bank balance trapped her at the lake. There would be some more time to explore the relationships—if she wanted. Did she? That was a question she didn't want to think about. All the yoga sessions in the world wouldn't relax *that* cramped muscle.

"Ben, check it out! Rayne brought food from the Crab Shack!"

Ben had known that fact on his first step through the door from the garage. Even without the two large plastic sacks that stood on the counter, the distinctive aromas of the Deer Cove restaurant's deep-fried spicy batter and clam chowder saturated the room.

He peeled off his jacket. With the storm over, the clear air had turned freezing cold as soon as the sun set. They might get the first hard frost tonight. Soon it would be time for Quin to pull the boat and store it in the old barn, but the boy was firmly in denial. Ben understood completely. Quin would figure it out without advice from him. He watched Quin pull two huge baskets of French fries out of one sack. Each cardboard bowl contained enough for four hungry high-schoolers. "How many others are coming for dinner?"

"What do you mean?" Quin asked, looking over the piles of fish-n-chips, cartons of chowder, cole slaw, and garlic roles. "This is all for us."

Rayne blushed as Ben raised a brow.

"I got a job," she said quietly, but he heard a hint of excitement in her voice. Ben's own breath seized in his throat, and he tamped down hope before it swelled out of control. A job didn't mean she was staying.

"She's playing music for Bibs at the Beauty Barn, and they're *paying* her," Quin said, as if he couldn't believe anyone would shell out money for such a thing.

"It's just twice a week," Rayne said, "plus a couple extra times right before Thanksgiving. I play two sets of four or five songs, then lead everyone in some sing-a-longs."

She must have caught some expression on his face, because she jumped in again.

"I know it sounds a little hokey. Okay, *really* hokey. Danny would die if I told him about it."

Ben felt his face tighten at the drummer's name.

"Who's Danny?" Quin asked, stuffing a half-dozen fries in his mouth.

"Oh, uh, he's a friend who lives overseas," Rayne covered and turned back to Ben. "Anyway, I need to earn a little money, so when she asked me…well, she thinks it will really help her business during the holiday season. Plus, it gives me some practice time. She's even got a decent piano hiding in the back of the barn, and she's bringing in a tuner tomorrow. Sooo…what do you think?"

Ben opened his mouth, but no words came out. Did this mean she was making a place for herself in the community? Or was she earning money so she could leave?

Finally he said, "I think you can fill us in on all the details over dinner. I'm starved and half-frozen."

Rayne sent him a smile that warmed him to his toes.

CHAPTER TWENTY-TWO

Raoul did a double take the next day as he coaxed his sputtering Super Beetle down the hill toward Deer Cove. Parked in front of the big barn sat an oxidized red Ford Bronco. He checked the license plate to be sure it was Conner's, then turned right at the corner past the barn and drove a ways down a rutted dirt road before pulling off behind some brush.

Conner could be driving it, or the teenage girl, though Raoul had seen Conner leave in his F150 pickup early, and the spiky-hair girl usually didn't come around the house until afternoon.

Raoul exited the car and pushed through red-leafed brush until he reached rusty strands of a barbed wire fence. After squeezing between them, he walked across the field where the harvest festival had been, to the back of the barn. He'd been so close to Regen van Onweer that night, right beside her, talking like two new friends, old friends. Marielle's eyes had gazed at him with interest, wanting, desire. If only they'd had more time. And privacy.

Save your last breath for me.

He'd allowed Regen van Onweer to perform, but it had galled him to let her leave with Conner and the boy. The syringe had lain heavy in his pocket. One prick, depress the plunger, and lift her slumping body. So close. He could have her at his cabin right now. It was all prepared. Waiting.

He swiped his wet brow with his sleeve as he slipped between piled hay bails and two small sheds, merging with the shadows obscuring the rear wall of the barn. Piano music came through the gaps in the boards. No, not exactly music. Each key was being hit several times, and the tone changed slightly.

The old barn siding had seen better days. Cracked and split, many of the boards looked ready to tumble to the ground, and they also had several missing knots. He knelt on the damp earth and peered into the dim interior. He couldn't see anything from the first several holes, but finally he found one that gave him the view he wanted.

Regen van Onweer sat on an old trunk, watching intently as a gray-haired man played a key and reached through the open top. Some sort of electronic tuning device sat on the music tray.

Raoul dismissed the man, turning his attention to Regen van Onweer. With short auburn hair, she looked so different from her stage presence. Gone were her long, black tresses.

The jeans and T-shirt she wore disgusted him; she looked cheap, common. Regen van Onweer belonged in ornate gowns made of satin or silk, knee-high boots, long gloves, and Celtic jewelry. Marielle was precious, and he would take care of her, preserve her. When she came to him, he'd dress her properly with her own things he'd brought from her house. She'd be so grateful to have her own clothes against her skin again.

In the dim barn interior, Regen van Onweer smiled at the old piano tuner and put her arms around him.

Raoul's gut twisted at the sight, and he jumped to his feet and stormed away from the building. When he reached the car, he threw himself in. The humid interior stank of mold and spoiled food. He deserved better. And he would have it—one day. But first it was his destiny to have Marielle.

Soon.

After the tuner left, Rayne practiced on the old upright piano until she got a good feel for the instrument's action—and until Bibs clamored for her to move into the main beauty shop. Rayne stood by helplessly as seven customers and operators pushed and pulled the heavy piano on its cantankerous metal casters that squealed on the concrete and found every crack. A woman with foil and curlers swarming her head carried the stool.

Bibs directed everyone on where to place the piano, and soon all were gathered around Rayne. Bibs motioned expectantly, so Rayne sat and began to play the old Irish tune, "Bí Liom," one that Enya's sister, Moya Brennan, had written and recorded. Rayne knew just enough Gaelic to get through the haunting piece, feathering the keyboard so the strings barely sounded. It had always been a favorite but, being far too mellow, not one she could ever use in her concerts.

The lyrics spoke of love never letting go, of having courage in the mist, being alone without love by her side, and seeking a new song. In some ways it mirrored Marielle's story, and the regret of not finishing the girl's story rose in Rayne's chest. The performance at the Ahoy Rotterdam had been one of those magical moments where everything came together so perfectly. Well, nearly. She would never have a chance like that again.

As the last plaintive notes faded away in the high rafters of the dusty old barn, Rayne let her hands rest in her lap. Only then did she look around and see the tear-stained faces surrounding her.

"Well," Bibs sniffed loudly and passed around a box of tissues, "I can see we're not going to get much business done if you keep on like that, young lady." She shooed everyone back to their stations, giving Yvonne orders on how to curl Mrs. Eberly's blue hair, and hurrying Becky to get started on Olivia Hamilton's shampoo.

"I'm going to have her play that at my funeral," Bibs' sister, Irene, proclaimed to no one in particular before heading back to her rocking chair and knitting needles.

Before following Becky, Mrs. Hamilton leaned in and squeezed Rayne's arm. She smelled like Rayne had always imagined a grandmother would, a combination of soft powder and baking spices. The spices reminded Rayne of Lorna, and she fought back tears.

"Thank you, my dear," Mrs. Hamilton said. "That was absolutely beautiful. It's so good to have you back." Then she gave a little wink and said softly, "Quin thinks so, too."

Rayne had no time to react as Bibs stepped between them with hands on ample hips. "Now, how about playing something a whole lot more upbeat? If you can't, I'll have to tune in that hip-hop station on the radio." A chorus of protests erupted around the room, and Rayne had no choice but to dig through the dozens of old songbooks Bibs produced and find some lively songs.

Forty-five minutes later, she'd played and sung a dozen songs. Her left bicep cramped as she prodded the muscles for one last number. Somewhere in the middle of "Red River Valley," Rayne imagined Danny walking through the barn door and seeing her here, surrounded by a crowd of twenty or more women, many singing along. She flubbed a chord, imagining his dismay—or disappointment. Then she thought of Ben and Quin standing there, smiling, and maybe singing along with the women. How could her two worlds be more different?

Begging an end to the session, Rayne stood and stretched her aching body.

"Remember ladies, she'll be back tomorrow for her regular show," Bibs said, "then Tuesday and Thursday next week. Be sure to tell your friends to call for their appointments early so they don't miss out. I'm bringing in Connie Franco and her team from Mission Peak for manicures and pedicures, and there's a discount if you get both done at the same time." A number of appreciative murmurs rose, and women rushed Irene who manned the appointment book. One woman said something about bringing veggies and dip.

Rayne limped around to the back of the piano and leaned on the old upright as the women thanked her over and over, gushing about who they were going to call. Today was supposed to be tuning and practice, but it had turned out to be a mini concert. And she had to be back tomorrow. She had the feeling that "a few songs and some sing-a-longs" as Bibs originally requested would grow each session.

Several women made requests, and Rayne wrote them down. Soon had a list of everything from Bob Dylan to Stephen Foster, a dozen hymns, standards of Frank Sinatra and Bing Crosby, and a few by Elvis and the Beatles. People were starved for songs that touched their souls. So much music on the radio today merely filled the air with noise. The requested songs reminded them of better or simpler times, or perhaps of a time when a loved one still lived. And Rayne knew it wasn't just the old songs that moved them. New songs like Marielle's story could as well. She'd proven that twice now.

Later, as she drove home in the early dark, she reflected on the dichotomy of her audiences. In Europe, most in the crowd were under twenty-five, sported multiple piercings and tattoos, and wore leather and metal, while here in Storm Lake—at least at Bibs'—the age averaged seventy, and they wore clip-ons and sensible shoes. Though, eyeing some of the spunkier old gals, Rayne had wondered if there might be a few hidden tattoos.

Irene's prediction of her own death not withstanding, how much of an impact could Rayne have in these women's lives? Was her destiny to reach young people or old? Maybe both at the same time? Now that would truly be an accomplishment.

As she rounded the bottom of the lake just past Flume, an old Volkswagen passed her on a blind curve and cut in sharply in front of the Bronco, forcing her to hit the brakes and skid to the side of the road.

"Idiot!" The Beetle's weak taillights faded into the night, never slowing to see if she'd wrecked.

CHAPTER TWENTY-THREE

Friday night hadn't come soon enough for Ben. His week had been a crazy mix of both new work and emergency repairs for potential customers whose regular security companies had flaked on them. With the post-Thanksgiving shopping season fast approaching, it seemed everyone wanted additional security cameras to ward against shoplifting. He and Kurt had worked non-stop since dawn, and Kurt was going back tomorrow to fix the surveillance system at a clothing boutique in Mission Peak.

Ben checked the digital clock as he turned on East Lake Road at Flume: six forty-five. Addison, Mandy, Sam, and Star would have arrived an hour ago, and Ben had planned to barbecue, even though the temperature hovered in the low forties. Nothing stood between the Conner brothers and barbecued tri-tip.

He urged his truck a couple of miles per hour over the limit and switched on the fog lamps against the dark forest pressing the sides of the road. Many a deer had met their maker on these curves, and Ben had no intention of landing his truck in the body shop with a smashed grill. He'd driven Lake Road thousands of times, knew every rut and pothole and who had fixed them last year.

Suddenly, oncoming headlights careened around the curve he'd just entered, the yellow orbs cutting the corner into Ben's lane. He twisted the steering wheel left toward the open lane, but the other driver had the same idea. Tires squealed and the anti-lock braking system pulsed and growled as Ben put all his weight on the pedal under his foot. He desperately swung back to the right, heading toward the sloping bank, but the other driver followed his move. They were like two pedestrians on a sidewalk. With no time to turn back left, Ben kept his foot on the brake as the truck sped toward the steep bank.

He tensed for the collision. Mentally he knew he should relax his arms to avoid breaking anything by gripping the wheel too hard, but his body reflexes took over. Both vehicles headed toward each other and at the hill.

An instant before Ben closed his eyes, the other car whipped back toward its own lane. Ben glimpsed dark paint as his side mirror smashed back into the truck's side window. Glass shattered at the same time his right front tire plowed into the roadside bank.

The airbag exploded, punching him in the face. The g-force pushed him deep into the seat springs as the nose of the truck bounced skyward. He was thrown right, then left, slamming his ribs against the door and robbing his breath. His briefcase ricocheted off the ceiling and burst open, launching papers, pens, and business cards. Something whacked him in the cheek hard enough to loosen teeth.

Tree trunks flashed by on the right side, and the frame groaned as the truck tilted at a forty-five degree angle. But then the left wheels lurched back onto the pavement and the pickup righted itself. It slid to a creaking stop amidst a shower of rocks and dirt. Dust swirled in the headlight beams where they shone across the road at an odd angle, and papers fluttered to the floor and seat. He coughed and fanned away the dirt cloud swirling in the missing window.

His right leg, still locked on the brake pedal, shook with palsy as he tried to relax. Outside, the clatter of rocks had disappeared, and the only sounds were the quiet purr of the running engine and Karen Carpenter singing "Have Yourself a Merry Little Christmas" on the radio. A cold wind leaked in the driver window.

Carefully, Ben released the brake pedal and let the vehicle roll ahead a few feet. The left front wobbled like a bent wheel would, but nothing rubbed or fell off, at least not that he could determine. He turned on the emergency flashers and drove slowly about a quarter of a mile to a pullout. After shifting into Park and setting the emergency brake, he stepped out on rubbery legs, accompanied by a shower of quarter-inch glass bits. Hot pain knifed his left side, and he wrapped his right hand around his ribcage as he walked around to the front of the car.

The reflection of the headlights off his clothes gave enough light to check the damage which, amazingly, didn't seem too bad. He'd have to have the alignment and frame checked at a shop, but it looked drivable.

Back inside he found his cell phone on the passenger floor, its screen shattered. He'd have to wait to call the sheriff. No other cars came by since this side of the lake tended to be pretty quiet by this time of night, especially in the fall and winter season. He crept along at ten miles per hour with his emergency flashers on until he reached the safety of his driveway.

Raoul's breath came out in a cloud of frosty white as he stepped into his rented cabin. He pushed the thermostat up to ninety degrees, but nothing happened. No heat in the car, freezing outside. Now it seemed the house heater had failed too.

He sank into an armchair by the stony fireplace. The stiff leather crackled and leeched body heat right through his jacket. He hated the cold. California was supposed to be warm. The Rose Parade on TV always showed people wearing shorts on January 1st, waving to the cameras from under palm trees. They probably all went for a swim at the beach after the parade.

He'd been born during a New York winter so harsh dozens had died. While briefly in military service, friends had been stationed in warm places all over the globe, but he'd been sent to guard an obscure base in Alaska. Guard from what? Polar Bears? Even the summer hadn't hit sixty degrees. They said you got used to it; your blood thickened. His never had, especially not in his adopted country, Germany.

With a sigh, he rose and threw some newspapers on the cold grate. He hadn't paid extra for firewood delivery, so he broke up one of the maple kitchen chairs and added the wood. His match fired the paper immediately, and it pulsed yellow and warm. He stretched his hands toward the heat, but the flames were gone before they could ignite the thick chair legs. The last of the paper crumbled to black ash, only the edges glowing red. It was all over in less than two minutes.

"Story of my life."

He turned on all the burners of the apartment-size gas range. At least that still worked. It wouldn't force air to the back bedroom, but it was better than nothing. He sat down in one of the remaining chairs around the dinette and switched on the television. He flipped through the camera feeds until he came to one that showed the Conner kitchen.

Ben Conner sat on one of the bar stools, surrounded by people. He didn't look too bad after their run-in on the road. It wasn't something Raoul had planned. He'd been watching from his hiding place up on the road above the Conner house when the brother and family arrived. After awhile, he realized he'd be better off using the video cameras he'd installed, so he'd been hurrying back to the cabin. Sure gave him a fright when he'd rounded the corner and nearly met the truck head-on. Hadn't even realized it was Conner until the VW headlights lit up the man's face right as the two vehicles passed.

On the TV, Raoul recognized the brother, Addison Conner, and the tall girl with short black hair. When Regen van Onweer joined the group, he dismissed the others, focusing on each tilt of her head, the way her lips curved when she spoke to one of the others who all circled her bright star. She carried a white first-aid box that she placed on the counter beside Conner. Standing beside him, she used a cotton ball and carefully cleaned his right cheek where blood left a wide trail from eye to jaw. Raoul's teeth clenched when he saw her leg touching Conner's as she dabbed. Her left hand cradled his head, and her breast grazed his shoulder.

Too close! She belonged to him, and no one else. He nearly swept the television from the table before he got control. Instead, he careened from the chair and backed to the paneled wall, as far as he could get from the flickering images. Breath came in ragged gulps. He didn't want to watch, but couldn't tear his eyes away from the scene on the television. It was almost as if the camera zoomed in on the couple, demoting the others to lesser roles in the stage play, off the edges of his viewing angle.

He shook his head to clear it. *Have to think. Have to plan.*

He yanked a yellow legal pad, sending the local phone book to the floor and scattering a half-dozen empty beer cans.

Clutching a pen hard enough to break it, he scratched words into the top sheet, which promptly ripped. He tore it away and began again, this time more deliberate, with marginally less force.

Save your last breath for me. You live among others, but I'm waiting for you. You're mine. Now, and soon to be forever. I'm coming, Marielle. I'm closer than you think. Watch. Save your last breath for me.

CHAPTER TWENTY-FOUR

Rayne stretched her feet toward the hot fire, its noisy crackle filled the room with comforting sound. The big couch creaked and shifted as Quin took the far end. She returned his smile as he opened a boating magazine and propped his feet on the coffee table beside hers. Ben had crafted the sturdy piece with rough-hewn edges and a rock hard satin finish to take the abuse of shoes and feet. He said furniture should be completely functional as well as good looking. Only a man would think using a coffee table as a footstool qualified as functional.

The other half of the Conner family had left and, despite Ben's accident, the evening had been enjoyable. Other than the brief meeting at the festival, this was the first time Rayne had been around Addison and Mandy's soon-to-bes, Sam and Star. She had to admit, they were a fun bunch. Sam Riley leaned toward the quiet side, as did Addison. In stark contrast, Mandy brightened any room and infused energy in every activity, while Star's megawatt grin and wild red hair outshone them all.

Rayne hadn't been sure what to do when Ben hadn't come home to start the barbecue, but Addison suggested Quin fire up the grill and put on the meat. He let Quin lead every step of the way, from arranging the briquettes to dousing them with lighter fluid and tossing in a match. Then they stayed out on the patio in the freezing cold, warming themselves as the coals burned down to a white hot pile. Addison came in to get the meat, and she'd asked him what they were talking about out there.

"Male bonding stuff," he answered, giving her a wink. "You wouldn't understand." Then he headed back outside with the pan in one hand and giant tongs in the other. Addison held the pan while Quin levered the marinated chunks onto the grill. Smoke from the searing meat wound into the dark, and Rayne could almost taste the spices as Addison shook the containers.

Watching the two through the windows reminded Rayne of a silent film, the actions and expressions communicating the message without sound. *Father to son.* Or in this case, uncle to nephew, but the passing of tradition from one generation to the next was exactly the same. One day, Quin would teach his own son or nephew the manly art of barbecue.

In the kitchen, Sam drew in Star as they prepared a fantastic salad that included homemade candied pecans, dried cherries, and oranges. Sam explained it was a favorite of her aunt, Rowena Riley, who had collected at least fifty all-time great recipes from the potlucks and dinner parties she'd attended during her years in Perilous Cove. If the other dishes were anything like the salad, Rayne couldn't wait to taste them.

Fortunately, the meat had cooked and was staying hot in the oven when Ben limped in all bloody and battered, otherwise it would have burned to a crisp while they gathered around him and heard his story.

As Ben spoke, Quin grew increasingly still, his color going white as Ben told how the other car sideswiped the truck. No doubt the boy remembered his dad's fatal accident. Mandy draped her arm around his shoulder. She was an amazing girl.

Rayne retrieved the first-aid kit and, when no one else stepped forward to help, she cleaned and bandaged Ben's wounds. It seemed natural to everyone that she tend to him. But standing close and gently dabbing on ointment, it seemed a much more intimate moment than even the pantry kiss. That scared her more than anything.

Now, with everyone gone, Ben had groaned his way upstairs to shower. After two hours of family time, his body had begun to shut down, adrenalin long drained away. Addison had wanted him to go to urgent care, but Ben argued if he could drive home after the accident, he could wait until morning.

Rayne wasn't so sure, and had promised Addison she and Quin would check on him later. Although Ben hadn't hit his head while thrashing around in the cab, he certainly tweaked every joint in his body as well as banged his ribs. He'd be really sore in a day or two.

And what if he needed help in the shower or getting dressed? Would everyone expect her to help with that, too? After all, they'd been husband and wife. She jerked as sudden heat suffused her body. From the end of the couch, Quin glanced up, his brow furrowed in question. She gave him what she hoped was an assuring smile and lay her head back on the cushion.

With the wedding coming soon, she couldn't ask Addison for days of help; he'd already been gone too much for business as it was and Sam was strongly hinting he be around more. And it was one thing for Mandy to help with Rayne's physical therapy, but caring for her uncle wouldn't work at all. If Ben needed help, Rayne would have to do it. What would Ben think about that?

She pulled her shirt out and flapped it, trying to cool her skin, then she rose and headed to the cooler kitchen area.

She wiped down the already clean counters, then polished a couple of fingerprints off the microwave door. She looked around for anything else to do, but Sam, Mandy, and Star had washed and dried every dish and even given the floor a quick Swiffering. The trashcan was half full, so she pulled the bag out and twisted the top into a knot. Ben's jacket hung by the door; she slipped her arms into it, probably looking like a stick in a gunnysack, but it would do for a quick trip to the trash bin.

It couldn't have been more than forty degrees in the garage, but that seemed toasty compared to what greeted her when she opened the back door. Cold lake air snatched her breath and ballooned under the coat, washing away her body heat. She pulled up the hood and clutched the drawstrings in one fist as she shuffled down the length of the garage to where the containers were stored, grateful for the slight shelter as she rounded the far end. An overhead motion light switched on, throwing trees and rocks into sharp relief. Tree branches thrashed, twisting in a ghostly dance to the roaring rhythm emanating from the treetops.

Dodging a swirling column of leaves, Rayne deposited the bag in the proper bin before running for the shelter of the garage.

Once inside, she shut and locked the door, flipped off the backyard light, and took a step toward the kitchen door. It was then she noticed a faint *beep*. Ben had always kidded her about her overly sensitive hearing. Every rattle and squeak in the car drove her nuts until she found the offending pen or coins or rubbing plastic parts. He'd even put a small container of silicone spray in her Christmas stocking, only half-joking.

Ben's damaged truck was still outside in the driveway, so she walked to the center of the empty bay and rotated 360°, listening. There it was again. The beep lasted for about a half-second, then all grew quiet for twenty or thirty seconds. Slowly, she walked around the Bronco to the outer wall of the garage. The next beep seemed louder here, but as she continued moving, the next was softer again. She retraced her steps, even bending to look under the old truck. The rusty undercarriage glared back, silent and cold.

Beep. So faint, she wondered if it was from upstairs or out in Ben's truck.

The workbench was her next target. The man owned a dozen tools that all seemed powered by batteries. A row of charges lined the back of the cluttered space, red and green LEDs glowing like animal eyes in the night.

Beep.

Tiny feet crept up Rayne's spine, producing an award-winning shiver. She told herself it was the cold concrete sucking the heat from her body, but the internal joke didn't seem funny.

Beep.

She flipped back the jacket hood and shook out her hair. The movement caused her to focus on the ceiling for a moment, and it was then the next beep sounded. It seemed louder. Head tilted back, she walked around until she stood under the trapdoor stairs and waited the half-minute. The next beep seemed to come from above the ceiling.

"Rayne?"

It felt like she jumped a foot, but she knew that wasn't possible. Even so, she spun around so fast her left leg nearly buckled. Quin stood silhouetted in the kitchen door, hopping back and forth in his socks on the concrete step. He rubbed his arms.

"What are you doing out here? It's freezing!" He looked around the space, perhaps expecting to see something meaningful.

Rayne willed her heartbeat back toward normal. "I heard a noise...a beeping sound." Quin cocked his head and listened, but didn't venture farther into the frigid garage.

"I don't hear anything." He rubbed his arms harder, hugging heat to his bony teen body clad only in a T-shirt.

"It's probably nothing," she said, heading toward him. "Maybe an electrical component or something. I'll tell Ben about it later. Let's get inside where it's warm." The boy didn't have to be told twice and jumped back into the bright kitchen. With one last look around the garage, Rayne turned off the lights and closed the door, firmly twisting the deadbolt until it sounded a reassuring *thunk*.

Quin fixed himself a huge bowl of ice cream, while Rayne shivered at the very thought and added several more logs to the fire. She didn't think any fire was big enough to warm her chilled core.

Quin had just plopped on the couch with his quart-sized bowl when a crash sounded upstairs.

Quin raced ahead of Rayne on the stairs as she pushed her hurting leg. She heard Quin cry out and hurried faster. Quin was in Ben's bathroom, kneeling on the floor. Ben, clad only in a towel about his waist, lay at the base of the toilet in the large master bathroom. Blood ran freely from a new gash on his forehead, and a stream dribbled from his mouth. He clutched his left side, moaning in pain. Puddles of water covered the dark slate floor, and his chest hairs were matted in moisture. She grabbed a hand towel as she painfully lowered herself to the floor and pressed it against the wound.

"Ben." She stroked his cheek. "Can you hear me?"

"Ben. Wake up, please!" Quin's cry produced only more moans from the man soon to be his adoptive father. Ben coughed, a rattling shake that sprayed bright blood on Rayne's arm.

Rayne clutched Quin's shoulder. "Quin, listen to me. Call 9-1-1. Tell them we need an ambulance." The boy hesitated, looking from her to Ben with eyes the size of saucers. "Go now!" Quin sprinted from the room.

The next moments passed in a blur. She remembered gently drying Ben's chest and hair, careful not to move him. Quin returned with the portable phone, and she spoke with the 9-1-1 operator who gave assurance an ambulance was on the way. Ben didn't cough up any more blood, but she prayed help would arrive fast. She had Quin go put on his shoes and heavy jacket and take a large flashlight to the top of the driveway where it met Lake Road.

Fire rescue arrived first. Men and equipment flooded into the house, up the stairs and into the suddenly cramped bathroom that had seemed so spacious. Rayne was led to Ben's bedroom where she sank to the end of the bed next to Quin. She put her arm around his shoulders and pulled him tight. Radios crackled like static electricity as the men knelt around Ben, all but obscuring him from her view. One man asked her questions about Ben's medications, about which she knew nothing. She told him about Ben's accident on the road. He relayed the information to the paramedics and went to search the medicine cabinet.

Minutes later, another siren wailed its way closer until even more flashing lights painted the bedroom windows with pulsing red, blue, and white. Ambulance techs trudged through the bedroom with unending loads of equipment, but within minutes they prepared to move Ben.

Rayne suddenly realized they were taking him away. A foolish thought, really, since that's exactly what she'd hoped. She had to get dressed.

Her shoes were right where she'd left them near the sofa. Once tied, she pulled on Ben's coat again. Quin refused to stay behind, and she couldn't blame him, but the fire she'd added all the logs to still burned so hot she didn't feel it safe to leave, so Quin got several glasses of water and doused it. Wet smoke clung to the air in the great room, banishing all the former cheeriness.

By the time she'd located her purse and Ben's wallet for his insurance card, the ambulance techs and firemen had maneuvered Ben down the stairs and were wheeling him onto the front porch. An oxygen mask covered his mouth and nose, and his skin looked white against the dark blanket covering him. Four men lifted him down the porch steps and into yawning doors of the waiting vehicle. Icy air poured in the open front door, chasing all warmth from the house and freezing Rayne's heart. These men carried Ben down his own stairs, the very ones he'd carried her up just weeks ago. As she stood watching, a hand slipped into hers. Quin's skin matched the pallid color of Ben's.

"He'll be okay," she assured him, squeezing his hand.

"How do you know?" His eyes never left the ambulance, and his tone wasn't accusatory. But it was devoid of hope. She had no answer. Ben *had* to be okay. He was too strong, too vital. As the ambulance doors closed and the vehicle drove up the driveway with lights flashing and siren wailing, she realized something else about Ben Conner: he was part of her.

Perhaps a bigger part than she'd ever known.

Raoul stepped out of the hot shower into the frigid bathroom. Moisture streamed down the wallpaper and dripped from the light fixture above the sink. Even with the door to the hall shut, the walls radiated cold. Perhaps he could buy some firewood at the general store in Deer Cove tomorrow. He dried quickly and dropped the towel in the pile with the others before pulling on his clothes. The air in the hallway was even colder than the bathroom, but it warmed as he entered the living space and neared the kitchen where the stove's gas burners warred against the cold. Maybe he'd sleep out here tonight.

The refrigerator still held a half a package of pre-formed hamburger patties, so he pulled the frying pan out of the sink and set it on the surging gas flame of the front burner. The meat patty sizzled when he dropped it in, sending grease spatters flying. Raoul stepped back, avoiding the burning globules as they rained on the range top and floor. He could have covered the pan, but that's what his cleaning deposit went for. Let them earn it.

When he'd assembled a hamburger from his limited supplies, he carried the plate to the dining table and settled into one of the remaining chairs. He took a huge bite and used a paper towel to wipe the hot juices and ketchup from his chin.

"Let's see what's on the Conner channel." He picked up the remote and clicked on the television. As the set warmed up, his first thought was that the system had failed. Pulsing light filled the screen. Then he caught movement and checked the front yard camera.

"What in the…" Raoul dropped his hamburger on the plate and cleaned his hands. He switched to the camera that covered the great room and saw a fireman charge through. Quickly flipping through all the cameras, Raoul scanned each room for Regen van Onweer.

There! She'd backed into the upstairs hallway then disappeared from view as more men maneuvered a rolling gurney through the doorway she'd just come through. Conner lay on the narrow pad, covered by something dark, with broad straps crossing his legs, waist and shoulders. The men rolled it toward the stairs, and Raoul changed to the great room camera again. The angle was bad, but it showed enough for him to know they took the gurney out the front door.

He selected the yard camera again and squinted against the flashing lights. Bulky vehicle shapes littered the yard, but the strobes overwhelmed the security camera's pickups so they were nearly useless.

Raoul sat back, mesmerized by the lights and the events unfolding like an episode of *Law & Order*. Had Conner been seriously injured in their earlier close call? Raoul had seen the truck's lights bouncing wildly in his rearview mirror, but he hadn't stopped to see if it had crashed. And he'd seen Conner with the rest of his family as Regen van Onweer attended his wounds. Maybe the man sustained internal injuries?

A smile pulled his mouth tight. One could hope.

CHAPTER TWENTY-FIVE

Rayne checked the clock on the wall. Past midnight. Saturday morning—the day she'd planned to fly home, leaving from right here in Mission Peak at 2:35 pm, twelve hours from now, connecting through Los Angeles and New York, then landing at Schiphol airport in Amsterdam. One of the routes she'd checked to go home.

Home. What a strange concept it now seemed. Was it that the destination no longer fit the word? She rubbed her face, willing some sensation into numb skin. Quin stirred where he lay stretched out on the extra-firm seating, his head in her lap. She stroked his hair, and he stilled.

The flight had been a fantasy at best. Truth was, she hadn't enough money to buy the ticket. Yes, she needed to get back to the Netherlands, regain control of Elusive Hope before it slipped away forever. The band's name had taken on an ironic prophetic meaning. The more she tried to hang on, the farther away it got.

The volatile music industry used up and spit out dreams and dreamers like a machine. It cared little if one had talent or even thousands of fans. Even hit songs made the charts for only short periods, measured in days or weeks, before the next new one pushed it off the page. One misstep, one poor outing, and the next group stormed in to take your place. Dolina Macgowan was already establishing herself as a worthy successor to the injured and absent Regen van Onweer. Out of sight, out of mind.

And who *was* Regen van Onweer? Did she have real substance, or was she simply a fictional character on a European stage? Make that *former* character. *Where* was Regen van Onweer? Her house had been destroyed, her band had continued on without her, and she had effectively disappeared. No one had heard from her in months. No blog entries—at least none by her—no emails answered, no interviews. She might as well have died. Actually, her death would be much bigger news than her existence now. She'd been eclipsed by other events.

Marilyn Monroe had it right: "Fame is fickle, and I know it."

In ten years, Regen van Onweer would be the subject of an VH1 special: "Where Are They Now?" They'd show old band photos of her onstage in her fancy gowns, grainy video clips of her singing, and the show's hosts would pontificate about her talent or lack thereof before moving on in their countdown. Even in a show about past shining stars, she'd be pushed off the screen as they moved to the next interesting target.

For the first time in many years, Rayne wondered what her future held.

"Mrs. Conner?" A lab-coated doctor with a stethoscope looped around his neck stood in the waiting room doorway. A shock of brown hair waved unkempt above the deeply tanned face, and dozens of laugh lines at the corners of each eye matched his creased and worn Converse high-top tennis shoes.

Rayne liked him immediately. Quin sat up, then rose with her. United, they stepped forward.

"Is Ben okay?" Quin asked, rubbing sleep-crusted eyes. The clock above the drinking fountain clicked another minute: 2:36 am. Rayne had watched each minute creep by.

"I think he'll be fine," he said, addressing Quin and putting a hand on his shoulder.

He introduced himself as Dr. Fall. Any other time that might have been funny. But he seemed nice enough. Rayne prayed he'd graduated at the top of his class. The doctor turned to her.

"We need to keep him in the hospital for a couple of days." He explained that Ben had a serious bump on the back of his skull where he'd struck something in the bathroom, and they wanted to monitor it. He'd bloodied the inside of his mouth as well, the source of the spitting blood. That was a relief to Rayne—she'd thought of a lung injury. Ben's two broken left ribs were his most pressing injury. He'd probably cracked them during the accident on the road, the doctor said, then had the bad luck to fall on them again in the bathroom.

Quin gripped her hand harder, and she shifted her weight off her bad leg and put her arm around him. Bad luck. She shouldn't have let him shower by himself. But what was she to do, climb in with him? Soap his back?

"It's a good thing you called the ambulance right away, Mrs. Conner." Neither she nor Quin corrected the doctor's assumption of her relationship with Ben. Sometimes staying mute produced better results. The doctor explained about head injuries and how they could be very serious.

All Rayne could think about was how close she'd come to losing him twice in one night. He could have died on the road, upside down in a burning vehicle, or on that cold bathroom floor while she sat by helplessly. For the last several weeks, he'd been her rock. No, that wasn't true. Whether she admitted it or not, he'd filled that role for fifteen years, always a phone call away if she'd needed him. But she'd never called, never reached out or let him reach her.

And tonight, it had nearly gone completely away before… before…

Suddenly it felt like a sumo wrestler climbed atop her chest. She couldn't get air, couldn't breathe. The room spun, and Rayne sagged to the end of the vinyl-covered couch.

"Rayne!" Quin's voice punched a thick cloud surrounding her, but he was distant, obscured by a blanketing gray fog. Her scalp frizzled and her hands went numb with freezing cold.

Far in the distance a man yelled, "Nurse!"

Time passed slowly. Through the fog, she could both see and not see that wretched clock above the drinking fountain. The hands barely moved, kept reversing. One notch forward, two back, then three back. Could time reverse itself? Could she go back in time? And do what exactly? Change things. But everything was so fuzzy, so…

Something tickled her nose. A fragrance, an aroma. With her next breath, white-hot ice picks shot up her nasal passages and pierced her brain. She made the mistake of sucking in more air. Batting with one hand to get the thing away from her nose, Rayne nearly fell off the couch. A colorful smock materialized before her eyes, then moved back and took the shape of a woman.

"Mrs. Conner?" the woman asked, flanked by a concerned Dr. Fall.

"Umm?" Her nasal linings felt scorched by the strong odor emanating from the small packet in the nurse's fingers, and her stomach lurched, threatening to cover the pastel woman's shoes with her barbecue dinner. Rayne pushed the hand farther away.

"Just lay still a minute," the doctor soothed. He probably excelled at bedside manner in doctor school. "You fainted," he added unnecessarily.

Rayne willed consciousness, blinked for clarity. Seeing the scared look on Quin's face, she thought it best to sit up sooner rather than later. She worked her way up to a reclining position.

"I'm okay, Quin. Sorry about that. I haven't fainted in years." She coughed a laugh, a forced, ingenuous noise, but Quin didn't seem to notice, and his lips curved into a small smile.

The doctor—after telling them Ben was sedated and would sleep for several hours—excused himself, while the nurse insisted she call someone to drive them home. She even went so far as to pocket the Bronco keys from Rayne's purse.

She had to call Addison. Why hadn't she called him last night? It had been ten-thirty or eleven when Ben fell. The next hour plus was insane with emergency workers, the departing ambulance, her and Quin's drive to Mission Peak in the old Bronco. But as she reflected on her wait through the early morning hours, she had no answer for not calling then. She'd spent most of the time stroking Quin's soft brown hair as he lay with his head on her lap, and thinking about Ben and his love for the boy. And then Ben's love for her. Tears had fallen as she realized for the first time how much she'd screwed things up, and the old clock ticked off another minute.

Ben's brother had arrived shortly before 3:30 am, and he hadn't been happy. Rayne couldn't blame Addison and, although she'd apologized for not calling him right away, he'd stormed away to find Dr. Fall. Sam Riley paused to give Rayne a bewildered look, then trailed after him.

After the doctor assured them Ben would be out for a few hours, Addison drove Rayne home in the Bronco, followed by Sam and Quin in their car. Even with the heater belching warm air into the old truck, the atmosphere had been chilly at best. Addison barely said a word; he didn't have to. In her own mind, he read her the riot act.

Rayne had messed up by not calling him. He was Ben's brother, had been at the house for dinner a few hours before. Quin was his soon-to-be nephew. Why hadn't she called him, let him know his only sibling had a serious fall and was in the hospital? She had no answer other than her fear for Ben had immobilized her, and she couldn't tell him that. She'd disappointed Addison fifteen years ago by leaving Storm Lake and hurting his brother, and he expected no less from her this time around. Now she'd let him down again.

Music was the only thing she'd ever succeeded at. Certainly not married life with Ben. And no one as unreliable as she was could be even a substitute mother to Quin. She needed to go home.

But as they drove down the curving driveway and the headlights washed across the sturdy steps and porch of the increasingly familiar house, Rayne's heart ached at the thought of leaving. Disaster nipped at her heels wherever she went, and no place felt safe anymore. Even if she hurried back to Holland and moved into a secure building, how long would it take for the basic feeling of safety to return? What if they never caught the man who attacked her?

In the garage, she thanked Addison, then stood in the biting wind at the open door while Quin exited Sam's car. Addison climbed in and they drove away. As she followed the boy into the dark, cold house, Rayne realized her biggest fear was that if she stayed at Storm Lake, her attacker might find her here and bring that danger to Quin and Ben.

CHAPTER TWENTY-SIX

Ben woke just after sunrise, rays streaming across a soft tan blanket covering his legs. Cool green walls, a wall-mounted TV, and the chrome bedrails were all the clues he needed. Hospital.

An intravenous line snaked from his left arm to a hanging bag of clear fluid, so he used his right hand to rub the sleep from his eyes, finding a tender bump on his jaw. He worked the muscles of his face, feeling the effects of medicine-induced sleep. He'd gotten as far as the accident on the road in trying to piece together the events, when a cheery volunteer's tennis shoes squeaked in the door and around the end of the hanging curtain.

He shifted his weight, noticing the tight wrappings around his chest and a dull ache on his left side. Back in high school, he'd been trussed up like a mummy for three weeks after a right tackle from a rival school blindsided him during a Friday night game. Coach said the guy must have flunked a few years of high school; he looked old enough to have finished college, and outweighed Ben by fifty pounds or more.

A bustling all-business nurse named Betty checked his vitals, poked and prodded until he threatened her—which she ignored—then told him nothing. She left to locate the doctor who was, she informed him, "Probably taking his own sweet time over coffee in the cafeteria."

Gingerly, he shifted position in the firm bed, easing pressure off his numb back and butt. A knock drew his attention to the door.

Addison, dressed in a knee-length camel overcoat and looking like an ad for GQ, stepped into the room. "Hey, bro. How's the bod doing this morning?"

"Other than hoping you got the license of the Mack truck that ran me over, I'm doing okay."

Addison laughed, then shucked his coat and sank into a side chair. He wore a black dress shirt without a tie, and black pants.

Ben pointed. "Pretty fancy duds for a hospital visit. Going somewhere?"

"San Francisco. I have a meeting at noon with a client. They have a string of retail stores from there north and are being eaten alive by shoplifters."

"On a Saturday? It *is* still Saturday, isn't it? I haven't lost a day or anything, have I?"

"I told them it was today or not at all. Sam will run *me* over with a truck if I go anywhere the next two weeks. Bad enough going today. Had to promise her to paint the house with the money I earn from this one, so I'm charging them extra." He grinned.

Most women would ask for a bigger diamond or a new car, but Samantha Riley wasn't the least bit materialistic. It was one of the things Ben liked most about his future sister-in-law. Well, truth was, he liked everything about Sam. She was Addison's perfect match. His brother was lucky to have found her, especially after that maniac had tried so hard to kill her last year.

What was it about guys trying to kill the Conner women? He thought again of the man who'd shot Rayne. The Dutch police weren't very forthcoming with information on the case, nor was Rayne's contact with the FBI who had been brought in after the threatening message at her mother's condo in Atlanta. They all seemed stalled. Maybe Addison could check into it—after the wedding, of course. His brother was a crack detective and, as much as he enjoyed working as a security consultant, Ben knew he missed active police investigations.

Ben mentioned the idea to Addison. "What do you think?" He was surprised at the frown that sprang up on his brother's face. "What's wrong?"

Addison sat silently for a minute before responding. "Ben, please don't take this the wrong way, okay?" Addison waited for Ben's cautious nod before continuing. "I'm not so sure you should keep getting in deeper and deeper with Rayne. I know you still care for her, but I have a feeling she's going to leave again as soon as she can."

Ben rubbed his eyes. "I know. But I've stayed out of it too long already. It's her life, Addison, and she's in touch with the contacts she has. But that's not enough for me any longer. I *have* to help her."

Addison shifted in the vinyl chair. "Is it wise to get your hopes up? I know you don't want Quin hurt, either."

As much as Ben wanted to defend Rayne and tell Addison to stay out of their business, the Quin card hit home. His brother was right: Quin was still fragile. When Quin's sister and her husband had told him about their dad's death, Quin had run out the door into a cold night. It took them an hour of hunting before they found him curled in a ball on the metal floor of his boat—the one his dad bought for him.

Ben wasn't foolish enough to think some of those emotional issues wouldn't surface during the teen years, even though he'd been impressed with Quin's coping ability. And the lake community helped immeasurably, providing a stable environment, like what Ben hoped to provide in their home. Bringing Rayne there had heaved stability out the window.

Addison said he'd think about it, then left for the Mission Peak airport a few minutes later. The empty room left Ben time to think about all those things he'd been successfully avoiding until now.

Rayne turned on the porch and yard lights, then peeked out the front door window to the barren driveway. With a sigh, she consciously stopped wringing her hands. Her mother did that; Rayne refused to copy the habit.

Addison would be arriving soon with Ben and Quin. She'd declined Addison's half-hearted invitation to ride along as they checked Ben out of the hospital and brought him home, but Quin jumped at the chance to go. Although Rayne had taken him to visit Ben on Saturday, Sunday, and Monday afternoons, the boy needed the extra assurance Ben was on the mend, and she couldn't fault him for it. She needed it, too.

On Sunday's visit, Addison and Mandy had arrived shortly after Rayne and Quin, making for a rather full hospital room. Fortunately, Ben's roommate had been discharged that morning, so they had the space to themselves. But even the extra space put her a little too close to Addison, who plainly still regarded her with suspicion—for what Rayne wasn't entirely sure. She hid out by the other bed, letting Mandy and Quin dominate the conversation. Ben shot her several questioning looks, but she had kept her distance during Addison's presence.

Rayne stepped away from the front window, wishing she had something to do. She'd already straightened the room, plumping the pillows on the couch, and dusting the tables. Simmering spaghetti sauce filled the room with tangy tomato aromas, and steam rose from the pasta pot, waiting for her to turn up the heat and drop in the noodles. She'd fixed a green salad and garlic French bread. A pan of brownies cooled on a wire rack. She hadn't been this domestic in years. Fifteen to be exact.

The opening to the hall caught her eye and, before she could be distracted, she walked to the piano room. She'd already played for nearly two hours at the Barn today, and she needed to practice some of the old songs the women requested. Although in the past she could adequately sight-read music, she'd grown lazy during her years with the band. Her own music sprang from within, so by the time she showed her charts to the rest of the group it was indelibly etched in her head. Plus, with Pieter on keyboards, she didn't accompany herself anymore at practices or performances. She was rusty.

Adjusting the bench, Rayne opened the keyboard cover and let her fingertips slide across the silky white. Every key matched its neighbor in height, adjusted and restored to perfection by Ben's talented hands. His gift for an absent wife who, except for an attacker's bullets, might never have known about it.

Before the guilt knife slipped too far into her heart, Rayne sifted through the sheet music on the rack. A yellow sticky note popped off one piece and fluttered to the keys. It read "Simple Things." She'd made the note after her first drive to Bibs' Beauty Barn.

Rayne forgot her plan to practice the old songs, and within fifteen minutes she'd filled a yellow pad with lyrics and two notation sheets with melody and chorus. She told the story of treasuring simple things in life: a homemade gift, the night sky and shooting stars on the beach, popcorn by the fire, the warm embrace of a lover, and a convertible with the top down in freezing weather with the heater on full blast—all things she'd shared with Ben during those brief months of their marriage. She sang of a child's treasured toy made by his grandfather and passed down, scuffed paint and all, a mother's gift of something old on her daughter's wedding day, the first taste of hand-squeezed lemonade, and Rice Krispies treats around a patio fire.

The melody coursed like blood through her veins, firing messages to arms and fingers, and ultimately to the restored instrument whose strings hummed with beauty and meaning. A boy remembered the sound his Christmas tricycle tires made on the gravel driveway, a girl combed a favorite doll's hair while hiding under a tented sheet and whispering future secrets, an old man walked the seashore and mourned the love of his lifetime lost to old age.

Simple things, simple things,
Things we find in every day.
Take me to your favorite places,
Share your secrets, your treasures, your life.
Protect the things that truly matter,
Keep them close as your heart.
Sing the song of simple things,
Don't let them slip away,
Don't let them slip away,
Don't let me slip away.

Rayne let the major chord fade and lifted her foot from the pedal, wondering where "Don't let *me* slip away" had come from. Those weren't the words she'd written on the page.

Clapping hands sounded behind her and she spun around. Quin stood in the doorway, a wide grin covering his face as he clapped enthusiastically. Ben towered over him with as big a grin. Except for blond versus brown hair, they looked like father and son. Embarrassment coursed through her at getting caught singing a half-done song, or maybe it was the last line of the lyrics that caused her hot cheeks and neck. She rose from the stool and was astonished to see Addison behind Ben, applauding too. A smile curved his mouth and reached his eyes.

"Wow, Rayne. That was beautiful!" Quin charged into the room and nearly knocked her over as he hugged her waist. She marveled how natural it felt. They'd become closer these last few days since Ben's injury, fishing off the dock together, and spending long hours in front of the fireplace each evening as Quin finished homework and Rayne jotted song ideas or perused cookbooks and asked his opinions on recipes about what he and Ben liked. He'd talked more about his mom and dad, but also about how much Ben meant to him now. Even Rayne with her limited kid experience knew such conversations were rare for a middle-schooler.

"Thanks, kiddo. I didn't even hear you guys come in." She ruffled his hair and dropped her hand to his shoulder, pulling him tight. Her eyes rose to Ben's. "I'm glad you're home." Oh, man, that sounded like June Cleaver welcoming Ward home after a day at his mysterious job.

But she couldn't look away when Ben's blue eyes shone as they did, seeing her soul, uncovering longings in her song as well as pain—and fear. Ben loved her, had always loved her; she knew that without doubt. Over his shoulder, Addison lifted a brow in unspoken question directed solely to her: Was she staying or leaving?

If only she knew.

CHAPTER TWENTY-SEVEN

Ben used the table for leverage as he eased up from the kitchen chair. For two days he'd avoided the cushy furniture, unable to rise without help from Rayne or Quin. He poured another cup of coffee—not the best decision since his nerves were already zinging, but he needed something to do. His truck had been towed to Deer Cove Auto. The owner, Mark, had called and said in addition to the side mirror and door glass, the damage was confined to a bent right front wheel. Guess the truck lived up to its "Ford Tough" sales pitch. But he'd been very lucky last Saturday, in more ways than one.

The phone rang, and he snatched it up, grateful for the distraction. He'd bend the ear of a telemarketer if he had to.

"Hey, bro. Ribs all healed?"

Ben laughed. "Only werewolves and vampires heal in a few days." He and Addison had been fans of campy horror movies from the time they were kids and they still loved watching them on Ben's 50-inch plasma now that Addison had moved back from Missouri. Sam, Quin, and Mandy thought the brothers were crazy, but Star loved the old flicks, too, though she tended to squeal and hide her eyes a lot.

He and Addison chatted about wedding plans, but Ben couldn't work up much interest in those, even if the wedding was only a week from Saturday. Funny how after fifteen years certain subjects were still in his off-limits zone. Evidently Addison heard his sigh and changed the subject.

"I called to talk about Rayne—specifically her shooting. I've done a little digging."

This surprised Ben, for he assumed his brother's suspicions of Rayne's departure had sidelined Ben's request for help.

"She isn't here right now if you want her on the line, too." Rayne had taken the Bronco for her Thursday singing job at the Beauty Barn, leaving Ben marooned in his own home. Technically he wasn't stranded. He had a 1969 Triumph 650 motorcycle under a tarp in the garage, but he wasn't stupid enough to take it out with cracked ribs. Newer bikes had better power to weight ratios, but the throb of the venerable British machine still made his blood pump on the curving county roads.

"No, that's okay. I called in a few favors and ferreted out some contacts I've made with security firms with European offices." Ben knew Addison often consulted with companies that had international branches. Sometimes the other firm led the project, but other times Addison drove the show. He covered everything: shoplifting, employee theft, building security, bomb threat procedures, emergency phone lists. Basic to advanced, and he excelled at it all.

"What'd you find out? Have they made any progress?"

"Some. I'll fill you in when I get there. And warm up the big screen, I'm bringing some video."

"Another horror flick?" Ben laughed. Addison had probably picked up *Abbott and Costello Meet the Wolfman*, or something.

"You have no idea." His brother sounded all too serious as he disconnected.

———

Raoul lifted his high-power binoculars and checked Bibs' Beauty Barn again. The Bronco sat right where Regen van Onweer had left it, along the north side of the building where the staff parked.

In order not to arouse suspicion, he'd parked his VW on the curving road entering town from the north. He smiled at his perfect, broad-daylight hiding spot. Although the car was tucked into a turnout, if anyone stopped to check on it, he'd explain it broke down, not unlikely after a look at his decrepit wheels. His cabin farther up the road would corroborate his story. He hadn't seen a cop since arriving at Storm Lake, but he'd heard they patrolled periodically.

Darkness finally slid across the street and stole the sunlight. Even the fates blessed his plan by providing early nightfall. Depositing the binoculars on the backseat, he retrieved a night vision monocular he'd purchased from a helpful man at Rory's Military Surplus in Mission Peak. Although only 3x magnifying, it gave a clear view of the building and parking areas as the night deepened. Lights flicked on in houses and buildings scattered through the tree-lined hills. Fortunately, the Barn sat at the extreme north end of Deer Cove, separated from the main town area by a couple of flat fields and one small hill.

Any minute, Regen van Onweer would exit the building. *Marielle.* Raoul shifted into a comfortable position, the old seat creaking beneath him. He'd waited so long; *too* long. She should have been his the night of the concert in Rotterdam. All that preparation wasted. But tonight would be different. He felt it as surely as blood coursed through his veins— blood of a wolf.

Today, Thursday, was the chosen day.

Save your last breath for me.

Ben hunched forward in the dining room chair Addison had carried into the TV room for him, the ache from his ribcage an irritating thorn as he scanned the video footage flickering across his 55-inch flat screen. Six feet away was almost too close, but he demanded every detail, no matter how menial. A clipboard on his knee overflowed with scribbled notes, squares and arrows.

Fortunately, Rayne's finale concert producers had hired a professional company to film their biggest show, with plans for airing on one of the Dutch television networks. The recording company used nine hi-def cameras, so there was plenty of footage to sift through. Each time he and Addison ran the movie, he studied a different area of the screen.

Some of the footage was raw: no dissolves from camera to camera, just straight through from each camera's location, including jerky repositions of the handhelds and hundreds of zooms, pull-backs, and focuses. Those images were eerie without the soundtrack yet to be added in postproduction. But other segments, like the one onscreen now, had the audio track synced, and the music pulsed through Ben's 7.1 Surround Sound system.

His jaw muscles tightened as the now familiar image filled the screen. In a cloud of yellow fog, Rayne, in her guise as Regen van Onweer, stood with arms stretched overhead, every part of her body taut with effort. Her skin glistened, a mix of sweat and glitter dust. With every viewing he gained new respect for her. She sang with a passion unmatched, telling the operatic story of Marielle, a girl who'd been betrayed in love, then rose above it and conquered. Bass and drums pounded, anchoring the orchestra and choir. Rayne's voice soared above them all. A bell-like soprano much of the time, she could dip to smoky alto with ease, more than holding her own against all the other performers combined.

The first time through the video, he'd brushed tears from his eyes. Instead of watching for threats, he'd been caught up in the musical experience, weeping like some sappy teenage girl. He'd caught his brother dabbing his eyes, too.

But, as amazing as the production was, it wasn't the theatrics that held his eyes prisoner—it was Rayne Evans as Regen van Onweer.

And he was not alone. An overhead cable camera swept across the audience, revealing rapt faces reflecting pain, tears, rapture, and hope, all the things Rayne dreamed of communicating through her music when they'd first been married. And here on his TV was proof that she'd done it. *Magnificent* failed as a descriptor.

The picture shifted again and Ben tensed, knowing what was to come, powerless to stop it. Mid-song, Rayne wrenched sideways and fell to the narrow platform at the top of the stairs. Even at the third viewing, Ben cringed at the pain she must have felt that exact moment. Singing beside her, Dolina Macgowan shifted her eyes sideways to the downed star, clearly confused. Then she extended her right hand to Rayne and mouthed something he couldn't make out. But then the young woman jerked once, toppled over Rayne, and rolled out of the spotlight's circle toward the rear of the stage.

Addison said witnesses stated Macgowan had tumbled off the platform and plunged twenty feet, striking prop support bars and breaking an ankle before slamming onto Lorna Nairne, Rayne's hair and makeup assistant, who was standing on the main stage deck behind the stairs. The woman's unlucky position probably saved the young singer's life, though Nairne sustained a serious neck injury and broken leg of her own. Addison didn't know how Nairne was doing. Macgowan had been shot in the shoulder, fortunately missing the bone, and spent a week in the hospital, followed by outpatient physical therapy.

Rayne hadn't been as lucky. Ben slow-motioned the DVD and the sound vanished, leaving only his and Addison's breathing in addition to the whir of the DVD player. After Macgowan's disappearance, Rayne struggled to her knees, a bewildered expression on her porcelain face. Ben's heart nearly stopped as she opened her mouth, preparing to continue the song. He willed her to be safe, for no more bullets. But, as with the previous showings, the left sleeve of her gown rippled like someone had struck it with a tree switch. Rayne wrenched forward, reaching with her right hand, but she'd been too close to the grand staircase. She missed the platform and landed on the next step down, throwing her off-balance. In slow motion, she began her long tumbling fall.

Ten times she rolled and bounced. In the single frame mode, Ben watched the red stain on her sleeve grow from one tumble to the next. At the drummer's setup near the bottom of the stairs, Danny Haynes toppled backward, feet in the air, drumsticks flying as Rayne undercut him. Her sheer momentum scattered drums, cymbals and mic stands into the guitar and keyboard players, and into the fans pressing the front of the stage.

Like ketchup on a clean white T-shirt, Rayne's life-force stained her white satin dress. Her left arm was a bloody mess when her body slid to a stop amid tangled cords and instruments. In a macabre postscript, the automated pyrotechnics exploded on cue, pulsing in time to music that no longer played.

The TV image switched to raw footage from one of two handheld cameras that had been filming onstage. Although silent, the picture quality was still perfect, and this angle showed the audience's reactions in bizarre variety. Some grinned and cheered, obviously thinking it was part of the show, while their companions stared in horror. Others screamed in silent pantomime. Hundreds—maybe thousands—had cell phones pointed at the stage during the concert. Addison said footage of the shooting had hit YouTube, Flixxy, and dozens of other music and video sharing sites within minutes, racking up hundreds of thousands of views before the next day's end.

Panicked expressions told Ben exactly when the fire alarm klaxons sounded. Strobes lit the crowd in pulses, and many fans bolted for the exits. Some went with the tide, but others climbed on seats, continuing to film or take pictures with their phones while friends fled.

Addison read from a translated synopsis of the police report. *"All hope of containing the shooter in the building was lost in the chaotic aftermath. Police are reviewing the video, looking for anyone suspicious, but they determined the shooter fired from a small alcove room high on the back wall near the projection booth. The alarm box in the hallway near that small room was the one that triggered the fire alarm."*

One of the handheld cameras swung back to the devastation onstage. Ben pushed *Pause* on the remote control, freezing Rayne where she lay like a broken rag doll in the center of the screen. This woman—this beautiful, talented creature—had been his friend and lover. His wife. And some madman had deemed it okay to end her life.

The second bullet had broken Rayne's arm, but fortunately—if a shooting injury could ever be called fortunate—the impact had been several inches below the shoulder.

Ben dropped his head into his hands. In time, the physical wounds would heal—they nearly had during the weeks since these scenes were recorded. But she'd never told him—not in detail anyway—how bad the attack had been. He hadn't wanted to pry it out of her, but now he felt cheated that she didn't trust enough to tell him.

"She's safe here." His brother's hand rested firmly on Ben's shoulder. "The Dutch police are staying in touch with Atlanta PD. It's an international investigation. They'll find him."

Ben stared at the horror on the screen. Perhaps. But in time?

CHAPTER TWENTY-EIGHT

Rayne smiled as Bibs locked the Beauty Barn doors with an ancient padlock at least four inches across. "Wow, that should keep them out."

"Always has," Irene said, her knitting bag slung over her boney shoulder.

"From the front doors at least," Bibs sighed. "Young Billy Humphrey broke in last year by pulling off some of the rear boards." She tilted her head back and looked lovingly over the front of the barn.

"You caught him?" Rayne asked, imagining Bibs and Irene walking in on a burglary. Memories of Rayne's own destroyed house in South Holland sent a shiver up her spine.

"Neighbor noticed him riding his bike with an armload of hair dryers. Cords kept tangling in his spokes." Bibs laughed, but Rayne was still thinking about the torn clothing, shredded bedding, and deeply scratched walls.

She watched the two other women pick their way across the dark parking lot using a penlight. They climbed into a 70s Buick and the engine roared to life in a cloud of dark smoke. As the headlights came on, Rayne waved and used their light to walk around to the side of the barn where the Bronco sat forlornly now that the other beauty technicians had all gone home. She'd stayed far later than she planned, but Bibs had bent her ear about songs that held special meaning for certain customers, and Rayne wanted to get some notes down and search through a couple of boxes of sheet music.

Crickets filled the hay-scented damp air with their songs as Rayne unlocked the truck and climbed onto the cold seat. She twisted the key in the ignition, pumping the gas and adjusting the choke as the engine cranked, but it wouldn't start. After letting it rest for a few seconds, she tried again, but there wasn't a hint of catching or sputtering as there usually was.

"Come on, you old mule. Don't do this to me." She turned the key repeatedly, trying not to flood the engine by pumping the accelerator too much, but it simply wouldn't catch.

She looked around the dark parking area. There were only a few homes farther up the road, and most of those were vacation houses, locked and boarded up for the winter. The road surface gleamed, damp and deserted. It was at least a quarter of a mile back to the houses in Deer Cove where she could find a phone, and her leg ached just thinking about such a long walk after a long day. Kicking herself for not leaving sooner or at least having a cell phone, Rayne retrieved her dad's battered flashlight from under the seat and opened the door.

Raoul watched through his night scope, barely able to keep it steady in his shaking hands. Cold had seeped into every joint as he waited, but it was excitement, not the wintry air that caused the trembling. The two old women had left Regen van Onweer alone.

This is the night! Right now.

Save your last breath for me.

He dropped the scope on the passenger seat. "Time for the wolf to come to the rescue." He turned the ignition key. The engine cranked sluggishly three times...and quit. His jaw dropped open. He switched the key off, then tried again. The motor gave a half-hearted moan and stopped.

"No. No. No!" He pounded on the plastic steering wheel until it cracked and warm blood ran down his wrist. "Tonight is the night.

Tonight is the night!" He shoved the door open, kicking it when it bounced back at him. A satisfying snap of breaking metal followed the third application of his boot, and the door hung at an odd angle.

He climbed out and began running down the road, toward Regen van Onweer. Toward Marielle, his destiny.

———

"Man." Ben rubbed a hand over his face. His eyeballs felt gritty from staring at the TV. They'd been scanning Rayne's concert footage, reviewing all the angles, looking for any clues that might help. "What time is it?"

"Almost six-thirty," Addison said, standing and twisting side to side. Then he stopped and stared at Ben. "How late does that singing job go at Bibs'?"

Ben hurried as fast as he could down the hall to his office, flipped on the light, and searched through a pile of phone books for the thinnest one, the local lake community. He scanned the pages and finally located the number. He let the phone at the Beauty Barn ring ten times, then searched the book for Bibs' home number and dialed. She answered on the third ring.

"Hi, Bibs. This is Ben Conner. I was wondering if Rayne left with you?"

"Oh, hi Ben. We've sure enjoyed having Rayne with us. She's such a—"

"Bibs, Rayne isn't home yet. I'm wondering if she had car trouble. Did she leave before you did?" Ben listened to Bibs' description of the timeline. He hung up while she was expressing concern that everything was okay. He'd apologize later.

Addison stood in the doorway. They'd both just spent ninety minutes watching someone shoot Rayne. Ben didn't even have to ask before his brother pulled out his car keys.

"I'll drive," Addison said, and sprinted for the front door.

Two minutes later, Ben gripped the armrest of Addison's Audi SUV as they rocketed onto Lake Road heading toward Deer Cove. The Q7 had all-wheel drive, and Ben appreciated how it hugged the corners on the wet asphalt.

Addison flipped him a cell phone. "Start calling people. I'd do it, but I don't want to break too many laws at once." Addison's high-speed driving training as a cop paid off, and they were passing Flume before Ben connected with the sheriff's office. The dispatcher said the nearest patrol car was working an accident south of Perilous Cove. She'd have them come as soon as they could.

Ben gritted his teeth at every corner and dialed the only numbers he could remember: Doc Arnold's office and Mark at Deer Cove Auto. Both were closed. He kicked himself for not bringing the phone book with their home numbers. They were approaching Deer Cove, so he dropped the phone in the center console. Addison kept the lights on high beam, and Ben squinted through the windshield, willing the Bronco to appear along the side of the road, but it never did.

Ben's brother gave the two Deer Cove stop signs a passing nod as he barely slowed in the town, then he floored it all the way to the Beauty Barn.

Addison twisted the wheel and bounced into the parking lot. Ben grunted, but didn't say anything. He'd do the same if he were driving. The Bronco sat to the right of the barn in the gravel overflow lot, its oxidized hood up. Something had happened. But where was Rayne? Addison left the Audi running and pointed at the Bronco as they climbed out and walked in circles around the old Ford and surrounding parking lot. The lights shone through a barbed wire fence at the edge of the cleared area and into the field beyond. Crickets filled the night with their winter-slow song.

"Rayne!" Ben's voice sounded impossibly loud in the still night. "Rayne Evans!"

Addison was heading around the other side of the barn, when an approaching car turned into the main lot. Ben closed on the vehicle as Bibs and Irene climbed out. She had a heavy housecoat buttoned up to her neck and calf-high UGG boots with fur around the tops. As odd as she appeared, her eyes were all business.

"Did you find her?"

Ben shook his head. The sisters lived on the other side of Deer Cove in a small Craftsman style house a block off Main. Obviously Rayne hadn't walked to their house, if she even knew where it was. Ben heard Addison calling Rayne's name from the other side of the barn as Bibs headed for the front doors, keys out and jangling.

"We'd better call in some help," Bibs said as she slid the big padlock free of the hasp. Ben helped her push the heavy door aside enough for them to enter. Bibs and Irene hurried in first, and a few seconds later lights came on, painting a giant rectangle across the outside blacktop. Then the classic outdoor barn light that hung above the doors bathed the parking lot in yellow.

Ben wasn't sure what to do. Get in the Audi and start searching the side roads? She had to be somewhere between here and Deer Cove. There wasn't anything much up the other way on the road except a few cabins before the road became little more than a Jeep trail. She wouldn't go that way.

He'd reached the Bronco and opened the cab door, hoping for some clue when he heard the scream.

CHAPTER TWENTY-NINE

Ben reached the barn doors as Addison barreled around the far corner of the barn holding a pistol in a two-handed grip. Ben ignored the pain from his ribs and ran through the building's entrance. He slid to a stop when he spotted the two owners behind the glass counter. Irene leaned on the countertop, drawing great gasps of air and holding her other hand to her chest like she was having a heart attack. Bibs was bent over double, her expansive backside hiding everything else from view.

Rayne!

Ben rounded the right end of the counter while Addison, gun now pointing at the ceiling, cautiously circled from the left.

Rayne sat on the floor in front of Bibs, wrapped in a quilt. Smeared blood covered the left side of her face from hairline to jaw, and tears streamed from red eyes. He dropped beside her and gathered her into his arms. She twisted her fists in his shirt so hard he thought she'd break another rib. A button snapped off and bounced on the concrete. She trembled and shook as sobs wracked her body.

"I… started to walk, but it was… too far. Then he… called my name. Ben, he called my name. I didn't know what to do," she blubbered against his chest. "I wasn't…it can't…" He tucked her head under his chin. Addison caught his eye and raised an eyebrow. Ben had no answers, not for any of his brother's questions.

"Shh, shh. It's okay, baby, it's okay. No one's going to hurt you. You're safe." He continued making soothing sounds as he rocked back and forth on the hard floor. The cold radiating from her body chilled him to the core.

She quieted after a few minutes and let out a sigh but kept her head buried against his flannel shirt. This was where she belonged, locked in his arms, safe. He wanted nothing more than to hold her forever.

Rayne finally relaxed her grip on Ben enough so they could move when the deputy sheriff strode in and demanded some answers to the scene he found in the barn. Addison went to check the Bronco, but Ben never left Rayne's side, keeping his arm around her or holding her hand in a grip that said he was afraid she might disappear.

After this evening, she wanted to. Another shiver tiptoed up her spine, and Ben pulled her closer, if that were possible.

"I'm afraid I don't fully understand," the deputy said, removing his wide-brim hat and scratching his head. He accepted a foam cup of coffee from Irene.

Rayne didn't blame him for being confused. They'd all asked so many questions, she was getting mixed up too. She inhaled the rich French vanilla from her own cup. This was the good stuff, not what Bibs kept going all day during business. Now, if it would only clear her mind.

"Your car won't start," the deputy stated, reviewing his spiral notebook, "so you decide to walk to town. Then you change your mind, double back, and hear a man calling your name. But instead of answering, you break into the barn and hide under this old blanket." He gestured to the valuable hand-stitched quilt as if it were a common mover's pad. His eyes met Rayne's. "Why didn't you answer whoever called your name?"

Why indeed? What was it about the man in the dark who'd called her name? Why had she reacted with instant terror? But she had.

"I don't know. There was..." What had sent her into panic mode?

She'd been a hundred yards down the road when she changed her mind. That's when she heard him calling. Her first instinct had been to run behind the barn, putting it between her and him.

"There was what?" the deputy prompted.

Rayne took a deep breath, forcing her nerves into submission. "Something about his voice. Or what he said." The tension headache plowed into her head in pulsing waves that felt like someone wrung her brain like an old dishtowel. "I'm sorry, I can't remember."

"Did you fall? Is that how you cut your head?" the deputy asked. Bibs had brought a washcloth from one of the hair washing sinks, and Rayne still dabbed at the cut with the wet rag.

"No. I scraped it when I crawled through the gap in the barn wall."

"Where you'd pulled off the boards," he reviewed his notes.

"Yes, that's right." She'd remembered the story of Billy breaking into the barn by removing some boards. She knew her way around the back room a little from using the piano there the first day.

"Why didn't you use the phone and call for help?" the deputy asked.

"She couldn't call," Bibs answered for her. The deputy turned to the woman.

"And why not? It's right there on the counter." He pointed to the phone, resting in its base unit on the glass.

"Because it's a cordless phone, not one of the old fashioned ones wired in from the phone company. Has to have electricity to work, and the plug up front is on the switch with the lights. No lights, no phone." Bibs gave a pointed look at Irene. "Told you buying that fancy phone wasn't a good idea, but you just had to have it."

Irene's chin raised and jutted out. "Never been a problem before."

Addison drove home much more slowly, but every turn in the road made Ben wish he'd brought some pain meds along. He and Rayne rode in the back seat, holding hands in the dark. She leaned into him, head on his shoulder, reminding him of high school days when he'd double-dated with Beth Griffin. A pothole taxed the Audi's superior suspension forcing a grunt as Ben tensed.

"Sorry, bro," Addison said, lifting his eyes to the rearview mirror. "Didn't see that one." He slowed down a little more as they passed through Flume and the Perilous Cove road junction.

From Flume to the house, the road left much to be desired and Ben tried to hold his breath when they came to places he knew to be rough. He relaxed a little when they finally turned down his driveway. Ben's Ford truck sat in front of the garage. Mark must have brought it by when he finished work on it—they'd probably passed him on their race to Bibs's barn.

At least it gave them a running vehicle to use while he figured out the problem with the Bronco. Addison pulled to a stop next to the truck and, with teeth clenched, Ben climbed out. He turned to help Rayne.

"I think I should be the one helping *you*, surfer boy. You're white with some green around the gills," she said, her fingers wrapping tight around his right arm. But she continued to lean on him as Addison led the way into the house.

"I guess we make quite a pair," Ben said as they stepped into the warm room. He wanted nothing more than to lie down on his pillow top mattress and pull up a blanket...preferably with Rayne beside him. But the daydream vanished when he spotted Addison a few feet in front of them, turning slowly toward the hallway. Music drifted from the far end.

"That's my music." Rayne looked at him, fingers digging into his arm. "How did you get it?" Her eyes grew large, and he saw the fear returning. Addison jogged down the hallway and, before Ben could say anything, Rayne broke loose and followed as fast as her leg would allow. Ben brought up the rear. He remembered putting the DVD on Pause before their mad dash to Deer Cove. It must have restarted automatically after some interval and was playing in a loop.

When Ben reached the doorway, Addison and Rayne stood just inside. In the middle of the room, Quin sat in the same chair Ben had used earlier, eyes glued to the onscreen performance. The crescendo of "Indigo Sun" filled the room and they watched Rayne's body collapse. Dolina reached down for her fallen comrade, then toppled out of sight. Then began Rayne's tumbling descent down the steep stairs. The music boomed as she scattered the drums and instruments, and the pyrotechnics exploded. The sound cut off as the video cut to the non-edited footage.

Quin turned at Rayne's gasp, confusion clear on his young face. "Rayne." He turned to the screen, then back to Rayne. "That was you singing." There was no question of the boy's recognition of Rayne.

"Yes." Her breathy whisper barely registered in the cushioned media room. Ben stepped close and put his arms around her. "That was me…as Regen van—"

Suddenly, she jerked away from Ben and paced around the room, pinching her brow.

"Rayne, what is it?" He reached for her, but she waved him off and danced out of his way.

"Wait. There was something…" She continued her head-down pacing, dodging chairs, mumbling, "Regen, Rayne. Regen, Rayne." The TV filled with people shouting in silence, climbing over chairs, then it switched to shots of the choir and orchestra as Rayne paced in front of the big screen. Abruptly her head popped up, wild eyes darting between Addison and him.

"Rayne?" Ben asked gently, afraid he'd spook her.

"The man," she said, her breath coming in shallow gasps. "He called me Regen van Onweer."

Rayne checked the blue display on the bedside clock: 2:14 am. She'd fallen into a deep sleep around 11:30 only to wake two hours later, and she'd been tossing ever since. Sighing, she threw back the covers and pulled a sweatshirt over her pajama top. Still without slippers of her own, she stuffed her feet into a pair of white Moon Boots Mandy had loaned her, and shuffled toward the kitchen.

The house rested quietly even if she didn't. Even with the lights out, enough LEDs shined from the phone, cell chargers, and stereo equipment to guide her path through the great room. The small mantle clock ticked away the sleepless seconds as she passed. She smelled coffee and saw dim light from the kitchen. Her boots squeaked on the hardwood as she rounded the corner.

One of the under-cabinet lights was on low, and soft blue light from the refrigerator water dispenser splashed like a shallow pool on the tile floor. Across the kitchen, Ben half-turned where he stood staring out the window above the sink into the blackness beyond. He was barefoot.

She hadn't seen him barefoot since... Memories flooded her mind. Their little cabin that first winter had been drafty and cold, and she-of-the-perpetually-cold-feet sought his rough but warm ones as they snuggled in bed, laughing as he howled and tickled her in return for her icy intrusion. Did he still have calluses from his years of surfing? An ache began down deep in her chest. She had missed so much.

Her eyes scanned up again, taking in rumpled pajama bottoms with some sort of hunting scene, and a gray T-shirt with big letters spelling out Storm Lake Bait & Tackle over a hooked trout thrashing above the water. Blond stubble softened his jawline, and his hair stuck up in ways that made her want to smooth it with her fingers. She stopped just inside the room and leaned against the granite counter, unable to breathe easily, as if she were the one with the damaged ribs.

His eyes regarded her in hooded silence. But then they'd both enjoyed solitude, even while together in the same room, or on a hike along the lake or in the hills above the group of cabins called Gift. Although she spent so much time making noise with her music, it was tranquil quiet from which she drew strength and rejuvenation, bringing new messages to share and the passion to proclaim them.

With Ben, though, she'd rarely known his thoughts. Oh, she was confident he had them. Deep intelligence snapped behind those blue eyes like the plasma ball globes she used in some of their Elusive Hope concerts. But—at least when they were first together—she'd been left to wonder what he felt. When the cancer struck his mom, he'd had such a difficult time talking about it. And when Rayne wanted to leave to pursue music, he'd been mostly silent, which she interpreted as not caring—at least not enough.

Then he hadn't come after her. Yes, she'd been the one to leave, but *he hadn't come.* For years she expected him to show up at one of her concerts. Every time a tall, blond man entered the door of a club where she played, her heart stuttered, and she squinted against the spotlights. Not Ben Conner.

Never Ben Conner.

Rayne blinked away the wet on her lashes as she turned away from the kitchen and walked to the French doors leading to the patio and lake beyond. The night's cold radiated off the black glass like an open freezer, and she wrapped her arms around herself, chilled in spite of the thick sweatshirt. Far across to the northwest, a few lights from Deer Cove shone bravely across the rippling water.

She knew when he stood behind her, close but not touching. Maybe it was his body heat or the soft sigh of his breath that caused her to lean back. Whichever, it felt right, just as it should. His arms wrapped her tight against his warm chest, and her eyes closed, blocking out the cold beyond the glass, the cold in her soul.

Ben Conner had come for her tonight. When she'd crawled through that pitch-black barn, bleeding and terrified, and buried herself in that old quilt, it was Ben she wanted, him who she prayed would come. And he had. Broken ribs and all.

Ben rested his chin on her shoulder, their heads touching as he rocked her side to side. In rare quiet moments when she was alone in her house in Boskoop and dared open her heart and let her feelings emerge, this was what she missed the most. They fit together, yet they were so different, from different worlds. But one thing Rayne knew well: as much as she'd accomplished in music, she'd missed so much more. She'd missed Ben.

"I'm sorry." His words were a bare whisper tickling her hair, communicated as much through his warm arms as by his voice.

They were quiet for a long while. Rayne stared at the distant lights, but saw only the ghostly couple reflected in the hard glass. She drew a shallow breath.

"Me, too."

CHAPTER THIRTY

Ben hung up the phone in his office and tilted back in the desk chair. Addison had been burning up the lines with the Dutch police as well as the authorities in Atlanta, but neither group were convinced the would-be killer had tracked Regen van Onweer to Storm Lake, California.

After all, Regen was a well-known figure throughout Europe's music circles. Elusive Hope had three CDs in circulation worldwide with Regen's photo on the cover and in the liner notes, and the band had several Internet fan sites devoted to their music, with hundreds of concert and publicity photos.

A simple image search would bring up dozens of photos of her and the band. Blog postings tracked the members' personal travel, relationships, and diet. Girls were captivated by Regen's fashion, and guys by her stunning onstage outfits, fan-blown hair, and siren's voice. The authorities argued that Regen at five foot eleven inches stood out in any crowd. How could it be unusual that one person—an innocent fan, perhaps—recognized her, especially after she'd just sung at a public festival at the lake?

Addison's frustration had practically singed the phone line when he told Ben the men he talked to hinted at his lack of professionalism for letting her out in public at all after an attempt on her life. If she wasn't going to hide from view, there wasn't anything they could do from across the nation or across the Atlantic. Addison officially disagreed, but he and Ben could do nothing other than take their own precautions here in Storm Lake.

Ben certainly wasn't convinced a fan had called out Regen's name in the dark by the barn. And if it was a fan, where had he gone? No, Ben didn't believe it for a second.

He closed his company job folders on the desk and dropped them into his briefcase. He'd spent the morning scheduling new security work and talking to Kurt about repairs and installations on jobs Ben couldn't be at for a few days. Kurt's cousin was helping for a few weeks since Ben wouldn't be in any shape to shimmy through crawl spaces.

The call from Addison left Ben wanting nothing more than to get out of the house, even though the doctor wanted him confined for a couple more days. Heaven forbid the doc find out about his high-speed race last night.

A noise from the main part of the house drew him out of the office. Rayne sat on a barstool drinking a cup of coffee and eating what looked like a scone. Then he saw the box of Bisquick on the counter and a cookie sheet in the sink.

"Got any more of those?" he asked as he rounded the breakfast bar.

"Only a dozen or so." Rayne tilted her cup toward the counter by the stove. "But I suspect the count will change rapidly when Quin gets home." The dark circles under her eyes indicated she hadn't gotten much sleep either.

Ben hoisted one of the monster pastries off a wire cooling rack. He hadn't even known he *had* a cooling rack. He broke off a sizable chunk of the scone and popped it in his mouth. "Wow. This is *good*."

"Glad you like it." She rewarded him with a smile. "Special recipe, plus some of the dried cranberries I found in the pantry."

"I think Quin bought those for trail mix." Ben chewed in silence for a moment as he regarded her. She needed something to put color back in her cheeks. He checked the digital clock on the microwave: nearly eleven o'clock. "You up for a little trip? I want to check the Bronco."

Rayne narrowed her eyes at him for a few heartbeats, then headed for the coat rack by the front door. He appreciated that she didn't try to talk him out of another road trip. He stuffed the last of the scone in his mouth and wrapped another in a paper towel before following her out.

Rayne drove, handling the big truck with ease and missing most of the chuckholes Addison had plowed through last night. At the Beauty Barn parking lot, she steered around to the right where the Bronco sat among the workers' vehicles. The sun broke through high clouds as they climbed out, and Rayne turned her face to the warmth, eyes closed, a smile pulling at her full mouth. It amazed Ben she could appear serene after last night's trauma. She was remarkably stronger now at thirty-five than she'd been as a twenty-year-old newlywed, but he still glimpsed that youthful innocence, especially when he surreptitiously watched her talking with Quin.

She had changed in the past fifteen years. Ben had too. He couldn't expect them to fit back into old routines, but down deep he wanted another chance, a chance to do it right this time around.

Rayne raised the Bronco hood and used the bumper as a stepladder to hoist herself up with her good leg so she could see better. It took only a second to spot the coil wire hanging loose. Ben plugged it back into the distributor cap.

"I don't understand it. I just put new wires on and this is the second time it's come off. They're a good brand." He tugged on the wire—it was stuck tight in the plastic cap. "Want to give it a try?" he said, handing her the keys.

She climbed in and turned the key. The engine cranked several times without success.

"Are you choking it?" he called from the front of the vehicle. She answered affirmatively. He could see the throttle linkage moving as she pumped the accelerator, and the smell of gas filled the engine compartment. After a couple more rotations she turned the key off.

Ben started checking all the wiring connections. When he pulled on the coil wire again, this time it came off at the coil end. "What in the world...?" He shoved it into the coil until it bottomed in the socket, then leaned around the hood. "Try it now."

The engine roared to life. Rayne shoved in the choke as it warmed up and the motor slowed to a smooth idle. She hopped out and joined him at the front. He explained about the loose wire.

"It never missed a beat when I drove here yesterday. Hard to believe it came loose at both ends." She looked to Ben and he nodded in agreement. "Of course the wire did come off with Mandy that time. Guess it could happen."

Ben wasn't so sure, but then again, he had no proof. If the wire or other parts had been missing altogether, that would have proved tampering beyond a doubt. As it stood, they were left wondering about the reliability of the Bronco, and the motives of the man who'd called her *Regen.*

"Hey, Rock Star," Mandy called as the front door banged behind her, cutting off the sound of Tori's car leaving. A huge grin covered her face as she slid onto the bar stool beside Rayne.

Rayne shot her a world-class knock-it-off glare, but it slid off the peppy teenager like an egg off Teflon. Almost before Rayne could focus, the girl had hopped off the stool, grabbed a mug out of the cupboard, filled it with coffee, milk, and sugar, then was back on the stool. It made Rayne's head spin. It didn't help that she was dead on her feet from lack of sleep, hence the third cup of coffee this afternoon. Her insides were dancing the caffeine jitterbug, but her brain still felt like a low-lying Holland bog.

"So, I checked out some of your music last night after Quin called," Mandy said over the rim of her mug. The two soon-to-be cousins had tied up the phone lines after Quin saw the video of her concert and shooting. "Wow. You guys are *so hot.*" Mandy took another sip. "Can't believe I didn't know about you—*and* your cute drummer. What's his name again?"

"He is way too old for you, young lady. Don't get any ideas." Danny had turned twenty-eight in August—nearly twice Mandy's age.

"Sooo...have you two like dated or anything?" Mandy asked, shoulder-bumping Rayne, the grin growing wider, if that were possible.

"I'm way too old for *him,*" Rayne said. Truth was, they *had* dated a few times, informally, movies or a picnic, but she'd never reveal that to Mandy. Danny was a dear friend, but a relationship beyond that had never felt right, at least not to her. Seven years older seemed like a lifetime, especially when Rayne compared Danny to Ben who was eleven years her senior. She did a quick mental calculation: Ben was eighteen years older than Danny. It made Danny seem like a teenager.

"You're not too old," Mandy countered, undeterred. "Besides, Rock Star chicks *always* date younger guys, and only cute ones."

"Your dad lets you watch too much television," Rayne mumbled.

"YouTube." Mandy sipped her coffee, apparently unconcerned about her uncle catching her again.

"What?"

"Elusive Hope is all over YouTube. There are tons of videos. The quality isn't great on most of them, but they're still amazing."

Rayne knew the music videos were up on dozens of video sharing sites. Her producers were torn between demanding they come down due to copyright violations or leaving them up for the buzz they generated for concert ticket sales. Generally the audio wasn't the best quality, so present consensus was to leave them up. Suddenly Rayne realized what other videos might be up there, but before she could bring it up, Mandy huddled over her coffee mug.

"I also saw parts of your last concert—and the shooting," she said in a voice so low Rayne had to strain to hear. "I'm so sorry. It must have been awful." She stared into the cup.

Rayne put her arm around the girl and hugged her close. "Yeah. But I'm past it and healing up fine, thanks to your help. I'll soon be good as new."

Silently, Rayne wondered if that were true. In time she would heal physically, although she might have lingering aches and pains from the trauma to her body. But what about the psychological damage? One guy calling her name last night had flipped her into full-on panic mode, resulting in her tearing off barn siding with her bare hands and crawling through a dark room to hide under a quilt.

Had she overreacted? What if it *was* only some poor fan who'd recognized her and wanted an autograph? How long would it take before the sight of a tulip—glued hybrid or not—would seem normal? She didn't want to spend the rest of her life looking over her shoulder, or tensing for a bullet every time she walked on stage.

She rose and took her cup to the sink. The cool water running over her fingers felt normal. If only her life were so.

"Rayne?" Mandy still sat at the bar. "Are you scared?"

Rayne's back stiffened at the simple question. Enough of the little girl remained in this near adult that she wanted reassurance everything would be all right. Rayne could tell her the authorities would catch the bad guy and lock him up forever, that she would be free again to write new, amazing songs for a band that was slipping away from her. Tell her even that she and Ben would get back together. Rayne had no idea if any of those would happen, or even if she wanted them all to.

"More scared than I've been in my whole life," she admitted. About *all* the unknowns.

Mandy let out a big sigh and nodded. "Thanks for being honest with me." She took her own mug to the sink and rinsed it out.

Rayne swallowed her own sigh. It was time to lighten the mood. "Other than pestering a crippled rock star, did you come over for a reason today?" Mandy gave a little smile, heaviness temporarily forgotten.

"Yes." The girl dropped her gaze, suddenly interested in the tile floor. "I, uh..."

"Mandy. What is it?"

"I still haven't decided on a dress for the wedding."

"What?" Rayne shook the girl's shoulders. "Mandy, that's a week from tomorrow!"

"I know, I know," Mandy whined, frown lines appearing on her smooth forehead. "I just... I wondered—I mean, after seeing your sense of fashion and all from the videos—if you'd help me shop for one?" She smiled sweetly.

Rayne narrowed her eyes, then flicked them to the clock on the microwave. Not three-thirty yet. They could pop down to Mission Peak and hit some of the stores, maybe grab some dinner. Tomorrow was Saturday, so Mandy wouldn't have to be up for school. Rayne hoped *she* could stay awake.

"And," Mandy interrupted Rayne's thinking, "I could get in more driving experience." Her smile grew bigger.

Rayne leveled a stern gaze at the girl, but she couldn't maintain it and burst out laughing. "You are really good, young lady. I didn't stand a chance, did I?"

Mandy lifted the Bronco keys off the bar where Rayne had left them and dangled them from a finger. Her lips formed a seductive pout. "Kind of sad, isn't it?"

Rayne laughed again. It felt good. She'd missed Mandy since Tori's hours were decreased for winter at the Shelter Cove store and she couldn't give Mandy a ride as often.

Rayne called up the stairs to Quin and told him a pot of chili for dinner was in the refrigerator along with French bread buttered and wrapped in foil. She gave him instructions on what to do and where they were going. She grabbed her wallet and jacket, and they headed for the garage.

"Hey, Rayne?" Mandy stopped in the doorway, face sober.

"Yes?" Rayne asked, concerned at the girl's sudden seriousness. Was she worried about her own safety around Rayne? Maybe she feared for Quin, that he might get hurt. "What is it?"

One side of the girl's mouth twitched. "Just how old *is* Danny Haynes?"

Rayne turned toward the Bronco, Mandy's laugh at her back. The brat had known his name all along.

CHAPTER THIRTY-ONE

From the floral, overstuffed chair in his cabin, Raoul regarded the fist-sized holes in the wall. Drywall dust, rendered pink in the low afternoon sun streaming in the front windows, lay in a cloud across the plank floor like colored confectioner's sugar. A deeper red smeared the knuckles of both his hands where they lay on the rounded arms. Someone had thought the sun-yellow fabric with giant roses and peonies pretty. Someone insane. He rubbed his knuckles into the yellow. His blood didn't quite match the dusty red of the leafy petals. Perhaps Marielle's would.

Comforting lassitude suffused every cell in his body, and dragged him down into the deep cushion. It was always this way after he released the wolf inside. Now he could objectively analyze the hunt.

Last night he'd failed. He'd thought the timing perfect. Everyone had left the barn and only Regen van Onweer remained.

He tried not to think about her, but she filled every corner of his mind. Marielle belonged to him, and he'd almost made her his own. In his haste to have her, he'd made one simple mistake: he'd called Regen van Onweer by her real name, not the pseudonym she used in this community. Rayne Evans. What was that? Weak, puny. A commoner's moniker, that's what it was.

She should be proud of a name like Regen van Onweer. It carried power. Rain Storm. Like his own name, Raoul Kloepper. Wolf Hunter. Worthy adversaries: her beauty and his unstoppable strength.

Marielle.

They must be together.

He flicked his finger at a drop of blood, dried to a hard ball on a white peony imprinted on the fabric. What if last night hadn't been a failure? Perhaps he'd gone about this all wrong. Where was the victory in taking her in private? His hunting skill deserved to be showcased as a masterpiece. In Rotterdam, he'd nearly taken her in a most dramatic way, but he'd felt the loss of not being able to touch her, hold her, feel the release of his Marielle. Distance robbed him of the pleasure.

Yet last night hadn't been right either. There was no audience, no one to appreciate his accomplishment. A private capture didn't give his talent proper exhibition. The world should know him in his moment of greatest strength.

"I need to do both," he proclaimed in sudden revelation to the drywall dust. "Take her publicly, someplace where everyone will notice, and then privately. Let the people mourn her disappearance even as she becomes mine."

He rose, ignoring the pain as his battered fingers tore free of the fabric, and checked his watch. There was time. Not much, but enough. Using a bloodied fingernail, he lifted a magnetic business card from the refrigerator, carried it to the phone and dialed the printed number.

"Deer Cove Auto, Mark speaking," the voice on the other end answered.

"Yes. I wonder if you might be able to help me. I've suffered a breakdown in my car."

"Sure, where's it located? Wait. Hold on." The man's voice grew muffled for a few seconds and papers shuffled. "Okay, go ahead."

Raoul gave him directions to the VW and told him the symptoms.

"Okay. Half mile north of town, dark gray '75 Super Beetle," Mark repeated back. "Let's see...yep, I can go get it right now. What's your name and the best number to reach you?"

Raoul hesitated. Bad enough to call local help, but another thing altogether to reveal too much. He hadn't bothered to register the car, so his name wasn't on any of the records.

"E. Hope," he told the mechanic, smiling at his cryptic joke. He told the mechanic he'd call first thing in the morning to review the projected repairs. That done, it was time to plan.

He embraced the pain when the cuts along his knuckles cracked open as he searched the tiny local newspaper. Only a dozen pages long, it came out every Thursday, and he'd picked up a copy at the gas station. There—an ad on page six. Sunday afternoon and evening. Shelter Cove Holiday Fair, to be held on the other side of the lake at Shelter Cove, just north of Conner's house. Booths with holiday foods, locally made gifts, lighting the giant Christmas tree, and—ah, yes…live entertainment.

Raoul walked to the four-by-five-foot cork board he'd propped against the wall at the end of the dining table. His fingers trailed over a dozen photos of Regen van Onweer singing at clubs, strolling by quaint shops in Boskoop, exiting the front door of Bibs' Beauty Barn. Though only two-dimensional, Raoul stroked the matte surface, imagining the texture of her clothes, her skin, the hair that should always be long and black as midnight.

"Will you be at the Holiday Fair, Regen van Onweer? Will you sing?" She lived close enough—right down the road. His blood fizzed with absolute certainty. "Oh, yes. And I'll be there, too. We'll be together at last, Marielle."

Save your last breath for me.

"The craft fair? Are you out of your mind, Bibs?" Ben shouted into the phone that had rung the second he'd stepped in the front door. "No way she's performing Sunday after what happened, and I don't care how many people have asked for her." He tried to shuck his jacket while holding the phone, wincing as he tweaked his ribcage.

Against doctor's orders, he'd driven to a job site today to help Kurt with an estimate for installation of door and window alarms at a "Hollywood home," as Kurt called it. Owned by a producer from Los

Angeles, the house sat on a low bluff with a three-hundred-degree view of the Pacific. The monstrosity was huge—at least compared to the typical two thousand square foot or smaller homes in the coastal area north and south of Perilous Cove.

"When people have more to lose, they call us," Ben had told Kurt as they inventoried windows and external entry points seemingly without end. They'd passed at least four wall-filling flat screen TVs and multiple smaller ones, even in the bathrooms.

Kurt had grinned while enthusiastically filling in his estimate sheet. "I'm smelling Christmas bonus."

But Ben wasn't grinning now as Bibs carried on about how much they needed Rayne. The Shelter Cove Holiday Fair generally attracted only locals as it wasn't promoted outside the area—kind of a family celebration after all the seasonal crowds left and the lake reverted to the quiet community so many remembered from past decades. Attendees traded and bought homemade goods, from fruit spreads to quilts, gift baskets to hand carved clocks. People could set up tables or popup tents if they wanted, but no one collected fees.

According to Bibs, Butch Murray, a guitar-playing cowboy poet from Paso Robles—this year's entertainment—landed in the hospital with bronchitis yesterday, leaving the stage bare for Sunday, just two days away. Ben couldn't care less.

"No one knows where this whacko is, Bibs, or even *who* he is. He might be from out of town, but that doesn't mean he isn't staying in one of the houses. He could know about the fair."

"Yes, I guess that's true. But he wouldn't know Rayne was singing. No one would know until she got up there." The old woman sighed across the wire, obviously struggling with the request. "I know it's a lot to ask. But we'll all be there, Ben. We'll double-team her tighter than the NBA, and you can whisk her away the moment she's finished. You remember the sheriff is my second cousin? He owes me a favor, and I intend to call it in." Bibs wasn't only built like a bulldog, she had the will of one, too.

Ben pinched his forehead. True, the crowd would be much smaller than the fall event at Bibs's barn, and he could ask Addison to come up as added security. But if this guy at the barn was the same nutcase who'd shot Rayne and Dolina Macgowan…

"Just ask her, Ben. Okay? It would mean so much to all the people who worked hard on the fair. It'd be a shame not to have some live music."

Ben reluctantly agreed to ask Rayne, silently fearing her response, then hung up the phone, wishing he'd never answered it. A clank from the kitchen drew him through the great room. Quin stood at the stove stirring what looked and smelled like chili.

"Rayne went dress shopping with Mandy, so I'm fixing dinner." The boy's face showed determination as he carefully scraped the sides of the pot with a large wooden spoon. "The garlic bread is in the oven."

"Wow, I'm impressed," Ben said, bending over the pot and inhaling the savory spices. "This your special recipe?"

The boy grinned widely. "Nah. Rayne made it earlier. I'm just warming it up. I sure wish I could cook like her. She makes good stuff."

"What? Better than me?" Ben gave Quin a stricken look.

Quin didn't waver. "Yep. Better than you." Then they burst out laughing.

Ben wasn't a terrible cook, but from what people around the lake said, Quin's dad had been a cut above the norm. He'd won a couple of local prizes for his bourbon barbecue ribs.

Ben grabbed a soda from the refrigerator and popped the tab. He raised the can in salute. "Here's hoping you take after your dad in the kitchen department." Ben took a sip. "Maybe we should enroll you in cooking classes right away so you can get started."

Quin considered that as he finished stirring, tapped the spoon on the edge of the pot, and adjusted the flame to simmer. He turned to Ben. "That would be cool."

Ben raised his eyebrow. He'd been joking, but Quin was serious. Maybe there was more of the old man in the boy than Ben first thought.

Quin lit the logs in the fireplace, then ran upstairs to finish his homework. Ben, still not trusting his ability to get up from the soft leather chairs, lowered himself onto the edge of the coffee table and stretched his legs toward the growing fire. Fragrant smoke curled into the room before the chimney built up a draft.

He loved winter at the lake—the nights so cold and clear, "You can pick a dozen or two stars and make a moon pie," his dad used to say. Next month would be three and a half years since he'd died two weeks before Christmas. It made the holidays rough. But more than Ben's own loss, he wished his dad could have known Quin. The boy might not be technically carrying on the Conner name, but Ben was already proud of the man he was becoming. He also wished Dad could have met Rayne as she was now—a woman, not a girl.

When it came to Rayne, the future was still a dark mystery. Whether she would leave or choose to stay, he was thankful for this time. And recently he'd begun to wonder why he'd never gone after her when she left the first time. Sure he had lots of reasons: his mother fell ill and his family needed him, money was tight, and he'd have lost his job. But Rayne was his wife, and he'd lost her instead.

He had committed to her and should have followed. Not to drag her back like some caveman, but in support. Looking back, it had been the biggest mistake of his life. A plane ticket to Holland now seemed a small price to redeem fifteen years.

In the warmth of the fire, Ben let his eyes close and watched patterns flickering on the inside of his eyelids like images from a projector. Rayne and Mandy shopping—now there was a vision. Mandy had been such a perfect match for Sam Riley a year ago, strengthening the woman in ways neither Ben nor Addison fully understood. And now Mandy played much the same role for Rayne, offering far more than mere physical therapy. The girl had the gift of encouragement and genuine depth. He was proud of her, and knew Addison was as well.

All the Conner children and soon-to-be children were survivors. Mandy lost her mom and had been shot; Star's parents abandoned her as a toddler and then her grandmother died; and Quin's mom deserted the family before his dad died in the accident. But it wasn't those experiences that defined them or even made them strong. No, they were strong before those events happened. Their strength brought them through. Whether due to genetics, God's grace, or both, they'd each come through tough times as better people.

Rayne fit right in. Her fortitude never failed to surprise him. Most women—men, even—would hide out if someone hunted them. But not Rayne. Nope. She was out shopping with a teenager.

Quin's padded steps sounded on the stairs and Ben heard him do a sock-skid stop by the fireplace. He cracked one eye open to find the boy staring at him, head cocked to one side.

"Why are you smiling, Ben?"

CHAPTER THIRTY-TWO

"Well, then, I'd better start practicing," Rayne told Ben, then picked up her coffee and headed toward the piano room.

"Rayne, wait." The concern in Ben's voice stopped her, and she turned to him. "Are you sure?"

Worry lines creased his brow, and her fingers twitched with her desire to smooth them away. The poor man hadn't slept well last night, especially since she and Mandy were gone until after eleven o'clock on their girls' shopping excursion.

After hitting the stores in Mission Peak, they'd swung by Sam and Star's in Perilous Cove where Mandy tried on the three dresses she'd picked out. Then Star ran to try on *her* dress to see which of Mandy's matched the best. The mini fashion show lengthened considerably when Addison arrived. Sam microwaved popcorn and whipped up a batch of brownies more gooey-chocolate than cake, and the evening had turned into a party.

During the party, Rayne observed the still-forming family in action. Addison sneaked glances at Sam constantly, like he couldn't get enough of her. And when Sam caught him staring and they both blushed like teenagers, they often moved together and entwined their fingers.

Rayne and Ben had that same easy intimacy once, hands finding each other as they walked the coarse sand at Perilous Cove Beach, or while snuggled in a darkened movie theater. They could sit for an hour reading in chairs at the lake, summer-heated water lapping their toes, and suddenly he'd take her hand or brush a wayward strand of hair from her face. Her body had always moved toward him naturally—like that night in the pantry...and the kiss. She envied Addison and Sam for what they had and hoped it would last the rest of their lives.

Obviously Mandy and Star were comfortable with their coming-together home situation. In their minds they were already a family, the upcoming wedding just an excuse for a party. For the first time, Rayne found herself relaxing around Addison. When she and Ben had married, Addison and his first wife, Elizabeth, lived out of state, so the two couples spent only a few days together here and there. Then, as the strain began with Ben, Rayne had opted out of a few family gatherings with his parents. She realized now that her pulling back made it easier to leave.

In some ways she felt more guilt today than in those first few years after separating from Ben. Initially, she'd been so focused on music and career, she barely had time to do anything but survive week to week, taking part-time jobs, playing in clubs, fronting as a singer for various bands, or filling in on keyboard when someone got sick. She went many a day with only one meal that first year. The more time passed, the less she dwelt on Rayne Conner. Music had filled her hours, her life, her heart.

Returning to Storm Lake—to Ben and everyone in the close community—had changed that. For the first time she saw the damage she'd caused. Admittedly self-absorbed, she always thought the hurt was to her alone. But she'd hurt Ben and others, and it weighed on her now. With a few facts changed, theirs could have been a twist on Marielle's story. The anguished feeling of betrayal, the tearing separation. The names had been changed to protect the innocent, as the narrator said, but all players lived the pain. The final chapter in Marielle's life brought a chance of vindication and victory, of reunited love. Rayne wondered if that paralleled her own life as well.

As she watched Addison and Sam's new family, she understood how much she'd missed. What if she had stayed? Even the salted popcorn and brownies failed to settle her stomach as she realized she'd put far more effort into her career than their marriage. Some days it sucked getting wiser as she grew older.

Eventually the evening had wound down, and she'd called Ben and told him not to worry. Addison had insisted she drive his Audi and leave him the Bronco. Still, Ben had been waiting by the fire when she had come in the front door.

This morning, sunlight streamed through the east-facing great room windows, washing wood and leather with buttery warmth. Those same rays cast shadows in the deepening lines at the corners of Ben's eyes. Rayne sighed and returned to the kitchen bar where he leaned, always seeking a comfortable position for his ribs. She slid onto the stool next to him.

"No, I'm not sure," she answered his question about performing. "I'm not sure of anything in my life right now." It was the truest thing she'd admitted in weeks. She'd been stalked, shot, then stalked some more. She'd kissed her ex-husband—and enjoyed it. Wanted more. Mandy had become a friend, a sister, someone to trade inside jokes with, girl to girl. And Quin...she loved sitting with him by the fire, reading, or talking. The fishing trip on his boat had been special. She wanted more time with him and his Rice Krispies treats. The thought of going back to her house in Boskoop and living alone ran like an icy river down her core.

As much as she missed her band, it was more the *concept* of the band she missed. The only one who might miss her was Danny. She'd never been that close to Pieter, Hans, or Eva. Professionally they clicked, but they had little in common socially. Those three liked the rock star status and lived it to the full, partying after every concert and landing in jail a couple of times. That wasn't the image Rayne wanted for herself or Elusive Hope.

Beyond the patio doors, the lake community from which she'd once fled now called to her in ways that triggered creativity—totally the reverse of what it had been all those years ago. Simple things like this dumb holiday fair at Shelter Cove sent her mind into high rev. Her fingertips itched with ideas for new songs.

Could she have a life here, with Quin and Ben? Could it really be that simple? *Yes*, instead of *no*? She glanced at Ben, his face close, so familiar.

He wore a plaid flannel shirt, and she longed to bury her face in the soft warmth and inhale his scent, let him hold her and make everything all right.

"Rayne." Ben's voice brought her back to unwanted reality. "He might be here at the lake. He could show up at the festival. There's no guarantee we can keep you safe." Life fell again on her shoulders like one of the old feed sacks in the back of Bibs's barn, unclean and messy. She laid her hand on his forearm.

"I won't let fear chase me away, Ben," she said, then realized she should have spoken those words fifteen years ago. She'd been scared of losing out on a music career. Well, she'd gotten what she'd wanted, hadn't she? She took a breath. "It was different in the barn's parking lot alone at night. And I can't even be sure I heard what I think I did."

"You were sure then."

She sighed and nodded. "Anyway, at the fair I'll be surrounded by … people." She wanted to say *family* but the word wouldn't quite come. Instead, she forced a reassuring smile—hoping it worked better on him than on herself.

She'd been surrounded by people in Rotterdam at the Ahoy, and that hadn't stopped the gunman. The barn incident had shaken her more than she let on, and one thing she couldn't stand was the thought of putting anyone else in danger. Lorna and Dolina could have been killed.

But it just didn't make sense that the shooter had tracked her here. No one outside the lake community knew where she was, except her mother. Much as they didn't get along, her mother would never let that secret out. Plus, her Atlanta condo had gone on the market, and she was spending most of her time in Florida.

Rayne headed toward the piano room. "I have some new song ideas for tomorrow."

"Of course you do. I'll have Quin drag you out for lunch and dinner." Ben's grin gave her confidence.

She prayed it would be enough.

Ben's ribs grated as he stirred the thick soup bubbling in the Dutch oven. "Should have used the microwave."

"What's that, cowboy?" Rayne came up behind him and placed her hand in the small of his back. She leaned over and inhaled. "Um. Smells good. Enough for me?"

He was surprised she'd come up for air after being sequestered in the piano room for several hours, but he held the thought when her fingers drew warm circles on his spine. If she'd keep that up, he'd feed her the whole pot while doing a one-armed handstand, sore ribs and all.

Instead of the handstand, they ate on the patio where Quin had a winter-chasing fire roaring in the pit. Crackling bursts propelled tongues of flame and fragrant oak smoke into the night. Rayne sat with Ben on the bench, a blanket wrapped around her back as she sopped up the soup with large chunks of hot, crusty French bread. She caught him staring.

"What?" she asked around a huge mouthful, and he laughed out loud.

"You eat like a prisoner just released."

"Well, I'm hungry." She tore off another chunk of warm bread and pointed it like a gun. "Music's hard work, buddy boy. Not like laying around in attics all day playing with wires and cameras."

Ben put his hand over his heart. "Oh, you wound me, woman." Quin laughed, and Rayne threw a small chunk of bread, popping him squarely on the nose, which only caused him to fall on the ground in exaggerated hysterics. A bread war ensued until Rayne declared a truce so they wouldn't starve.

Sitting around the fire like this, they could have been any happy family around the lakeshore taking advantage of the clear, chilly evening, and Ben's heart ached with could-have-been's and might-be's. He'd been a fool to let her go without a fight, and he'd come to a firm conclusion: he wanted her back. A decade and a half separated them from those two headstrong young people. He wanted to know this woman who dressed in Gothic costume and commanded thousands of screaming fans, but could entertain a beauty shop of old ladies just as easily.

"Tell me about your home in Boskoop and about your music." The words were out of Ben's mouth before he thought about them.

The large piece of bread dripping with hot soup slipped from Rayne's fingers and landed with a splat on the cold pavers unnoticed, and her mouth hung slightly open.

"I'd like to know," he said, realizing they were words that, had he spoken them fifteen years ago, would have made all the difference.

He watched Rayne's face transform as she told them of her home. How her neighbors, old Mr. and Mrs. Ostrander, had planted at least two hundred new tulip bulbs every year for the past thirty years along the canal bank. And, when they bloomed, boats would come from miles around to cruise the canal and take pictures. The flowers ranged from black to blood-red to yellow so bright you had to wear sunglasses.

"And then I wrote the story of Marielle. She's an innocent young girl who trusts too much and is betrayed. But she's a fighter and gets stronger with each experience. I themed the songs around colors that matched the emotion. I matched the lighting cues to the lyrics and used scrim and a projector for background images and..."

Excitement poured from her as she told of the music production, the arrangements, playing in venues large and small, indoors and out. Sometimes she slipped into Dutch for a few words before catching herself. Quin found this hilarious and kept asking her to teach him words for *fire, log, soup,* and *bread.* The boy joined them on the bench, sitting on the other side of Rayne forcing her closer to Ben. She told about eating bread thick with butter and chocolate sprinkles for breakfast. Quin liked that idea, but wasn't impressed with French fries served with mayonnaise at *broodjeswinkels,* small sandwich shops serving inexpensive lunches.

Ben listened hard, fascinated by this woman he'd never known. Since coming to his house, he'd seen her as *his* Rayne, the way she'd been at twenty, simply older. He recognized his error as she described traveling to Britain, Germany, the Czech Republic, Poland, and a dozen other countries in Europe, moving with confidence through peoples, cultures, and languages. She'd grown into a capable, independent, professional woman. He wondered if she had someone special in her life across the globe. Maybe that was part of the reason she wanted to get back there.

His eyes narrowed at the thought of someone else caring for her, touching her, calling her name in the quiet of the night. She hadn't mentioned anyone, but then he'd never asked. Just assumed there wasn't anyone.

And—even if she didn't have anyone special in her life—was there room for him any longer? Or, in spite of the spot on his back that still tingled from her touch earlier, had she moved on?

Without him.

CHAPTER THIRTY-THREE

Sunday morning, they drove down to meet Addison, Sam, Mandy, and Star at Perilous Cove Community Church. Ben and Quin attended most weeks, but this was Rayne's first time since she'd been back. When they were first married, she and Ben had gone regularly with his folks.

Her heart thudded as they reached the top step and stood before the double doors. She couldn't seem to force enough air into her lungs. Ten thousand screaming fans were easier to face than the congregation waiting inside.

"They won't bite," Ben whispered in her ear as an elderly couple turned toward them.

"Maybe not *you*," she growled low enough so only he could hear. She pasted on what felt like a totally fake smile and shook the greeters' hands. Ben chuckled behind her as Quin led them into the chapel.

More than a few curious faces turned her way as they made their march down the center aisle, eyes zeroing in on Ben's proprietary hand heating the small of her back. Leave it to Addison to sit way down front. He probably did it on purpose.

Although she recognized a few older faces, she wondered even with her old haircut and Ben's proximity if they knew who she was. A few mouths dropped open.

Okay. Answered that *question.*

Since they had arrived right as the service began, there was no time for introductions, which suited Rayne. They slid into the pew with Addison, Sam, Star, and Mandy—the soon-to-be Conner crew, officially to be united right here in six days. Mandy reached across Quin and squeezed Rayne's hand. Rayne was sandwiched between Ben and Quin, the picture of a happy family to anyone who didn't know them, yet there was nothing conventional about their family makeup. They weren't even a family—at least she wasn't.

She tried to ignore glances swung her way as they all stood for the first hymn. Some undoubtedly recognized her as Ben's former wife, but what would their reaction be if they knew she dressed in elaborate costumes and performed in a rock metal band? She had to stifle a laugh. What a contrast of lives and associates. Many of her fans considered body piercing and tattoos mere fashion accessory—alternative beauty, they called it—and she'd seen every color of spiked Mohawk imaginable on both male and female. Danny joked they should sell their own Elusive Hope brand black eyeliner, and perhaps he wasn't wrong based on their audiences' tastes.

But she'd never been one to think God discriminated, allowing only the proper into his buildings while relegating the unseemly to a view through the windows. When home in Boskoop, she attended a small congregation in town, and the members always welcomed any of her fans who came out of curiosity, no matter how bizarre their wardrobe. Actually, it was her fans that were shocked at her understated Sunday dress and the fact that she attended church at all. A few of them had become regular attenders, and that made Rayne feel her music had reached across boundaries where simple words could not.

Up front a small band played a mix of modern worship songs and old hymns. Though many of the tunes were the same as at her church, it seemed strange to sing in English instead of Dutch. The drummer and lead guitar player were particularly talented and had Rayne wondering if they played professionally or only on Sundays. If she decided to do a bigger concert locally, they could provide good backup.

The pastor, who Ben told her had come to the church three years ago, spoke about the power in giving thanks, both for things from God and from man, and not just at the Thanksgiving holiday. Without thankfulness, people became indifferent consumers, taking from others but not responding or offering something in return. Believers in God should be examples of *thanks*-giving, first to God for the beauty of his love, then to all those around.

Did her music with Elusive Hope call people to appreciate others? Did it answer their needs and desires? Yes, she told stories of hardship and overcoming, the latest being Marielle's, stories with a strong moral, but could she do more?

Then another thought struck her so hard she jolted in the seat, and Ben's eyes cut to her in concern. She managed a quavering smile, enough to reassure him, but the guilt wouldn't go away as easily and bent her shoulders under its weight. Thankfulness for Ben had been the furthest thing from her mind when she'd fled their marriage. It had all been about her, a consumer, offering little in return. Without a backward glance, she'd set off to pursue her own career at the expense of her wedding vows.

Rayne dropped her head, grateful the pastor chose that moment to end the service with a prayer of thanksgiving and a time of silent reflection. She fished a tissue from her bag and dabbed her eyes. She guessed one of the purposes of church was to confront each person with their shortcomings, areas of life that could benefit from a do-over. There was plenty of that in her life. She could do better. *Would* do better.

When the service ended, Rayne excused herself to the restroom while several people greeted Ben and Quin. In the small room off the vestibule she blotted reddened eyes with a damp paper towel, then she escaped out a side door that led downhill to the parking lot. Situated a few blocks above the tiny town, the church afforded an unobstructed view across the rooftops, harbor, breakwater, and out to a vibrant Pacific of shifting greens and blues. The cool ocean air cleared her lungs, and she considered following the meandering footpath toward the harbor.

"Rayne!" Mandy bounced down the church stairs and trotted over. "Do you want to walk to town?"

Rayne glanced back to the church steps where Ben and Quin stood talking in a small group, then back at the harbor. Beyond the sunny patches, an ominous gray wall darkened the northwestern horizon, beginning its relentless advance on a breeze that sent a shiver up her spine. They'd have rain by sunset. She hoped the festival would be over before the storm hit.

"Hey," Mandy said gently, touching Rayne's arm. "You okay?"

Rayne regarded the teenager and discovered not a kid who wanted to go to the waterfront, but a young woman with kindness in her eyes. A friend. "No. But I *would* like to walk down to town."

"Got it." Mandy jogged back to tell Ben and Quin, then she joined Rayne for the downhill jaunt.

They walked in silence broken only by waves, birds, and the occasional barking dog. After a few minutes, Rayne turned to the girl.

"Sitting in church, I realized something." She paused to find the right words, the right way to say it. But there was no way except straight out. "I shouldn't have left."

Mandy was quiet for half a block, then she stopped in the middle of the sidewalk, put her head back and looked at the cirrus clouds speeding by high overhead as they led the storm ashore. "My mom shouldn't have died from cancer, either, Rayne. She was so beautiful, and Dad and I both needed her so much." The girl's eyes glistened.

"I'm sorry," Rayne said, feeling worse for making Mandy cry. "I didn't mean to stir up painful mem—"

"No no, that's not it," Mandy cut her off and faced her from a foot away. She gripped Rayne's upper arms. "If Mom hadn't died, Dad wouldn't have fallen in love with Sam. I wouldn't be gaining a sister. We'd probably still be living in Missouri, and I wouldn't have met you."

Rayne opened her mouth to respond, but nothing came out. Mandy turned and fingered some greenery spilling through a picket fence that lined the walkway.

"Don't get me wrong. I wish my mom was alive," Mandy said in a soft voice, "I really do. I don't know how it all works, but we don't get the chance to go back, only forward. I love Sam and Star. No one would want to lose one to gain the other. But I'm glad Sam and Star came into our lives." Her next words were so soft Rayne had to strain for them. "I'm glad *you* came."

Mandy turned back, gave Rayne a hug. "Sorry. I'm not making any sense." She slipped her arm through Rayne's, and they continued their walk.

Rayne again marveled at the young woman at her side and at what she'd said. Life took weird turns, either by external circumstances like the death of a spouse, or personal decisions like escaping a marriage. She'd chosen to leave Ben, and fifteen years had passed. There wasn't anything she could do to change that. But that didn't mean she couldn't begin again right now.

Life was full of choices, some in the past, but some still ahead. Addison and Sam had laid aside the pain of the past and fallen in love. Could she and Ben let go of a decade and a half and start again?

Rayne tugged Mandy tight against her as they rounded the corner on Harbor Street. "How did you grow to be so wise?"

"Practice." For a second, Mandy's eyes were filled with experience beyond her years, then she grinned, and it broke the seriousness of the moment. "Plus, I listen a lot in church."

Soon they mingled with other tourists strolling down the shop fronts and stopped to peek in windows at artwork, gifts, T-shirts, and cooking gadgets. Mandy slipped into a kite store to look for a gift for Star's birthday, and Rayne retraced their route to the previous window to look at handcrafted jewelry. A cold wind snapped the colorful flags mounted along the storefronts, and she stepped inside to warm up.

The storekeeper, a woman in her sixties with leathery skin crinkled by laugh lines, called a greeting from her messy work bench covered in jewelry-making materials. A small torch hissed blue flame as the woman joined silver wire. There was only one other customer in the store as Rayne worked her way around the perimeter of the shop, impressed by the jewelry maker's skill with stone, beads, and wire. A three-inch Celtic cross caught Rayne's attention, and she lifted the heavy silver to examine its intricate detail. She'd had one similar, but it was missing from her home after the vandalism. She liked this one better.

"Hello, there. I don't think we've met."

The curt voice swept away Rayne's peaceful shopping as effectively as a needle skipping across a disk jockey's LP. She turned and found a petite woman in a dove-gray dress standing too close with hand outstretched.

"I'm Kayleigh O'Hara. Are you new here? I saw you walk by the window with Mandy Conner," she explained to Rayne's questioning look. The sharp angle of the woman's wrist and tense stance contrasted with the friendly greeting, suggesting a business encounter with a competitor rather than a casual meeting.

Rayne took a half step back before accepting the woman's hand. "Rayne Evans. I'm…uh, just visiting." The woman's hand was cool and a bit too firm.

Flaming red hair cascaded over skin so fair it appeared translucent, and dustings of freckles floated across her nose like tan dots on the surface of a cream sea. Her hazel eyes slightly ruined the green-eyed Irish stereotype, and Kayleigh's voice held not a trace of the accent Rayne expected from her own trips to the Emerald Isle.

"Oh. Are you visiting Ben and Quin?"

Rayne opened her mouth to respond, but Kayleigh launched into a monologue about how she, Ben, and Quin had attended the Storm Lake Community Picnic in July, how she'd brought fennel baked chicken stuffed with mushrooms and brie, endive salad with blanched asparagus spears, and traditional Irish cookies from her grandmother's secret recipe. Rayne couldn't imagine Quin eating anything of what she described, except the cookies—maybe.

Just when it seemed Kayleigh showed signs of winding down, she sprinted ahead with a blow-by-blow of the Labor Day Festival in Perilous Cove when she and Ben danced on Harbor Street beneath paper lantern strings while a Mariachi band played. The muscles in Rayne's jaw twitched as the redhead described the warm, romantic evening. Rayne was pondering which of a dozen retorts she'd use when Mandy slid up beside her and linked their arms.

"There you are," she said to Rayne, then turned to the woman. "Hello, Kayleigh." Mandy's smoky alto hummed with subtle power and, not for the first time, Rayne wondered if she'd ever tried singing. With her looks and voice, she could fill a club just by reciting the lyrics. But if she could sing, well…

Side by side and both near six feet tall, Rayne and Mandy towered over the other woman. Kayleigh backed up a step—then another—to even things out.

"Mandy," the woman gave up the barest nod, her storytelling finally at an end. "How are things in *high* school?" Rayne choked back a laugh at the blatant reminder to Mandy of her place among adults.

Mandy lifted a brow, then turned to Rayne with her characteristic lopsided smile. "Ben's *asking* about you." Her husky stage whisper held a promise of things to come the eavesdropping redhead couldn't miss. Then Mandy, eyes round and innocent, faced the woman. "We're all going down to Wave Pizza before heading back to the lake. You're welcome to join us, Kayleigh."

After such blatant claim-staking, Rayne expected Ms. O'Hara to jump at a chance to insert herself into lunch, but her brows knitted, wrestling with the invitation.

"Ben and Quin are going for the meat lovers special," Mandy said, "and Sam and Star want the four cheese and pepperoni. And I *love* their salad bar—they have the best iceberg lettuce and ranch dressing." She actually licked her lips. If possible, Kayleigh's alabaster complexion blanched for a moment before she regained composure.

"Oh, well, I'd better not." The redhead pulled a lipstick out of her purse and touched up the already perfect bow using a compact mirror. "I have to go down to Mission Peak to meet a friend. A man. Man friend." She snapped the compact closed and narrowed her gaze at Mandy. "Maybe next time," she said, and fled out the shop door.

"Oh, sure. Bye Kayleigh," Mandy sing-songed sweetly to the woman's retreating back, then blew out a breath. "Another good deed done," she mumbled almost too low for Rayne to hear.

"What was that?"

"Kayleigh's a health food nut," Mandy said, as if that explained it all. "Let's go find Ben. I'm starved." She led the way out into the wind.

Rayne hurried to catch up and looked around. "Where is he? I thought you said he was asking about me?"

Mandy lifted the corner of her mouth. "I didn't say *when*, but he's *always* asking about you."

Rayne mulled that over as they walked. But had Ben really danced with the Kayleigh O'Hara right here on Harbor Street? Rayne hadn't considered Ben dating, but he could have been married and divorced several times during the years she'd been gone, and she wouldn't have been the wiser. The thought of him dancing with a snuggling Kayleigh O'Hara had sweat breaking out on her neck. *Minx.*

They spotted Ben, Quin, and Addison's family exiting a bookstore in the next block.

"Hey, Ben," Mandy called. "We're hungry and want to go to The Wave for the meat lover's special. You guys up for it?"

Quin's yell of delight nearly drowned out Ben's, "That's *Uncle* Ben to you, young lady."

Rayne tugged Mandy's arm, stopping the girl in the middle of the sidewalk. "Mandy. Ben wasn't planning on going to get pizza until you brought it up just now. Why did you tell Kayleigh we were already going?"

"Well...that's not *technically* what I said," she dodged. "I said, 'We're all going down to Wave Pizza before we head back to the lake.' And..." she pointed where Quin and Star were jumping up and down... "we *are* going."

"Yes, but it wasn't a sure thing while we talked to Kayleigh."

"Have you ever tasted Wave Pizza?" Mandy asked, as if that ruled out any other possible decision.

Ben *had* come home with pizza one night. Wherever it came from, the melting cheese, toasted onions, and triple meat had been to die for. She opened her mouth to voice another question, but Mandy went on.

"Besides, Ben and Quin *always* order the meat lover's special, and Sam and Star love the four cheese and pepperoni. No brainer there."

"Iceberg lettuce and ranch dressing?"

The girl licked her smiling lips. "Yumm."

"You're really good, young lady." Rayne shook her head in mock disappointment. Mandy pasted on such round-eyed innocence, Rayne's disapproval cracked. Then she hooked the girl's arm and lowered her voice to a whisper. "Does Ben really ask about me?"

Mandy's eyes grew bigger. "Of course he does. He says, 'What's up with my Rock Star chick?'"

Rayne laughed and hip-bumped the girl. Still, she recalled Ben's hand on her back as he'd escorted her down the church aisle. She had to admit, the spark still smoldered. Rayne turned to the teenager beside her. "Kayleigh never stood a chance, did she?"

Mandy set her mouth in a sad pout. "Kinda sad, isn't it?"

They both burst out laughing and turned toward the others' curious looks.

Raoul parked his VW in the hidden spot above the Conner house. Earlier, he had watched Van Onweer, Conner, and the boy climb into the big truck and drive away. Raoul had cautiously followed them all the way to Perilous Cove, stopping a block from the church parking lot and making sure they were going inside before heading back to the house.

He opened the car door and stepped out into the quiet of the day. They'd be in church for at least an hour. It gave him time to accomplish his goal.

Everything was in place. His car was repaired, although it cost over two hundred dollars for a new battery, spark plugs, and other tune-up parts. Worthless piece of…

He took a deep breath, forcing himself to exhale slowly. Calm. Calm. The automobile was a tool, an instrument for a purpose. His purpose. Today, Regen van Onweer would be his.

The exterior garage door opened easily with the duplicate key he'd had made at the hardware store in Perilous Cove. He slipped inside the silent garage, the only movement being dust motes gyrating in noiseless sunbeams radiating through the rollup windows. Most people never bothered to lock the door from garage to house, and Conner was no exception. Raoul walked into the warm kitchen, sliding his hand across the cool stone countertop and fingering the range controls. He could make a cup of tea, and no one would know.

Proud of the power he wielded, he relaxed and settled for the last cup of coffee from the Black & Decker unit on the counter. He reheated it in the microwave, using a mug with a black line around the rim. He'd seen Regen van Onweer walk through the house with the same cup, caressing its hot surface with her lips. Raoul slid his tongue along the rim.

He strolled through the house, sipping coffee as he peeked into bedrooms, bathrooms, and closets. In the small office, he found Conner's checkbook and removed half a dozen non-sequential checks. These he dropped into the shredder, recoiling as gnashing steel teeth sounded in the room. He smiled at the thought that Conner would wonder where the checks had gone, maybe even call the police about a theft, close the account. He deserved it.

Returning to Regen's room, Raoul lingered, inhaling. Her scent permeated everything, just as it had in her house in the Netherlands. It didn't belong here in Conner's house. Soon it would be Raoul's home filled with her scent.

He'd first seen her two years ago. Elusive Hope had been setting up in a mid-sized club in Germany, appropriately called The Wolf. Dressed in black jeans and a turquoise T-shirt, she'd hauled in equipment with the guys, sweating from positioning amps, cables, instruments, and microphones, before going to clean up and change. If he'd been in charge, the work would have been done by the others. Regen van Onweer shouldn't do manual labor. Even then he'd known she was destined to be the queen.

When she stepped onto the stage, she took his breath away. Clothed in a flowing white gown with black leather corset and boots, she wrapped long, sensuous fingers around the mic and sang in a soprano so pure he had to sit. His fingers clutched his chest where his heart ached with a longing he'd only known twice before, once when he was sixteen, while on an extended stay with his parents visiting relatives in Germany.

The girl then, Antje, had long, midnight hair like Regen's, a creamy complexion, and a wide voluptuous mouth. It had been her mouth that ruined his plans, broke his fantasy. She swore at him the first time he touched her, then tried to slap him and began cursing in German. He couldn't understand all the words, but he recognized the twisted sneer on that luscious mouth. All he wanted was to care for her, love her, for them to be together. But she wouldn't have it.

What resulted was her fault. His first blow shocked her, and she stumbled to the ground, looking up at him with a dazed expression. If she'd shown any submission right then, he might have relented. But that mouth had opened again, spewing derision. Two hikers found her body three weeks later in the hills above Baden-Baden after animals had scattered her remains.

For several years he had contemplated that first—event. Taking her life hadn't been his goal, but he had to admit that level of control over another was intoxicating.

In Regen's open closet, he let her simple clothes drift like silk through his fingers. And, like the closet, the large chest of drawers in the bedroom was mostly empty. He stroked the few pieces. He'd planned to take a souvenir, but anything he took might be missed. No matter. He had all the clothing she'd need for their night together.

He lowered himself onto the leather sofa in the great room. The cold fireplace stared back, but he imagined it roaring with a warming fire. Eyes closed, he laid his head back. Regen van Onweer reclined next to him, snuggled against his side.

The telephone rang in the kitchen, and Raoul listened to Conner's answering machine greeting. The woman at his side disappeared.

Eavesdropping on phone calls was such an intimate act, almost like being part of the family. He sipped his cooling coffee. Perhaps he should have invested in wire tapping equipment. His amusement died as the caller began his message.

"Hey, Ben, this is Mark over at Deer Cove Auto. Uh … I'm not sure how to put this. Don't want to get anyone in trouble or anything. Well… maybe straight out's the best." The man cleared his throat. "You know when I fixed your truck mirror, you explained how the other car had clipped yours and practically ran you off the road? Well, I worked on a car yesterday, an old VW, and, well, it had this long scrape right on the roofline above the driver door. And the transferred paint color on your truck's broken mirror looked like a dark gray primer, just like the paint on that V-dub. Don't know if it's anything or not. The VW owner wasn't a local, but he's staying around here—I towed the car from a quarter mile north of the cove. Kind of funny, though, that he wouldn't give me an address or phone number. But I know I've seen that V-dub around the cove here for the past week or—" The message cut off with a beep. Evidently the answering machine had a time limit. The device gave the time and date of the call.

Raoul slammed the coffee mug down on the table and ran for the kitchen. In a second he found the ERASE button on the machine and, as he fled for the garage door, a woman's mechanical voice proudly proclaimed: "All messages deleted."

Mark from Deer Cove Auto was only supposed to fix his car, not meddle in Raoul's business. This could mess up everything. He slipped and slid up the wet hill behind the garage, but still made it to his car in under a minute. As he climbed into the Super Beetle, a phone began ringing somewhere down the hill.

CHAPTER THIRTY-FOUR

Rayne's hip bumped the passenger door of Ben's pickup when he bounced around a sharp curve on Lake Road. Quin, in the middle seat, steadied himself with a hand on the dash.

"Sorry," Ben said, eyes on the road. "I let the time get away from us." Rayne's stomach lurched and pressed against her lungs. She shouldn't have had that last piece of meat lovers pizza. Too late now.

"It's okay. I had a good time," she sent him a quick smile. The outing with his brother's forming family had been relaxed and fun. She'd sat next to Sam and had a great time hearing about the woman's whale watching tours and her reputation as an authority on boating safety after her own experience in rescuing a boy who had fallen overboard on one trip. Actually red-headed Star had related the details of the rescue since Sam was too modest, but near as Rayne could tell, Sam had nearly drowned while saving the boy.

Another pothole bounced Rayne back to reality, and she glanced at the dashboard clock. They'd barely have enough time for a quick stop at home before driving the few minutes to Shelter Cove for the festival. She made a mental note of what she needed: music, change clothes, a warm sweatshirt and hat for the cooling afternoon.

Outside the truck window, the previously blue sky had turned leaden, and clouds twisted in angry knots as they sped down the length of the lake. The predicted big storm appeared to be on time. Rayne added a poncho to her list.

Inside the house, Rayne limped for her bedroom while Quin and Ben ran upstairs to change out of their church clothes. While pulling on a long-sleeve T-shirt, she noticed her left arm ached deep in the bone. *Must be the change in weather*. She retrieved the music books and sheet music from the piano room and stuffed them into a canvas grocery bag. It wouldn't keep them dry if a downpour began, but she could tuck it up under her jacket. At that point, everyone would be running for cars and cover anyway, her part in the festival over.

She came back into the great room right as Ben and Quin descended the stairs. On the table in front of the fireplace sat the coffee mug she usually used.

"That's odd," she said, lifting the mug. Coffee dripped from its base.

"What?" Ben asked.

"I thought I put this in the sink before we left for church."

"You sure?"

Rayne shook her head. "I…well…"

"Just leave it for now." Ben opened the front door and Quin headed for the truck. "We've got to get going so you can get set up."

Rayne replaced the mug, picked up her music, and hurried through the door.

Within a few minutes they'd arrived in Shelter Cove, and Rayne walked across a freshly mowed area to where a ten-by-ten green pop-up covered a low wooden platform flanked by two tri-pod-mounted speakers. Bibs' electronic keyboard sat on its stand with a single metal folding chair behind it. Cables snaked from the keyboard and mic to a sound mixer off to one side where a young man adjusted knobs and bobbed his head in time to the country music flowing from the speakers. He introduced himself as Terry, and said he'd be ready for sound check in a couple of minutes.

Rayne stood on the platform, waiting while trucks and cars

surrounded the little green. Like busy ants, people set up open-sided tents, tables, and chairs, while kids raced each other to the simple play equipment. Someone switched on strands of lights already stretched between the large trees that dotted the area. The warm glow did little to offset the gale whipping up whitecaps on the lake. She shivered and rubbed at the ache in her arm.

As if reading her thoughts, a man lit the teepee of logs in the stone fire pit on one side of the forming circle. The stiff breeze fanned the flames quickly, swirling pine and oak smoke around the grassy area. Kids ran to the fire, but its intensity soon had them backing away. Even at fifty feet, Rayne felt the welcome heat on her cheeks and hoped the man had a good supply of wood. She inhaled the fragrant scents of barbecuing chicken, lake mist, and mown grass, and let her eyes close in sensory ecstasy, her mind churning with the music these potent smells evoked. Children's laughter mixed with the creak of swing chains.

"This might be the shortest Shelter Cove Holiday Fair on record," Bibs said as she waddled across the grass, drawing Rayne out of her musing. The stout woman swung one leg onto the platform, then impatiently motioned for Rayne to help. Rayne took Bibs' outstretched hand and heaved her up. To Rayne's surprise, Bibs grabbed her in a fierce hug, although her large stomach kept them somewhat separated. "Thank you, Rayne," she whispered earnestly. "I know Ben didn't want you to do this."

Rayne smiled at the short woman's wrinkled face. "I wouldn't be anywhere else, my friend." And, to her surprise, she meant it. This community had gotten under her skin as it never had fifteen years ago. Regret spiked like acid reflux in her chest. Fortunately she had no time to linger on what might have been, because Terry was ready for sound check.

She sang through the old Irish hymn, "Be Thou My Vision," while Terry tweaked knobs on the small PA. For the second verse, she sang in Gaelic without the keyboard. When she finished, she looked up to find all setup flurry had come to a standstill. Men stood with chairs half unfolded, women were frozen in place, boxes of pies and jams tilting dangerously from careless fingers. Even a couple of children not at the playground knelt in front of the stage, rosy faces upturned, mouths slightly open.

Embarrassed at the response to a simple sound check, Rayne dipped her head and swiveled away from the keyboard. She was about to step off the back of the platform when she noticed Ben leaning against a small tree nearby, hands fisted in the front pockets of his jeans. The desire in his hooded eyes nearly caused her to gasp. She feared he'd stalk across the separating space and kiss her in front of everyone. For a moment she wished he would.

No longer cold, she stepped down. Muttering her thanks to Terry, she told him she'd be back in ten minutes for the official start of the Holiday Fair. Ben straightened from the tree as she came closer.

"I need to use the bathroom. Then I want to sit in the truck and stay warm until I sing."

"Okay." His voice was rough as he handed her the truck keys. "I'll be right here."

Rayne didn't look back as she walked to the simple building that housed two restrooms, but she knew his eyes were on her back. And it felt good. Once inside the structure she let out a ragged breath, then leaned on the cold porcelain basin and stared at herself in the mirror. Ben's need had always scared her. She'd always doubted her ability to live up to his expectations. But what struck her now was the yearning she felt for him, for family, a sense of community. She ran from Storm Lake all those years ago, but now it held everything she deeply desired.

Elusive Hope, Danny, the rest of the band—all seemed so distant, no longer part of the real world, her world. Instead of continuing as a performer in Europe, was this the next step in her life?

She finished in the bathroom and headed for the truck, the most direct path taking her on the other side of the stage from where Ben stood talking with two men. One had on a sheriff's uniform. Rayne acknowledged Ben with a small wave and watched him as she passed the circle of tents.

Outside the protective ring, the wind cut through tree branches with vigor, raining leaves, needles, and twigs on the parked vehicles. She hurried as much as her leg allowed, skirting a rusted Toyota camper to get to Ben's Ford. She waved at Ben again, and he lifted a hand as she climbed in the passenger seat of the crew cab.

The interior lamp faded out and plunged the still-warm space into deep gloom, but not before she noticed something on the driver's floor mat. Now that the light was gone, she couldn't make it out. Lying across the seat, she reached with her right hand until her fingers closed around what felt like a stiff branch. Rayne struggled back to a sitting position and turned the object toward the weak light coming in the rear window. It was some kind of flower. Her chest constricted as she made out the glued-on pedals of a rose and tulip.

A shadow moved in the rear seat. Rayne drew a deep breath for a scream as a hand clamped across her mouth.

CHAPTER THIRTY-FIVE

Ben planned to accompany Rayne to the truck, but Sheriff Derrek Cabot wanted to discuss the procedure for canvassing the crowd. As Ben watched Rayne travel from the restrooms to his pickup, which was parked just outside the main circle of tents, he half listened to the older man. He shifted a couple of feet to his left so he had a clear view as Rayne unlocked the truck and climbed into the passenger side. He knew she'd lock the doors as they'd discussed.

Addison arrived a couple of minutes later and made his way to them while Sam, Star, and Mandy unloaded jars of homemade jams onto a small table.

"Afternoon, Derrek." Addison shook hands with the sheriff. "Glad to have you here." Addison had worked with the sheriff's department several times in the last few months, doing security reviews for construction plans and suggesting ways to make commercial buildings safer from burglary. Sometimes Ben got an install referral. Sheriff Cabot was a good man, attested by the fact he'd been in office for nearly twenty-five years.

"Ben," Cabot began, "since I'm in uniform, I suggest I stay close to Rayne and the stage when she's there. This uniform alone is often enough to make someone think twice about trying anything. Why don't you and Addison circle the crowd when she sings, each going in the opposite direction from the other? That way you can update each other twice each round if you notice anyone suspicious."

They both nodded in agreement.

"Be sure to check the parking lot and cars, too." Cabot gestured to the area where more cars were arriving each minute. At least forty vehicles were already crammed into the graveled area bordered by logs. Newcomers began parking along the road. It looked to Ben like the 'locals only' concept had expanded. He wouldn't recognize as many of the people as he'd thought.

The disk jockey cranked up the volume on a Tim McGraw song, and the young people gathered around the bonfire. The wind sent a spray of sparks into the cold air as someone tossed in another log.

"Where is Rayne now?" Addison asked, looking around.

"She's in my truck staying warm before she sings." All three men turned toward the lot. In the twilight, Ben could barely make out Rayne sitting in the Ford's cab. She lifted a hand and he waved back. "She's due to sing in a few minutes, but sometimes the smoke from the fire bothers her throat."

The sheriff said he was going to take a look around, and Addison left to hit the restroom and help Sam for a minute. Ben turned toward the truck, but Quin ran up and asked if he and Star could buy a snow cone. Ben shivered at the thought of eating ice on such a cold day, but he handed the boy a ten-dollar bill as Star joined them. They sprinted off together toward the vender who, Ben noted, wore fingerless mittens and a ski jacket with the hood up. The man had good sense.

Again Ben turned to the parking lot and saw Rayne safe. But four cars away, Olivia Hamilton struggled to lift a heavy box from the trunk of her ancient Chevy. Ben jogged over to help and carried the box and a card table to the craft area as she followed leaning on her cane. Her husband, John Hamilton, had spent years carving duck decoys. Olivia had painstakingly painted each one until they were difficult to tell from a real bird. Now, ten years after John's death, she still had a few boxes left that she brought to the craft fairs.

Doc Arnold took the stage and welcomed everyone. He told a few jokes about the cold weather and predicted storm, perfect for Storm

Lake. Then he introduced the committee who organized the event each year. Doc did a good job as an MC and the crowd showed their appreciation with applause, though the increasing wind seemed to blow away the sound. He brought up two teenagers who performed stupid human tricks. One stuck his whole fist into his mouth while the other lifted his shirt and sucked in his stomach until it nearly touched his spine. The girls liked that one especially.

Mandy joined him and rolled her eyes at the guys' behavior. "Dorks," she muttered, but her lips curled into a lopsided grin.

"And now we're privileged to have Rayne Conner come sing for us," Doc announced with an expansive wave of his arm. This time the crowd cheered as well as clapped. Ben turned to Mandy.

"You want to run and tell Rayne it's showtime? She's in the truck." He pointed to where it sat. It had grown too dark to see inside the cab. Rayne was probably watching, but she might not have heard her introduction.

"Sure." Mandy sprinted toward the vehicle as Ben scanned the nearby crowd.

Sheriff Cabot stood ready at the side of the stage. Star and Quin ran by, mouths stained blue from colored ice in paper cones. Addison was positioned opposite Ben near Sam's table where a few people tried samples of her jam.

"Ben!"

He turned at Mandy's cry. She was running toward him, holding something in her outstretched hand, but it was too dark to make out. Behind her, the door of the truck stood open, the interior light illuminating the seats and spilling onto the ground. Ben reached her as she entered the tent circle, only yards from the truck.

"She's not there! And this was on the seat." The girl thrust a flower at him in a shaking hand, her eyes large and round. He took it and turned so one of the overhead lights shined on it. It was mix of rose and tulip petals, crudely attached around a central stem with what looked like hot glue. A five year old could have done a better job.

It took only five minutes for all of them to search the grounds and all the cars. Bibs came huffing up, shaking her head after checking the restrooms. "I'm so...sorry, Ben," she gasped between breaths. "I should have...been with her...like I said." Irene embraced her sister who suddenly looked every one of her years.

Ben seethed in frustration. He should have stayed with Rayne like he'd said, too. But he'd just seen her in the truck, and she'd waved at him. It hadn't been four or five minutes—just the time for the two boys to do their act on stage. But as Addison said in his frequently requested lectures, five minutes was a lifetime when it came to security.

Sheriff Cabot's radio squawked, and he moved away a few steps to talk. Addison, Sam, Mandy, Star, and Quin huddled around Ben, silently pleading for answers that didn't exist. Then the sheriff rejoined them.

"That was one of my deputies. He's about three minutes south of Flume, and he'll set up a roadblock there at the Y. The Highway Patrol is sending another unit, and together they'll search every vehicle leaving the lake area. Meanwhile, I suggest we start looking within the area. There are a lot of empty cabins this time of year." He turned to a group of four men he'd gathered and began giving them directions on how to determine which cabins were vacant. Others circled around, contributing what they knew and compiling a list of addresses.

Many in the crowd still didn't know what had happened, only that Rayne hadn't shown up to sing, and a flurry of activity had resulted.

Ben walked a few paces away toward the lake, letting the icy wind jolt his mind. He had to think. Assuming her stalker took her—and of that he had no doubt—where would he go? The east side of the lake had the communities of Gift and Shelter Cove, while the bottom of the lake had Flume. Deer Cove was the only thing on the west. Problem was, there were cabins scattered in between all those areas, most hidden in the trees or up winding driveways. Searching them all could take hours, days.

He ran his hands through his hair. It was his fault. He never should have allowed her out of the house after Thursday's incident at the barn.

A door slammed, and he looked up to see Mark from Deer Cove Auto approaching him.

"Ben. I just heard about Rayne on my police scanner as I was driving over."

"Yeah." Ben didn't feel like talking to anyone. Except Rayne.

"Say, did you get my message about the car that I think hit your truck?" Mark said, following Ben as he walked away from the crowd. Mark never knew when to take a hint.

"Look, Mark. Now isn't a very good time, okay?"

"Well, yeah, okay. I get you." Mark turned back toward the people. "But I thought you'd be interested in the guy since he's a foreigner and all."

Ben grabbed the man's shoulder. "What are you talking about?" It came out more growl than polite, but he didn't have time for riddles.

"Didn't you get my phone message?"

Ben explained they'd been late and hadn't checked the machine before coming to the Holiday Fair.

"Well, when I fixed the VW that I described in my message—the one I left on your machine—I had to open the front hood to check the wiring. Ya see, the luggage compartment release on the '75 model is inside the glove box, so I had to—"

"Mark, are you going somewhere with this? We haven't got all day."

"Oh, yeah," Mark recoiled, then his brow wrinkled in concentration. "Well, ya see, there was so much junk stuffed in the glovebox, I had to pull it all out to get to the release knob."

Ben gave him another look, and Mark cleared his throat.

"See, there was a bunch of paperwork. I didn't mean to look at it, but I couldn't help it since I had to straighten it all out and everything."

"Ughh!" Ben shouted at the wind and threw up his hands.

"Okay okay. Sorry. Well, there were these rental papers for a cabin here at the lake. See, that's what I told you on your message machine, that the guy rented a place here."

That got Ben's attention. Could it be this easy? A foreigner renting a cabin? Of course lots of foreigners rented during the summer and fall, so it might be nothing.

"Funny thing, though," Mark continued, rubbing his chin. "The rental papers were made out to a Raoul Kloepper, but the guy on the phone gave his name as E. Hope."

Ben ran the name through his head. *E. Hope.* Rayne's band was named Elusive Hope. Was this some sick joke?

"Where's the cabin, Mark?"

Mark held out a piece of paper with an address printed in careful block letters: 12 NORTH LAKE ROAD. "Old Mrs. Lambert's place, but she don't own it anymore—some rental agency now." Ben turned toward where the sheriff stood.

"Derrek!" The sheriff and Addison came running just as marble-sized raindrops began pelting them all.

CHAPTER THIRTY-SIX

Ben made a very brief stop at the house. He was loading a magazine for his 9 millimeter semi-automatic when Quin came to the door of the office where Ben kept the gun locked up.

"I want to go with you, Ben." Quin watched Ben's preparations.

Ben sighed. At thirteen, Quin was outwardly a boy. But like the other two Conner children, he had an internal maturity beyond his years. But Ben still shook his head.

"She's the closest thing I've had to a mom," Quin whispered.

Ben closed the distance between them and hugged him tight. "I know, Quin. I know." He kissed the top of the boy's head, damp hair smelling like campfire smoke and everything wild and fresh at the lake. Then he stepped back and looked Quin in the eye.

"I won't insult you by saying you need to stay here to protect Sam, Star, and Mandy while Addison and I go." He gave Quin's shoulder a squeeze. "But I can't let you go. You know that?"

Quin stared at him for a long moment, then nodded. "Just find her. Bring her home, Ben. Please."

Two minutes later, Ben chewed on the boy's words as Addison raced his SUV around the lake road in a déjà vu repeat of their previous run.

Bring her home. He should have done that years ago. Stubborn fool. Now that he'd finally grown a brain, he hoped it wasn't too late.

The SUV bucked over a washboard of rocks and mud, and Ben grunted. He wrapped his right hand tighter around his ribs.

"Sorry, bro," Addison said, squinting through the windshield as the wiper blades hurled water off the glass. Heavier rain took its place as the clouds opened up.

"Faster," Ben grunted again, and the car surged ahead.

The sheriff had stopped briefly at Flume to confer with the officers where the lake exit road went west, first instructing Ben and Addison to wait for him at Bibs' Beauty Barn. They'd approach the cabin together. More Highway Patrol and deputies were coming from across the county, but it would take the first cars twenty minutes to reach the lake. An icy fist in his stomach told Ben they might not have that long.

Bring her home.

After checking the cabin's driveway and seeing no car, the sheriff, Addison, and Ben had approached through the trees and were hunkered down about sixty feet from the back of the cabin, behind the big propane tank. Reinforcements would be here in thirty minutes, but Derrek didn't want to wait. Neither did Ben.

Night had fallen, dropping the temperature, and unleashing rain that pelted the sheriff's flat-brimmed hat like gravel hitting a tin roof. Fortunately, the noise of the storm drowned out their voices, so they could talk freely.

"Okay, here's how we'll play it. Listen up, 'cuz I don't want any of us shot."

Ben tried to calm his racing heart as he listened to Derrek Cabot describe the plan. Cold water trickled under his coat collar and soaked his back, and his pant legs were wet up to his knees. He dismissed his own discomfort and focused on the wood-framed house.

Little useful illumination leaked beyond the home's rear-facing curtained windows. From this position, they couldn't even see the light from the front porch. The yard might contain a myriad of objects suitable for tripping over. Water sheeted off the roof in a twelve-foot-long waterfall.

They each carried flashlights, but these were reserved for the interior in case the lights went out. Ben kept his pistol tucked in his jacket pocket to protect it from getting wet. He couldn't afford a misfire.

Addison would go in the back door while Derrek and Ben knocked on the front door with the story they were checking all the cabins because of the storm. Ben protested if it *was* Kloepper inside, he wouldn't buy the ruse. All they were doing was warning him before he opened the door. But Derrek insisted they do it that way since it could be someone innocent inside with no knowledge of Rayne.

Once agreed, the lawman wasted no time. In less than a minute, Addison waited at the back door while Ben and the sheriff mounted the wooden porch illuminated by an anemic yellow bug light. Ben moved to one side of the door while Derrek covered the other side and rapped sharply.

"Hello? Anyone home?"

If there was movement inside, they couldn't hear it over the din of the rain hammering the porch roof. After what seemed like several minutes but was probably only thirty seconds, Derrek pounded the door again. "Sheriff's Department! Open the door!" No niceties this time. The man waited ten seconds and kicked the door right beside the handle.

The sound of splitting wood accompanied bright light as the door flew inward and bounced back at them. Derrek shouldered it aside as he rushed through in a low crouch, gun held two-handed in front of him.

As much as Ben wanted to dive in after him, his ribs wouldn't cooperate, so he waited until he heard, "Clear," and an answering echo form Addison.

The first thing Ben noticed when he entered was several fist-sized holes punched through the wall board beside the cold heater. They destroyed the cheery wallpaper apples, oranges, and pears, and white drywall powder and plaster chunks littered the floor. Then he spotted four large screw hooks, two of them about five feet apart and head-high, and two more at floor level—perfect for tying someone against the wall in a spread-eagle position.

But those first impressions evaporated when he noticed the large bulletin board propped on the end of the dining table and leaning against the wall. Dozens of pictures of Rayne covered its cork surface, tacked in place with clear pushpins from an open box on the table. Next to the box was a copy of the local newspaper.

Most of the photos were concert shots of Rayne's band singing in small venues, but one near the bottom caught his eye: Rayne exiting from Bibs' Beauty Barn. Clearly taken in late afternoon, her white T-shirt glowed amber in the fading sun, and her auburn hair shimmered like a smoldering fire. Her face was turned upward to catch the last light, and a slight smile touched her lips.

The sheriff took one look at the picture board and radioed for a crime unit. Then he used a pencil eraser and rotated the open local newspaper. An ad for Shelter Cove Holiday Fair had been circled with black marker.

On the other end of the dining table, an aluminum case housed a box with several knobs and flashing LEDs. Ben traced the coiled coax wire and found it was connected between the incoming cable TV wire and the cabin's television, which sat on an oak entertainment stand nearby. The TV was rotated to face the table instead of the living room.

"What's this?" Addison asked, coming in from checking the back porch more thoroughly. He leaned over the table beside Ben. "Security monitoring around the cabin?"

Ben shook his head and pointed to the coaxial wall jack. "He wouldn't connect it to the cable company feed if all he needed was outside cameras. Looks like some kind of modulator and camera control, though. Okay to turn on the TV?" he asked Derrek.

At the sheriff's nod, Addison punched the power button, and a black and white image took shape as the set warmed up. A ladder, coiled hose, rakes, brooms, and shovels filled the screen.

"Looks like the inside of a garage, but this house doesn't have one," Derrek said as his radio crackled. Ben had a sick feeling. He didn't wait for permission this time as he twisted one of the box's knobs. Another image replaced the first. The screen showed a living room and a view into a kitchen. A woman at the bar turned toward the camera.

"Oh, no," his brother muttered. "It's Sam." Her lips moved like a silent movie as she spoke to someone off-camera. Mandy paced into the camera's view, stopping in front of Sam, arms raising and lowering in agitation.

Ben sagged into one of the colorfully painted chairs. "He bugged my house."

CHAPTER THIRTY-SEVEN

Ben pressed his cell phone to his ear as he watched the picture of his home on the screen. Both Sam and Mandy turned toward the phone at the same time, but Mandy was faster.

"Hello?"

"It's Ben." He tried to keep disappointment out of his voice.

"Did you find her? Is she okay?" On-screen, Mandy put the call on speaker phone so Sam could listen too.

His heart felt like a lump of lead, cold and still. "She isn't here. Neither is Kloepper. But this is definitely where he was staying." He told them about the photo board. Then he said he could see them on TV and that the house was bugged.

The two women spent the next minute following his directions until they were staring right into the camera, hidden at the corner of the ceiling. It was only when they looked closely that Mandy spotted the miniature device. The tip of her finger filled the screen as she pointed it out to Sam.

"You know," Addison said, "it's possible he could have another setup somewhere else where he could monitor the feed." He looked around the room. "He might even be monitoring *this* place, though it's unlikely." That small probability didn't keep them from looking into all the corners.

They'd obviously found Kloepper's lair, but one thing Ben knew: this sicko was intelligent and patient. He'd planned this operation thoroughly, and he'd have a backup plan. The first thing was to cut off his information.

"Mandy," Ben broke into her stream of questions about where Rayne might be. "I think he's using the cable TV line there at the house to send the camera video. I need you to cut the cable feed to the house. Can you and Sam do that?"

"Yes," Sam replied, and her onscreen person nodded a split second later. "Tell us where to find it."

"On the far wall of the garage. Outside. You'll need a flashlight and a step ladder."

"Did he tap the phones?" Mandy asked.

Ben swore. He hadn't thought of that. Just because there wasn't audio over the cable line, didn't mean Kloepper hadn't separately bugged the phones. There wasn't any audio equipment on the table, but he could be routing it to a portable device he kept with him. Quin came into view, already shrugging into a hooded jacket.

"Just cut the cable TV line for now." Ben told them to get wire cutters from his toolbox. He scrubbed his face with his free hand. "But ... well, watch what you say, just in case. And keep the doors locked. We don't know where this guy is."

Not wanting to pile Sam and the kids with more worry, he didn't state the obvious, that Raoul Kloepper had been in their house. He'd violated their privacy and could be anywhere now, even very close by.

And what did Kloepper plan for Rayne? Ben stared at the hooks in the destroyed wall. Was she still alive? He checked his wristwatch and was shocked to see it had only been an hour since she'd disappeared. They had to find her. Fast.

"We'll see you soon." Ben clicked off. The sheriff gripped his arm until Ben focused on him.

"Why don't you and Addison go back to your house? I've got to stay here to secure the scene until my backup or the crime unit arrives." He looked around the room. "Kloepper may still come back here if he doesn't know we found this place. I'm going to set up surveillance outside and wait."

Ben eyed the splintered front door. Kloepper would know he'd been found out as soon as he saw it. And Ben had the feeling this was a closed chapter, as if Kloepper already knew not to return. The question was, where would he go? Ben hoped the deputy had blocked off the lake exit below Flume before the man got away.

CHAPTER THIRTY-EIGHT

White noise roused Rayne from sleep. The sound techs must be balancing the amplifiers, shifting the signal from speaker to speaker, checking the outputs. Was she late for sound check?

Something dug into her cheek, and she moved her hand to push it away...or tried to. Her hand didn't move. It was stuck behind her back.

She struggled to pry open her eyes. Flickering light danced as she blinked repeatedly to clear her vision. A dozen candles burned atop an old dresser rotated at a right angle to her view. The side of her face was pressed into a musty pillow, and she moved her head off what felt like a button sewn on its front. The slight movement sent her stomach heaving, and bile filled her mouth. By the barest of margins she avoided vomiting, holding still while the nausea subsided.

Not white noise, she realized. Rain. Hammering hard against the roof, as if demanding entrance and shelter from its own deluge. Rayne longed for a little of that cold water on her heated brow. Howling wind tested the windows and walls, like a wolf seeking a weak point.

The smell of vanilla filled the room. Probably from the candles. Such a gentle scent, made for lingering soaks in the tub with a glass of white wine as the light of the day waned over the canal outside her home.

But this was not her home. Holland was far away. She'd get home someday and take a bath in her own tub.

Then the recent memories resurfaced. The hideous flower. The shadow in the truck's backseat. Movement. She clenched her eyes tight against the man who had held the cloth over her face.

Terror pumped adrenaline through her system, energizing her, demanding her escape, even into the raging storm. Somewhere safe.

To Ben.

Gritting her teeth against the nausea, she tried to swing her legs off the bed. They didn't move. She kicked her legs and tugged at her arms, but her only reward was the creaking of open bedsprings. Her breath caught as a man moved in front of the candles, momentarily obscuring their light. He sat down in a straight-backed chair beside the dresser, leaned toward her, and steepled his hands.

"Hello, Regen van Onweer. It's good to see you again."

His accent sounded German, and there was something familiar about him, but pressed down on the pillow, she was sideways to him. She lifted her head a little, straining to remember. He smiled, but it transformed only his mouth, not his eyes.

"Yes, we met at the harvest festival." From his pocket he pulled a black mask and held it across his eyes. "Ev'nin, little lady," he drawled, and dipped his head in a slight bow. The German accent had vanished. "May I have the pleasure of this dance?"

White outfit, white hat, black mask. The Lone Ranger. He'd shared her hay bale. But this creep was no western hero. He looked so ordinary, like someone who might clerk in a store or work as an accountant.

His balding head tilted back as he laughed. "What a delightful event that was. Halloween. Americans make so much of it, don't you think?"

The good humor drained from his face like melting wax, and he leaned toward her. She shrank back as far as her bonds allowed, tied as they were to the metal head and footboards of the bed. What did he want? He'd already tried to kill her. Was he going to rape her?

"*Ich habe spezielle Pläne für uns,*" he said in German. *I have something special for us.* What was he planning?

She'd learned by watching television, the best way to survive a hostage situation was to build rapport with the kidnapper. Much as it repulsed her, she wetted her dry lips and asked, "What's your name?"

Addison had just driven past Bibs's barn on the outskirts of Deer Cove when Ben's cell phone rang.

"Hello."

"Ben!" Sam sounded frantic, and he put it on speakerphone. "The kids. They're gone!"

Ben felt like someone sucker punched him. His stomach pressed against his lungs, and he struggled for air. Before he could respond, Addison shouted at the phone.

"Sam, stay calm. Who's gone and where did they go?"

"Mandy and Quin."

"And Star?"

"No, she's here with me. They went out to cut the wire. Next thing, I heard the garage door opener and the Bronco start up. I ran outside as Mandy backed out of the garage." Her voice cracked, and a sob escaped.

"Where did they go?" Ben asked, finding his voice.

"I tried to stop them." She sobbed again, then got hold of herself. "Before driving off, Mandy said she thought he took Rayne to the old cabin, the one you lived in when you were first married. She said to tell you to hurry."

"We're coming, Sam. Keep the doors locked."

Addison floored the SUV and it rocketed through Deer Cove. He kept his thumb on the horn and flashed the headlights. What little traffic there was wisely scattered.

"Crazy girl," Addison growled. "She's grounded for life. What is she thinking?" He gave the steering wheel a sharp rap and turned to Ben. "Does she even know where that cabin is?"

"No, but Quin does. If Mandy's right about the cabin, she understands very well how long it will take us or the sheriff to get up there." The cabin he'd shared with Rayne was in Gift, about as far up the east side of the lake as the road went. He'd shown Quin the place one day when they were out on a fishing trip in the boat. They'd pulled to the shore and hiked the short path to the house. The place wasn't much, a few hundred square feet, one bedroom, one bath, with plywood siding in need of paint. Ben had simply said he'd once lived there. The boy never forgot a location on the lake.

He glanced at the lighted speedometer which wavered between seventy-five and eighty, and calculated the time: ten minutes to Flume at this speed, then five more to his house, another five to Shelter Cove, then another eight or ten to Gift and the cabin. Close to thirty minutes. That was if they didn't crash. Fortunately the rain had stopped.

He punched in Derrek Cabot's phone number, but had to try it twice more because of the weak signal on this stretch of the road. Once on the line, the sheriff said he'd send one of the deputies at the roadblock and be there himself as soon as someone relieved him. Ben disconnected as the man began a string of instructions about being careful, waiting for help, etc.

"I think Mandy may be right on this," Ben said. His brother flicked a glance at him before turning back to the road. A brief straight stretch let him accelerate to over a hundred miles per hour. Trees flashed by outside Ben's window like irregularly spaced pickets on a fence. Ben hadn't driven this fast since high school, but he trusted Addison's police training. He just hoped all the deer were hunkered down under shelter somewhere.

"Explain," his brother said.

Ben gripped his ribs tighter. "Well, Kloepper had only minutes to snatch Rayne from the last time I saw her in the truck. If he didn't get out of the lake and didn't make it back to his rented place up here, where did he go? We all expected him to go south since that's the only road out. But what if he headed toward Gift?"

"How would Kloepper even know about that place? Did you take Rayne there?"

"No." Ben had thought about taking her there, but felt it might push her too much, causing her to run from him again. "But if he's been spying on us long enough to set up those cameras and video feed, he could have checked the public records."

"What are you talking about, bro? What would Kloepper find out?"

"That I own it," Ben admitted. "I bought it four years ago."

Addison shot him a look Ben chose to ignore. As they approached Flume, the rain hit again, this time with hurricane force, showering the road with branches and small limbs. Addison slowed to forty and still they drove blind. Water sluiced over the windshield like a carwash, the wipers unable to make a dent.

Suddenly a large branch ripped across the hood, and the passenger-side wiper arm disappeared as the greenery scraped over the roof, leaving the orphaned left wiper to soldier on.

Ben squinted into the blurry night, as if he could identify a threat before it wrecked them. But the darkness was as indecipherable as his future. He hoped the bigger trees had healthy roots.

CHAPTER THIRTY-NINE

Raoul Kloepper. Rayne silently ran the name over her tongue.

A New York born German who lived in Germany and traveled frequently between the US and Europe for work as an independent auditor for auto parts manufacturing companies. And, as a self-styled poet, he liked symphonic metal music. After reading some of his truly appalling poetry to her—that she'd pretended to like—he'd left the room, promising to return shortly.

Rayne closed her eyes as another wave of nausea seized her stomach. Each bout was less intense than the previous, but her head still felt like it was filled with sticky molasses instead of brain matter. When the sickness passed, she opened her eyes again. Dark windows lined the front of the room, two on each side of a door with its upper half glass panes. This was obviously the living area rather than a bedroom. Through the headboard bars, she could see the far corner of the space where a potbellied stove sat on a brick hearth. Candles covered the flat top of the cold stove. If only Ben were here, he could use kindling from the brass wood holder to light a—

In an instant, the fog cleared from her thinking. She knew that hearth and stove! Frantically, she searched the walls for other telltale signs. There! Above the front door two wooden curtain rod holders stuck out where Ben had mounted them to keep his favorite fishing rod. She'd kidded him that one time he'd walk through the door and snag his own mouth on the dangling trout hook.

Their cabin. This madman had brought her to their old cabin. Her piano—the one Ben restored and resided in his new house—had faced the windows on the left of the door.

Tears stung her eyes as the memories of those first days were overlaid with the painful ones, until the good times disappeared. Until *she* disappeared.

"Regen van Onweer," Kloepper's lilting voice sounded behind her where the hallway led to the one bedroom, bath, and screen back porch. "I have a surprise for you."

She forced her self to lie still, let him think she was recovering from whatever drug he'd given her. She'd have a surprise for *him* if she could get free of these bonds.

"Get ready to kill your lights," Ben said as they drove through the tiny community of Gift. No more than thirty homes sprinkled the hilly area, each set a respectful distance from another. The main road twisted like a coiled rope through trees and houses. Only one structure had lights on—probably a visiting family on one last trip before boarding it up for the winter—but that cabin wasn't their destination.

Ben directed Addison to the left on a road that led down toward the lake, then right on what looked like a path for an ATV. Their vehicle slipped between two trees growing close to the path. "Now."

Addison plunged them into darkness with a flick of his wrist. He braked to a stop. "I can't see a thing." The lone wiper valiantly whipped water left and right, but did nothing to light the blackness before them. "How much farther?"

"Maybe two hundred yards. There's one more house on the right about half way."

"No sign of the Bronco. And I wonder where the deputy is."

"He should have been here before us." Ben checked his cell phone. No coverage; never was out here. If the deputy wasn't here somewhere, they couldn't wait. If Mandy had driven straight to the cabin, Kloepper might have them, too. He shuddered, thinking about what they would find.

"Now, don't you look lovely? Like Regen van Onweer should." Kloepper's hands were clasped right over left, like some fashion designer admiring his spring line. He tilted his head to one side as he walked an appraising semi-circle around her.

Rayne stood on tiptoe, arms stretched above, her cloth bounds replaced by shiny handcuffs. Her over-the-elbow black gloves kept the metal from cutting into her wrists. The cuff's connecting chain looped over a large hook he'd screwed into the ceiling. The chain was long enough so her toes touched the floor, but she couldn't get her feet under her to jump and flip the chain off the deep hook.

He had trained a gun on her while she dressed in one of the costumes she used for concerts, a fitted black bodice with broad burgundy skirt over ruffled black petticoats. It had been at her home the night of the concert. Too bad he hadn't brought the thigh-high leather boots with the steel toes she wore with the outfit, but the man was smart enough to stand to her side where she couldn't get leverage for a kick. Then he chained her up. He'd gagged her briefly, to keep her from biting him, he said. It also prevented telling him what she thought of him. That alone had probably kept her alive—so far.

The windows flashed, and thunder boomed a few seconds later. Getting closer. Rayne shivered as Kloepper reached into a large paper bag and removed one of her concert wigs. He combed his fingers through its long black curls, closing his eyes as if in ecstasy from the experience. Everything about him made her skin crawl. He'd invaded her life, injured her and her friends, and chased her halfway across the globe. But she knew the longer she cooperated and drew this out, the more likely someone would find her.

After a few minutes lost in his fantasy world, Kloepper moved behind her and settled the wig on her head. With clammy fingers, he tucked her own hair up under the wig and smoothed its cascades.

"There. Almost *perfect*," he breathed in her face. Fortunately, he turned to the dresser top before her involuntary wince. Turning back, he held up a small makeup bag. "I'm afraid I'm not an expert like you—or Lorna Nairne."

Lorna. Rayne closed her eyes at the memory of her friend. She'd talked with Lorna once after she'd been hit by Dolina's falling body. Her spinal injury had caused partial paralysis in her legs. At least Rayne's bullet wounds had healed.

For what seemed forever but was probably only twenty minutes, Kloepper applied foundation, powder, eyeliner and lipstick. Three times, he wiped off an area before doing it again, each time growing more frustrated. Rayne held as still as she could, trying not to inhale his stale breath as it touched her face and nose. He took pleasure in brushing her cheeks with the back of his fingers, leaning his body against hers.

Finally finished, he once again stood back to admire his craftsmanship. Satisfied, he replaced each item in the makeup bag and zipped it closed.

She had a hard time reading him. Certifiably crazy for sure, but Kloepper wasn't dumb. Could she trick him, get him to trust her? If she had a clear shot, she would get out the front door and take the lake path south along the shore. She still knew the route well, remembered the boulders and bigger trees it snaked around. Kloepper would be at a great disadvantage.

Lightning crackled and the immediate boom rattled the windows so hard she expected them to burst into the room, followed by wind, water, and fury. She wished for that—anything to alter the situation. Instead, it rained with more intensity, and dust drifted before her face from where the hook went in the ceiling.

Kloepper lifted a camera and smiled. That grimacing attempt was the most frightening thing he'd done yet.

CHAPTER FORTY

Addison shut off the car and opened the driver door. Ben followed his lead. The interior light pierced the night as they stepped into two inches of muddy water running across the road. When they shut the doors, the blackness closed in like a night in Carlsbad Caverns. They stood in the rain for two or three minutes while their eyes adjusted. Not that it did much good as the sky alternated between pitch black and blinding lightning.

Steady rain beat the SUV's roof and splattered sideways into their faces. Ben was weary of being wet and cold, but his suffering was minor compared to what Rayne must be going through. Providing she was still alive.

"Let's go," his brother said.

A small beam lit the ground in front of the car and began to move down the road. Ben pushed the button on his own flashlight and followed.

After several minutes walking, Ben pointed out the hulk of a house on his right. "Here's the Stenner place. The creek is just ahead."

"And there's the Bronco." Addison directed his flashlight to the carport on the far side of the home where the old Ford dripped water onto the gravel floor. They ran the short distance, knowing the vehicle would be empty before their lights covered every corner of its interior.

"Man, I hate this," Ben said. They hadn't opened the Bronco's doors, not wanting the dome light to go on. It was bad enough to have some psycho after Rayne. But having Mandy and Quin in danger…

"We'd better hurry," Addison said, leaning into the escalating gale as he trotted toward the road.

Water ran down Ben's neck, soaking his shirt and even his underwear, but he ignored the icy cold that sapped his strength. Rayne, Mandy, and Quin were all that mattered. Every splashing footfall jarred his torso, and he wrapped his right arm around his ribs. It did little good, and soon his world narrowed to the constant pain and bouncing circle of light.

Ben gave himself a mental slap, forcing pine-scented air into his lungs in an attempt to clear the cobwebs.

They hardly needed the flashlights at times, the way lit by periodic blasts of lightning so bright that everything—tree trunks, branches, even raindrops—burned in sharp relief on their retinas even after the light faded. After each flash, their handheld beams seemed to die out before they reached the ground. Ben stumbled along behind Addison, trusting his brother's eyes were faster to recover than his own.

They heard the creek before they found the old road bridge. Made of thick telephone poles and sturdy three-by-twelve planks, it spanned the twenty-foot gulley that normally held a trickle of water. Not tonight. The creek had morphed into a river and rushed by, inches below the structure. Logs and branches crashed into the upstream support pole, sending vibrations through the boards, but there was no thought of slowing down as they hurried across.

Ten yards ahead, Addison's light disappeared. Ben slowed to a walk and found his brother standing beside the trunk of a large redwood. Ben switched off his own flashlight. An old Volkswagen hunched nearby. Through the sheeting rain, Ben saw the dull yellow rectangles of the cabin windows.

"Not very bright, and looks like it's flickering," Addison whispered, though it wasn't necessary as the wind bent the trees and propelled pine needles like miniature stinging missiles.

"I had the power turned off a month ago for the winter. Must be a lantern. Or candles." As they watched, five bright flashes lit the inside of the windows, followed by another four. A camera strobe. Ben hoped if Kloepper was taking pictures, Rayne was still alive. *Please God. Protect her.*

Ben started walking, feeling his way by the texture of the gravel roadbed and the flashing lights from both the sky and house. It reminded him of a disco dance, and he had to concentrate to maintain his balance in the bizarre nightscape. There was still no sign of the deputy or the kids.

A jagged bolt speared the sky, lighting the area like a nighttime football game. They both froze. As soon as it faded, Addison led a sprint for the edge of the front porch. They knelt in the mud where Rayne had once planted all kinds of flowers, only to have the deer come each night and harvest them like their personal salad bar. She never gave up trying to find something the animals wouldn't eat.

A lump rose in Ben's throat as he and his brother caught their breath. How would the next few minutes play out? Chances were, someone would die, and he vowed it wouldn't be Rayne.

"Thank you for bringing my real clothes."

Rayne wanted to say more, but Kloepper had been like a zombie for a full three minutes, staring, mouth slightly open. The camera dangled from his left hand. She had no idea if he saw her here and now in this mountain lake cabin, or if he was seeing Regen van Onweer on stage at the Ahoy. Or maybe something else entirely. She forced herself to wait for his reaction. If he laughed, he wasn't going to be tricked.

Confusion clouded his eyes, then awareness flickered, and he bowed from the waist. "Of course, my dear."

Rayne almost collapsed on her heels in relief, but the handcuffs were cutting her wrists as it was, and her left arm screamed from the stretching. *One step at a time.*

She'd spent her whole adult life performing, and what she did these last few years—crafting elaborate stories and telling them through song

—was as much theater as it was rock concert. Lorna always said Rayne could act. But this little cabin room was the most important stage she'd ever played, and pleasing the audience of one, her biggest challenge.

Although it sickened her, she drew the tip of her tongue across her upper lip. His eyes tracked its movement, left to right. When she drew her tongue inside, she tasted the lipstick he'd applied—her regular brand. She inhaled a steadying breath.

"I'm ready to go home," she said. His eyes rose to hers, but his face revealed no hint whether he accepted the words. He took a hesitant step forward, eyes wanting to believe her, but not quite knowing. Her heart pounded like a bird trapped in a net. "But I'm tired, Raoul. I need to lie down for a little while." Her use of his first name brought a smile, and she swore shyness overcame the man.

He stepped closer, his smile bigger. "We can rest on the bed. Together."

We? His arms encircled her, lifting her off the overhead hook. Before she remembered to knee him in the groin, he set her on her feet and shifted to the side, keeping her firmly anchored by an arm around her waist.

No! She didn't want him on the bed, touching her as he had when he'd stripped and dressed her. The thought of him lying beside her, rubbing his body against hers, caused the bile to rise in her throat.

Pretense, that's what counts. Aunt Ruth's sassy voice filled her head, and Rayne smiled at the psychopath. "Yes, Raoul. On the bed. Together."

Kloepper swung her into his arms like a bride and laid her on the bed. This was her chance! As he put one knee on the mattress to follow her, Rayne rolled to the far side, nearest the door. The bed sank as Kloepper's full weight came down on it, and she pulled her legs up to jump free.

Fast as a snake, his arm wrapped around her, snagged her cuffed hands, and pulled them above her head. With a practiced move, he snapped another set of cuffs around hers, through the bars of the headboard, and around his own wrist. They were chained together on the bed and her planned escape vanished as quickly as the lightning that lit the window every couple of minutes. The bed shook as he scooted closer.

"Now this is nice." He snuggled against her back, spooning her like a playful lover. In spite of the freezing room, sweat covered her face. "We're meant to be together. Forever."

She had no idea if he'd seen through her ruse or if he'd simply outmaneuvered her. But either way, she was a mouse caught by a very deadly cat.

CHAPTER FORTY-ONE

Thunder crashed after every electric bolt seared the sky. Ben swore one must have struck a tree not far in back of the house, because he heard a crash of branches and felt a ground-jarring thud.

"We're going to have to rush the cabin," Addison whispered in his ear. "With your ribs, I think you should go in the back while I go in the front.

"What ribs?" He could almost see Addison's smile.

"I'll give you two minutes—exactly one hundred twenty seconds—to get around back and be ready. You do have a second hand on your watch, don't you?" Ben assured him he did, and pressed the stem to light the dial. "Good. If you see the kids back there, tell them to get their butts far away from the house and lie low."

He tapped Ben on the arm, and they both checked their watches. "Go."

The safety of Addison's gun made a small click as he switched it off, and Ben pulled his own gun out as he stumbled toward the back of the house.

As he rounded the rear corner, his foot caught on a tree root, and he went down, crashing hard onto a three-foot-round boulder he'd forgotten protruded from the earth halfway to the porch entrance. Knife-sharp pain shot through his left side, and he rolled to his right, off the rock and splashed on his back into the mud, breathing shallowly as he bit his lip to keep from crying out. Water from the sky ran into his mouth and he spit it out.

The boulder hemmed him in on his right, and he really didn't want to roll onto his hurting left side. He held his watch over his head and pressed his watch stem. The little light flickered to life. The crystal was shattered in a dozen radial lines, but before the light permanently blinked out, he noticed the second hand wasn't moving.

Gritting his teeth, he rolled left.

Regen van Onweer thought she had fooled him. Raoul smiled into her hair. Only it wasn't her real hair, and it smelled like paper bag and damp dog. His fists clenched until his longer fingernails cut the skin. He'd had it all planned: the isolated cabin north of Deer Cove, the restraints, his camera, and ability to connect directly to the Internet so he could update his blog. Conner had almost ruined it.

Luckily, Raoul had found out about this place. And so fittingly appropriate, too. The quaint cabin she'd once shared with Conner, she now shared with the Wolf. He sighed. It wasn't the best, but it would have to do. He stroked her shoulder. Let her believe the lie a little longer while he imagined the outcome of his next move.

She lay in front of him on her right side, the warmth of her body pressed seductively against his. She wanted him. Too bad this couldn't go on forever. Slowly, without disturbing her, he reached back with his left hand and found the knife. The candles on the dresser behind him glinted in the ten-inch blade's surface as he brought it forward. He'd sharpened it on a stone, then finished it on his leather boot like his father had showed him, honing the edge to the sharpness of a razor, tested against the hair on his arm. With no effort, they'd fallen away in a soft ball of fuzz.

Using the blade tip, he parted the curled black mass of her hair. A smile curved his lips.

Save your last breath for me, my lovely white dove,
  Don't sing too loud or long.
  Yellow fades and black overwhelms, like cold fog.
  I will release air from your lungs,
  Embrace my gift of freedom.

The first cut would be down her back. She would arch away from the liberating blade, but the handcuffs would keep her close.

Dark rain will fall from your eyes
  From your body, like notes spilling from a score.
  I drink its life; you sustain me.
  Give me what you promised.
  Save me
  And I will remain with you always

Then he'd bring the blade to her front, thrusting up through her lungs. Her last breath would be his, and he'd hold her until the last dark rain fell from her body. Only then could Marielle be released, and they would be complete. Only then would he post the pictures on his blog and claim his power.

Raoul slid back slightly, putting a little space between their bodies. He turned the blade of the knife and positioned it near her left shoulder blade.

Come to me, my Marielle.

The candles hissed and flared, as if they sensed the importance of this moment. His was the power to freeze the present and create history. He pressed the steele home.

CHAPTER FORTY-TWO

Ben stepped through a waterfall cascading from the roof, and stepped quietly as quietly as possible onto the old back porch. He counted silent seconds, guessing at the elapsed time.

A timely boom from the sky allowed him to twist the doorknob. Not locked. *Thank you, God.* He held the door closed, remaining stock still as a puddle spread around his feet. Rain drummed on the roof, masking his labored breathing.

There'd been no sign of the kids outside. He prayed they were sheltering under some tree and not being held prisoner on the other side of the flimsy door. How much time had passed? A minute and a half? Two and a half? Should he wait for a noise or just break in?

Searing pain, hotter than molten steel, traced a path down Rayne's back. She screamed and jerked away from the slicing agony, even as Kloepper pressed the blade hard. She hadn't seen the knife; thought she had more time. But this was the end, what he'd planned all along. Using all her strength, she kicked backward with her feet, smashing her heels into his shins.

The front door banged inward, and a man entered, water sheeting from his clothing. He held a pistol raised in firing position.

The blade in her back fell away, and the bed groaned as Kloepper moved. Then her captor's hand appeared across her body, holding a gun of its own.

Before she could think, he fired twice and the man fell back out the open door. The explosions from the black barrel, mere inches from her face, stung her nose with pungent gunpowder. Her ears rang like one of Danny's biggest cymbals.

She whipped her arms upward as much as her restraints allowed, knocking his gun upward. A shot from the front door boomed over their heads, and Kloepper hunkered down behind Rayne. Her body became the coward's cover. She had to get free of the handcuffs.

CHAPTER FORTY-THREE

Rayne's scream pierced the night, cutting through the pounding rain and straight into Ben's heart.

He wrenched the door open as gunfire cracked. Two shots rapid fire, then another deeper round.

Rayne!

Ben held his gun in front as he sprinted down the short hallway and into the main living area. The front door hung crazily on only its bottom hinge. Through the opening, he saw Addison peek above the porch edge as another shot came from Ben's left. It took a split-second to recognize Rayne, dressed as she was in over-the-elbow black gloves and long black hair. She and Kloepper were on the old bed that had been in the back room. Through the spindles of the metal headboard, Kloepper swung his gun at Ben. Rayne slammed her head back into his face as he fired, and the shot whistled past Ben's head.

Ben dropped to the floor and raised his own gun, but Rayne was tangled with Kloepper. She rotated her body so they were face to face, and wrapped her legs around his. She head-butted him again and again. Though her hands were secured over her head, she pummeled him with her elbows, screaming in his face like a banshee in her highest soprano.

Ben scrabbled backward toward the tiny kitchen as Kloepper fired again. Candles on a table inches from Ben's head exploded, spraying him with glass and hot wax. He dove the other direction toward the old potbellied stove, realizing too late there was no cover there. He overturned a single straight-back chair, faint protection against bullets.

Kloepper fired two shots at the front door, blasting wood chips from the frame. But Rayne was a hellcat, shrieking and writhing violently like Linda Blair.

Then Kloepper did something completely unexpected. He put down his pistol and grinned at Ben.

Ben rose to a sitting position and risked a glance toward the front door. Was Addison all right? Ben looked again at the bed. Rayne thrashed furiously, alternately kneeing and butting Kloepper who had suddenly gone calm. Then Ben saw why. The man's left hand came up with a huge carving knife, gripped for stabbing.

Rayne went still as her eyes focused on the blade suspended above her body.

"No!" Ben shouted and raised his pistol. Too close or not, he had no choice now. He was squeezing the trigger when a movement from his left caught his eye.

Mandy rounded the corner of the hallway, rushing toward the bed. She had a two-handed grip on a heavy wooden axe handle, lifted above her shoulder like a baseball bat. The metal axe head glinted in the flickering light. His axe. He'd sharpened it for splitting firewood and stashed it in the Bronco.

As the knife descended, Mandy swung at Kloepper's arm. The roar from her throat raised the hair on Ben's neck. But Kloepper was fast, and jerked his arm back. The axe head sliced through his sleeve, but caught enough flesh so the knife clattered into the dark.

The axe head continued its deadly arc, smashing into the top of the dresser, shattering candles before embedding itself deep in the wood paneled wall. Kloepper punched Rayne in the face, then he flipped himself half-off the side of the bed in a scrambling search for the knife.

"Mandy! Get back!" Ben shouted as he struggled to his knees, aiming the pistol for a clear shot. Side pain robbed his breath as he tried to get a bead on the thrashing man half hidden between the bed and dresser. Ben aimed high and squeezed the trigger. The gun bucked in his hand and a framed picture on the wall shattered and dropped to the floor, the noise lost in the gunshot. He'd hoped to cause Kloepper to stop fighting, but instead the killer's free hand came up with the knife raised high in triumph.

Mandy dove for the extended arm.

CHAPTER FORTY-FOUR

Before Rayne could react, Kloepper clubbed Mandy in the face with the butt of the knife, and the girl crumbled to the floor. Then he pushed off the dresser and leapt half onto Rayne, his weight crushing her into the dusty mattress. Over his shoulder, she saw the dresser bounce off the wall and rebound toward the bed.

Candles, the oil lamp, and the jug of lamp oil slid across the scarred top. The lamp's chimney glass toppled sideways, and the wick flickered as it arced toward the bed.

The jug landed first, smashing on the iron bed frame and splashing fuel across the mattress and Kloepper's back. The lamp followed, igniting his oil-soaked clothing and the mattress.

Heat rose as fast as Kloepper's scream. He thrashed on top of Rayne, trying to escape the flames, but he couldn't elude his own clothes. The mattress burned hotter as candles tumbled to the oil-soaked surface, adding their burning wicks and hot wax to the mix.

In a frantic move, Kloepper flipped across Rayne, trapping her between him and the flames that were now mere inches from her. Their chained hands were hopelessly twisted and wrapped around the headboard bars. Rayne felt her blood soaking into the mattress beneath her. With it went her strength. Kloepper continued to scream and thrash, trying to smother the blaze eating at his clothes and skin.

As the mattress burned brighter, Quin appeared on the other side of the flames and wrenched the axe out of the wall. She feared killing Kloepper wouldn't do any good now. Manacled as she was to him, she'd never be able to get free of the burning bed.

Addison rose over Kloepper the same time she heard metal crash against metal. The headboard's old bars fell loose under assault from Quin's axe, and Rayne's arms came free.

"Hang on, Rayne," Addison said. He reached across the burning Kloepper and grabbed two handfuls of her ornate costume. With a heave, Addison dragged her away from the fire and writhing man, and into his arms.

"No!" Kloepper rolled with Rayne. Chained together, he pulled until his face was inches from hers. "You can't leave me, Marielle," he whispered.

In his gray eyes, Rayne saw madness and love, hatred and longing. Flames licked his back, and the stink of burning flesh gagged her. But Kloepper now seemed oblivious to the fire eating his body.

"Marielle," Kloepper rasped as Addison shifted his arms, trying to drag her farther from the man. "You're mine. We are meant to be together. *I will release air from your lungs, Embrace my gift of freedom.*"

Rayne recoiled from the words. He still wanted to kill her. His obsession with Marielle had deprived him of sanity, carrying him into a dark world she could only imagine. But he'd pursued her for weeks, months. Attacked her friends. And she wanted free of him right now— forever.

Her dress ignited in a bright burst. Multiple layers of petticoat fabric temporarily insulated her, but they wouldn't last long. Already the heat singed her legs. Soon, the fabric would be reduced to ash, and the fire would devour her as eagerly as it was devouring the man she was bound to.

Addison backed up, the linked chains dragging Kloepper partway off the bed. But with each lunge, Rayne's wounds gaped, and her blood ran free. Lethargy suffused every fiber of her being, but she resisted its pull. Help was here. She couldn't give up.

"Dad!" Mandy's scream behind Rayne brought her mind into focus, and she saw Kloepper's left hand as it rose from behind his back. Fire raced up the shirtsleeve, blistering the skin of his wrist, and on to his blackened fingers where he clutched the big knife in a stabbing position.

"Save your last breath for me," he said, and brought the knife down.

A man's hand caught Kloepper's fiery wrist, grasping tight enough Rayne could see the knuckles turn white against the flames. With a wrench, the knife fell away, and Ben's face appeared.

"Get her out of here, Addison," Ben wheezed. He was bent over, his left arm tight across his torso, and his face shone with sweat.

Had he been shot? Rayne longed to wipe his brow, comfort him, but everyone jumped into action around her. Addison turned Rayne's feet toward the door and yelled at Mandy and Quin to help pull on the chains and drag Kloepper. She could hear the fire crackling beyond the man as it devoured the bed and spread to the dresser and fuel-saturated floor. Quin joined Mandy as they pulled the chains still attached to Rayne's wrists.

Like a surreal game of tug-o-war played with handcuffs in a burning room, the kids dragged Kloepper's flaming body outside, while Addison carried her and Ben limped beside them.

Addison didn't stop under the sheltered porch, and Rayne tried to ignore the thumping sound of Kloepper's body hitting the two stairs leading down to the yard. Addison settled her onto the soaked ground.

Pouring rain extinguished her dress, transforming the material into a sodden compress against her scorched skin. Kloepper's body hissed in the deluge where he moaned and writhed next to her.

In less than a minute, the icy cold water had soaked through to her skin, and she began shivering. The shaking of her body wore her wrists bloody under the metal cuffs, even through the long gloves, and Mandy held them still. Rayne closed her eyes against the pain of her butchered back.

Addison sprinted off into the night to retrieve his SUV. Ben sank in the mud on his knees, blocking her view of Kloepper and sheltering her face from the worst of the downpour.

"Rayne," he whispered as he cupped her face and brushed the water from her eyes with his thumbs.

His hands were so warm against her frigid skin. As much as she wanted to gaze into those blue eyes, it was too dark. The lightning flashes were less frequent now, but the rain intensified.

"Stay with me, Rayne," he pleaded and touched his forehead to hers, his breath warm on her face as he cradled her.

She didn't know if he meant now or forever, but it didn't matter. He'd come for her. After all these years, Ben Conner had followed her and brought her back. As weariness coursed through her body, she realized that was all she had ever wanted.

The yard began to glow as flames spread through the cabin and ventured out the open door. Reflections in the water running across the yard lit Ben's face, and she could almost make out his eyes.

Just a little more.

But darkness deeper than the night encroached the edges of her vision as blood drained from her body and joined the rivulets on their journey to the lake.

EPILOGUE

The water sparkled like diamonds as a boater sliced an arrow-straight V across the surface, the outboard motor purring and growing fainter in the distance. Rays from the warm sun filtered between the tall pines and tickled Rayne's face. She rested her head against the chaise cushion. So peaceful.

A gentle breeze stirred the colorful flowers that surrounded the yard and overflowed planters around the patio, filling the air with their sweet scents. The unusually heavy rains of winter had finally given way to a gorgeous spring.

She wiggled her back against the cushion. Even with nightly lotion rubs, the eight-inch scar still itched. Her body shuddered involuntarily at the events of that November night: the raging storm, gunfire, the handcuffs and knife, Kloepper's burning body steaming in the rain-soaked yard. Then the wild ride to the hospital in Mission Peak, led by wailing Highway Patrol and sheriff's vehicles that had joined them in Shelter Cove.

Rayne had remained chained to her would-be killer as they sped toward the hospital, Kloepper in the cargo area of the SUV, Rayne in the back seat, and the stink of seared flesh everywhere. She'd only been freed when a policeman at the Emergency Room entrance produced a key and unlocked the handcuffs.

Even then, the still conscious Raoul Kloepper faced her from his gurney for a moment. His eyes—calm and filled with longing—tracked her every movement. As they wheeled her gurney away, he whispered, *"Save your last breath for me."*

He'd died before morning.

The memories weren't quite as vivid now, but vanilla candles still gave her the creeps.

And she was glad the medical doctor insisted on counseling sessions for Mandy, Quin, and her. It had been eerie hearing Mandy talk so calmly about her intent to hack off a man's arm. She explained to the counselor that she knew right from wrong, and if using the axe was what it took, well then so be it. Rayne's respect for the girl had gone up immensely. She was a warrior in a teen's body.

Quin had held Rayne's hand during most of the sessions, quietly absorbing, and just as determined as his now-official cousin, Mandy. As they'd talked through the events several times, Rayne had no doubt she would fight just as fiercely to save Mandy, Quin, or any one of the Conners.

Kloepper had been an insane monster, intent on killing. Killing her. However, even the logical, rational understanding of the 'why' of him, as the psychologist put it, didn't diminish the sheer brutality of Kloepper's actions, nor the lingering terror of his spying and stalking. She wondered how long it would be before she could undress in a room without first checking the ceiling corners for hidden cameras.

"Rayne?"

Quin's voice roused her from the troubling musings, and she turned to the boy, Ben's legal son of two weeks. He'd grown an inch in the last five months and stood tall and handsome in black trousers and the crisp long-sleeve white shirt she ironed for him.

"There's someone here to see you." A smile tugged at his mouth.

A man appeared behind the boy, his bowl-cut blond hair hung in his eyes like one of the early Beatles.

"Danny!" Rayne jumped from the lounge and raced across the flagstone, meeting him halfway where he grabbed her waist and swung her in a circle. He kissed her cheek, and she twisted her hands in his hair when he set her down.

"This is new," she ruffled his hair where there hadn't been any the last time she'd seen him. "Guess I can't call you Kojak anymore."

"You like?" He grinned and smoothed it back into order. "I'm still getting used to it. Sure takes a lot more work than shaving it."

"So why'd you grow it?" Rayne couldn't stop grinning at him. He stepped back and tucked his hands in the front pockets of black jeans.

"Don't know, exactly. Seemed like everything was changing. Maybe time for me, too." He dropped his eyes momentarily. "Guess that sounds pretty weird." Rayne pulled his hands free and held them in her own, rubbing her fingers across the familiar calluses.

"No, it doesn't. You're right—a lot *has* changed." She hated the somber tone and shook it away with a toss of her hair. "But I'm okay. Look!" She lifted one of his hands aloft and twirled under it like a dancer. Her leg was back to normal.

"You look good, Regen. Sorry...Rayne. Wow, talk about change. That might take me a while." It had taken him months to switch from Rayne to Regen when she'd changed her name the first time.

Rayne hugged her friend again, holding him tight as the memories raced through her brain like electric charges. "I just can't believe you're here."

Danny stuffed his hands into his pockets and suddenly found his shoes fascinating. "I'm sorry about the band and—"

"Danny." She tilted his chin up until their eyes met. "It's okay. Really, it is."

And it was. Dolina Macgowan had accepted the position of Elusive Hope's frontwoman, while Danny and Pieter shared the decision-making. Rayne had called Dolina and wished her the best, glad the group wouldn't have downtime from Regen van Onweer's departure.

"Just promise me one thing," she said, squeezing his shoulders.

"Sure, anything."

"If you guys tour anywhere near California, come and play a concert here. Okay?"

"Count on it, babe." They hugged again before he said, "Oh, almost forgot. I brought someone else."

She pulled back. He was grinning ear to ear.

"Who? *Tell* me!" Danny pointed over her shoulder to the interior of the house, and Rayne spun.

Rayne's mother stood talking to a woman in a multicolored dress. Dark curls concealed the side of her face and hung to her waist. Then, leaning on an ornately carved cane, the woman turned. A neck brace held her firm, but her eyes sparkled when they locked with Rayne's. A wide grin split her brown face.

"Lorna!"

They met at the doorway and Rayne hugged her gently for a long minute, rocking, remembering. Good, bad, and back to good. Her hair smelled like cinnamon, and that alone brought tears to Rayne's eyes. Rayne mouthed "thank you" toward Danny.

"Hey, now," Lorna said as she pulled away and handed Rayne a tissue. "Don't you be ruining your make-up for me, baby girl, or I'll have to help you redo it. You must look beautiful for your perfect day; for your perfect man." Lorna studied Rayne's cream gown and nodded approval. Then she ran her fingers through Rayne's hair, fluffing it away from her face.

Rayne let out a sigh. "I'm kind of nervous about this, Lorna," she confessed. "I never thought I'd be getting married again, certainly not to Ben. And to become an instant mother..."

Lorna gripped Rayne's shoulders. "You may not think it, but you are ready for this."

Addison and Sam came through the front door with Mandy and Star. He wore a black tuxedo, and Sam and Star were dressed to the nines. But it was Mandy that turned every head in the room.

Confident on three-inch heels that sent the tips of her spiked black hair reaching at least six foot three, Mandy owned the room as she strode toward Rayne. Black and turquoise earrings matched her form-fitting one-shoulder dress that revealed flawless golden skin.

She made her way to Rayne and hugged her. "Hey, Rock Star."

Rayne introduced Lorna, and then turned toward Danny.

"Danny Haynes, I'd like you to meet Ben's niece, Man—"

"Amanda. Amanda Conner," Mandy interrupted smoothly with her deepest alto, and extended her hand. Danny accepted it with a somewhat awestruck expression. The corner of Mandy's mouth twitched, and she winked at Rayne as she linked arms with the drummer and drew him away. "*We* have a lot to talk about," she said, leading him to a corner of the room. Rayne could have sworn she heard the girl ask Danny how old he was.

Addison smiled and said, "Everyone ready to go?" and they were soon climbing into cars for the drive to Perilous Cove.

Perilous Cove Community Church shone brilliant white in the noon sun, and people streamed in through the tall double doors as Addison stopped his brand new SUV at the base of the steps. Bibs and Irene waved to Rayne as she stepped out of the car, then the two women scurried inside to their seats.

Rayne lifted her face to the warm sun, closed her eyes, and breathed in the salty coastal air. Feeling good to be alive seemed cliché, but that's how she approached each day. Before they left the house, Lorna had told her, "*Life comes in chunks, baby girl. You take what comes and wring every bit of good out of it. No regrets.*"

And Rayne had none as Quin pecked her cheek and then followed Addison around the corner and through the garden toward the side door, while Rayne waited in the small vestibule.

When everyone was in place, the pianist began playing Rayne's instrumental arrangement of "Fathers And Sons." She adjusted her bouquet, fingering the smooth waves tattooed on her right wrist. One for each letter of Ben's name, visually representing the lake where—at least for a brief time—she'd been the happiest. A special reminder to no one but herself.

She began her walk down the same wood-planked aisle she'd traversed nearly sixteen years ago.

The men waited at the front. Addison, Quin, and Ben, all *soon-to-be's* in one form or another: brother-in-law, son, husband. Except this time all the soon-to-be's were *hers*. Ben's grin filled the building, and Rayne grinned right back. His brother elbowed him in the side, but Ben's eyes never left hers.

The music swelled, and the lyrics—printed in the handout—poured silently from Rayne's heart. At first, she'd planned to use "Indigo Sun," a last chance to finish Marielle's story. But that was *Regen*'s job, and another life.

On the left side of the room, Mandy and Star stood with their new mom, Samantha Conner. On the right, Ben waited with Addison and Quin. Today celebrated family, no matter how unconventional its makeup. Mandy winked at Rayne, and her redheaded sister flashed a brilliant grin.

This was the beginning of a *new* legacy, and Rayne thanked God she had a chance to be part of it. Her mother, Doc Arnold, Bibs, Irene, the women from the Beauty Barn, Danny and Lorna—all were here. Rayne wanted everyone to hear *her* story.

A NOTE TO READERS

Thanks for reading *Storm Song*!

Please consider writing a review at your favorite retailer site. They help other potential readers, and advertisers look for how many reviews a book has. Sometimes it's why they will accept a book in this competitive world.

I'd love to hear from you. Tell me what you liked or <gasp!> didn't like, and why. Your feedback will make me a better writer.

I have a great team of test readers and editors, and we work hard to catch every error. But if you find one that slipped through, please let me know! Just send a short phrase I can search for in the master document.

richbullockwriter@gmail.com

ACKNOWLEDGMENTS

A book is always a group effort, and an author relies on many people for expertise. For Storm Song, my thanks go to Cher Floria Nelson and Phil Kingsley for help with Gaelic translation of the song, "Bí Liom." It really helped me set a mood in my own mind.

Deborah Raney and Julie Carobini gave early feedback on the opening section. Lyle Carlson encouraged me and introduced me to metal bands I'd never heard about. James Scott Bell's mentoring group at Mount Hermon Christian Writers Conference was a terrific way of gaining months of experience in four days.

Thanks to Rebecca L. Miller for editing: rewriterewordrework. wordpress.com; Sally Apokedak for story edit; and Sis Hammack, Diane Diggs, Lee Starkey, Carol Dickerson, and many initial readers who sent corrections and suggestions.

Rob Henslin at www.rhdcreative.com designed another awesome cover.

BOOKS BY RICH BULLOCK

<u>Perilous Safety Series</u>
Perilous Cove
Storm Song
Desperation Falls
<u>Glass & Stone Series</u>
Shattered Glass
Glass Revenge
Killing Callie
<u>Lake Effect Series</u>
Night Skyy

<u>Nonfiction</u>
Beyond Us: The Writings of V.M. Narrano
Wild Life: The Writings of V.M. Narrano

The Shortest Book On Marriage,
with Sheryl Bullock

ABOUT THE AUTHOR

Rich Bullock writes stories of ordinary people put in perilous situations, where lives are changed forever. Storm Song is his second novel.

Fortunate to grow up in small-town San Luis Obispo, California, he developed an eye for settings that remind people of home. He now lives and writes in Redding, California where, on most days, he sees Mount Lassen, Mount Shasta, and the inside of a coffee shop.

Connect with Rich Bullock
www.perilousfiction.com
richbullockwriter@gmail.com

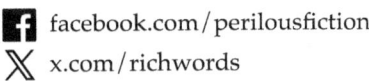

f facebook.com/perilousfiction
X x.com/richwords

www.ingramcontent.com/pod-product-compliance
Lightning Source LLC
Chambersburg PA
CBHW070739180626
46818CB00007B/2921